WILD
VIOLETS
GROWING UP IN THE
1940s And 50s

Also by Joseph P. Cody

THE TIGER'S FURY

DRAGON FANG

HUBOT - Human Robot

METANOIA - Total Conversion

PHANTOM TEAM

FIND SPARTACUS

WILD

VIOLETS

GROWING UP IN THE
1940s And 50s

JOSEPH P. CODY

A Novel

Autotech Industries

St. Paul, Minnesota

This is a work of fiction. Any resemblance to persons living or dead is purely coincidental. Names, characters, places and events, except where noted, are products of the author's imagination and are fictional. The views expressed herein are solely those of the author.

This book is written, printed, and bound in the United States of America

First Edition: 2015

ISBN-13: 978-0-9791167-7-3

A Publication of:

Autotech Industries
688 – 11th Avenue NW
St. Paul, Minnesota 55112

Autotech Industries is a publisher; it does not sell books. This and other books by Joseph P. Cody may be ordered from Amazon.com or any book store.

To a special world that has slipped away and now exists only in my memories.

INTRODUCTION

This will be the story of my earliest memories and growing up years that includes the things that shaped my life of necessity fictionalized in places—a lot of places. At times I will have to step out of my young life to explain things or much of what I say would not be understandable, or at least not fully so, to the modern reader. Indeed, though they were part of everyday life then, I did not understand why they were, or how they might have differed from times before or after. They just were. As a result, there are places where one could say that a child could not possibly know something that is narrated and he would be right. I ask that you, the reader, accept this and put the adult things in a different pocket from the things of the boy.

It is my hope that in reading this you will try to connect to that different time. As I write this I recall a program, *The Lone Ranger*, that we listened to on the radio. At the beginning with the opening bars of Rossini's *William Tell Overture* playing in the background the narrator would say, "Let us return now to those thrilling days of yesteryear." In this adventure we are returning to the days when that program was the highlight of many kids' day which for us, today, is as much yesteryear as the old west was to us back then. If you let yourself go a little we could almost start the story with . . .

Once upon a time . . . .

PRELIMINARIES

Earliest memories

I'm three years old plus a month standing in the backseat of the '38 Chevy looking over the front seat out the windshield. There isn't much to see because it's all white. This is the earliest memory I can put a date to. I know my age because it's a March blizzard in 1944 and we're taking my new brother, Mikey, home from the hospital in Deep Woods, the town nearest to where we lived. Beside me is my brother, Tommy, two years older than me. The exchange of words between my parents in the front doesn't remain in my recollections other than they are both tense. They are probably arguing. I recall my father saying years later that when a man gets married he learns that anything worth doing was worth arguing about. For now, the snow is blinding and my father operates the floor shift causing the sound of the motor to change. We are starting up the hill that will lead to the long driveway into our house. Looking back, I think it was the prospect of the driveway that was causing concern. The first half of the drive was through woods and on a slight up-grade. Emerging from the trees it turned to the left a little, went level for a distance and began a gradual down slope. In the open flat area the snow drifted the driveway closed first.

I have recollections from before this but have no way of fixing a date to them. Other than the winter ride in the Chevy a lot of my early memories concern the war, World War II, that is. We lived on a farm in central Minnesota. My father, at thirty-six, was not drafted because he ran the farm alone and the war needed food. I knew about the war in odd ways almost from when it started. At Christmas time when relatives sent Christmas presents, frequently they were in the form of War Bond Stamps. We each had a war bond, a small booklet with rectangular squares on each page. You licked the stamps like postage stamps and pasted them in the book. It had no meaning for me other than it was fun to lick and paste the stamps. My stamps were all red with a picture of a soldier on them. These would be saved for my education sometime in the far distant future.

The other Christmas gift I remember was a small cardboard tube and a couple of paratroopers. The tube was decorated with small pictures of paratroopers falling under their silky canopies. When you pulled the top of the parachute of one of the paratroopers it collapsed the canopy because the shroud lines were made from toothpicks. Inserting the whole affair into the tube you were supposed to point the tube up and blow on it. The paratrooper shot out of the end, the chute opened and it floated to the floor. That was the idea anyway. More often than not you didn't point it up but rather aimed it at your brother and shot the paratrooper out like a bazooka shell.

Rationing was hard for the big people but my only personal recollection in that regard is toward the end of the war we had our first introduction to artificial sweetners. Kool-Aid had not come on the market yet but we had Nectar. It was a liquid concentrate containing no sugar. There was a small bottle of little white pills that came with it. You'd drop a pill in a glass of water and wait until it dissolved and then add a spoonful of the concentrate. If you used your imagination it tasted sweet.

The war permeated everything, news, conversations, and shortages. There was a shortage of rice. I guess, that's another thing that affected me. I could remember Rice Krispies that went Snap, Crackle, Pop when you poured milk on them. I thought they were so good until they were simply not obtainable. Most rice was imported and there were no imports. Rice Krispies came in a box smaller than corn flakes. One day in town I saw a display of boxes in a grocery store window and said, "Dad! There's some Rice Krispies." I'll never forget his reply. "Those are just small boxes of corn flakes."

Other than that, for a kid life was good. We had enough to eat and wood to heat the house, even if it did get awful cold by morning. By the time I was five I was sleeping upstairs in a double bed with Tommy. Our room was on the north side of the house, and the window had a crack in the glass so when there was snow and a north wind, there'd be snow on the floor in the morning. Mom didn't call us until there was a fire in the heater in the living room. We'd grab our clothes, step around the snow, and make a mad dash down the stairs. We'd pull a chair up close to the heater and dress. It was life. It was what we had and we didn't question it. The big people knew what they were doing—most of the time. To this day I can't remember why it was, but in all things I trusted my parents except with the possibility that the house would burn down. I could see myself standing in snow with bare feet and no place to go. Each night after being tucked in I laid awake praying the house wouldn't burn down.

Red Feather

I am Red Feather from among the human beings, *änicinábek* in our tongue, Indians in white man's tongue. White man has other words that included Indians as well as white men and even black white men. But, we are *änicinábek* and white men are not.

In the moon of the falling leaves one of our warriors returned to us wounded. The warrior's name was Running Wolf. I am his grandfather. Upon his return he talked with me for one day and one night before he began his last journey. After that I did not know if he slipped over the borderland from this life to the other. Two nights after Running Wolf left I had a dream visitor who told me that Running Wolf's story was true. Those we meet in dreams are called *pawáganak* and are among the persons in the other-than-human class. These stories, or *täbátcamowin*, shall be repeated around the fire in proper season. It is so.

Running Wolf came to know a boy who was the son of a white man. The boy came to Running Wolf's aid in mysterious ways. He became blood brother to Running Wolf who gave him a name of the *änicinábek* that was given to Running Wolf by a *pawáganak*.

It was the time of the greatest war since *Atahocan*, the Earthmaker, finished making the soul of the first one who would be of the likeness of himself. Running Wolf told of crossing a big water in a boat of great size as well as many things we had not known about the war in the far away place. Mostly his story was about his return to our land and his time with the white boy. The boy had great power that he said came from what he called a guardian angel. Clearly this guardian angel was a *manita*, a general word for a person of the other-than-human class. This, now, is the story of Running Wolf and his little blood brother.

CHAPTER 1

Spring had fallen upon the land like a glorious shower of fairy feathers. I was outside setting on the bench under the elm tree by the house. I liked being outdoors so spring, summer and fall were much preferred to winter. Sliding was fun in the winter, but the cold would drive us in sooner than we liked.

The world around me impinged on my senses though I was not aware that it did, or at least only as aware as a six year old would be. The bench on which I sat was the wash bench that mom put the wash tubs on when she washed clothes. Otherwise it was used for sitting. The elm tree, located on the east side of the house about fifteen feet from it, stood right in front of the cellar door. The door was closer to flat to the ground than standing on end. Firewood was thrown through this trap door to get it into the basement which meant the tree was in a most inconvenient location. It was left there because along with other elm trees close to the house they provided shade in the summer which kept the house cool.

The sun was warm but the wind was still chilly so I wore a coat and my winter cap with the ear flaps up. The flaps folded into the cap rather than out. The trees were budding and it was in the time of the moon of the deep water. I didn't know it was called that yet, but I would. My legs were too short to reach the ground so my feet swung back and forth out of phase. I was lazily watching two birds chasing each other around the yard to the south.

The grass was green and there were bright yellow dandelions here and there. It had rained yesterday, the day after we finished raking up the leaves and dead grass from last year. I say "we" because we as a family did it. Mostly, I watched though now and then I helped carry leaves and grass to the pile in the driveway where we burned them. Carrying leaves was work or close enough to it so it didn't matter. I hated work because there were always so many other things to do, like what I was doing now.

With a start I saw the dark figure on the gravel road a quarter mile to the south coming down the hill toward town. We owned the land across the road too as the road headed through our property southeast to north-west. But, we didn't own the road. Dad said that was everybody's. It was odd, though I didn't think it was odd because six year olds don't think like that, but he was heading toward town rather than away from it. Well, since the road went both ways, so could a man on foot, I supposed.

We had two driveways, the real one that passed twenty feet to the south of the house headed out in a westerly direction and met the road at an angle an eighth of a mile later. The other, what we called the field road, started near the barn proceeded south until it came to the gravel road. A hundred yards, or a little more, to the south of the buildings was a low spot where the field road crossed the outlet from a slough. After a rain it was muddy and a car would get stuck in the ruts at that spot.

As I watched the figure progress to where our field road met the gravel road he turned without hesitation and started down the sloping road to the farm. My legs stopped swinging. It looked like a peddler, and that always put mom in a bad mood. She always said, they'd sit in the kitchen all day if necessary until she bought something. Sometimes they sold brushes, other times it was small square bottles of stuff for cooking. Mom said they were square so more of them could fit in the wire frame case they carried.

I hopped down from the bench and ran to the screen door and yelled, "Mom, peddler's commin' down the field road."

Coming to the door she said, "Darn, and I was about to start supper. Well, he can sit all night for all I care."

See what I mean, peddlers were not a good thing. On the bench again, my feet were hardly swinging at all as I followed him with my eyes. Funny, I thought he was using a walking stick when he started into the field road but now he wasn't. He had come to the muddy part of the field road and without a pause deftly shifted from one high spot to another. All the time I expected to see him slip with a splash in one of the water filled ruts but he didn't.

This was not the usual peddler as he carried a satchel on his shoulder not the grip at his side containing his wares. He was soon under the trees twenty yards to my left front continuing up the grade toward the house with a slight limp. With that, Chips, our dog, spotted him and in his usual way let out barking as he ran toward the figure. Pausing, the man said a few low words and Chips settled down as he sniffed his feet and ran around him.

The man was headed in my direction not toward the back door of the house. As he approached I saw his jet black hair, not to his shoulders, but longer than people around here wore, and black eyes. His face was squarish and darkly tanned with a shallow crease down the left side from eye to chin. His hands were large and terribly strong. What I could see of his nails were dark and chipped. His shirt was faded and could have been part of an Army uniform. Worn blue jeans covered his muscular legs leading to scuffed pull-on boots—no laces—another thing not common around here. A wide belt encircled a slim waist and passed though the scabbard of a long bone-handled knife on his left. His belt buckle was large and shiny with the image of a wolf tooled on it in such a way that the wolf stood forward from its background.

Chips was still not sure, but seemed better than around most strangers. Turning his broad shoulders the man unburdened his load and swung it to the bench. As he turned his head I saw a red scar under his left ear. Standing square in front of me the black holes for eyes took me in as a slight twitch came to one side of his mouth. "Good dog you have there. What's his name?"

"Chips."

"Kind of an odd breed, but a fine dog. Now, there, young man," his voice was like wind through tall grass with a hint of thunder in it, "do you suppose you could find a dipper of water for a thirsty traveler?"

With wide eyes I was looking almost straight up so close he was to me. "I'll tell mom."

Slipping off the bench I scooted past him to the back door, Chips at my heels. The screen door slammed behind me as I dashed from the porch to the kitchen. The dog stayed out because he knew he wasn't allowed in the house. Mom was at the stove. "He's not a peddler, mom. He's a traveler and wants a drink of water."

She slid a pan to the side so it would be off the heat of the wood fired kitchen stove and walked to the window that looked east in the direction of the barn. The man had turned to take in the place. "Good Lord, an Indian," was all she said. We had no running water in the house and like all farms had a pail of drinking water on a stand with a dipper in it. We all drank from the same dipper and if you didn't drink all the water you had dipped out, it went back in the pail with the dipper.

She filled the dipper and said to me, "Jamie, you stay in here." I watched through the window as she took the water out to the man. I could hear through the open door.

"Thank you ma'am," he said as he reached for the dipper. He drank it spilling none like it was precious. Handing the dipper back he said, "Wonder if I could have a word with your man when he comes in?"

Mom was uneasy, but having been brought up to be kind to strangers and most of all not to be rude to anyone, she was unable to say anything but, "Well, sit on the bench if you like. He'll be coming in for supper before long."

Shifting his bag to the ground on the far end of the bench he sat down. I guess mom thought I'd stay put, but I was always in trouble for being disobedient, naughty, unruly and other words I didn't exactly know the meaning of, though they all seemed 'bout the same.

Mom had the pan on the hot part of the stove again and I slipped out. Peeking around the corner of the house he saw me. With an ever so slight a smile he said in that same unusual voice, "Come on, I don't bite."

Walking toward him Chips mostly kept in front of me. He saw it. "He's a good dog. He's keeping himself between you and me. He's protecting you. How about you taking the other end of the bench, I'll stay put and we can pass the time."

I wasn't sure what "pass the time" meant 'cause it seemed it passed whether or not we cared anything about it. I liked to talk and mom and dad said my mouth was going all the time. Right now, it seemed there was nothing to say, as in, "cat got your tongue?" was what big people said when I met a stranger.

"Nice place you have here," he said. His words were clear and distinct like he cared about each one and wasn't about to abuse them. "Do you have any brothers or sisters?"

"Yeah, my older brother, Tommy. He's eight. He can read pretty good, but not like big people, yet. He's in the house reading a book now. I can't read—go to kindergarten mornings. I'll be in first grade this fall. Hope I can learn to read. We don't learn anything in kindergarten, just draw pictures with crayons and stuff like that. I been doing that for a long time. You never know about big people. They must think it's important." There I go, once I start the mouth won't stop.

"Can I see your knife?"

He looked at me a little funny. "It's just a knife. All knives are about the same, like the ones your ma uses in the kitchen."

He wasn't going to show me his knife. Big people were like that with kids. If I were a man and asked him, he'd show it to me.

"Where'd you get the shiny belt buckle? It has a nice picture of a wolf on it."

"Made it. I've done some silver tooling for others and one time decided to make something for myself. What's your name?"

"Jamie, Jamie Landon. What's yours?"

"Justin."

"That all? Seems like most people got two names even if we don't use both of them much, just the first one. You got another name?"

"Yes, it's Merchner. Do you have any other brothers and sisters?"

"Yeah. Another brother, Mikey. He's pretty small yet but he doesn't cry so much anymore. Boy, when he was littler he cried all the time. Mom said he had colic. I think that means his stomach hurt. Are you really an Indian? Mom said you were."

"Yes, I have some Indian in me."

"That's funny because you sound more like the Lone Ranger than Tonto."

"That's because I had a teacher who insisted we speak properly, and came down hard on us when we didn't. He said we'd have a hard enough time in life without the stigma of our perceived culture being held against us."

Chips had settled at my feet so my feet couldn't swing so I pushed him with my foot. No good, he wouldn't move. The man noticed it.

"What kind of dog is that."

"Just a dog, dog. We got him as a puppy from the neighbors who live at the end of the driveway. I don't think we paid for him because they were giving away puppies. Dad says he's a bulldog up to his neck, then he turns into something else." He had the wide stance and strong fore body of a bull dog, even had only a stump for a tail. But the head was more like a normal dog.

"When he was a puppy we kept him in the kitchen and Tommy and I had to take turns wiping it up every time he went piddle on the floor. Our last dog was a real collie called Skippy. Problem was he would spot a car coming over the hill on the road," I said pointing to where Justin had come, "and take off running across the field so he'd get to the car where the road came the closest to the house. I never thought he'd make it because it's quite a ways, but he always did. Then he'd run along side the car barking at it. The neighbors didn't like that so dad had to shoot him. Chips is okay."

Justin didn't say more about the dog, only nodded. "That's some barn you have. Looks like somebody started to build the world's largest teepee and then part way along changed his mind."

He was referring to the big barn which was round. I had never thought about it but the roof was like a large inverted funnel with the stem being the cupola on top. It had a lightning rod sticking out of it with a weather vane half way to the end of the rod—never saw lightning strike it, though.

That was when we saw dad coming down the field road on the tractor with a plough hung on the back. Justin took an interest in it. "That's dad coming. Dad says the tractor is a 1940 Ford. He likes the rubber wheels it has. He says it's a good tractor. I can remember the tractor we had before it had iron wheels. The back ones even had iron cleats sticking out of the rims so it wouldn't slip. They got it stuck in a wet place up the field. Dad and the hired man worked two days getting it out."

"Does your dad have a hired man now?"

"Nah. He says you can't get a good man with the war going on."

Dad stopped the tractor by the old barn. "That's the old barn where he stopped. The big red one is the big barn, but we didn't call it the big barn. That's just the barn. The old barn is called old." Chips had gone to meet dad, and for some reason my feet were swinging pretty fast.

Justin said, "You'll wear out your knees if you keep that up."

"Yeah," I said. "It's funny when my feet are happy they swing away."

Dad approached. He was wearing his felt hat and bib overalls and a blue button shirt, but you couldn't see that because he had on his black flannel jacket. He was a little over six feet tall and slim but strong. He worked a lot. His eyes were blue like mine and his face was tan from the sun and wind, and had a few creases in it. This would be his night to shave so his whiskers were showing. He nodded as he approached Justin.

"Hello. Haven't seen you around before," dad said a little guardedly.

Justin said, "I'd been walking a mite and stopped for a drink of water which your wife was kind enough to give me. Your son said you didn't have a hand and I'm wondering if you'd give me a chance. I'm part Indian and look all Indian and most folks in these parts don't want much to do with the likes of me. No mistake, they're good people, but I know how it is."

The screen door slammed and mom came out with a basin of water, a bar of soap and a towel. "It's supper time and I hate to see a hungry man on his way at meal time. Might as well eat with us." She set the things on the bench and went back in the house.

Dad said, "I guess that does it. Wash up, you're invited for supper."

As usual, dad washed up in the sink in the kitchen and then I washed my hands, too. We had a cistern that collected water that ran off the roof of the house and that's what we used for washing. A hand pump by the sink brought the water up. We got drinking water from the well down by the slough.

We sat down to eat and said our before meal prayer. Justin put his hands on his lap and bowed his head. Tommy had not known that Justin was even here so naturally he was curious. We passed around the food. There was pork of some sort, not too bad if you could get the fat off. Then there were boiled potatoes that were still from last fall and were all wrinkly before they were peeled. And there was most always gravy as there was now. We had the first asparagus of the spring, and of course bread and butter. Asparagus was the first fresh vegetable of the season. It grew wild and if it was cut when it was still a single slender stalk, it was good to eat. Some kids hated asparagus, spinach, and stuff like that, but as long as there wasn't too much of it, I didn't mind. Tommy hated it.

I knew enough not to talk because this was big people time, especially with a guest, especially, especially with a strange guest. There wasn't much talking anyway while everybody was digging in. These were hard working people and meal time was no joke, they took their eating seriously. Justin was holding himself back I could see, but every time mom passed something to him, he helped himself.

Mom had baked a cake yesterday so there was enough to go around. The pieces were a little smaller than normal. She had to cut it so there was one more than expected. Justin looked about to refuse it, but must have decided it would not be nice if he did.

Finally dad said, "You boys, run along."

Tommy and I ran into the living room but stopped out of sight beside the door to listen. Tommy was always the one to know everything before me and felt left out. I wanted to listen because I kind of liked Justin and wanted to know if dad would take him on as a hired man.

Dad began, "Have you ever milked cows? I'm milking fourteen head by hand and could use some help there."

"Yes, sir, that I have."

"How are you around horses, I mean work horses, not riding."

"Used a team a lot a few years back. I seem to get along well with animals. Never ran into a horse I couldn't get the upper hand with."

I could tell dad must have been stifling a smile at that because Daisy, the smaller of our two horses—Nellie was the large one—was hard to handle. Dad had said a couple of times that before long she'd earn herself a ticket to the glue factory. I took that to mean that horses were in some way used in making glue, and the men at the factory had special tricks to make rambunctious horses work better. At other times I guessed he thought there must be some hope because he mentioned making an appointment for her out behind the barn with Dr. Winchester.

There was no talking for awhile. Then dad said, "That would be a help because the gasoline ration stamps aren't stretching so I have to use the horses whenever I can, but that small one is a headstrong nag if there ever was one."

The rationing caused by the war included almost everything. The place we saw it was in the gasoline stamps and sugar stamps. Gasoline stamps were guarded more closely than gold would have been guarded if anyone had any gold, which they didn't. Since we raised a lot of our own food, the rest of the rationing didn't hurt us as much as it did the town people. Dad said it wasn't that there wasn't enough gasoline, but there wasn't nearly enough rubber for tires and the war used a lot of tires. The idea was that if tires were rationed, people would run their cars and tractors until the tires were worn out and then their machines would be useless when they couldn't get new tires. With gasoline rationed people made as few trips as possible. We had a few more gasoline stamps than others because we had a farm tractor.

There was more silence. "Well, how about we do a little milking now and see how you do. If you stay on it'd be two and a half dollars a day, but only half that for Sunday because all we do is chores. That's about the going rate."

I didn't know how mom would like that because washing sheets and clothes for a hired man was a lot more work for her.

Dad continued, "We have a room upstairs that you'll find suitable."

He hardly got it out before Justin broke in, "No sir. That won't be necessary. I've been sleeping out a lot these past years, so I'll manage outside. Maybe hunker down in the barn if it rains if that's okay. When it's needed, I handle my own bathing and clothes washing, too. I have extra cloths in my pack."

"No smoking in the barn, though, never."

"I know enough to not do things like that, sir."

"Let's go, then."

I could see Justin was a proud man and he didn't like to take orders, but the food seemed to be to his liking and he seemed to need a job so he'd handle it.

I watched through the kitchen window. Justin went to his bag and as he hoisted it on his shoulder he staggered a little. Dad noticed it. As they proceeded to the barn Justin had that limp again.

CHAPTER 2

Red Feather

Running Wolf called himself Justin Merchner for the white man. We living grandfathers never liked that teacher who insisted on teaching white man ways to our boys including that each boy should make a white man name for himself for when he went out in the world away from the human beings, *änicinábek*. Many *änicinábek* mixed with the white man and were lost to the nation. No *änicinábek* were required by white man's laws to join the Army but many did. They were great warriors and were much desired. Running Wolf returned from the great war with many wounds. He was put in the Army hospital in the city of St. Cloud. That city was in the white man nation of Minnesota. That is where his wounds started to heal and his life became wounded.

The man who shared his room with him in the hospital that he called the VA Hospital because it was run by something called the Veterans Administration had bad wounds that would not heal. He was a bent man and the poison from his past deeds would cause him to die before many days. Running Wolf spoke with him and learned that he would have gone to prison for life so he slipped off and joined the Army under a false name. Now, he was back in St. Cloud where he did not want to be—the place of his crimes. His friends visited him and saw Running Wolf doing silver tooling. Growing up Running Wolf had received powers from a *Midé* who was a man of great power who performed the *Midewiwin* ceremony. With this power Running Wolf could shape silver into likenesses of living things. They wanted his power for their own foul deeds. But, Running Wolf would not help them until forced to do it to save his life.

The day the other man died, the bad men with a helper in the records room, switched his records with Running Wolf's so the Army thought Running Wolf was the one who had died. The bad men told him what they had done and unless he did work for them the police would find him. He would then go to prison for the other man's crimes. He was too wounded to leave so he did what they wanted. When he had finished they left but said they would come back. They came back when Running Wolf was mostly healed and gave him more work to do for them. But, he left the hospital before the work was done and without being properly released. He found a ride with a man who said he was going to Deep Woods. The man was a farmer whose farm was some miles from the town so Running Wolf had to walk the rest of the way. His plan was to reach the train station in Deep Woods for his journey north to the Nation where he could finish healing in safety. He was forced to stop at a farm because his leg hurt from an unhealed wound. He changed his travel plans when he found he could work at that farm so he wouldn't have to travel where either the police or the bad men might find him.

Next morning Tommy and I were getting ready for school and dad and Justin were in for breakfast having done the milking already. They talked about work stuff and I didn't pay much attention. Dad had a trailer he pulled behind the car for hauling the milk to the creamery. He'd drop us off at school and we'd walk home—it was less than two miles.

While we ate dad told Justin that he wanted him to use the horses to take the hay rack to bring in a load of hay from a stack in the meadow. It was too early in the year for the stock to eat grass so we were still feeding hay. Dad pulled the load of hay up to the outside manger and filled the manger from it each morning. I liked to go along to get hay if I could because it was fun riding back on the top of the load of hay.

"Get your stuff, boys. Time to go," mom said.

It was cloudy today and I dreaded the thought of having to walk home in the rain. The room above the kindergarten room was a spare room and sometimes the big kids would be up there rearranging the chairs. It sounded like thunder and that terrified me. But, the thought of walking home in the rain was silly because if there was even a hint of rain, mom would be there waiting for me. It still didn't matter.

It didn't rain, in fact it was warm and sunny for my trek home. Sometimes people would stop and ask if I wanted a ride. I'd always accept. It seemed they knew who I was, but they were strangers to me. It was like that. A kid on a lonely country road getting into a car with a stranger—nobody worried.

During dinner dad and Justin were discussing Daisy. I wanted to laugh and maybe dad did too, but neither of us did. Any horse was a valuable piece of property and this one wasn't doing what it should, and that was serious. Maybe it made dad feel good that he wasn't the only one who had trouble with that horse.

I didn't follow the discussion at the table because I was in a hurry to finish eating and go outside. I had to check on the mayflowers. When I was real little Tommy and I were in the woods north of the house in the early spring shortly after the snow melted. We found these pretty flowers poking up out of the brown leaves. There were no green leaves from the plants, nor on the trees or brush, only the flowers. There were bunches of them everywhere. It was the prettiest and most unexpected sight I had ever seen. We picked some and when we bought them in the house mom said they were mayflowers, and she put them in a glass of water for us.

The next year I went out and there weren't any. When I asked what had happened to the mayflowers, dad said it was too early but he took me into the woods and found a big plant of mayflowers still under the leaves. There were only little fuzzy buds with their heads bowed. He said we'd have to cover them up with leaves again or else they'd freeze at night if it got cold. But he poked a stick in the ground to mark the place. Every day I went to check on them and saw their progression from buds to flowers. When they finally bloomed, the woods was full of flowers like the year before. That plant was maybe ten feet north of a big oak tree and even though the stick dad had used to mark it was no longer there, I could still find that big plant. Years later I went back in the summer and it was still there.

After lunch, dinner to us—we had breakfast, dinner and supper—I changed clothes and went outside. Chips was there to meet me wanting to be petted like always. Lickety-split, I headed for the woods to see how the mayflowers were doing. The buds were getting ready to open in a day or two, that is, they would if I could keep the dumb dog from crushing them all as he pranced around me wondering what could be so interesting in the leaves. He could be a pest at the worst time. But not for long because he popped up his ears and in a second was gone to chase a rabbit. The rabbit always won. Whenever Chips chased a rabbit in the woods we could hear him bark. Tommy and I could never decide if he was barking at the rabbit or yelping as he ran into stuff.

I looked around and saw a mayflower that was blooming already. To a kid, it gave a sense of continuity to life. Here was something that happened with no help from anybody. You could count on it, every year would be the same. It left me with a good feeling. The only odd thing, that odd business again, was they always bloomed in April even though they were called mayflowers. Every year I said they should have been called April flowers.

I walked back to the house thinking about everything and nothing. Being little was great if I had only known it. There were no responsibilities, no problems, no worries. Mom always said, "Youth is wasted on the young."

Nearly at the house, I saw movement in the barn. From the house you would go east slightly down hill to the bottom floor of the barn fifty yards away. Halfway there you'd cross the driveway. It ran along the south side of the house and then turned north as it passed to the east of the house. The garage, which we called the shed, was set off to the northeast of the house. Half way between the garage and the path to the ground floor of the barn, the driveway split and also went up to the second floor of the barn. From where the drive entered the upper barn to the path to the bottom floor there was a hill that was steep enough to slide on in the winter which we did a lot. We went down that hill on sleds, skis, pieces of cardboard, and just about anything else—thousands of times.

Once in the upper barn you were in the place where the hay wagon was stopped to unload the hay by means of ropes and pulleys. With no wagon parked there, it was a nice open area that was good for all kinds of fun things. Today Justin had a harness laid out on the floor. He was working at one of the straps.

"How can you tell what to do?" I asked. "That is such a jumbled up mess of straps."

Without looking at me he said, "This is a perfectly normal harness. Every strap is where it is supposed to be. Since the horse before Daisy was larger, we think it might not fit her well and hurts her when she pulls."

I stooped down to watch. I suppose I was too close and he wanted to swat me away, but that didn't occur to me because he didn't swat me. With a special tool, he punched a round hole in a leather strap. He aligned the new hole with an old hole in another strap and poked a small metal thing—he said it was a rivet when I asked—through the holes. Using another tool he squeezed the rivet so the end squashed out. I was talking all the time and he was answering. I liked him. I could see other places where there were shinny new rivets. He gathered up his tools and went to a shadowed place by the wall where I saw his leather pack. He placed the tools in the pack and buckled the straps. He was still limping a little.

"Now, lets see if it fits the old nag a little better."

He gathered it up in a special way and walked down our sliding hill to the lower level with it slung over his shoulder. The horses were in their stall. He walked between them and slid the harness on Daisy's back. The collar was still on her. The collar was a large pad that fit around the horse's neck with a strap and buckle under the neck to fasten the two ends of it together. The front of the harness engaged the front of the collar so when the horse pulled, it was pushing on the collar with its shoulders to draw the load.

After checking it thoroughly he said more to himself than to me, "That should work better."

The wagon with the hay rack on it had rubber wheels. We still had an old one with iron wheels that dad used for hauling manure to the field. With the horses both harnessed, he took them out and hitched them to the old wagon and brought it to the back barn door to start cleaning the barn. That meant loading the manure from behind the horses and cows into a wheelbarrow and then wheeling it out the back door to the wagon. A plank from the barn to the side of the wagon worked as a bridge for the wheelbarrow. Thinking back it was terribly unsafe but nobody seemed to get hurt. It was a lot of work because out in the field where it was used for fertilizer he had to pitch it off again.

Knowing what Justin was doing I wasn't interested and started to the house. Then I remembered that one of the barn cats had kittens awhile back and decided to check if they had their eyes open yet. I found them where they were playing on some hay in a corner by the calf pens. Sometimes Tommy and I came to the barn to watch the kittens. They'd chase each other around. Then one would crouch low like it was waiting for a wild animal to approach so it could attack it. Then it'd leap on the other kitten and the two would roll around having a great time. I petted the kittens for awhile and then the mother cat, too.

It was then that I heard Justin let out a low groan. He had finished behind the horses and was working on the gutter behind the cows. But, he had sat down in front of the feed trough and had his left pants leg pulled up. I was back where there wasn't much light and he didn't see me because I was looking between boards in a calf pen. There was a purple wound on his leg below the knee and it looked bad. He was squeezing it and stuff drained out of it. Then he wrapped a dirty rag around it, pulled his pant leg down and stood up.

I hadn't moved and made no noise. For some reason I sensed he would not be happy if he had known I were watching. He went back to work and I went to the house. On the way I thought I should tell mom or dad but wasn't sure. Justin would say something if it were necessary and I shouldn't stick my nose into his business. Big people knew what to do. It still bothered me, though. Every time I got a scratch they put iodine on it and it stung like crazy. They said the iodine was necessary to kill the germs.

When I was four I had gotten my middle finger pinched in one of the cow stanchions when the cows were out of the barn and dad was cleaning barn. It was torn badly and really hurt. Mom took me to the hospital and the doctor said it was too crushed to stitch up so he cut a strip of metal with a scissors and bent it into a "U" shape that fit over the end of my finger to hold the pieces together. Then he wrapped lots of clean white cloth around it. I remember that as he was cutting the metal he said that I shouldn't try cutting tin cans with my mother's scissors.

It healed pretty good but I still have a big scar from the tip of my finger to the first joint. They were all surprised when the fingernail grew back almost like normal. Anyway, they checked it every day and put more iodine on it and they always used new clean cloth for the bandage. They said we had to be careful so it didn't get infected. It looked like Justin didn't have any iodine or clean bandages so his leg had gotten infected.

What was I going to do? I liked Justin because he talked to me more than anybody else. Tommy was the one who did things first being the oldest—things like going to school. This meant he was the center of attention. Coming second, they thought they had it all figured out and didn't notice me much. Everything was supposed to be the same for me as for Tommy and when it wasn't I got scolded.

Maybe Justin should go to the doctor but he didn't have any money. Mom had a drawer full of old clean sheets that we used for bandages. We could at least give him clean bandages. Coming from the barn, I didn't go into the house but sat on the bench. Chips laid down by me. I had to think about my problem. Other than praying that the house didn't burn down at night leaving me standing in the snow with no place to go, and worrying about having to walk home from school in the rain, I wasn't supposed to have any problems, but I had one now. Those little kittens tumbled and played on the hay while their mother watched. They didn't have any problems—the mother cat knew what to do. How come I had problems?

My attention was diverted from my thoughts because a barn cat had happened to be coming from the woods headed toward the barn. Chips saw it and was off after it barking. Those cats were quick because he was always chasing them. It climbed a tree to the first branch and sat there smugly looking down at the dog. He barked a few times and gave up. The dog never went into the downstairs of the barn and the cats never came close to the horse. That is unless mom decided to have a house cat. Sometime in the fall she'd take a cat in as a mouser. Somehow she managed to make peace between that one cat and the dog.

After supper Tommy was reading aloud at the kitchen table and I was listening. It was still cool enough in the evening so we stayed inside. After milking dad came in and was washing up. He mentioned that Justin was limping a little more each day. Mom said she had noticed it, too.

I felt I had to say something. "That's because he has a bad sore on his leg by his knee."

They both looked at me, Tommy stopped reading. Mom asked, "How do you know that, Jamie?"

"I saw it this afternoon. It hurts a lot."

"Did he show it to you?"

Shaking my head I said, "I was playing with the kittens where he didn't see me. He sat down and pulled up his pants leg. He squeezed it and stuff ran out. He has a dirty bandage on it. It's all dark and I bet it's infected. Maybe he doesn't have any money to pay for a doctor."

Dad said, "You and Tommy go into the living room."

After that we heard mom and dad talking in low voices for awhile.

The next morning we got ready for school like usual. As soon as we finished eating, Justin went outside. Dad went to the phone on the wall in the living room. After picking up the receiver, the operator would say, "Number please." Dad gave the three numbers. I knew the phone number for my cousin who lived in town was 433. That was the only number I knew.

We were lucky because we only had one other house on our line and our phone didn't ring when they got a call. The people further out had party lines and you knew the call was for you by the long and short rings that came through, like a code. Of course, everybody listened in on everybody else's calls. When we visited one of our neighbors once I remember him saying that a call came at two in the morning for somebody or other, by the code they knew who it was for. He and his wife discussed whether it was worth getting up to listen in, but in the end curiosity got the better of them and one of them did.

"Hello, doctor. This is Fred Landon. Sorry to be calling so early in the day. I took on a hired hand a few days ago and he's a hard working, responsible man—something hard to find these days. But he has an infected sore on his leg and that has to be looked at as soon as possible or I'm afraid he'll end up loosing the leg."

After a short pause, "Thanks for the offer, but this looks serious. He'll need a hospital. We're about to take the kids to school. Can I stop with him then?"

Another parse, "Well, there's something you should know. He's an Indian, and I'm not sure how folks will take to him being in the same waiting room with them."

Dad was shifting his weight from one foot to another. The doctor might have been wondering if it was dad who was concerned about what people would think when they found out the he had hired an Indian. It wasn't that anybody had anything against Indians other than they had a completely different culture. It was the way people always seemed to be toward those who were different than them. They had ideas stuck in their heads, and facts had no bearing on anything. In this part of the state everybody was white and that meant everybody. There was enough trouble keeping peace between the Germans and the Scandinavians.

"Okay, I'll do that. Thanks."

Dad hung up the phone. Mom was standing with a dishtowel in her hand and an expectant look, "What'd he say?"

"I'll put a straw hat on him and drive around to the back of the hospital. He'll meet us with a wheel chair. I think Justin will understand."

The drive to school was made in silence. I could see Justin was not pleased with any of this, though he had been limping even worse this morning. There wasn't much choice for him. He had some folded papers in his hand which I thought was strange. Anyway we were dumped off at school with still nothing said. Tommy had his dinner-pail and I would be home to eat.

CHAPTER 3

Even though the big kids were bumping around chairs above the kindergarten room so it sounded like thunder, it was sunny out so I had some hope that I could walk home without getting soaking wet. After we were released from another morning of, well, nothing, I was off walking fast. I couldn't help thinking about Justin. As I walked I prayed for him. He would be no good to dad with a missing leg. Plus, I had seen a man on main street sitting on his crutches with a raw stump for one leg. It looked terrible. I prayed some more.

When I got home mom said they hadn't heard anything about Justin. The afternoon went slowly. When it was getting close to supper time the phone rang. After mom hung up she said dad was in the barn and I should go get him.

When dad came in the house mom said, "They had to operate on his leg and he should stay in the hospital over night, but he refuses. The doctor is still there and will wait for you if you go in right now."

Dad washed quickly and went to the car—still the '38 Chevy. After dad left, mom was digging around upstairs and came down with an arm load of old quilts. "Tommy, you and Jamie carry these out to the haymow. I know that stubborn man won't sleep in a bed, even if it kills him. Well, good enough for him if it does." She said it but I could tell she didn't mean it.

Mom had started supper and I was getting hungry. Finally dad got home with Justin in the passenger seat. He stopped and backed the car up into the haymow like mom had expected. We were all there to watch as dad helped Justin get the crutches to where he could use them. Dad made a pile of hay near the wall and put a quilt and pillow on it.

Looking at mom dad said, "Doc says he can't have anything to eat this evening so you might as well put supper on for us. I'll help bed him down."

It was awkward as dad tried to help with Justin just about pushing him away. He was a proud man, but he allowed himself to be assisted a little. There were two quilts lying beside him, but the day was warm.

Dad said, "I'll be out in a bit to check on you and bring some water."

Justin nodded. He didn't make a sound but his face said it hurt a lot.

While we were eating dad told us what the doctor had said. "Justin was in the Army in Italy and was wounded pretty bad. When he got back to the States, he got an honorable discharge with disabilities and then they put him in the VA Hospital in St. Cloud to complete his recovery. Justin was concerned about a mix-up of records in St. Cloud, so with good sense he brought along the papers he got when he arrived in New York. He had gotten two Purple Hearts for being wounded in combat, and a Silver Star for bravery. Doc said a shell went off close to him and he took a lot of shrapnel. One of the effects was he doesn't hear much with his left ear. They dug out all the shrapnel or so they thought. But, they missed a small jagged piece stuck in the bone below his knee. They get so may wounded men and they do as good a job as they can, but there's always another one. His body was trying to get rid of the foreign object by festering, but it was stuck. They did x-rays in the hospital and the doctor is sure they got it all now.

"The thing is, he is badly infected and he may lose his leg. Time will tell. He had previously been given shots for tetanus but Doc gave him some more. He also left some sulfa drug in the wound before he sewed it up. He said they have a new drug called penicillin that's supposed to be really good at curing infections. But, all that they can make goes to the active military for now. But, if it goes well, he'll be up and around in a few days and doing light work in a week or so. I guess, we can keep him around. We owe those guys something."

Mom was looking worried, "Feeding him won't be hard, but how much will the operation and everything else cost?"

"Doc's sure the Government will pay the bills. They've come through for less severe cases than this. He will submit the charges to the government so in any case we don't have to worry about it now."

After supper dad took a two quart jar full of water out to Justin. I was about to go, too, but he said I had to leave him alone so he could rest. We said our night prayers and at the end we always said "God bless mama, daddy, Tommy, Jamie, Mikey, Justin, Chips and the soldiers." Tonight we added a special prayer for Justin.

It was still April but had gotten comfortably warm so Tommy and I didn't need the heavy wool blanket on our bed. That was more than a blanket. I watched them when they made it. They laid out a large piece of cloth, took an armful of wool from the spring shearing that had been cleaned of the sheep's natural oil. Dad said the oil was called lanolin. They spread the wool evenly over the fabric. Then a second piece of cloth went on top and it was sewed all around. Yarn pieces were poked through and tied every few inches to keep the wool from bunching up. That kept us warm on the coldest nights. When the night was warm it caused us to sweat.

I opened my eyes and it was night but not dark—bright moonlight streamed through the window. Someone had called my name. I listened but there was no other sound. Who could have called me? I thought it might have been Tommy, but he was asleep or he was pretending to be. He liked to play tricks on me sometimes, but never at night like this. It couldn't have been mom or dad because the house wasn't burning down. I thought of Justin but he was out in the barn.

I closed my eyes and tried to get back to sleep but it wasn't working. The voice calling my name had been so clear that I couldn't forget it. Justin came to mind again. Why did I feel he needed me? It was not logical that I could have heard his voice this far away, but logic was not a big thing for a six year old kid. I had to go see. I slipped out of bed and put on my pants over my pajamas while sitting on the floor so I wouldn't wake up Tommy, then my socks. About to put on my shoes I stopped. They would make too much noise. Mom and dad slept on the first floor and the stair-door was by the door to their bed room. At the bottom of the stairs, I open the door and stepped into the living room. There was no sound.

I knew the drawer where the flashlight was kept in the kitchen so I went to get it. Everything in the drawer was shades of gray so I felt around until I found it. The door to the porch would be the toughest. Of course, it wasn't locked. Nobody locked their doors at night. But, it made noise when it was opened. Sure enough it made a screeching noise like from that place we were told we would go if we were bad. But, maybe it wasn't so bad because nobody came to scold me for being up.

Chips slept on the rug outside the door and I stepped on him. He made a short yelp and I thought I was done for. But, I must have had the door closed enough so the sound didn't get into the house. He was up, sniffing and wagging his non-existent tail like he always did. With the porch screen door quietly closed I was out. The moon was so bright it was almost like day. I ran toward the barn and my feet were instantly wet and cold from the dew on the grass. When I reached the driveway the small stones poked at my feet so I slowed to a walk. As I entered the shadows in the barn I switched on the flashlight.

Justin had rolled off the pile of hay dad had made for him and was on his stomach. The jar of water had been tipped over. He looked into the light and his face was all red and dripping with sweat. "Water," he said in a rasping voice, "Get me some water."

"Justin," I said, "You're awful sick. You need a doctor."

"Water," he gasped out again.

"Okay, I'll get dad."

I ran like the dickens over the pebbles and all. I let the screen door slam behind me and opened the kitchen door with no care about noise. In the dining room I punched the light switch, dumping the flashlight on the dining room table, and ran to the bedroom.

Beside the bed, I said, "Dad, come on. Justin's real sick and needs some water. Come on!"

I said it again. "Wake up, dad." Finally, he was sitting on the edge of the bed running his hand through his hair.

"I went out to see how Justin was doing and he needs help, probably the doctor."

Mom was awake by this time and everything was in confusion. She immediately thought one of the kids was sick. She went to the little room connected to their bedroom to check on Mikey.

"Come on," I kept saying. "Justin is real sick and might be dying." That was a little fib because I hadn't given any thought to that up until that moment. Justin hadn't said he was dying that was for sure.

After being sure I was not hurt and not terribly crazy the lamp beside bed was on and we were moving toward the living room so we wouldn't wake up Mikey. Dad had his shoes in his hand, and put them on. He was tired but resigned. "Might as well go out and check," he said. He went to the kitchen and I heard him go out.

"Why did you go out to Justin?" was the first question from mom as I expected.

I was thinking fast because I didn't know why I had done it. Dream. Yeah, a dream. Big people had dreams the same as kids. "I had a bad dream that Justin was real sick so I got up and went out to see if he needed anything. His face is all red and dripping with sweat. He had tipped over the jar and was asking for water."

This interrogation continued. Mom put her hand on my forehead to see if I had a fever and was delirious.

The kitchen door opened again and dad went to the phone and in a few seconds said three numbers. He waited and we watched him wait. "Doc, this is Fred Landon. Justin has a high fever, never saw anything like it. I think he's dying. Can you come?"

There was a pause, "Yes, we'll do that." More pause, "Okay, thanks."

He looked at mom. "He'll come, and he wants us to heat a big kettle of water, not hot, just warm. We'll wet his clothes with it to bring down the fever. If it's too cold it will send him into shock, if too hot, it won't do any good. Start a fire and I'll take some drinking water out to him.

I was forgotten which for once I felt good about—no more questions.

Mom and dad had decided to make the water too hot because they could always add cold water to it to make it the right temperature. While the water was heating dad carried the half full ten gallon can of drinking water to the barn.

Car lights shown in the driveway and Chips went out and barked to let us know he was doing his part. Dad came out of the house carrying the kettle by two handles and potholders. He had the light on in the haymow, but it was one small bulb in a very large space so wasn't terribly helpful. The doctor also had a flashlight, and I saw them going to the barn. I went out and followed at a distance. This was not something I was going to miss.

Dad held the flashlight and the doctor looked at Justin. He immediately asked for the warm water. Too hot! Dad had the can of cold water and pored some in. Just right. Using the drinking dipper that they had brought along, the doctor proceeded to wet all of Justin's clothes. Mom had sent out a towel and that was wet with cold water and put on his forehead.

Justin moaned now and then but seemed to be asleep. The doctor shook his head and said, "He's bad. If he'd been in the hospital, we would have caught it sooner. As it is, it's lucky you decided to check on him. He'd 'a been dead by morning."

I felt better than I could ever remember feeling.

The doctor said he'd stay around for awhile and then would let dad or mom stay with Justin. He didn't want him left alone because he wasn't sleeping, he was in a coma and still might die. I didn't know what a coma was, but it must have meant real sick. I was, of course, corralled and put to bed. Tommy hadn't even stirred.

Next morning everybody was tired except Tommy but off to school we went and they'd keep an eye on Justin who still hadn't come out of the coma thing. It was strange the way your life can be going along pretty much like normal and can seem pretty boring, then something happens that makes you think normal isn't so bad. Dad needed a hired man; Justin had been working out better than others he'd tried. They weren't about to turn their backs on him in his condition, but it increased the load on the family rather than lessening the load. But, we were good Catholics and here was a man in need even if he was pretty stubborn.

All the other hired men dad had tried would work a week or so and they'd be gone for whatever reason I didn't know. There was one man in town who always hired himself out. That was what he did for a living. He had a wife and kids and was a nice man. He was good and was usually not available because everybody wanted to hire him, but he helped us sometimes. His name was Hank Cooper. Previously, mom mentioned him, but dad said he knew Hank had solid work for the summer.

The doctor came back in the evening and headed to the barn. I heard him mention to dad that if his fishing buddy, a veterinarian, heard about this, he'd never live it down. Justin was still not awake so as to talk, but they got him to drink lots of water. The doctor said that was what was keeping him alive. Most of the time when people got like this they wouldn't drink. I wondered what he did when he had to pee, but nobody mentioned it and I didn't ask.

The next morning as soon as I was dressed I ran out to the haymow. Dad was there and Justin was awake and setting up but he was weak and laid down again. As we went to he house dad said he might make it. It was strange because we were talking about a man like we would talk about a sick cow.

CHAPTER 4

Two days later when we were eating dinner mom mentioned that Justin was eating enough to stay alive and could move around a little. He was eating soup mostly, but it was staying down and he was feeling better. The leg was doing fine. The doctor came out each day and changed the bandage.

After eating I headed for the barn. There wasn't much for a kid to do and this was the event of the day. Justin was laying down but looked up as he heard me coming. He nodded and said, "A good man. It looks like you are the one who saved my life. That means a lot to an Indian, more than to white folks. Tell me why you came out to me in the middle of the night."

I couldn't get over the way he talked, the same as a white man, sometimes even better than some of the neighbors up the road. There was a stump of wood a foot in diameter and about as long that I rolled over by him. I tipped up on end and sat on it. He watched with interest as I did this. Maybe it was the curiosity of watching a child do things in a way he had learned must be done because his size and strength prohibited doing it the way big people would.

It was hard to tell him why I had come out so I said, "I was sleeping and someone called my name. At first I thought it was Tommy playing a trick on me but he was sleeping. All I know is I thought about you out here all alone and decided I had to come out and see if you were okay. I told mom and she said it must have been your guardian angel that came and called me. We all have guardian angels, you know."

He laid back on his bed on the hay looking at the roof. Here and there was a bright point of light where there was a hole in the shingles. After awhile he said. My grandfather must have called you. To us grandfather doesn't mean only my father's father, but can be any of those who have gone before. We call them *pawáganak*. It is a belief of my people, my father's people, that there are spirits of the dead that sometimes help us and sometimes are bad to us."

I had never heard things like this so didn't know what to say. So, I asked, "Who were your mother's people."

He raise himself enough to put his arm under his head so he could face me. "My father was an Ojibwe. They are the Indians from mostly the northern part of Minnesota and to the east. My mother was Sioux, also called Dakotas. They are mostly in the western and southern part of the state and in North and South Dakota to the west. That makes me a half-breed to both tribes, though all Indian. It's the Ojibwe nation where I'm registered." After a pause he asked, "Weren't you afraid coming outside alone in the middle of the night?"

"Nah. I had the flashlight and Chips was with me. I didn't need the light to get to the barn because the moon was so bright. I never saw it so bright. It was shining like a silver ball in the sky. I used the flashlight in the barn. You really scared me the way you looked. I remember the prickly gravel on my feet coming out, by didn't notice it running back."

"That was the moon of the deep water shining on you. It starts the growing season. If you're an Indian you have blood that runs close to the earth and that makes you one with the world around you. We can feel the full moon pull on us. That moon was pulling on me and helped me to call to you for help. Maybe you have some Indian blood in you. After this, our lives will pull on each other at times when we don't expect it, especially at the full moon of the deep water."

Chips was by me and I was petting him, something he liked a lot. I pretended I wasn't too interested in what Justin was saying, but I didn't miss a word. It was funny things he was saying and I didn't understand most of it. Finally I said, "If you're all Indian being half of each, do you have an Indian name, you know like on the radio, like Eagle Feather or something'?"

He smiled and waited. I waited, too. Finally he said, "Yes I do. It's Running Wolf."

"Why are you called that? It's a good Indian name—just wondering."

"Indians get their names in many ways. Sometimes it has something to do with how they were born, or some characteristic about them when they are babies. Other times it's taken from the things they do when they are young and still others from when they are grown and do brave or odd things. Most times how we are named is finally settled by a grandfather based in part by something he learned from a dream visitor. I had mine from as long as I can remember. If it came in a dream the grandfather would not tell why it was given because it is bad luck to reveal dreams."

"Could it have anything to do with the big knife with the bone-handle you always wear, the one you didn't want to show me?"

"No. That knife was passed on to me by a man in the Veterans Hospital in St. Cloud. They gave him a drug, morphine I think, for his pain. When the drug took effect he'd relax and go to sleep and he was afraid someone would steal it while he was unconscious. Since I was doing well and nearly ready to be released, he decided to give it to me for safe keeping until he got better. He said it was a special knife, special in ways a knife usually isn't. From the way he said it, it seemed it involved a secret. I tried to get him to say what that meant but every time I mentioned it we were interrupted before he could tell me. He died before he could let me in on the secret, if there were one. It's odd, he was getting better each day and then one morning he was gone. The doctor said he had died in the night." He turned to the wall of the barn and produced the knife from in the hay. Slowly he pulled it from its sheath. It was shinny, but not silver shinny, a gray shinny.

He turned it over laying first one side and then the other on the palm of his hand as if admiring it. The handle wasn't really part of a bone but more like part of the antler of a large animal. That made the handle rough and easy to grip tightly.

"The dying man had visitors quite often and they seemed to be unsavory types. I felt reluctant to give the knife to any of them because the man could have done it himself on any of several occasions. Then something happened that had nothing to do with the knife and I left the hospital a little before I should have. If I hadn't left early, that shard of metal in my leg might have been found before I was released. But, things work out the way the do and there is no telling why that is so."

Justin slid his thumb across the flat side of the blade. "By the gray shade of the metal you can see it is not the usual steel used to make knives. I don't know what kind of steel it is but it takes a keen edge. It can be sharpened to a finer edge than other knives I've used. It can cut clean through bone in one slash."

He handed it to me saying, "Here, you can hold it but be careful not to touch the edge or you will cut yourself."

It was heavy in my hands as I looked at it, my eyes glistening. It was a real man's knife and I longed to have one like it even if I was just a kid and could hardly lift it. As I turned it over in my hand the side of my thumb touched the edge and without feeling it I was cut.

"Wow," I said softly. "It's heavy."

"Not so heavy as it must seem to you. It's a throwing knife and a knife that is thrown must have mass or it won't penetrate what you hit with it."

As I handed it back to him I saw the blood on my thumb. "I cut myself," I said.

"I thought you might have," he replied. "Here, now we'll do something. I'll be the *manidookaazo* which in Ojibwe means one who takes it upon himself to perform a ceremony. It has to be that way because we're limited here with respect to Ojibwe trappings such as a *midewiwin* which is a medicine lodge and a *Midé* which is a man of special powers." He made a slight cut in his thumb, too, and said, "Now, press your cut against mine."

He reached over and took my hand and held my thumb against his. "The blood mixes and I become your *miskwi niijikiw*, or blood brother, and you mine. We become blood brothers of the moon of the deep water. It is so. You saved my life and now we are brothers."

After that he deftly took the knife and slipped it into the scabbard. The way he handled it, it seemed to be part of him, like it knew what he wanted it to do.

I wrapped my handkerchief around my thumb until it stopped bleeding. The cut wasn't bad and would heal fast. Then I put the end of a piece of hay in my mouth and chewed on it like we sometimes did as the things he had said rattled around in my head. "That full moon sure was pretty and I was glad I was out to see it, but I don't think it pulled on me. I think it was your guardian angel that saved you. We have a picture on our bedroom wall of two kids chasing a butterfly by a river and there is this big beautiful guardian angel with pretty wings watching over them so they don't fall in the water and drown. The angels especially help kids, but they stay around when you get big, too. And, they only do good for you, never bad like your 'ancestor spirit' things. They are also messengers that tell God that you need help with stuff.

"Last year I was running through the tall corn when Tommy was cutting corn with the corn knife. He made a whack and cut my leg as I ran by. Dad said he would have cut my leg clean off, slick as a whistle, if Tommy hadn't hit the corn stalk first. That really hurt. They took me to the hospital and the doctor used five metal clips to close up the skin so it would heal. It really itched after a couple of days and mom said that meant it was healing. All I have is a white scar below my knee now. My guardian angel put that corn stalk in the way of the knife so my leg wouldn't get cut off."

Justin had laid back on his bed and was staring at the roof of the barn giving no sign that he had heard me. Finally he said, "If your angel had put two corn stalks in the way you wouldn't have been hurt at all."

"Nope. I was running and my leg would have run into the knife anyway."

"Suppose so."

Chips pulled away and turned on his side and scratched his belly with one of his hind legs. Then he was back with his cold wet nose coaxing me to pet him some more. "Go away, that's enough. Find a cat to chase."

Looking at Justin slumped back on the blanket on the hay I asked, "Has your leg started to itch yet?"

He didn't answer right away like he did a lot of times. "It does sometimes. The part that is the hardest is how weak I am. The doctor said it will pass and is because of how sick I was. The fever ran down my system and now it needs time to get better. It's hard not to be able to work. In the Army I didn't mind when I was laid up because that meant I wasn't being shot at."

The news on the radio and discussions when big people talked was most of the time about Germans, lots of time called Krauts and Japs too, of course. The only thing I really knew about them was they were really bad. So bad that when Tommy and I set fire to the pile grass and leaves in the driveway while we were raking we had said, "Let's pretend it's a Jap house."

"Did you shoot any Germans?" I asked.

Once again he didn't answer. It was colder today than yesterday so I got up and ran around the haymow with Chips chasing after me. The dog didn't have much to do, either, most of the day so when I was out he was with me a lot. Tommy spent more time in the house than I did, but sometimes we had good times outside together. I came back and stood on the wood stump and looked down at Justin.

I was about to leave when he said, "I don't know if I directly killed any, but we sure shot at each other a lot. I was in demolition so it wasn't my job to close with and fight the enemy directly."

"What does demolition mean?"

"It was my job to blow things up."

"What kinds of things?"

"Bridges mostly. What most slows down an army are things like rivers and deep gorges so bridges are very important in a war. Sometimes we'd blow up trees so they'd fall on a road to slow down the enemy. Other times we'd blow up buildings to they'd have to sleep outside in the snow. We even blew up our own tanks and trucks sometimes to keep them from falling into the hands of the Germans. Worst of all we always had to drive around with a truck full of explosives. The only good thing about that was if the truck ever took a hit, we wouldn't suffer."

I was sitting on my little stump again wishing he would keep talking but it seemed that was all he was going to say. I said, "When dad left you at the hospital he said the doctor knew that you got a lot of scrap-in-all in you. What's that?"

It must have been that I said it wrong that made him look at me and respond right away. "The word is shrapnel. Artillery shells are like great big bullets that they shoot up in the air at an angle from a long ways away and they rain down on you. These shells have a lot of gun powder in the center and packed in around the explosive are a bunch of lead balls the size of marbles. When the shells explode the balls fly out in all directions. I was hit by four or five of them. The outside casing also splits into small pieces and they fly around, too. It was one of those pieces that was stuck in my leg bone that the doctor removed in the hospital. Since I still had all my arms and legs, the Army doctors didn't take much time with me so they missed that piece when they were digging the shrapnel balls out of me."

Justin was staring at the roof and talking as if he were far away. He even sounded different, like he was talking to himself, or someone who wasn't there. "Bearfoot was my partner. We signed up together. We had known each other from when we were small. We were pushing the Germans back and they were fighting hard because they knew they could escape across a river on an important bridge if we got too close. They already had it fitted with explosives so if they had to retreat across it they would blow it up so we couldn't follow them. It was our job to get around behind them and blow it up before they could go across so they'd be trapped between the river and our army.

"Bearfoot and I swam down the river at night and were working by the bridge at dawn when we were spotted. Shells started exploding all around us. They might have been German shells trying to stop us, or our shells trying to damage the bridge. One went off close to us and I was hit with a lot of shrapnel. We were both left for dead. Bearfoot was dead and he saved me by stopping the balls from hitting my head and upper body. He was a good friend and I miss him."

"I'll bet your guardian angel kept you from getting killed."

"Then Bearfoot's angel must have been asleep."

"I don't know. Mom says that when God says your time is up, you die so I guess even his angel couldn't go against what God wanted." With hardly a pause I continued, "It's getting cold and it might rain. Mom says you should come in the house."

"It's enough that I stay dry when it rains. It's nice to hear the rain on the roof and smell the hay. I'll get well and help your dad. I can walk a little bit now. Your mother is a good cook. Pretty soon I'll be able to come to the house to eat and save them the trouble of coming out here."

He sat up and pulled one of the quilts over his legs. "This is like being in a fancy hotel for me." He smiled and laid back again. The rain started to patter on the roof so I said good bye and ran for the house with Chips ahead of me.

CHAPTER 5

The next morning was Saturday and the sun was shining. The mayflowers were all blooming and the tree leaf buds were starting to become small leaves since it was the end of April. In a few days the wild violets would be blooming. They came out after the mayflowers wilted. We had purple and yellow violets. The mayflowers were special to me because they were the first sign of life in the spring. But, I liked the violets the best, especially the violet ones. They were of such fine shades of violet and the flowers had a fascinating shape.

We called them wild violets so I supposed there must be tame violets that people planted in flower gardens though I had never seen any. I guessed it was like we had real plumb trees that had plumbs a little larger than walnuts. Then there were wild plumbs that had plumbs the size of acorns and had large seeds, but they were real sweet at the right time. From that I took to understand that things that grew with no help from people were wild, like wild rabbits and of course wild violets.

There were more dandelions now, too. And, the poison ivy would be leafing out in the woods so I had to be careful of that. One year I had been picking violets and managed to get poison ivy that covered the back of both hands. The itching was terrible until mom figured she had to wash my hands with hot soapy water. That worked. She'd make a pan of water so hot she couldn't put her fingers in it and used a washcloth to wash my hands. She said she couldn't understand how I could stand such hot water. It made my hands feel like I was scratching them all over at the same time. The feeling was so satisfying I never forgot it all my life. That kept the itch away for about a day, then she'd do it again.

After checking the flowers, I went to see Justin. He was sitting up with dishes from his breakfast beside him and he looked better. "How ya feeling, Justin?"

He smiled. "Better, much better, Jamie."

There was a square stick beside him that had been cut off a board to make it narrower. He got up on his knees and using the stick to help, stood up. "I've been working at it and can walk around a little today," he said. Leaning on the stick he took a few unsteady steps.

As he was practicing walking I wandered away not having a very long attention span for slow repetitive things. I sure wished I had a knife like Justin's. There were old machines and various piles of junk behind most of the farm buildings so I looked for something to make a knife out of. It was hard going because whenever I saw something that would work it was attached to something bigger and besides it was all rusty. Then I saw something that was light gray. It was light for its size and not rusty so it wasn't iron, and it was a little too long but close. It was a funny metal as I handled it but it seemed that was the best I'd do. There was a rock large enough to sit on behind the shed so I started to rub the square end on the rock. It seemed to shape pretty fast as small pieces rubbed off. Every time I stopped to rest I looked at it to see how close its shape was to Justin's knife. It wasn't very good, but I kept at it. Normally I would have stopped long before this, but I really wanted a big knife. Finally my arms were tired and my hands raw so I had to stop. It wasn't finished, but it showed promise.

I hid my work under a rotten board and walked to the barn. There were kittens in the back of the machinery room, which was the room under the third floor. I went to see if I could catch one. They were old enough to be playing around so I went in and after cautiously crawling near finally caught one. There was a large wooden box in the corner with yellow powder in it and the kittens had been walking in it. I came out carrying one and showed it to Justin who was sitting on his bed again.

"Every year a cat has kittens behind the box of yellow powder and they end up getting covered with it. What a mess. I hope it's not poison."

Justin was immediately interested. "I'm doing pretty good at this walking, why don't you show me where the powder is?"

"Sure." He slowly got up using his stick and followed me into the machinery room. There was a few pieces of machinery that dad used in there, but mostly it was junk. "There it is," I said as I put the kitten down. It ran to where it's litter mates were.

The box had various boards and pieces of iron over and around it so Justin had to get to his knees to be able to reach the powder. He took a pinch of it between his thumb and finger and smelled of it, tasted it and spit it out. "Hmmm . . . ." was all he said.

"What is it?" I asked.

"Something that's best left alone. It's not poison, but best left alone."

He hobbled back to his bed on the hay and slowly sat down. He reached over and lightly scratched his bandage through his pants leg. "It's itching now so the wound is healing. It's the weakness that's bothering me. My biggest problem will be keeping from doing too much too soon. In the war that happened a lot. A man would have his wounds healing well and he'd be sent back to the front before he was able. Combat is hard work for strong men and if you're still recovering from wounds or illness, it'll kill you. I saw it happen."

"Why didn't they send you back to the front?"

He smiled. "Good luck or bad luck depending on how you look at it. After that shell went off so close I couldn't hear anything. They thought I'd never be able to hear again which meant I wouldn't be any good to them so they let me out. I hate to leave a job half done, but I'm not going to sign up again, either. My hearing is back in one ear, but this side," he said pointing to his left ear, "isn't doing too well."

"Maybe God thought you'd be needed here and He had your guardian angel save you, but not good enough to stay in the Army."

He shook his head. "Whatever you do, keep that simple faith for as long as you live. I saw men die, some good, some bad. The ones with faith managed it the best. Never had much taught to me about religion other than the Indian ways and that's not religion the way you think of it. The Indian way is good for looking at life when the tribe is close to nature, when life and death are all tied up with the sun, the rain, and the seasons. With your people having so many ways to keep nature away from you its hard to be an Indian. The Army and the war was much different from how I was brought up so dying worried me some. That's why I didn't mind having a load of explosives behind me in the truck. If it ever exploded, I wouldn't have time to worry. Still, there were times like when I was trying to sleep in a pup tent wondering about what would happen before the night was over."

He laid back on the hay with his hands behind his head. Looking at the roof he said, "If I'm needed here, what am I doing laying like a lump of meat on the hay?"

"You'll get strong again. The hard work comes when it's time to make hay. Most of the time now dad sits on the tractor while he's plowing and planting."

"You know about the cycles of life. That's good. You're lucky you're growing up on a farm. Its closer to the Indian ways than living in a city. Some of the men I served with had no idea even of the phases of the moon. You have the run of the place as far as you can run and it's all yours. It's not like the forests where I grew up, but better than most. You won't appreciate this until you're grown and see how society fences you in."

Then he was quiet again. Justin was a funny guy that way, but I guessed we were all different so that was what was different about him. I chased around the haymow. There was still a pile of hay that I climbed up on and tried to slide down but it didn't work because it wasn't steep enough.

"Jamie," Justin called.

I went over to him.

"Do you suppose there are some scraps of tarpaper around any place? Do you know what I mean, like they put on roofs?"

"Sure. Last summer dad used it to cover the roof on the gray brooder house." That was a small building on skids that in the past was used to raise baby chicks after they hatched but dad used it for baby turkeys.

Dad had six brooder houses of different sizes and shapes and the turkeys were getting bigger all the time. He brought them home when there was still snow on the ground. They'd be in cardboard boxes with round holes the size of a nickel in the sides. The holes were to let air in. When we took them out of the box we'd take each one and put it's beak in the feed and then the water so they'd know where to get food. Now, mom mostly did the feeding and watering of them while dad worked in the field. I helped sometimes putting the feed in the little feeders, but I spilled too much so I did other stuff. Tommy was good at that. No matter what they had me do I didn't do it very well. It was always hard work, and I hated work.

"Do you suppose you could find a piece of tarpaper that was cut off and not used. I need a piece at least this big," he said showing about a two foot square with his hands.

I ran out of the barn on my errand. It was nice to be needed as long as it was for something besides work. Chips was with me always hoping there'd be something fun to do. There was a few scraps of tarpaper that had been left where they fell. The men were always busy and didn't bother to clean up because if they had it would only make a pile of junk, anyway. The dead grass from last summer laid on it and the first piece I garbed tore and left a small piece in my hand. For the next try I was more gentle and it went better. Chips was there as I lifted it up hoping to find a mouse or something under it. He sniffed at the wet earth but found nothing. The piece I had was a lot bigger than what Justin had asked for but I dragged it across the lawn to the barn.

"Here's the best piece I could find."

He took it without a word and felt of it, flexing it as he did. Reaching over by the barn wall he brought out his knife.

"This knife is made for fighting though it is good for normal knife things, too." With the point of the blade he marked a pattern in the piece of tarpaper. Putting the knife back in the scabbard he flexed the sheet and the piece he had marked fell out. Even the tip of the knife was sharp. He had hardly touched the tarpaper with it and it had cut almost through.

I could tell he wanted to sit with his legs crossed Indian style, but that would upset his bandage. He shifted himself until his back was against the barn wall and considered the piece of tarpaper in his hand. He slowly started to bend it working his fingers along it as he did. Finally, he had it shaped into something resembling a cone. "If we laid it in the sun for awhile it would get softer and form much better, but this will do fine."

"What are ya making?"

"I'll talk to your father and if he agrees I'll tell you all about it."

"Gotta be going," I said as I ran out of the barn.

The sun was warm even if the air was still cool. I went to the swing hanging from a pole between two trees and started to swing. There was always so much to do. I wondered how big people found time to work.

42

CHAPTER 6

About noon I went to the house knowing it was time for dinner. Chips and I had been in the plumb orchard west of the house. The orchard started beyond what we called the front lawn and at one time had been a real orchard. In its present state it had perhaps a dozen large plumb trees but mostly it was brush. I had heard Chips barking so I went to investigate. He was digging in a hole under a tree where he had probably chased a rabbit but it could have been anything. After digging with his front paws he would stick his nose in the hole and take in deep breaths. It was clear he could smell the varmint, whatever it was. He dug like that sometimes when he really got irritated by the critters always getting away from him, but I never saw him dig far enough to catch one.

When I got to the house Justin was sitting in the chair by the window that looked out on the back yard. His back was to the window and his arms rested on the table. Tommy was there and mom, Justin and Tommy were talking about the weather and the war. Those were always the two main topics of conversation. He had cleaned himself up and maybe even put on a clean shirt. Seeing him in the full light I was surprised at how changed he was from that first day he arrived. It was obvious that he had lost weight and the skin on his face seemed loose. He was early for dinner and was uncomfortable. But, I guessed he hadn't know the exact time and had to allow for his slow movement. We heard the tractor pull up to where dad always parked it and the engine stop. So as not to be in the way when he came in, I washed my hands.

Dad stepped through the door and nodded at Justin. "Glad to see you're among the living." That was his standard greeting when any of us had been sick and then showed up to eat with the family.

"I've been coming along pretty good. Maybe I can help with the milking this evening."

Dad was washing his hands at the sink as he replied, "We'll see. Maybe the morning would be better. We'll see."

The meal passed with a little better mood than the past few days. Everybody wanted to be as considerate as possible of Justin, but the fact remained that dad needed help. About the time we were finishing dad looked at mom and said, "It's the end of the month today and we still have a gas stamp left. Will you go in and fill up the car. It's low enough so it will take the eight gallons we get with a stamp this month."

Mom nodded. "I need a few things at the store anyway."

Dad sipped his coffee and turned to Justin, "Those darned gas stamps are a real pain the way you can't use them beyond their expiration date. Have you ever had to deal with that?"

Justin shook his head. "Can't say I have. In the Army if you were driving a vehicle and could find a POL depot, that's Petroleum, Oil, and Lubricants—the Army abbreviates everything—all you had to do was say fill it up. If you had some Jerry cans on the back they'd fill them too."

"Well this isn't the Army. It would be one thing if a guy could carry over a couple of stamps especially from the winter when a guy doesn't need so many. As it is I end up with five gallon cans full of gas setting around in preparation to spring plowing—just doesn't make sense. And you never know how many gallons you can get with a stamp, sometimes it's as high as eleven or as low as eight."

Justin was listening intently. "I thought you could get all the gas you needed for running a farm."

Dad scoffed. "In theory you can. Here's how it is. Every year I have to go in and fill out a form as long as my arm saying how many acres of what I'll be planting. And they want to know all kinds of other stuff too like the horsepower of my tractor, if I have a forty acres five miles away, all that sort of stuff. Then, they assume I must be lying about something or other so instead of giving me enough gas to farm a hundred-twenty acres, I get enough for eighty."

Nobody said anything because we all knew gas stamps really got dad steamed. "Of course," he continued, "the bankers, the lawyers, the men who own the stores on main street seem to get all the stamps they want, and new tires too. I'll tell you a little secret. Ned Blevins who runs the Co-Op in town told me that the bankers and such people even come in with counterfeit stamps that they buy on the black market. He can tell they're not real but if he doesn't take them pretty soon nobody will sell him groceries. This war is tearing this county apart, I tell you."

He took another sip of coffee and looked into his cup. "Darned coffee is rationed, too, and they cut it with something so it's not all real coffee." Replacing his cup he looked at Justin again as said, "Ned even had a joke from a magazine pinned up on his wall. It showed bank robbers who had gotten the main vault open. The vault had new tires in it. There was money falling on the floor but the robbers were grabbing the tires. Getting tires is bad enough, but it's the gasoline that's really the rub.

"And then we come to the bad part," he said laughing a little, "if that's possible. The thing about this rationing program it that they have the worst people in society running it. Think about it. Most able bodied men are in uniform except for those who are needed to run the factories and farms to provide what is needed for the war. Somebody has to run the trains, power plants, and things like that. Suddenly they need thousands of more workers to pass out ration books. These come from what's left since all the productive people are employed. These are people who for one reason or another never held a job much of any kind or are retired people. Those in the first category are generally used to getting by without working and will take bribes whenever offered. The retired people aren't up to it and make a lot of mistakes. So when something is wrong or you ask to have your case reviewed they're lazy or tired and say no. They have immense power over people's lives and are the last people you'd want to have that authority."

Justin was leaning on the table intently listening to what dad was saying. When there was a pause he asked, "Couldn't this Blevins call the authorities and turn in the people who passed the illegal gasoline stamps?"

"No, and there are reasons. The first is that this all seems to be connected with organized crime so there are so many layers in the distribution of those things that they never get to the real problem—the guys that are printing them. Another reason is that a lot of what you think of as 'the authorities' are in on it, too. All we can do is hope this war comes to an end while we still have a country left."

As dad got up to go back to work, he said, "This isn't your problem. You've certainly done your part. It's irritating, that's all. As they say, life isn't fair."

After dinner I walked with Justin back to the haymow. He sat on the hay and rested for awhile deeper in thought even than was normal for him. Finally he said shaking his head, "As soon as I'm on my feet I'll have to work those old nags a lot harder. I hate to see your dad pressed so hard for gasoline."

"Yeah," I said, "Most of the time he doesn't say much about it but stuff bothers him. I guess having someone new to tell it to makes him feel better."

I had been walking around in the haymow and decided to find something to do when Justin asked me a question.

"You said your guardian angel kept your leg from being cut off when Tommy swung the corn knife. Has he done any other good deeds for you lately?"

He might have been "pulling my leg" as we would say, but I took it as an honest question. "Yeah, he helps me sometimes like last spring when I fell in the water." I moved closer and sat down on my little stump.

Justin was lightly scratching his bandage and I knew it must itch like crazy if it was a big wound and was healing well. Without looking up he asked, "Where was that?"

"Down in the woods with the mayflowers. There had been some real warm days and the last of the snow was melting fast. Because of the warm weather I went to check on the flowers but it was too soon. I could hear water running by the road and went to see what it was. It wasn't much further. The water from the snow melting was causing a river in the ditch. Where it come to a low spot it wasn't running fast. There I saw dry snow half way across the ditch like snow covering an island. I wanted to see if the water was running on the other side of the road, too, so I decided to jump to the island and then across to the road. But when I landed on the island I went right through it. It was only the top of a snow bank with water running under it."

I stopped talking. After waiting for me to continue and I didn't, Justin looked up and asked, "What happened next?"

It was funny but I'd never thought about it before. I couldn't exactly remember. After quite awhile when Justin didn't ask any more questions, I said, "I remember the big surprise I felt when I went right through the snow. I knew immediately that I had been wrong about there being an island and how dumb it was for me to have thought that. I remember the cold water and then I was soaking wet running though the woods towards the house. I wasn't crying because I knew I'd be scolded for being so naughty and careless for having fallen in the water. Tommy and I were always slopping around in water wearing our overshoes and floating pieces of straw that we pretended were boats down the streams made by the melting snow. When I got to the house it was obvious to mom that's what had happened. I peeled off my clothes and mom brought dry ones for me. My scolding wasn't as bad as I had expected."

To my surprise, Justin seemed genuinely interested in my story. "Try to remember what happened right after you fell though the island."

"Well, I remember the water was running a lot faster than I thought because it moved me to the side."

"Did your feet land on the bottom?"

"I don't remember. Maybe they did, but I should remember that."

"Did your face go under the water?"

"No, because I still had my cap on and it wasn't wet."

"Do you remember crawling out of the stream?"

"Nope, just running."

Justin was quiet again as was his way. It seemed he spent a lot of time thinking about things. It was warmer now that the sun was high in the sky so I decided to go outside and find something to do.

As I got up Justin looked up and said, "You think your guardian angel pulled you out of that stream of snow melt water?"

"I can't swim, my clothes were all wet, my overshoes were full of water, and I was never so cold in my life. Somebody helped me."

"Do you have any more guardian angel stories?"

"Why do you want to know this stuff?"

A strange look came over his face. Maybe he thought he shouldn't have asked because it wasn't any of his business. Most of the time he didn't like to tell stuff about himself.

"I don't want you to say things that are private, like you want to keep only to yourself. I'm curious because I've never heard anything like this."

Walking back a few steps I sat on my little stump again. "There is another one but if I tell it, you have to promise not to tell anybody else."

"Okay, it's a deal. I won't tell."

"Late last fall, the haymow was full of hay but it sloped down toward the driveway where the hay wagon is pulled in. Tommy and I slid down the hay sometimes but to slide on hay it has to be exactly the right angle or it doesn't work and this wasn't right for that. Other times if there were a sling rope hanging from the hay carrier over the driveway we'd swing on the rope. But this time dad had pulled the carrier back into the barn so it was out of the way.

"One day I thought I'd try to get a rope over the hay rail, you know that iron rail attached to the rafters." I pointed up and Justin nodded. "Up on the third floor the rail isn't so far away so I had an old bolt tied to a piece of binder twine and I threw up the bolt a hundred times trying to get it over the rail. Finally I got it. Then I tied the twine to the metal loop on the end of a sling rope and pulled it up to the rail, all the way up over and down again so I had both metal ends of the sling rope together. Do you know what a sling rope is?"

"I'm not sure."

"You'll find out when we make hay. It's two ropes that attach to a metal ring at one end. On each of the other ends a piece of iron is clamped on and the iron has a hole, making a small loop in the end."

I stopped because I didn't really want to tell it all, but Justin was waiting for the rest of the story. He seemed to like a good story. He nodded, "Then what?"

"Well, I tied the two metal loops together with as much twine as I could get though the holes in the metal ends. After that I pulled the rope over the rail until the twine was on the rail. That put the metal ring at the bottom, but it was too high to be used as a swing over the driveway. I soon found that if I pulled the rope to the top of the hay, it was the right height to sit in the loop of rope and still be above the hay. I shoved off and swung down angled across the driveway and up toward the wall on the other side. It turned out that my feet came up under the rafters where the roof meets the wall. You see that? The roof is pretty steep so the rail is a lot higher than where the roof meets the outside wall."

Justin nodded. "It's a good thing you put the rope over the rail where you did or you might have smashed into that wall on the other side of the driveway where we pull in the loads of hay. Is that where you think your angel helped you?"

"No. I never even thought of that. I was coming to that part. That was great fun so I found a short board to put in the bottom of the loop of rope so the rope wouldn't pinch my butt. That swing was odd in one way. You see there are hangers where the rail is attached to the rafters on about every other one. Well, when I pulled the swing back to the top of the hay where I started to swing, the rope pulled back to a hanger. Then, when I swung down, passed the lowest part and started to swing up it would slide on the rail to the next hanger where it would stop with a big jerk. It was funny that on the return swing when it slid back to where it started it would hardly jerk at all and the swing had lost most of its force. So, the main fun was only from that first mighty swing forward, but that was really great. See those electrical wires up where the roof meets the wall? My feet would just touch them.

"I loved doing things like that so I kept at it, time after time. Now we come to the bad part. I swung down like I always did and the rope slid forward to the next hanger like it always did and stopped with a big jerk. Coming back the rope slid back with its gentle jerk and the rope broke. I fell about a foot onto the hay. I knew immediately what had happened like my angel had spoken to me, like I heard my name called when you were sick. There were no words, but I knew. The rope should have broken on the first swing down at the hard jerk, not on the gentle backward swing. When I looked at the ends of the rope I saw that the twine had sawed through by rubbing on the rail as it slid back and forth. The rope wasn't damaged at all. Dad would never know."

Justin was leaning against the barn wall listening. He was slowly nodding. "The first time I was wounded my guardian angel must have saved me. It was almost mysterious and I don't want to tell it now. Maybe sometime."

It was surprising that he'd say something like that. He was a man, full grown, and big people have things under control which is why kids needed angels to help them.

He was working on something in is head and it was a little scary to see a man who seemed to have his mind all mixed up. Finally he said, "I can tell that what you said really happened and you know there is no explaining why you fell on the hay like you did. From the way things normally work the twine should have broken at the first big jerk and you'd be dead. The normal rules of our world were changed for you for that short time. I'll have to think about that."

He laid down on the hay like he was very tired and I decided to leave. "You promised not to tell dad." He didn't say anything or even move but I knew he heard me.

I went outside with less energy then I normally had. There were times when the swing accident came to mind but I put it off easily. Now that I had told it to someone, it seemed more real. What happened was done and there was nothing I could do about that, but it made me think.

Halfway down the hill from the second floor to the door to the bottom floor a couple of the barn windows were about my height. The sun was warm and there was a tabby cat laying on a window sill sunning itself so I stopped to pet it. It immediately started to purr. There were two kinds of cats. The first were the ones that stayed all the time. They were pretty much pets and most of them would let you get close enough to pet them. A few even let you pick them up. The others were what we called wild cats that only came in the barn in the winter to stay warm. They left when the weather got nice. I had never seen them in the woods or any place so I didn't know where they lived in the summer.

There was one black cat that came in during the winter that had a growth above one of his eyes. It was a lump of scabs the way it looked. It reminded Tommy and me of a pirate so we called him piratey. He had the strange habit of sitting on the back of one of the horses. Of course, it was a warm place to sit, and we never knew if the horse liked that or not. But we supposed the horse would have had a hard time getting him off if she didn't like it. No other cat ever did that.

CHAPTER 7

The next morning, Sunday, Justin milked a few cows. On the way to church, dad said it was a big help. We all felt better and were told to say a special prayer to thank God that Justin was getting well. After Mass mom and dad stopped to talk to some of the people. It was mostly about the war, but a couple asked about our hired man. The town was between two and three thousand people so it was a small gossipy community. Everybody knew everybody else's business. My mother was particularly sensitive to that. No matter what we did, she'd always say, "What will people say?" It was usually directed at me because Tommy always seemed to want to do what people liked kids to do. I didn't want to be bad, but when there were two possible things to do, I always wanted to do the one that was not on the approved "nice kid" list.

When we got home from Mass I changed my clothes and went out to work on my knife. It was so hard for me to stay at anything and I was nearly ready to give up on the project except that it was coming along so well. Finally, I had the shape right and then all I had to do was sharpen the edge. The metal was an eighth inch thick so I rubbed it from both sides and the edge looked sharp. But when I tried to cut grass with it, it was like a blunt instrument. It didn't matter, that was all I had patience for. In the work shop I found a small piece of wood and some string that I tied on for a hilt. It looked pretty good, at least to me. I sliced at the air with it pretending to cut down imaginary attackers with every slash. I felt pretty good so I went out to where Justin was resting on the hay.

"How do you like my knife. I made it all myself," I said with pride.

In a rare hint of a smile he looked at it. His eyes even seemed to smile. "That is a fine looking knife. I know a man's weapons are a very personal thing, but I'm wondering if you'd let me handle it. I let you see my knife."

Of course, I was hoping he'd ask that. "Well, be careful with it," I replied.

With solemnity he reached over and I laid it in the palm of his hand. He grasped it by the handle and considered it carefully as he turned it first one way and then another. "Not exactly Damascus steel, but pretty good. That material is called aluminum, did you know that?"

"Nope." After a pause I said, "It's not very sharp."

He nodded. "It's a good knife for you because you are still a little young to have a really sharp knife. The blade will sharpen, but because aluminum is a soft metal, it will never get a keen edge like steel. But, now you have a knife just like a man. Well done. If you were of the people, you might be called Little Boy With Big Knife or something like that. We will see."

When I left the barn I felt great that Justin said I had a knife like a man. I hid my knife in the shed and went to find something to do.

By mid week Justin was getting around pretty well. He couldn't do real hard work yet but kept himself busy. Dad always had a ton of things to do that he never had time for. One of them was blasting stumps. Our farm was originally all woods. My grandparents who settled it started by clearing the first land. Now, they'd cut all the trees on a chunk of land starting at the edge of the woods and moving in. The good logs were sold for lumber or saved and hauled to a saw mill to be made into lumber for our own use. The tops of the trees were cut up for fire wood and the brush was piled up and burned when it got dry. As soon as the trees were cut, the land was fenced in and used to pasture the cows. With no shade from the trees the grass grew fast. The problem was the tree stumps. Nobody wanted to wait long enough for them to simply rot away especially because the oak stumps would last fifty years. They had big bulldozers that could dig out any stump but they were expensive to hire so a lot of people blasted stumps.

I heard dad and Justin discussing it a couple of times. Justin had training and experience in using explosives and he was eager to do it. Dynamite was hard to get and we had the big box of yellow powder in the barn which turned out to be blasting powder. It was the type of light work that Justin could do, too. So, when I got home from school at noon Justin was in for dinner and he and dad were discussing stump blasting. He said he was going to try some of the blasting powder in the afternoon.

"Can I come along?" It was the only thing I could say. This really sounded like fun.

Mom immediately said no but I pleaded. Finally Justin said, "It'll take quite awhile to get things working and I may not even get to setting the first charge today. There'll be no danger."

From the look on her face I could tell mom wasn't so sure but finally she relented.

In the workshop on the second floor of the barn there always had been a thing that dad called the dynamite drill. It was a steel tube with a bar sticking out on each side of one end. The other end, the drill part, was a spiral ribbon of steel that was wound so about half of the space was open. Justin took that, a shovel, and a couple of those things he had made out of the tarpaper. There was also a coil of white rope. He said it was dynamite fuse. He loaded it all on the wagon with the iron wheels and hitched up the horses. He said if he were a little stronger he'd carry it all. We went out to the stumps.

As we drove along Justin was giving me instructions. "Absolutely the first thing you must know about this business is that it's dangerous, very dangerous. Do you understand, Jamie? You must always do exactly what I tell you to do. Do you understand?"

I had never heard him or even dad talk to me that way. "Yes, sir," was all I could think of to say.

"Good. In the Army, there were high causalities among the demolition squads. Part of it was from enemy fire, but an awful lot if it was from guys getting careless and blowing themselves to bits. I believe your stories about your guardian angel, but don't expect that to apply to blasting. Out here I'm your guardian angel."

I shouldn't have said it but my mouth was always going before my mind started to work. "If you're an angel where're your wings?"

Without a pause he replied, "You're a kid and kids can't see 'em."

As he said it he turned his face to the other side. I think it was because he was starting to smile. This was a case where he was for sure "pulling my leg." But, for once I was thinking. If I pushed the issue I might be sent home so I said, "Oh."

He continued with what he was saying before I interrupted him. "At first all I'll be doing is drilling holes, but when I start setting charges, that's the time to be careful. This is really dangerous, you have to believe that."

Boy, when he wanted to let a guy know something, he could really do it. For the first time in my life I was wishing I was more like Tommy. We bumped along on the wagon in silence like he wanted me think about doom—which I was.

He stopped the horses and tied the reins to a post sticking up on the corner of the wagon. He carefully placed the fuse and the tarpaper things which I assumed contained blasting powder, on a stump. He looked around and walked to a smallish stump. "We'll start with a small one to see how the powder works. The chemicals may have separated and it won't work."

With the shovel he dug the sod out between two large roots. Then he took the dynamite drill, placed it in the hole at an angle to the ground and began to twist it. Again and again he turned on the handles. When the spiral was all in the ground he pulled it out and banged it on the top of the stump so the dirt would fall out from between the spirals.

"This is too wet," he said. "If I had dynamite it wouldn't matter, but the water in the soil will soak into the powder before I can set it off and it'll be a dud. We'll give it a try on higher ground over by the fence."

He gathered up his tools and set off. When he had picked out a stump as his next intended victim, he sat down on it. "I have to take a rest so as not to overdo it. I still feel the weakness come over me at times."

So we sat, him on his stump, me on mine. He pulled a smoking pipe out of his pocket and then a small pouch of tobacco. I had never seen him smoke before. He filled the pipe and lit it. He saw me looking at him. "Everybody smoked in the Army, mostly cigarettes. If you weren't smoking you were picked for special duty while the smokers relaxed. I didn't like to smoke but had to start out of self defense. Smoking a pipe takes more time fiddling with it for the time actually spent smoking.

Along the way I got hooked on it, not as bad as the cigarette smokers, though."

As he took a few puffs I looked around. The day was beautiful with white clouds sailing in the blue like big puffy ships. "There's a cloud that looks like a cow," I said.

"Which one?"

"That one. See its head and feet, it even has a tail." I pointed and moved my outstretched arm to show the parts I meant.

"Nah. It looks like a hawk. That's not a tail, that's wing feathers."

"You're blind, Justin. It's a cow." That was the way Tommy and I would go at it.

"Well, if it's a cow, how come it's flying in the sky?"

"Justin! I didn't say it *was* a cow, I said it looked like a cow, and now it's changed so it doesn't look like anything but a cloud."

Justin laughed like he did at rare times. I laughed too. "It's fun being a kid, isn't it?" he said. He tapped his pipe on his stump to dislodge the ashes and stowed it in his pocket. "How about we try another hole?"

When he pulled out the drill this time the dirt was damp but not as wet as the first time. "This is better, still a bit wetter then I'd like but we'll give it a try." He ran the drill in the hole again and pulled it out full of dirt as before.

"One of those charges I made should be enough for a stump this size, but it will depend on the formula of the explosive. There were no markings on the box that give its composition and your dad bought it at an auction sale so he didn't know either."

He gathered up the makings. "Now, here's when we get to a place where you have to do exactly what I say. Do you agree?"

"Yeah."

"Okay. Since the ground is pretty wet, even where we are now I'll have to do this quickly. I'll tell you what I'll do so you will know what's happening. First I cut a piece of fuse," which he did with his fighting knife. "I could have made fuse from the powder, but with damp conditions that's unreliable. Your dad managed to find a hardware store in town that still had some fuse. This is water proof so it will even burn under water. It burns at exactly a foot a minute. I tested a piece so it's good. Now I'll put the end of the fuse in the tarpaper charge I made and tie the end of the tarpaper closed around the fuse with string."

As he worked he continued, "In the Army we had a sticky glue that I could have put on all the seams and made it water tight, but I haven't found anything to do that yet. After I poke the charge down the hole I must back fill the hole with dirt as tightly as I can so the blast doesn't escape out the hole. Then, when it's ready to go, I'll split the end of the fuse so some of the powder in the center of the fuse is open to the match. Do you understand that?"

"Yeah, I think so."

He looked at me. "Here, I'll show you. I want you to know how all of this works so there will be no reason for you to be watching me when you should be a long way away. Okay?"

That did it. The game was over, the jig was up. He knew I had a hard time doing what I was told to do and was trying as hard as he could to keep me alive.

He cut off a couple of inches of fuse and then cut into one end a half inch the long way and slightly parted the two halves. He took out a wooden match and flicked his thumbnail across the end to light it. When he put the head of the burning match into the split fuse it started to hiss. "Now, watch the other end. When the fuse burns to the end it will shoot out a small flame. That is what sets off the blasting powder."

It took a few seconds and, spit, out shot a flame just like he said.

This was getting real close to doing big people stuff and I wasn't so sure anymore. "Where do you want me to go?"

"That's a good question. I'd be the happiest if you'd go back to the house, but that being unlikely, I want you to be someplace where I know you'll be."

He stood up and continued. "First I'll drive the horses halfway back to the barn so the noise won't frighten them. Then we'll find a place for you."

When he stopped the horses he tied the reins to a fence post to be sure they'd stay put. Walking back we detoured into the uncut trees. He looked at the trees and then to where the stump was as if measuring the distance with his eyes. He looked up at the budding branches. Stopping by a big elm tree he seemed satisfied. "Here's where you'll stay. Do you understand that?"

"Okay, but I can't even see the stump from here."

"Doesn't matter. This is where you'll stay or you go back to the house. I'll keep checking and when I call you have to answer."

I hated to be talked to that way, but it was nice to know someone besides my parents actually cared that much about me.

"It'll take me awhile to set the charge so don't get impatient. Until I say all clear, you stay right here!"

I nodded but I was thinking, "Okay, okay. I have ears."

Justin went back toward the stump. I stood by my tree and watched him go wondering if I'd die of hunger before I heard the all clear signal. What if night came and he forgot about me and didn't say the magic words? What if after he lit the fuse Justin got one of his weak spells and couldn't move?

Waiting was always hard especially when I knew something was going to happen. Justin was on his knees bent over working by the stump, I could just see his back. Then he straightened up, still on his knees and faced my way. "Jamie, where are you? Wave your hand."

I yelled, "Here by the big tree," and waved.

"Good, don't move. I'm ready to light the fuse."

Oh, boy. This was the best. We were going to blast a stump. I didn't know what would happen because he said he expected it to only split the stump so we could hook the tractor to parts of it and pull them out.

Justin got up and started running slowly my way. Why wasn't he running as fast as he could, that's what I'd be doing. He arrived at my tree and took me by the arm and stood me right in front of him so we could see past the side of the tree.

"We can watch the explosion because nothing can fly fast enough to get here before we duck behind the tree. But as soon as it blows we'll pull close in behind the tree. Okay, shouldn't be long now."

It seemed like forever. "What if it doesn't explode?"

"Then we leave it alone and don't go near it for twenty-four hours. There's no telling when a slow fuse might decide to come to life again."

Suddenly there was a spray of black dirt up in the air and a second later a loud boom that shook the ground and my teeth. With a jerk, Justin had me pressed between him and back of the tree. I looked to the side and saw a chunk of stump tumbling across the ground not far away—in fact way too close! I could see why standing behind the tree was a good idea. Particles of dirt also rained down on the dry leaves around us.

"Well, it worked," he said.

"Wow! It worked a lot."

We walked—Justin walked, I ran after him—back to see what was left of the stump. There was only a black hole in the ground with yellow-green smoke wafting out of it. "Looks like this is a more powerful blend than they taught us about. I hope it doesn't mean it becomes unstable. But, for now it's what we have to work with so we'll be extra careful."

He looked around. There were chunks of the stump in the field across the fence. "That's what we want to avoid. Now, we'll have to pick up the stump parts when we pick rocks."

Sitting down heavily on a stump he continued, "Darn this weakness. We'll have to quit for today."

He lit another pipe and slowly took a puff now and then. Then Justin looked at me with an unusual expression and said, "One of the grandfathers visited me in a dream last night. Normally it is a living grandfather who gives names, but there aren't any here so I must do it. You are to be called Little Manknife to the people. We are blood brothers and one day you will be inducted to the tribe with that name. What do you think?"

"It's a good name, I like it. Will it be just between you and me?"

"For now I suppose it'll have to be."

When he didn't say more I said, "Is your real grandfather still alive?"

"No. But as I said most of the old men are called grandfathers. I have a living grandfather that you would call an uncle. His name is Red Feather. He was good to me when I was growing up and taught me many things about the woods."

Justin puffed on his pipe a few times. "What happened to your knife. I haven't seen you wearing it?"

It was an embarrassing question seeing as he had given me the name of Little Manknife but I had to answer because sooner or later he'd find out. "I showed it to Tommy and he said it was dumb so I threw it away. Does that mean I don't get to keep the name?"

"No. Not at all. When a name is given it stays. It's your initiative and desire to be a real warrior that is important. It shows a lot about what kind of man you will be."

It was okay, then. I didn't want Tommy to laugh at me, but I could keep my name which I liked a lot.

After some minutes when he didn't seem to be in the mood for saying any more—I was beginning to be able to sense those times—we started walking to where he had tied the horses.

In the following days Justin blew more stumps as he continued to regain his strength. He always did his share of the chores, too. Sometimes I went with him to blast stumps, but most of the time I stayed home because he had figured out how to seal the charges so they were water tight. That meant he could spend all day drilling holes and placing the charges. Then before he quit for the day, he'd light all the fuses one after the other so they'd all go off at about the same time. At the house we'd hear them booming away.

CHAPTER 8

After lunch one day when dad had left the house Justin said, "Jamie, I've got a little job for you this afternoon if you want to come along."

"Sure I'll come."

Mom was, by this time, less concerned about my going with him. After that day when we blasted the first stump I was interrogated at length about what had gone on. When I told her about how careful Justin was to keep me out of danger and how seriously he took the whole thing, she seemed to relax. I told her about how he had seen guys blow themselves to bits because they had become careless and how he had decided he'd never let that happen to him or me.

It was a nice day and we walked along, not needing the horses because the tools were left at the stumps and anyway, Justin was stronger now. As we walked through the area of the stumps I saw that most of them had "had the powder put to them" as Justin would say. Finally he stopped at the biggest stump of all. Sometimes when Tommy and I came out to drive in the cows in the evening we'd climb up on it and walk around on the top. We'd wonder about how big the tree must have been.

One of my earliest memories was of being out here in the woods on a cold fall day. Dad had hired two men with a great big chainsaw. The motor was on one end and the biggest man lifted it by two handles something like a wheelbarrow, but no wheel, of course. There was a handle on the other end of the saw bar for the second man. The motor always stayed level and the chain bar could be rotated to horizontal to cut trees down or vertical to saw the tree into logs. This must have been one of the trees they cut that day. Or maybe they were hired specifically to cut this tree. We were all standing out of the wind behind this one tree as the men talked. That's all I remember. It must have been spectacular to see it fall.

I saw that Justin had already drilled one hole under the stump. "Since this one is so big it will take at least three charges to even crack it. I can't set off one and then see what it did before planting another one. After the first explosion the dirt will be loose and that spoils any additional shots because the explosive gases escape before they can build up enough pressure to do any good."

It didn't make as much sense to me as it did to him so I said, "Okay."

"That means," he continued, "we must have three or four charges go off at the same time. So, I must dig holes from each side and have them interconnect under the stump. Then when I set off one with a fuse that explosion will set off the others so they'll all explode at the same time."

He had two sticks longer than I was tall laying by the stump. He poked one in the hole he had already drilled and then started drilling a hole on the opposite side. After he had worked at it for awhile, he poked the second stick in his hole and said, "Grab the end of the other stick and I'll poke around with my stick. When you feel yours moving let me know."

He poked and jabbed his stick in his hole but I felt no movement. "Nothing?" he asked.

"Nope."

Using the drill he worked at his hole again, then tried his stick once more. Still nothing. Then he drilled in my hole some more and we traded places with our sticks. Finally I felt mine move.

"It moved," I said.

He poked his around and mine jerked harder. "Now poke your stick in a few times."

This I did and while I was poking he did the same. Finally he pulled his out and it was shorter.

"Hey, you broke my stick," he said in mock surprise.

I said, "My stick won, it killed your stick." Pulling mine out I jumped around showing my stick with wet dirt on the end. "The winner. The champion."

Justin laughed. "Everything's a game."

He dug two more holes and eventually we got all of them to intersect. Then he started placing charges like he had forgotten me. His concentration was intense. After he had two in he looked at me almost in surprise and said, "Okay, time to vamoose."

"Where should I go?"

He stood and looked at the trees. The big elm where we stood the first time was a lot further away now but he pointed at it and said, "Go stand by that tree we used the first time. Do you see it?"

"Yeah. But, that's awful far away."

"And that's awful good," he said in response. "This will be a larger explosion. No argument, get moving, and don't dawdle."

He knew that about me too. I had a habit of becoming sidetracked when I started out to do just about anything.

When I reached the tree Justin was watching me. Assured I was where he intended me to be, he went about the job of setting the last charges. Finally he stood up and looked all around as if insuring there was nobody near enough to be hurt. He looked at me and I waved. Then he knelt down to where I lost sight of him. Seconds later he was up and loping my way. Arriving, he grasped my arm with his right hand and we waited. His left hand was jerking up and down as if he were counting something. "Should be any second . . . ." The words were hardly spoken when the dirt flew. The air shattered with a terrible roar, the ground shook and it was over.

I was almost off to see that had happened to the stump but he had not released his hold on me. "Wait! I think one charge didn't go. I could only detect three. We'll let it rest until tomorrow."

It was incredible that he could have heard how many charges went off. It was one big boom to me. But, there was nothing for me to do but to walk back to the barn with him.

Nearing the barnyard, a man appeared out of the trees from the north as if he had been waiting for us and chose that moment to reveal himself. The gravel road that went along the north side of our property had no driveway into the farm though there was a drive-off to the woods with a culvert under it. I remembered dad used it one time when he was returning with a load of lumber but he had to drive the tractor through brush. A car would never make it so the man must have parked his car on the road. That seemed strange. Why not drive a little further and come in by the normal driveway?

The stranger was wearing a leather jacket and leather gloves. He had the same kind of pull on boots that Justin wore. His hair was sandy and appeared tousled like he had been in a strong wind. Most striking was a small pointed nose and light colored eyes. Twenty steps away he opened his mouth to speak and a dark colored tooth was unmistakable.

"Heard the blast and knew you'd not be far."

Justin stopped stock still a short distance from the barnyard fence. Giving no sign of recognition or greeting, he waited.

"I asked around and heard you were working here. Quite a change from your last job, though from the sound of it old habits die hard."

Still no response was forthcoming from Justin which didn't in any way seem to put off the other man as if he were accustomed to it. "I'm here about some unfinished business you have with us. Would have tracked you down sooner but you were danged hard to find."

Justin replied, "I got an honorable discharge from multiple wounds. I'm out of the hospital and that's it. What about you?"

He grinned revealing the strange tooth again. "I'm not so dumb. I pretended I was shell shocked and crazy. Did a good job of it, too, because I've always been a bit unbalanced. Had 'em comin' and goin'. Of course I had to escape from the booby hatch. Suspect they were happy to be rid of me." After a pause, "Now to business. When I arrived back I hooked up with the gang and they told me about you in the VA Hospital. Tricky the way you managed to sneak away. Where are the goods, and more importantly where is *it*?"

A slight movement of Justin's hand that hung near his fighting knife caught my eye. Under other circumstances it would have been unnoticed except for me his hand was almost at eye level and Justin's whole body gave the appearance that there was about to be an explosion. Taking what I had learned from stump blasting to heart I sensed it would be best to be a safe distance away when the detonation occurred. As casually as I could I walked to the fence without giving any sign that it was anything but normal.

The barnyard fence was oak broads nailed to oak fence posts so I climbed over the fence and waited on the far side as I watched between the boards. The new arrival never took his eyes off Justin waiting for a reply. His feet were set a little further apart than normal and he, too, seemed ready to lash out, though I saw no knife or gun.

This standoff continued for some minutes until I wondered if both men had fallen into a trance. Of course, I was always impatient and hated to wait. Finally the stranger, probably realizing he could never stare down an Indian, especially Justin, who could have stood there for hours if necessary, said, "Well?"

Still no response. It was clear that if anything was to be decided the other man would have to do the deciding because he was up against a solid rock. "That business isn't finished and you're part of it so don't think that standing there like a post will get you off the hook. I'll be back—give you time to think some."

He turned and walked the way he had come. Until he was lost from sight among the trees Justin didn't move. When he did he turned his head and looked at me. "You did right in getting away and behind cover. That is a bad man."

Justin climbed over the fence and I asked, "Will he come back like he said?"

We walked toward the barn and Justin didn't respond right away which was nothing new to me. As impatient as I always was it didn't seem to bother me when Justin made me wait. Maybe it was because I knew that when he did speak he'd have thought it out and I could be sure of what he said.

"Can't rightly say," he finally responded.

Now, that answer wasn't much help. "What kind of business does he have with you?"

I probably shouldn't have asked that because it was none of my business, I guessed, but it was a case of my mouth going before my brain.

To my surprise he answered right away. "He was in demolition like I was. In fact, for awhile he was half of a companion team with Bearfoot and me. When you're in the business of blowing things up, sometimes you uncover things that should have been left alone. There have been people living in Europe for thousands of years so there are few places where people haven't been living, worrying, hiding stuff, and the like. More than once we found stuff left by the Roman legions two thousand years before. And, that has bearing on what he thinks."

The pasture still wasn't ready for grazing so the cows were in the barnyard, some wandering around, but most lying down chewing their cud. We walked among them being careful not to step in cow pies as they ignored us.

"Roads and especially bridges are built at the best place to cross a ravine or a river. If people in modern times picked the best place, you can bet the Romans had just as good an eye for things like that. A certain bridge we blew had been built on the remains of a Roman bridge. After a demolition we were required to go back, if possible, to see how well we did so as to report it to higher command. But, we all knew about the history of the place, especially where I was in Italy, so when we went back we were mostly looking for something of value."

This was better then a *Lone Ranger* program so I was intently interested in what Justin was saying . . . oops, just missed it.

We arrived at the barn and walked up on the foundation where there was a place for a man to pass between the end of the fence boards and the side of the barn but not nearly wide enough for a cow. He went first and I followed running a little to catch up hoping he'd continue with his story.

"Sure enough, Bearfoot and I each found a couple of gold Roman coins. It was finders keepers but that man, Rango, saw us pick them up. Since the Germans were counter attacking we had to hightail it out of there. Gold does things to men's minds and by this time he thinks we carried off a half a ton of it and he wants it. He says he only wants his share but he wants it all. The thing is, there isn't any."

"What'd you do with the coins you found? I'd sure like to see 'em."

"I sold one as soon as I hit New York for traveling money, and the other I sent home to my people."

"But, he'll come back. He said he would. What are you going to do?"

By this time we were around to where the path from the house came to the door to the ground floor of the barn. Justin ignored my question. "Your dad asked me to pitch out what was left of the silage in the silo when I was up to it, so I guess I'll have a go at it."

Here it is necessary to describe the barn in more detail. It was seventy feet in diameter. The idea of a round barn was that a circle enclosed more space than any other shape. Some "round" barns were really polygons, but ours was truly round. The siding boards had to bend from one vertical stud to the next. Nearly all farms had a silo for corn silage. Normally the silo was outside the barn right next to it. That had the disadvantage that the silage froze in the winter and had to be chopped out with a pickaxe. Our silo was inside the barn so the heat from the cattle on the lower floor as well as the insulation of the hay on the second floor kept the silage from freezing—a huge advantage. The silo was not in the exact center of the building but offset to the east so the west edge of the silo was nearly at the center of the barn. This gave room on the second floor for the hay wagon and team of horses to enter the barn. The silo was sixteen feet in diameter, of poured concrete construction and extended from six feet below the first floor level to the roof. The drive-in to the hay mow came from the west.

In the hay mow was a chute that was pressed against the side of the silo. When we boys were old enough to do chores, we'd first pitch silage out of the silo through square windows in the concrete into the chute where it fell to the first floor. Then, we'd distribute the silage into feed troughs for the cattle. After that we'd throw hay into the chute from the hay mow side. After supper we'd do the milking and then the hay would be carried to the feed troughs. The cattle did not have water in the barn, so they drank only during the day when they were outside.

My grandfather had worked all this out as he was something of an inventor. He also had taken to heart that one of the main expenses of a farm was construction and maintenance of farm buildings. As such, this one large barn was to serve as all the buildings in one. I have mentioned the machinery room on the second floor where the blasting powder was found. As one entered the drive-in to the hay mow that room was off to the right front with the hay mow to the left. To the immediate right of the drive-in was a door into the "feed room" that also had a work bench in it with hand tools which was call the work shop. There were also stairs in the shop that led down to the first floor.

Above the feed room was the granary where the grain was stored. The thing to remember is that oats was the most common grain fed to cattle and horses, and silage and hay made up most of their diet in the winter. But when large animals eat oats, they tend to swallow some of it without chewing it. As a result it passes through them undigested. For that reason up near the ceiling of the feed room, the underside of the third floor, was an oat grinder powered by an electric motor. The oats was fed into the grinder from the granary above and the ground grain fell into one of two bins. From there the ground grain was sent by means of one foot square chutes to small hoppers on the ground floor. After distributing the silage a topping of ground oats was added for the cows. After all, the milk you got out of a cow was a result of what you put into the cow.

What we called the third floor was on the level of the floor of the granary and covered the machinery room. It also extended over the inner half of the drive-in to the hay mow so when the hay wagon was all the way in to where it could be unloaded the horses would be under the third floor. All the while I was growing up, the third floor was not put to any particular use other than to store miscellaneous stuff that we wanted to keep dry. The strange thing was that to enter the granary you had to climb up to the third floor by means of a movable stairs and then enter the granary from it. But the door to the granary was located at a shear drop of nine feet into the drive-in to the hay mow. To enter the granary one had to step around open space as he grabbed the vertical 2 x 4 stud at the inside of the door. As dangerous as this was, there was only one mis-step in the entire life of the barn in this regard and that will play a part in our story. If this has left the reader bewildered, as it probably has, there is a sketch of this arrangement on a nearby page.

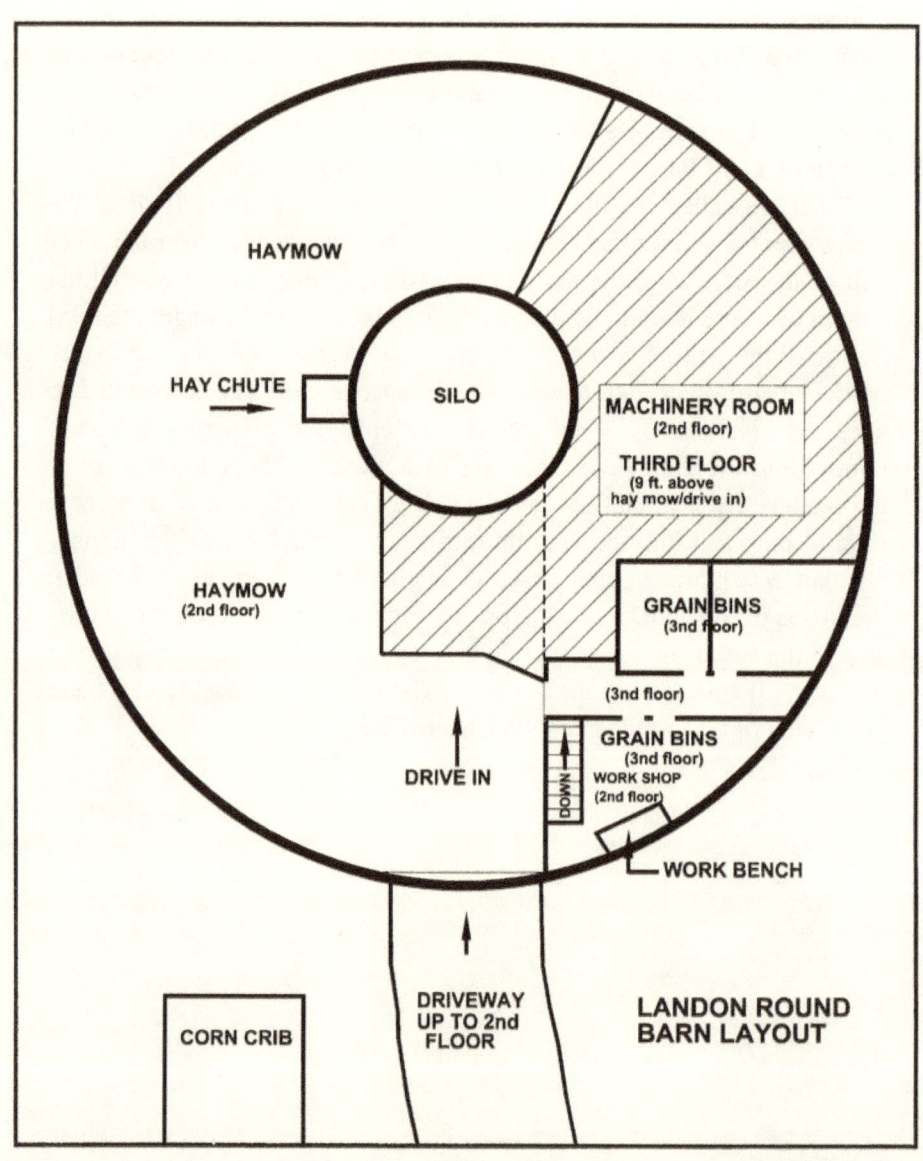

LANDON FARM CIRCA 1950

CHAPTER 9

May came and went and with it the hare moon, as Justin informed me and we were in early June. There came a day when the radio was the most important appliance in the house as everybody sat around it somberly listening. It was D-Day, the sixth of June, the day everyone was pinning their hopes on. The Allies had lunched an invasion of France. Of course, I didn't know what it was about other than it was important to winning the war. Discussion went back an forth about whether or not we could hold the beachhead or be thrown back. By the second day it seemed clear that our troops were holding on and breaking through to the interior of France and generally the mood lightened, except for the casualty lists.

At the time I knew little about families who had lost sons, husbands and fathers. It seemed that such things were kept from the kids as much as possible. However, in the years after the war it was common to see a picture of a young man in uniform hanging on a wall, or setting on a side table with perhaps a ribbon and a medal hanging on or near it. The war left no community and few families untouched. I lost first cousins. One was a pilot who took off from the east coast to ferry his plane to England and simply was never heard from again.

During these years I had an aunt who subscribed to *Life Magazine* and at times she'd drop off back issues with us. I couldn't read but I liked to page through them and look at the pictures of airplanes. Mom even let me cut out pictures with a scissors and I had a box where I saved them. Two in particular stick in my mind. One showed crews abroad an aircraft carrier wheeling a torpedo under an airplane on the hangar deck. Even though I couldn't read I knew the symbols of the major cars. This one was a Pontiac ad so I assumed torpedoes were made in the Pontiac factory. Another showed P-51 Mustangs with the Cadillac symbol.

All factories were converted to war production. While in high school I read a book by a fighter pilot who complained about his machine guns jamming a lot. His friend replied to the effect that what could he expect because the guns were manufactured on a washing machine line. Factories would bid on government contracts to stay in business because their normal products wouldn't sell due to a pronounced lack of disposable income and a shortage of raw materials. Later in life I worked for a time at a granite quarrying and finishing company in central Minnesota. In the Second World War they made, of all things, PT Boat bottoms. They were sent by rail to where the rest of the boat was assembled.

In spite of the mood of the country there was work to be done. Justin was back to his full strength and that was helping dad a lot. He was almost one of the family by now but he still refused to sleep in the house.

I haven't mentioned Tommy much even though he was as much a part of my life as anyone else. While we were blasting stumps he was in school and always lamented that he missed all the fun. With school finally out for the summer all the stumps had been sent to their final reward. The two of us had a lot of fun and we were outside together a lot. Tommy being eight did more work than I did. One of his jobs was driving tractor for such jobs as picking rocks.

I'll always remember the sneaky streak Tommy had that I never seemed to be able to acquire. For example, one day mom told us to wash our hands for dinner and to use soap since she knew we'd go through the motions and be just as dirty after washing as before. Tommy went to the washbasin and said, "My hands make soap." And sure enough he started washing never having touched the bar of soap and his hands lathered up like anything. I was dumbfounded. I asked him how he could do that and he refused to tell me. It made me mad but there was nothing I could do about it.

Some days Justin took to smoking a pipe, not every day, only some days. Dad smoked every day. He had a can of Prince Albert in the center pocket of the bib of his overalls and the little book of cigarette papers in another little pocket. Whenever he had a chance to take a break he'd roll a cigarette, light it with a wooden match and smoke as he worked with it hanging out of his mouth.

Well, one of the books Tommy was reading was *Huckleberry Finn* and he said the kid in the story had a corncob pipe and we should try making pipes for ourselves. Corncobs were no problem because there was cob corn in the corn crib so all we had to do was shell and ear of corn and there was a cob. And surprisingly the stem was no problem either. There was a strange bush that grew in the neighbor's pasture across the road to the southwest of the house. Dad had said it was called pipe-stem. So, taking it literally we walked over there, across the road, under the barbed wire fence and broke off some of the plants. The stem was a woody material and after a few experiments we found that the parts of the stem between the places where the leaves branched out was hollow. We had the rest of our pipes.

Back in the workshop in the barn Tommy put a corncob in the vise and with a hacksaw cut it off a couple of inches from the butt. Tommy had a jackknife and he used the smallest blade to dig out the soft pithy center of the cob. Then he used the tip of his knife to bore a hole into the side. After carefully cutting the ends of a four inch piece of pipe-stem he worked it into the hole, and there he had a pipe. Since it had worked so well he made another one for me.

Besides being sneaky, Tommy was good at planing ahead because he had already snitched some wooden matches which he had in his pocket. We were ready to give our pipes a try. I wondered what we'd smoke in them but Tommy had thought that out already. He led the way north of the barn to a large oak tree that we could sit under and have privacy. Under it's spreading boughs there wasn't much growing except a few short weeds. But, in the full sunlight around the tree grass was as tall as we were. Using dry oak leaves from last summer, we crunched them up and poked them in our pipes. It was important that we both had our own pipe so we could each work at our own pace without waiting for the other to make mistakes. Tommy had a match in his hand as I expectantly waited. But, there was nothing to strike it on. He tried it on the bark of the oak tree but that didn't work and only succeeded in breaking the match.

"We need a rock," he said. So, we both started tramping around in the weeds and then the tall green grass. There were always rocks when you didn't need them, but none now. Not far away was the iron wheeled wagon. "The wagon," he said. We went over to it. He stooped down and scratched the next match on the inside of the wheel and it came to life. He immediately held it above the bowl of his pipe, took a big puff and bent over coughing uncontrollably. Undeterred, I took the still burning match and lit mine with similar results. From there on we took smaller puffs until we decided dried tree leaves from last summer didn't make good tobacco. It was the only reason either of us could think of as to why we didn't enjoy a good puff on our pipes just like men did.

The next day Tommy told me he knew where we could get some real tobacco. As always he led the way. I followed to the ground floor of the barn. Next to the first stanchion where the cows stood to be milked was the milk room. That was where a ten gallon milk can would be placed. With the cover removed something called the strainer was placed on top. The strainer was a metal bowl that held about a pail full of milk. It had vertical walls that angled inward toward the bottom so as to fit into the top to the milk can. Inside the strainer was a place to put a white filter pad that strained the milk as it ran into the can. When I was very small they had a cream separator in that room. Then they only sold the cream and fed the skim milk to the pigs.

Anyway, along one wall inside the milk room were shelves. Up on the top one, pushed way back was a large round can of Prince Albert. Tommy said that was where Justin got the tobacco to refill the little pouch he carried. There was a stool about three feet high that didn't have a particular use now, though it must have had a purpose at one time. Tommy pulled it over to the right place and crawled up on it. He handed the can of tobacco to me and came down. Since dad bought tobacco in the small flat cans, there was always plenty of them around so we filled one of them half full and Tommy replaced Justin's stash making sure to turn the can so the writing on the side was facing out like it was before he had touched it. He was so good at thinking of stuff like that.

After climbing down, Tommy was about to move the stool to where we found it when he stooped down. Beneath the lowest shelf, pushed back in the shadows was Justin's large leather bag, the one he was carrying when he arrived.

73

"That's Justin's bag," I said. I felt good because Tommy had never seen it and I knew all about it. "When he was fixing Daisy's harness he had some tools for punching holes in leather and stuff like that. When he was done, he put the tools in his bag."

Tommy was tugging at it but it wouldn't move. "Better leave it alone," I said. But he tugged at it all the harder still with no results, I asked, "Is it stuck?"

He kept working at it but it wasn't coming. "It's real heavy," he said.

On his knees with is head only inches from it, he poked at it with his fingers. "It seems like it's full of a lot of small things, like nuts and bolts or something." He continued probing it with his finger near the bottom from one end to the other. "There seems to be some hard round things like short iron bars. Why would he carry around stuff like that?"

At that moment we heard the barn door open. Tommy jerked up his head, stood and pulled the string to turn out the light hanging above. We both eased back into the shadows of the room and froze. Someone came in and stopped abruptly. We waited, he waited. Then he started walking again. I could tell by the walk that it was Justin. Tommy would get us both into trouble. In the shadows I saw with horror that the small can of tobacco was still lying on top of the stool. Our lives were over! The mountains would fall in us and cover us forever, such was the fate of evil doers. We were stealing someone else's stuff. And we'd get caught, I knew it. Justin ran out of tobacco at this very time, I just knew it! God, deliver me and I'll never steal again, please! I was trembling I was so scared.

But . . . Justin didn't come to the milk room, he walked around in front of the feed trough for the cows. I heard the scrape of a pitchfork. Maybe he had come for that. Maybe . . . please, the pitchfork. That's all you want, no tobacco, not even thinking of tobacco, don't need any of that. Please . . . . The barn door opened and closed. We heard no more movement. We waited . . . and waited. Finally Tommy slowly looked out of the milk room toward the door and pulled back. "Coast is clear," he said and pulled the string to turn on the light. He took the can of tobacco off the stool and handed it to me. Then he brushed off a few crumbs of tobacco—he was so good at thinking of things like that—sneaky stuff— and then placed the stool back were we had found it.

He grabbed the can from me stuck it under his shirt behind his belt, and we scooted out. When we were safely under the oak tree, the site of our first abortive attempt to be like big people, I said, "Boy, that was close. What would have happened if Justin had come into the milk room?"

Tommy didn't seem too concerned. "I would have told him we were playing a game." What Justin would have thought about the can of tobacco on the stool wasn't mentioned.

Well, to work. Taking turns with the tobacco can we used twigs to poke tobacco into our pipes. Tommy even had a small rock in his pocket this time. With the match aflame, he held it above the bowl of his pipe, took a big puff and bent over coughing uncontrollably. This time I wasn't so fast to follow suit. I lit mine with slow small puffs, but ended up coughing a lot, too. This wasn't working at all well.

Finally Tommy got the hang of it. "Take a lot of real small puffs and each time hold it in your mouth, then it works," he said.

We spent the next half hour puffing away, refilling our pipes and doing it again. Finally, it dawned on both of us at about the same time that we didn't feel so good so we stopped the experiment. But the experiment wasn't finished with us. Our complexions turned white, we started to sweat all over, and then we turned green. It wasn't long before we were both barfing.

That evening neither of us had much of an appetite at supper and mom wondered if we were coming down with something. She put her hand on Tommy's forehead and looked at him. "You look a little pale. What have you two been up to?"

Tommy shrugged and said we ran all the way out to the pond in the woods, made a race of it and really got tired out. How could he think of stuff like that to say? It was obvious mom was skeptical as she said, "Be careful not to overdo it until you get used to the summer heat."

Justin kept eating away like he always did, but I thought for a second he glanced at me. We tried mightily to eat what we could and keep it down. For some reason, Tommy never mentioned smoking again. That was okay with me.

*   *   *

It was hay making time and we all pitched in. Dad had a mower that mounted on the back of the tractor and he was the one who mowed the hay. It lay in the field until it dried and then it was raked. We were still using the horse drawn hay rake and Justin did most of that. The rake consisted of a bunch of tines shaped like a half circle abut six inches apart. The tines were lowered and pulled along the ground catching up the hay in the half hoop of the tines. When the half-hoop was full he'd push a lever and lift the tines and leave the short row of hay as long as the rake was wide. Each time he came across the field he'd dump the hay in line with the last time so it made a windrow of hay perpendicular to the direction of travel of the rake.

Before my time, men would use pitchforks to pitch the hay onto the hay rack, but we had a hayloader. That was a machine that hooked onto the back of the hay rack. The tractor pulled the hayrack which pulled the hayloader. The tractor would straddle the windrow of hay and it would pass under the hayrack, too. The hayloader had rotating tines that swept up the hay from the ground and then transported it up a slide and onto the back of the hayrack. At the start of a load the hay fell onto the hayrack and one of the men pitched it around evenly. As the load filled up the man went up with it all the time spreading out the hay. Nearing a full load he had to reach down with his fork to get the hay as it came out of the top of the hayloader.

Before they started to load hay, they laid out one of the sling ropes on the hay rack so the metal ring hung over the front and the two metal ends over the back. The two ropes were spaced out a few feet from the center of the hayrack. After they loaded part of the hay they laid out another one and then later a third one.

A lot of the time we kids went along to the field to load hay. I don't know why they put up with us but they did. When I was very young and we didn't have a hired man, mom came along to drive the horses so I suppose we came so they'd know where we were. It was fun riding out because we'd sit along the side of the hayrack and hang our feet over the edge. As we moved along we'd try to catch grass or weeds between our shoes. While they loaded we walked behind and then they'd boost us up on top of the load of hay for the ride home. That was the most fun. We'd sink in a foot or so and it was like a huge pillow. The fresh hay smelled good and being way up in the air there was always a breeze.

Unloading was a real project but one that had been worked out over the years because bringing hay into a barn was something all farmers did. The way our barn was originally built, the hayrack was pulled into the barn with horses. With the rack in the unloading position, the horses were under the third floor. They were unhitched and there was room for them to turn and walk out single file between the load of hay and the pile of hay in the haymow when it began to fill up. But, using the tractor, dad had to figure out something else. He'd stop the tractor a short distance before it entered the barn. One of us would jump down and put a block of wood behind a wheel of the wagon. Then we'd unhitch the tractor and dad would back it around the wagon, turn and back up to it. He had made a second tongue on the back of the wagon and he'd back up to that and connect it to the draw bar of the tractor. Then one man, or small boy, would pick up the front tongue and steer the wagon into the barn as the tractor pushed it. As the wagon started to move it was my job to remove the block of wood from behind the wheel.

When the wagon was in the barn the center of the load was beneath the hay carrier that rode on the rail attached to the rafters. One end of a thick rope was attached to the bottom of the hay carrier. It came down and ran through two pulley blocks with hooks on them, and then returned up and around a pulley in the carrier.

To start the unloading the blocks were pulled down and the metal ring in the front of the sling rope highest up in the load was hooked to one block. The metal ends of the two sling ropes from the rear were attached to the tripper which was hooked to the other block on the hay rope. The big hay rope ran up through the carrier and all around the barn, behind the silo and then out beside the hayrack to the driveway. Horses, or in our case the tractor, was attached to the rope. When we were these ages Tommy drove the tractor backwards to pull the rope and I stood on the third floor where Tommy could see me and I gave arm signals to him as dad told me what to do. They were simple signals as in go and stop and come back up the driveway for the next bunch of hay.

Justin was needed for hard work. This may seem odd, but the hay had to be spread out in the haymow, too. If it were all dropped one sling load on top of another, as the pile built up the hay would roll to one side or the other. This was no problem for bringing the hay into the barn. But in the winter when it came time to pitch the hay out, it was a big problem. The stalks of hay were two to three feet long so it was not possible to start anywhere and begin digging up hay and pitching it down the hay chute. You had to take it out in layers exactly as it had been laid in. That meant that for the hay that would have rolled down the pile toward the wall, it would have been necessary to pitch it up over the center hump to the chute. Therefore, as the hay was dropped from the sling rope, Justin had to evenly spread it out.

When all was ready I signaled Tommy to start backing the tractor. As the rope tightened it first pulled the two pulley blocks together and then lifted the first big bunch of hay up off the hayrack. At this point the hay carrier was locked to a knob on the rail so the hay only lifted straight up rather than being pulled off the side of the wagon. When the pulleys got up to the bottom of the carrier they pushed a lever and the hay stopped lifting, released the carrier from the knob so it could now be pulled into the haymow. At the same time the part of the rope holding up the sling load of hay was clamped in place so the load of hay did not start to lower.

As the hay lifted the whole barn shook and it seemed to a small kid like me that the roof was about to fall in. But, time and time again it worked and the roof stayed up.

When the bunch of hay arrived at where dad wanted it he yelled at me to stop and I gave the signal for Tommy who stopped. Then dad or Justin pulled the trip rope attached to the tripper and the hay dropped with a big swish. My second job was to pull the hay rope up on to the third floor when Tommy drove the tractor back up the driveway for the next sling load of hay. This made it easier for dad to pull the carrier back along the rail to the wagon. With a sharp pull he locked the carrier back into the knob and the pulley blocks would lower to where the sling rope could be removed in preparation for the next sling.

CHAPTER 10

Sundays were always fun except that often relatives would stop by. If it was only big people it didn't matter. Some of my cousins were fun to play with but some weren't. Since we lived on the same farm where my father grew up, and he was from a family of thirteen kids, there were a lot of relatives. They all liked to come back to the home place and relax. All it meant for mom was a lot of cooking. My mother had one brother and three sisters so there were a few relatives on that side, too. Since my father was one of the youngest in his family, he had nephews and nieces who were older than he was—there were a lot of them and they had their own families. Hardly a weekend passed any time of the year when someone didn't drive into the yard. They all seemed to have enough gas to get as far as our house. The only thing that kept it at manageable levels was that a lot of them had gravitated to California so those only came at most once a year.

It didn't take Justin long to figure this out and he made himself scarce on Sundays. He'd be there for chores morning and evening but that was all. Mom and dad wondered a time or two where he went, though it was left at the fact that it was his time off and where he went was his business.

One Sunday in mid June we had gone to seven o'clock Mass as usual and were home. I had my clothes changed and was out fooling around with Chips trying to worry some critter to death under the corncrib. Chips would dig with his front paws and then I'd poke with a stick. We were pretty sure it wasn't a skunk because we'd have been able to smell it. Looking for a longer stick it brought me to the outside feed troughs that extended out perpendicular to the barn on the north side. From there I could see the barnyard. It happened that Justin was walking north away from the buildings. As he approached a tree he whipped out his big knife and threw it so it stuck in the tree. It was then I saw why he wore it on his left side. He'd reach across his body and grab it and then draw and throw it in one smooth motion.

He went to it and worked it up and down until it was free and replaced it in the scabbard. Then he continued into the woods and soon after that I heard a motorcycle on the road that ran north of the farm but there were too many trees to see it. From the sound it seemed to stop about the place where there was a turnoff from the road into the woods. A few minutes later I heard the motor start again. It sounded like it went east on the gravel road away from town. I waited to see if Justin would come back but got restless so went back to see how Chips was doing.

The next day when everybody was busy, I told Tommy that I thought Justin had a motorcycle in the woods. He was immediately ready to take a look. I started to the barnyard where I had seen Justin and Tommy stopped me.

"If we go that way we might leave tracks that he'll see and become suspicious. If he thinks we found it he'll hide it someplace else."

Tommy was so good at stuff like that. But, the woods north of the barnyard was free of brush because the cows trampled it down and ate the tree leaves that were low enough for them to reach. We had to go into the woods north of the house and work our way around. This was something we never did in the summer because we only wore short sleeved T-shirts and the mosquitoes were vicious in the woods. Into the woods we went, Chips along with us, sometimes in front, other times elsewhere. We had gone east nearly to where the thick woods ended and the cow pasture started. On our side of the fence it was thick. Most of the trees were no larger than a man's leg but there were a lot of them. And, there was underbrush that made walking hard. We were both swatting mosquitoes and had spread out as we neared where we thought the motorcycle might be.

We looked all around and found nothing. Finally Tommy suggested we go to the north edge of the woods where the drive-off from the road was. The approach was covered with weeds but we found crushed weeds and fresh tracks in the gravel that had to have come from a motorcycle.

However, once in the woods there were no clear tracks so we followed its progress by looking for crushed weeds and broken twigs but we lost it. Looking all around for any signs Tommy said, "Here's something."

He was standing by one of the few large trees in the woods. There was a place where someone had waited from the way the leaves were packed down. On our knees we swished around the leaves and uncovered cigarette butts.

"I think," Tommy started, "this is where someone drove or pushed his motorcycle into the woods and waited for Justin. Then he left and that's the motorcycle you heard. Justin stayed in the woods long after it left so nobody would see him coming back."

"But, I kept watching every now and then and didn't see him."

"Yeah. Maybe he went further east in the cow pasture and sat down and read a book or something."

At that moment we heard the throb of a motorcycle on the road, and it seemed to be slowing down.

"It's stopping by the turnoff into the woods!" Tommy hissed.

He grabbed my arm and we ran back in the woods until we came to another big tree which we crouched behind.

The driver drove the motorcycle right into the woods. It was really loud the way he had to gun the motor to get over some brush. Tommy whispered to me, "No matter what, if we don't move or make any noise he won't know we're here."

We could see well enough through the leaves as he stopped near the other big tree and turned off the motor. The silence was suddenly loud. This was a big motorcycle and there were two men on it. They both got off as the driver, the larger of the two, leaned it up against a nearby tree.

"Why couldn't he have brought it to town?" the small man said. "Why all the slinking around?"

"He's known in town by now, and he doesn't want to draw these folks into it. I don't know why, but he was really hard about that. Don't ask any more questions and let's see if we can find what we came for."

I wasn't sure, but the second one who had spoken, the bigger one, looked a lot like the man who had confronted Justin in the pasture when we were coming back from blasting the big stump.

Tommy looked at me, and it seemed he was as scared as I was. I didn't want those men to find us. And, that was a worry because the mosquitoes were eating us alive. We dared not swat them so we took turns slowly rubbing them off each other's back.

I wondered how long they'd stay when suddenly I jerked as the small man said, "What's this!"

"Not so loud, stupid, somebody might hear you," the large one said. "What's the problem?"

"This is the wrong one. It won't work. He'll have to do it again and work fast, too. We have to get started on production for September so we have time to get them into distribution."

The small man went to the motorcycle and opened a saddle bag withdrawing something wrapped in brown paper. Coming to the other man he said, "Somebody really screwed up. These are the ones he's supposed to have worked on. Boy, he'll be mad when we tell him all his work was for nothing. I have no choice but to leave him a note and tell him to start again."

Chips took that moment to come running through the woods towards us returning from the urgent matter of chasing a rabbit. When he heard the voices he immediately started barking and growling.

The men stopped talking for a moment. "See what I told you about talking so loud. Hurry up. We have to get out of here before someone comes to investigate."

"That won't work about the note. He thinks he has completed the job and won't come back here until he expects to pick up his pay. We have to send him a letter.'

"That's getting risky. We already sent him one."

"I'll leave him a note now, and maybe he'll check that we've been here to pick them up."

"Yeah. I'll tell him to leave a note for us as to when he will have them done, too." The small man went to the cycle and dug in the saddle bag for a pencil and paper all the while keeping an eye on the dog who kept barking. Both men were mumbling things that we were never supposed to hear, let alone say. He put the note in the brown paper, wrapped everything up, and shoved the package in a hole in the tree at the level of the top of his head.

"I'd better push the cycle out to the road. We made an awful lot of noise coming in."

They turned the machine around and pushed it toward the road leaving more bad words behind as they scratched themselves on prickly ash. It wasn't long before we heard the motor start and in seconds the sound was falling as it sped off.

We were both up and running for the edge of the woods to the south of us. At this point the woods wasn't very wide because a small field had been cut out of it for growing potatoes. Once out in the sun we both shook our shirts and scratched every square inch of skin we could reach and then took turns on one another's back.

"Dad said once that if you wash off the mosquito bites right away they won't itch so much. Lets run to the well."

We took off. Past the potato patch we ran up to the corn crib, past it, between the house and the barn and down the hundred yard slope to the slough and the well. Tommy started pumping and when the water came I washed my hands, arms and face. Then, I pumped for him. He suggested we take our shirts off and wash our backs too. After awhile we were both pretty wet, laughing, and having a good time. The sun was warm and there was a breeze. What could be better?

Finally we were sitting on the grass by the pump and Tommy asked, "What do you suppose Justin did for those guys? After he got well he worked all the time. And how did he get the wrong thing whatever it was?"

"He got a letter once," I said.

"How do you know that?"

"One day mom asked me to go get the mail. There was a letter for Justin and I took it to him."

"How'd you know it was for Justin?"

"I know my alphabet and the first name started with a 'J' so it had to be for Justin. I know my name and besides I don't get any mail. A few days later he sent a letter, too."

"How would you know?"

"Mom asked me to take a letter out to the mailbox. Justin left the house the same time I did and when we were outside he kind of quietly asked me if I'd put a letter in the mailbox for him, too. I said 'sure' and I did."

"Who was the letter addressed to?"

"How would I know? I can't read."

"Oh," Tommy said in a mysterious voice, "I see. If he had asked anyone else to mail the letter, they'd have read the name and address. You were the only one who was safe."

"He might have asked Mikey to do it," I said laughing and poking him in the ribs.

"Mikey is just learning to walk!" Tommy retorted as he poked me back.

"Yeah, but he can only say four words and you can barely understand them," I said snickering. "He wouldn't be able to tell what he did." Before Tommy could poke me again I was up and ran to the pump. There was still a small pool of water where we had pumped at first. Scooping up a hand full of water I threw it at my brother. We ran around for awhile with him chasing me. Even though I was two years younger, I could run faster.

Soon we stopped and Tommy said, "I need another drink." After taking turns pumping and scooping water in our mouths we started to walk back to the house.

Tommy was still thinking about the woods. "Maybe Justin sent the letter to one of those guys and told them to leave whatever it was in the woods."

"That must be what they did," I said, "but that must mean it's all real secret. I think the biggest man in the woods was Rango."

Tommy looked at me with surprise. "Who's that?"

I hadn't told Tommy about the day Justin and I met Rango in the woods and how he said he'd be back.

We walked up the field road to the buildings talking about it. Then Tommy said, "I wonder what's in his leather bag?"

"Don't know, but he moved it. I looked when they were milking last night. It's not under the bottom shelf in the milk room anymore."

That evening at supper mom said, "You boys are all bitten up. What were you doing today?"

I sat pushing potatoes around on my plate with my fork while Tommy answered, "We were in the plumb orchard looking for wild raspberries. The mosquitoes were pretty bad."

How he could come up with stuff like that without thinking I could never imagine.

CHAPTER 11

Red Feather

Running Wolf had seen the light go out in the milk room the day the boys were snitching tobacco. He did not hold that against them. They got sick from smoking and he thought it might keep them from developing the habit when they grew to men. But, he could see that this was their farm and they were everywhere on it. He could not have them snooping in his leather bag so decided it was necessary to hide it where it would be lost to them. Now, there is no more compelling notion than that there is a treasure lying about that only needed a little finding. And where small boys are concerned it becomes an obsession.

The next day we went to work. In true sleuth tradition, Tommy went first to the milk room and verified our quarry was indeed missing. It was. Using the stool Tommy stood on to snitch the tobacco he insured that it wasn't on any of the shelves. Anyway, it seemed it would have been too heavy for any of the shelves to support.

"Maybe he took stuff out of the bag and hid it in different places," I suggested.

"Yeah," Tommy said. "That would mean it would be real hard to find. But, the bag would still be around. We can find that."

We started on the first floor of the barn. The beams that supported the second floor were logs that had been chopped flat on opposite sides with an axe. The floor joists rested on them. It seemed logical that he would have hid the bag on top of one of the beams. It would be easy to see where he put it because the whole ceiling of the first floor was a blanket of cobwebs. But on the negative side there wasn't much light. The two foot square windows were set up rather high so a man could see out of the bottom. And, they hadn't been washed since the barn had been built.

"This is impossible," Tommy said after we had been looking for a half-hour.

"Maybe he moved it to the old barn," I suggested. "Maybe it's in the chicken coop." The chicken coop was in the south part of the old barn that had been added on to the original structure. "Maybe the chickens are laying eggs in it."

"Don't be dumb! He'd think of a better place than that."

"How about above the chicken coop, on the straw?"

That made Tommy think because that was a possibility. When my grandparents started the farm here the first building they built was an all purpose one. It was two story—it had to be. That was because the cattle were kept on the ground floor and the people lived on the floor above. It was a German thing, or so we were told. It had the advantage that the heat from the cattle would help warm the upper floor in the winter. Of course, it didn't always smell so good. But in a time when people only took two baths a year, it wasn't such a terrible thing. Besides, with no insulation, and normally only the outer wall boards and the siding—the studs were not covered on the inside—standing between the thirty below mornings and the inside, there was a lot of fresh air at all times.

The first improvement they made was to add on to the main building to the south. This addition was only one story high and the roof was continued from the main structure at a lower pitch to cover it. This addition was partly chicken coop and partly horse barn. The ceiling was no more than poles set at nine inch spacing with a thick layer of straw thrown on top of them. As the family grew the boys slept on the straw rolled up in wool blankets. It was told—if true or not was hard to tell—that when grandpa went to call the boys in the morning he could tell if they were still all alive by small wafts of steam rising from each one where their noses should have been.

Getting to the second floor of the old barn was sometimes easy and sometimes hard. That was because normally there was a step ladder leaning up against the barn below the upper door unless the ladder was needed elsewhere. If it were gone there were board steps nailed to the wall that you had to climb up. In that case going up was easier than coming down. Today the step ladder was in presence so it was easy both ways.

We were both crawling around on the straw—there was hardly room for us to stand up, let alone an adult. A window on each end made for enough light to see what we were doing. There was no leather bag in evidence and no sign that the straw had been disturbed to hide it. Well, another dead end. While we were there we looked around in the main part of the building. Most of the space was occupied by piles of lumber which left little in the way of hidey-holes. Above, in the peak of the roof there were cross beams with a few boards thrown across them at places. It would have been easy to see the bag if it were there which it wasn't.

After that we went into the haymow and sat on the hay. It still smelled new which was something I always liked. I could tell Tommy was frustrated. At this point he was more interested in finding the bag than I was. Maybe that was something that happened to you when you got older.

"It has to still be here," he said. "I don't think that it was something he would carry all this way only to give it to someone else."

"Maybe he buried it."

"Nah. It would get wet and rot. And, if he wanted to remove something, it would be hard to get at. It's hidden here someplace. We aren't thinking the way we should."

Well, Tommy should speak for himself. I was only six and didn't usually think much about anything other than to worry about the house burning down in the winter. And, worrying must not be the same as thinking or people would be saying I was awful smart.

"Maybe we should pray to St. Anthony. Mom says he's the patron saint for finding lost things."

"Might not work because we didn't lose anything. We're trying to find something that someone has hidden."

"I don't care. Tonight I'm going to pray to St. Anthony. Bet he'll find it for us."

* * *

The following day we didn't have much time for treasure hunting. Since dad had Justin this year he decided to stack the meadow hay by the hay mangers along the west side of the barnyard rather than in the meadow. That was Justin's job. Tommy and I went with dad to move the turkeys. This takes a little explaining. We got the turkeys right after they were hatched. There was still snow on the ground at that time. There were other farmers who raised laying turkeys who collected the eggs and then hatched them. We had six little brooder houses that were heated with fuel oil stoves. As the turkeys grew it became crowded in the brooder houses and dad built small pens behind them so the turkeys could be outside during the day. Each evening we drove them in and closed the little door for fear of foxes and other varmints eating them at night. Sometimes a weasel or something like that got into one of the houses and then it was all out war. Dad patched up every hole, set traps and if all else failed left poisoned meat near the house. One way or the other it stopped.

In early June, when the birds were big enough we drove them out to the field where dad had made a large pen out of woven wire. He had also constructed shelters which were open sided structures with only roofs. Poles ran crosswise a couple of feet off the ground. The turkeys sat on the poles at night since by instinct they would sit on tree limbs to sleep. This also provided shelter from rain and also the sun on hot days. The shelters were on skids so they could be moved by pulling them with the tractor.

Driving the turkeys out to the field was an all-family project. They didn't walk very fast and liked to sit down and dust their feathers in the sand wherever they found it. They also liked to wander off and eat bugs and grasshoppers in the grass along the way. We used poles with flags on the end to drive them. The flag being swung over head looked to them like a bird of prey and they instinctively ran from it. That's how we managed to keep them together and moving in the direction we wanted.

Keeping away all manner of wild thing that was looking for an easy meal was hard when they were first "on range" as we called it. When they became larger they were more of a threat to predators than the other way around. Turkeys are omnivores and relished meat. In fact turkey vultures have no feathers on their heads the same as turkeys. Dad said the reason that neither bird had feathers on their heads was so when they ate the innards out of a carcass they wouldn't get stuff stuck in their head feathers.

The first few nights on range dad slept out with them in a little hut with his shotgun handy. After that he hung kerosene lanterns from the shelters to make it look like people were around. This all worked pretty well until the summer before when dad was losing three of four birds a night. They were not carried away, but only had their heads missing. It was a big problem because if we lost a tenth of the flock that was the profit for the year.

In a magazine dad subscribed to that dealt only with raising turkeys, he had seen something about owls attacking the young birds. They could kill a turkey but it was too heavy for them to fly away with so they pulled off the head. The answer relied on the instinctive behavior of owls. If they were hunting something like mice, they dove on their victim the moment they saw it. However, as a mater of course, before attacking a concentration of prey, they would land on the highest perch in the area to assess danger. Out in the open fields it was a relatively simple matter to set up a pole which would be the highest thing in the area and put a trap on top. It worked. We caught six or eight great horned owls that summer. They were huge with spans of six to eight feet. I felt at the time it was too bad that such beautiful birds had to die so we could make a living. But, you take the most committed tree-huggers and have them miss a few meals and suddenly those beautiful birds wouldn't be so important.

The result was dad cut a ten foot piece of an old telephone pole and braced it up on a skid that could be pulled by the tractor. It became a permanent fixture in the turkey pen with the result that there were no more owl problems. That didn't mean we eradicated all the owls—far from it. Like any wild thing, the owls were canny when it came to survival. As dad had suspected, more than one owl attacked the turkeys each night. When the first one got caught in the trap, it hung helplessly by its leg screeching in terror. This served as a warning for the others to stay away.

This was our second year with the owl post and so far we had caught no owls. Each morning after breakfast dad took a load of feed out to the turkeys on the two wheeled trailer pulled behind the tractor. We road on the bags of feed. As we neared the turkeys we could hear them. Turkeys were odd birds in a lot of ways. If you make a sharp noise they will all gobble in unison. We called it turkey laughter. This morning they were laughing something fierce. As we drew near we could see an owl hanging from the post which was the object of the flock's levity. When we stopped at the gate to the pen, Tommy and I jumped off to open it and dad told us to go to the woods and get a club which we did. When we returned, dad took us to the owl. It had dug the claws of its free leg into the post and had its head up facing us. Dad said, "Look at that, you'll never see anything like it again and you'll never forget it." The huge yellow eyes were defiantly glaring at us as it hissed its hatred. I have to say I can still see it as clearly today as all those years ago. Then dad whacked it on the head threw it over the fence and we went to the job of filling the feed troughs for the turkeys.

We never had a problem with animal predators when the turkeys were on range. I guess that was because foxes, skunks, and similar animals foraged mostly in the woods and marshy areas where food would be more plentiful.

Turkeys were nearly always run on alfalfa fields. This was because of crop rotation. The small grain we grew was oats. I guess it gave the best yield per acre and for animal feed the hard hulls on it didn't matter. After the oats was planted in the spring, alfalfa was planted in the same field. Alfalfa took two years to mature so by the time the oats was harvested it was less than six inches high. The next year it fully matured and was cut two or even three times for hay and in the fall it was plowed under. Alfalfa was a legume so it put nitrogen into the soil. The year after alfalfa, corn was raised. Corn was terribly hard on the soil so growing it one year out of three was the only responsible way to husband the soil so it remained fertile for future generations.

Now, back to moving the turkeys. At the very first, the turkeys ruined the first cutting of hay, but the fertilizer deposited by the birds made what would have been the second cutting that much better. After the first cutting they were on stubble until the hay grew up. Every week or so all the vegitation was padded down and the pen became pretty rank from the droppings so a second pen was set up and the turkeys moved into it. When the cross fence was taken down to let them into the new pen, it was fun to watch as they delightedly made their way into the fresh hay. They snapped up the grasshoppers and any other insect in seconds. They also ate the leaves of the hay. All the shelters and feeders had to be moved, mostly by being pulled by the tractor. Tommy and I hooked the chain to the shelters, and then had to chase the turkeys out before we could move it. Then one of us walked in front of the tractor with a flag getting the turkeys out of the way.

After everything was moved we put up the fence again so they would not roam back into the old area. This was to reduce the chance of diseases being carried along. Since all the pens were temporary, they were only built as solidly as necessary. Sometimes a storm of something else would scare the turkeys—low flying airplanes were the worst—and they would run en masse toward a fence and push it down. The next morning we would spend a lot of time rounding up the flock and setting up the fence again. Maybe the reader will get the idea that living on a farm was a lot of work—it was—and we were all included. Some nights even at six years old, and even hating to work as I did, I fell into bed tired from work. Even though I didn't think of it at the time it gave a kid a deep sense of self worth.

The first thing after breakfast the next morning Tommy and I had to help dad sack up oats for the turkeys. First he'd back the two wheeled trailer up into the barn where we unloaded hay. Then we'd go to the granary in the third floor where Tommy and I held open burlap bags while dad shoveled oats into them from one of the grain bins. He tied each one shut after it was filled. We'd typically fill six or eight sacks. There was a long plank about ten inches wide and two inches thick standing on end on the right side of the doorway to the granary. Seen from the driveway that doorway was a rectangular opening in the wall at the height of the third floor with a shear drop from it to the driveway floor.

Dad would bring the plank to horizontal and slide it out of the granary door until the end rested on the trailer below. Tommy and I would go down and wait on the trailer as dad slid bags of oats down the plank. We would wrestle the bags to the side the best we could. After the last bag, dad pulled up the plank and stowed it again beside the doorway just inside the granary.

Today like most days we went out with dad to feed the turkeys. We helped in little ways like opening and closing the gate to the turkey pen for him. It was also our job to walk around and look in the shelters for dead turkeys. It was necessary to be vigilant for diseases, predators, and cripples.

If we found a couple of dead ones in successive days we'd take the carcasses home and dad would do autopsies. I remember one had eaten a stick that it could not digest and it had eventually stabbed itself right through the gizzard so that was an easily explained death. Dad always looked at the liver because if it had yellow spots on it the bird had died of a disease called blackhead and that was bad. But even then, there was a medicine for it and it worked.

Turkeys were never meant to live in a dense community of thousands. I didn't know how they acted in the wild but in a large flock the normal instincts sometimes were a little off. Like many birds they were attracted to shiny objects. Sometimes we'd throw a bottle cap on the ground. They'd all make a mad dash for it and a pecking contest would ensue to determine which one got it. As soon as one had a good grip on it he would start running. A long line of birds chased him until another one took possession of it. Then the game would start anew. Finally one would get far enough away from the flock to where the rest would give up the chase. He'd stop, drop the bottle cap on the ground, peck at it a few times as if wondering what all the fuss was about and leaving it there walk back to the flock. It only had value as long as others wanted it. They reminded me of people. I wonder why.

At other times one turkey would scrape its head and a little blood would appear. This made it stand out as different and soon others would start pecking at the wound. Occasionally when we came out to feed the turkeys we'd find one with a totally bloody head, but still alive. At other times it would be already dead. If still alive, dad would stick it in an empty feed sack and take it home. We maintained a small pen by the buildings for cripples of one kind or another. For the pecked heads we had a black pitch that dad would smear over the wound. It dried and formed a scab that eventually fell off. This was another case where they imitated people. Anyone that was not the same as the majority was subjected to ridicule, or worse.

CHAPTER 12

After returning from feeding the turkeys we were ready to start the treasure hunt again. The first place we looked was in the machinery room on the second floor. That was where Justin had found the blasting powder so we thought it might be there.

Tommy said, "We'll go slow and watch for spider webs. No matter where he went to hide the bag he would have had to brush aside webs. If there are tons of webs, it's not there."

It was a good thing Tommy was so smart because I would never have though about the spider web trick. "But," I said, "maybe he gives the spiders free flies and they like him so they'll spin webs over his bag."

"Don't be dumb."

It was hot and every place we stepped we stirred up dust. Sun streamed in from a couple of windows and dust motes filled the air. There were spider webs everywhere and there was no sign that anything had been moved recently. After awhile we both had to admit that it probably wasn't in the machinery room.

"Maybe it's in the shed," I suggested. The shed was big enough for two cars but only one side was ever used because we only had one car. The other side was used to store small machines and tools. Even though it appeared messy, dad knew where everything was.

Tommy thought a minute and said, "I don't think so. Dad stores stuff in there that he uses a lot. He might run across it."

"We're running out of places to look," I said. "And, I said a prayer to St. Anthony a couple of times. Mom says sometimes he makes you look a long time, but you always find it. Like last winter when she lost her favorite thimble. She looked for it for two weeks, but finally found it."

We walked to the south lawn and sat under the big trees. No sooner had we sat in the cool shade when Chips was there wanting to be petted. "Get away, dog," Tommy said as he pushed him. Then he came to me. I gave in.

"Think of the best hiding place you can," Tommy said. "It's someplace, I know it."

We sat looking at the trees and sky with no new ideas coming to mind.

"Tommy," mom called, "come in. I need you for awhile."

He got up heavily, not wanting to bestir himself any more than I would have. With him gone I got it in my head that I had better become scarce lest a similar fate befall me.

Since treasure hunting was on my mind, and it seemed the barn was the place it had to be that was where I headed. Walking into the cavernous haymow, now starting to fill up with hay, I figured it couldn't be there. If we hauled more hay in it might get covered up and Justin would never be able to recover it. Returning to the driveway where the hay wagon was stopped to be unloaded, it came to me that the workshop might be a good place. It wasn't very big but still there might be a place. I glanced around and found nothing. My penchant for expending as little effort as possible on any activity except when it was fun meant that I didn't move anything, look under anything or even look behind anything. Worst luck, no leather bag. The stairs to the first floor were there so I started down. After two steps I stopped and turned. From where I stood I could see under the workbench.

Something came to mind. Last summer when my cousins, George and Tim visited from California, we had played hide-and-seek. Quite by accent I had found the space under the workbench was not filled with junk as most other nooks and crannies were and it made a perfect hiding place. I had gone all the way to the wall of the barn behind a horizontal cross beam that extended a foot up from the floor. Nobody could find me. They all looked and looked until finally they gave up. I never told them my hiding pace figuring to use it again sometime. It seemed that the reason it was such a good hiding place was that the bench was placed up against a window. That gave the best light for someone working there.

The result was that when somebody looked under the bench it appeared abnormally dark compared to the light flooded work surface.

I crawled on hands and knees over to the bench six feet away, and stopped in the shadow of the bench top. In a minute I began to make out shapes as my eyes adjusted to the darkness. The top of Justin's leather bag was dimly visible behind the cross beam. Inching forward on my knees I was about to reach for it when I stopped. There were pieces of straw lying on top. If I opened the case they would fall off and he would know we had found it so he'd move it again.

What to do? If I looked carefully at the placement of the straw pieces, I might be able to replace them more or less the same unless he had a real good memory and could tell even a slight change to the arrangement. I was itching to open the bag and look inside. But, the close call we had when we were snitching his tobacco made me decide to leave and think about it, so I did.

I went back into the haymow and sat on the hay. Chips was there beside me. He knew I was a soft touch so I scratched him behind the ears. Not a minute later I heard steps coming up the drive to the barn. Justin appeared and went into the workshop.

Wow, that was close. I got up and walked over there. "Hi Justin," what 'cha doin'?"

He had placed an axe in the vice and was filing at the cutting edge to sharpen it. "After dinner your dad wants me to chop some of the brush away from the plumb trees. It looks like there might be a good crop and he wants to try to sell some. There's another axe that I'll sharpen if you want to help."

"Come on Justin. I can hardly lift an axe."

He smiled. "There's a hatchet hanging on the wall. That's more your size. How about it?"

"I'd probably chop my leg off and finish what Tommy started."

He didn't look up as he intently worked. Using slow even movements he stroked the file across the steel of the axe's flank. I was taken by the way he focused on his work. I said something that was characteristic of my speaking without thinking. "You treat that file and axe like they were your friends."

As usual he mechanically went about his work as though he hadn't heard me, in fact as if I didn't exist, so, I waited.

"They could be my friends. In our world, that of the Ojibwe, there are many persons in the other-than-human class. We are careful not to offend or abuse anything we encounter because we are never sure if they aren't a metamorphosed person greater than we are. If they are such a person who is a friend we wish to do them no harm, if an enemy it would be foolish to offend them."

"But the file and axe are iron. Do you think they're alive?"

"They could become alive in another sphere of existance, one that crosses into ours and then influence us."

"Like cutting off your foot?"

"Or, cutting down a tree so we'd have wood to keep us warm in the winter. It would depend in whether it was an enemy or a friend."

"Then, aren't you hurting the axe by filling some of it away?"

"No. The axe wants to be sharp because that is the way it is supposed to be. If it is a person of the other-than-human class I am doing it a kindness. Of course it could only be a chunk of iron, but I can never be sure."

"That sounds kind of funny, Justin. Do all Indians think axes and things like rocks might be persons?"

"In some rare cases, yes. That is our culture. Animals are more likely to be other-than-human persons, especially bears. When we dream we are visited by a person in the other-than-human class while we sleep. That is why we hold great store in dreams. They tell us about our lives and what will happen."

"Well I hope nothing bad happens for a long time. The oats is getting ripe and we'll be cutting grain soon."

Nodding, he replied. "Yes, if you notice the moon is getting fuller every day. In a few days it will be full and that will be the grain moon. All things that ripen in mid-summer happen in the grain moon. The wild berries will mostly be ready to pick about then. My people waited for that moon. In the old times, other than honey from bees, berries were about the only thing we had that was sweet."

Justin carefully pulled his thumb crosswise across the axe blade and nodded. "That will be good enough for what I'll be doing. When cutting brush the axe goes into the earth so sharp stubs aren't left to step on. That dulls the axe so there is no reason to make it terribly sharp at the start."

"Never knew when the plumb orchard was anything but a lot of brush. Last year Tommy and I worked our way through the prickly branches and sat under one of the trees eating plumbs. A lot of them were wormy, but we had a lot to pick from. Dad is sure glad you're here. He says he's getting caught up on a lot of things he never had time for. He even has time to do things with Tommy and me. That's real nice."

Justin opened the vice and turned around the axe head so he could sharpen the other bit and started filing.

I continued talking. "Dad even took us fishing twice so far this summer. I like to do that. We rent a boat and dad rows out with the oars the man gives him. Tommy is big enough to let down the anchor now. It's a paint pail full of cement with a rope on it. I even managed to put a worm on my hook this year. Tommy and I drop a line over the side of the boat but dad has a rod and reel. We let the line out until it stops on the bottom and then pull it up this much. If they're hungry they bite right away. A lot of them are awful small and we throw them back. But some are keepers.

"You ever been fishing, Justin?"

He nodded. "Yes. When I was a little older than you I started going fishing with the men. Most of the time we used nets, though. It wasn't a sport like you do. You would not be allowed to do that but on the reservation we can fish any way we want."

"I like to look down into the lake. If I'm on the side of the boat where the shadow is on my side sometimes I can even see the fish if the water's clear. It's so pretty seeing them swimming around like they were hanging in the water. When they see the worm they nibble at it. Dad says that when it disappears that means they have it in their mouth so to pull on the line. Works every time."

He looked through the dirty panes on glass toward the house for a second. "Your dad is in from the field so it looks like it's about dinner time."

Justin took the axe from the vise and stood it beside the door. We started toward the house for dinner. Once again I was talking. "I hope the axe is your friend because we don't want anything to happen to you."

Justin shot a quick glance at me with an odd expression. Being a kid, I didn't make anything of it.

After lunch Tommy had to help mom again so I went outside to play. Justin took the axe to the plumb orchard to cut brush. An hour later Tommy came out and I told him that I had found Justin's bag. That was great news to him. I told him about the pieces of straw on top of it. He said that was a good thing to notice, in fact real smart of me. I felt good about that. It didn't stop us from going to the workshop to see what we could.

Now that it was after dinner the sun was streaming in through the window in front of the work bench so the contrast in the light from the sunbeam and the darkness under the bench made it impossible to see anything.

"We need a flashlight," I said.

"Yeah, but mom would never let us have it. Batteries are too expensive and they don't last long. Anyway, what would we say when she asked us why we wanted it?"

"It's too bad the sun isn't shining in under the workbench."

"Wait a minute. What we need is a mirror."

"Yeah. There's a piece of a broken one in the shed in front of the car."

"Sure. We could take it and then put it back so nobody would know we used it."

We were both off to the shed. There it was, a jagged shard of mirror about the size of a saucer. Tommy took it and looked at it. "It's awful dirty. We need a rag and some water."

"There's a feed sack in the barn. Just spit on it."

"Might work. Otherwise we'll have to go down to the well."

In the barn Tommy spit all over it and rubbed it with the sack. It was a still pretty smeared.

"Let's try it," I said.

First Tommy stood back to where the sun fell on the floor and reflected the light under the workbench. I was up closer and said. "The light is too high up."

With some experimenting, Tommy held the mirror a couple of feet off the floor and closer to the bench. That made the light shine down at an angle.

"That's perfect," I said.

"Don't get any closer or touch anything. Here you hold the mirror and let me look."

We traded places and I held the mirror so light reflected under the bench.

"Don't wobble it around so much. Hold it steadier."

Tommy was on his knees with his hands on his thighs being careful not to touch anything. "There," he said in triumph. "I see a thread coming from the wall to the top handle on the bag. If I tried to open the bag the thread will be brushed aside and I'd never know it."

He looked up under the bench. "Bring the mirror back to where I put it at first and shine it up at the underside of the bench." Now he craned his neck to see up. He stood up and told me to shine the light at the top of the bag while he pounded on the top of the bench with a hammer. Small pieces of straw and dust fell on the bag.

A few steps away were the stairs to the bottom floor of the barn. We went down. I had told Tommy about how Justin had come in to sharpen the axe immediately after I had found the bag so we weren't taking any chances. It was cool in the lower barn which was nice.

"Here's what I think," Tommy said. "The pieces of straw fall on the bag whenever someone works on the workbench and aren't part of a trick to see if anyone has opened the bag. But, the thread is. He put that there on purpose. If we look in the bag we can sprinkle some dust and straw on the top and that would be okay. But we would have to be careful about that thread and put it back exactly the way we found it. It looks like it's from an old pair of blue overalls."

We sat and considered it for awhile. Then I said, "Wonder what those guys left in the hole in the tree?"

"Yeah," Tommy said. "Maybe what's in the tree is connected with what's in Justin's bag. It seems like the guys in the woods left it for Justin especially since you think one of them met you and Justin coming back from blasting the big stump. Wonder what it was?"

"How'd we get to it? It's pretty high up. The step ladder by the old barn would work."

"Nah. Somebody would notice it was missing. And, anyway it's too heavy for us to carry. We need something that's all over the place. Maybe there's an old log around the hollow tree."

"We could each carry a piece of wood from the wood pile and set them on top of each other."

"Yeah, Jamie. That's a good idea. Let's go."

Every chunk of wood that we thought would be good for our plan was too heavy. The ones we could carry were too small. "Here's a mostly rotten one," I said. "Dad said he should have left that log in the woods. But if we sat it on end it would hold one of us."

Tommy agreed and we dug in the pile looking for another one. Then we set off. When we came to the potato patch Tommy stopped. I dropped my load to rest. "What's the matter?"

"When we ran out of the woods we left tracks in the potato patch."

"We can rub them out with a branch like Tonto did in a *Lone Ranger* program."

"Sure. But, now we should go around the end of the patch so we don't leave more tracks."

"I don't know if I can carry my wood that far."

"Ah, don't be a whiner. Let's go."

It took quite awhile and we were bitten by a lot of mosquitoes again, but we made it. We set the two chunks of wood on end with the smaller one, mine, on the top. Tommy was the tallest so he climbed up and reached into the hollow in the tree.

"There, I can feel it, but it's not coming."

I could see him working away at it with his hand until finally he pulled it free.

"It's pretty heavy," he said.

"Now what do we do?" I asked.

"We take it with us, that's what. We can always bring it back. But, first we have to carry our wood chunks back into the brush so nobody will see them."

After we carried the wood away we returned. Tommy made sure there were no signs of our having been there—he thought of everything—and we left with him carrying our booty.

Again, we walked around the potato patch and provided more meals for hungry mosquitoes. We hid the package in the machinery room under some old straw and went to the pump to wash our bites. After that we sat down and didn't say much because we were pretty tired. It was hard to keep from looking in the brown paper package to see what it was, but we knew we had to be careful lest someone find us at it so we decided to wait until tomorrow. The day was wearing on and would soon be supper time so we headed back to the house.

We didn't get a chance to look at our treasure the next day because that was the day we started to cut grain and everybody was busy.

CHAPTER 13

The next morning at breakfast dad asked Justin, "Ever shocked grain before?"

"No sir, can't say I have."

"Well, nothing much to it. We'll start on the field up the hill from the house so you can see when we've been around a couple of times with the binder. Then come out and throw back the bundles so we can back-cut. After you've done that we'll stop for a minute and get you started shocking."

Back-cutting was necessary because the first time around the field the binder ran in the very edge of the field to avoid whatever was next to the grain—a fence or corn field. The way the binder was built it was necessary to go around the field in a counter clockwise direction. After the whole field was cut a final round was made in a clockwise direction to cut that swath the binder traveled in on the first round. Some of the oats was lost having been flatten by the wheels of the machines, but enough was salvageable to make back-cutting worthwhile.

The day before dad had pulled the grain binder out from where it was parked for most of the year near the woods on the west side of the potato patch. He greased and oiled all the bearings and other moving parts. Tommy would drive the tractor, dad would ride the binder, and Justin would shock. Dad had modified the binder so a tractor could pull it. Originally the binder was made for a three horse hitch. We only had two so the tractor was used.

Dad had to ride the binder most of all to operate the bundle carrier. That was a rack the extended out to the right side and caught the bundles as they were ejected after being tied with twine. That made it possible to carry along several bundles. The carrier was collapsed by a movement of the operator's foot to deposit bundles in rows of piles on the field so the shockers didn't have to walk all over the place collecting up bundles. The other thing the dad did was make sure everything was working properly. It was a complicated machine for its day and all manner of things could go wrong. He also yelled directions to the tractor driver some of which were hard to understand.

By mid-morning things were in full swing. Justin had taken to shocking where he'd pick up a bundle under each arm and set them down a foot or two apart and leaned them together on top. Then another two bundles on either side of those two making a long teepee out of a total of six bundles. They sat in the field that way for a couple of weeks so the grain would get nice and dry for threshing. Justin was getting pretty good at it, but not nearly as fast as Hank Cooper who helped us last year.

Mom got some things together in a basket and we headed up to the field. She carried Mikey and a basket and I carried a jug of hot coffee and a small pail with tin cups in it. When we got to the field she set the things down. Justin came over and on the next round Tommy stopped and he and dad came over for morning coffee, too. Of course, Tommy, Mikey and I didn't drink coffee. We had water and a cookie. They carried a jug of water out to the field with them in the morning. There were rags tied all around it that when wetted kept the water in the jug cool by evaporation.

After coffee, mom and I started to shock, too. She wasn't strong enough to take a bundle under each arm like the men did so she set one up and I'd have to hold it up until she got another one set up beside it and then she'd slap the tops together. We set up two shocks close to each other and mom put an old table cloth over them for shade and a small blanket on the ground for Mikey. There were a few toys left for him to play with as we went about shocking.

This was real work and I hated it. But nobody asked if I liked it or not. Chips rarely came to the field with us. He wasn't stupid. He knew work when he saw it so decided to stay at the house and sleep on the back step in the shade. After all, his job was to keep all manner of marauders way from the house, or at least bark at them. It was a hard job, but somebody had to do it and he was the one.

As we continued setting up oat bundles I couldn't help thinking about what was in the brown paper package and what would happen when somebody found it was missing from the hollow tree. From time to time mom had to remind me to pay attention to what I was doing. A half hour before noon mom had to go to the house and start dinner which was great as far as I was concerned. But, when we got to the house mom had me go to the garden and pull some carrots and clean them for dinner. More work and still no time to look in the package.

Dad carried a stump of wood along on the binder so he could put it under the tongue when he unhooked the binder from the tractor. That way they could all ride home from the field on the tractor. They arrived at noon and washed up. Tommy and I were outside as dad and Justin sat on the porch. Out of sight from them I said, "What happens when someone goes looking for the package and it's not in the tree?"

Tommy shrugged. "I don't know. They sure won't know we took it." At that mom called us for dinner.

In the summer we ate dinner and supper on the back porch unless it was raining. There was a large table that stayed on the porch all the time even in winter. The porch was screened in and was cooler than in the house on hot days. After dinner the men sat around for awhile talking before getting back to work. I helped mom clear the table and dried some of the dishes. I was still pretty small for that and she was afraid I'd drop and break the plates and stuff, so I only dried things that wouldn't break. I guess she thought it was good training because she could do stuff like that so fast that what I did didn't help much. It also seemed she was being sure to keep me occupied as if she though I'd get into mischief if I was out of her sight. Maybe it was only my imagination because I wanted to look in the brown paper package so bad.

With the kitchen work done mom put Mikey down for a nap. I thought this was my chance to slip away, but she had me stay in the house in case Mikey woke up while she went to the garden. It was getting late in the season for peas but she thought she could find enough for supper. When she came back I had to shell peas—worst luck—while she prepared sandwiches that she'd take to the field for afternoon lunch after Mikey woke up.

About the time I had the peas shelled Mikey was awake and we headed back to the field with lunch for the men. During the rest of the afternoon I helped mom and at times played with Mikey so he wouldn't cry while mom went on shocking the best she could alone. It was odd because mom didn't seem to be a very good shocker, but by the time we went home so mom could start supper she had a lot of shocks set up. I was hoping I'd have time to go to the barn on my mission when we got back.

At the house, I sat on a chair on the porch. I was pretty tired with walking to the field and shocking oats. Mom looked at me and said, "You look like you're bushed. You've helped a lot today and can go play until supper if you want."

I wanted to see what was in the package but being as tired as I was, it didn't seem so important now. But, I got up and went to the barn with Chips at my heels. He wasn't tired because he'd been sleeping all day. I got down on my knees and carefully reached under the straw and pulled it out. Since the straw was old there was dust and spider webs on top of it so Tommy had carefully lifted it up so as to disturb it as little as possible and slid the package under it.

Tommy had said it was heavy for it's size and it was. Maybe it was a flat piece of gold. Chips was there beside me sniffing at stuff. He put his nose to the package and growled. I knew he could smell the men from the woods. I pushed him away and told him not to bother me.

There was still enough light to see so I untied the string and unfolded the brown paper. I laid the open package in front of my knees and upon trying to pick it up discovered there were two things, like rectangular plates, about eight by ten inches and as thick as my thumb. I lifted up the top one and held it up to the light. It seemed to be made of a grayish silver metal. The back was smooth but the front was mostly covered with a pattern of squares about an inch on a side except for the top. On the upper right was a lot of small letters like a page from a small book. To the left of that was an area that looked like a blank form, only backwards. I had seen the blank forms that dad had gotten from the post office for his income taxes last winter. This would have been a small form. There were clearly words followed by a line extending to the left of them where something could be written in. But as I looked closely most of the letters were wrong. There was a large letter "A" that I recognized but most of the letters must have been from a foreign language.

I set it aside and noticed there was a sheet of paper that had been between the top and bottom plate. I set it aside and held up the second plate which looked like the other one.

At that moment I heard the tractor stop by the old barn and the motor turned off. Quickly, almost frantically, I placed the plates on the paper aligning them mostly with the creases and wrapping it again. There wasn't time to put the string back the way it was so I put the string under the last fold of paper and slipped the package under the straw. I rushed out of the machinery room but started to walk normally as I left the barn.

The men were making their way to the house but Tommy saw me and turned my way. Justin turned his head and looked at me only for a second. He was an alert man and not much happened that escaped his notice. He couldn't have known what I had been doing, though.

Tommy came my way and as he approached I could see his face was dirty. The fields were a little dryer than normal and the binder threw up dust when the grain was cut. "You're pretty dirty," I said. "Be sure you wash your face and arms good or mom will make us take a bath tonight." Almost always we only took a bath on Saturday night and that was too often to suit us. I could see Tommy wasn't thinking about taking baths.

"Did you look in the package?" he asked.

"Yeah," I said. "There're two metal plates with mostly squares on then and some writing at the top. But most of the letters are wrong. Must be a foreign language."

"Did you find the note?"

"I didn't see a note. There wasn't any, except there was a paper between the two plates. But, that wasn't a note because the paper only had printing on it."

"But, the guy went to the saddle bag on his motorcycle and got a pencil and paper. He must have left a note. Let's go look."

"Boys, come wash up for supper."

Tommy almost growled at me but we had to go to the house or we'd get scolded.

After supper Tommy had to dry dishes and by then it was too dark in the barn to see anything.

The next day went about the same as the day before except that they were cutting oats a long way from the house so mom drove the car out with the morning coffee and afternoon lunch. After dinner Tommy and I went to the barn to see if we could find the note that I might have failed to see and left laying on the floor. But, there was no note in plain sight and we had to leave before Tommy had a chance to look at the plates because dad and Justin were ready to go back to the field.

After supper Tommy went to the barn by himself even though it was getting pretty dark. He was back sooner than I expected. Dad and Justin were milking so we sat on the wash bench under the elm tree.

He whispered to me. "The note was under the package. They must have slipped it under the string and you didn't see it fall when you opened the package."

"Well, what does it say?"

It was still light enough outside to read as Tommy looked around for anybody watching and took it from his pocket. It was written in pencil, of course, and there had not been a good writing surface in the woods.

"It says—it's pretty hard to read: 'There was a mistake with the last plates. Not your fault but they are worth'. . . something. Let me see, ah, 'worth-less.' Yeah, that's it. 'The new layout is in the package with the plates.' That must mean the printed paper you saw between the plates. I didn't look for anything else after I found the note. Then it says, 'Leave a note here when you will have these done—you have ten days at most.'"

CHAPTER 14

Red Feather

That afternoon the man, Rango, had come back to see if Justin found the new plates. He was quiet when arriving and pushed the motorcycle into the woods. This meant the dog wasn't there to bother him. At the hollow tree he discovered the package gone, but no note saying when Justin would have his work done. Being late in the day he decided to wait until the cows came out of the barn after milking and then find Justin.

Justin was surprised to see Rango that evening because he had done the work that was demanded of him. But, when Rango asked about the second set of plates Justin thought back and remembered seeing Jamie coming out of the barn late in the day as they arrived at the buildings from cutting grain. The boys were normally around the house that time of day.

In the twilight of the haymow, Justin now went along with Rango as if he had the plates. He listened to what Rango said and then told him he'd have the work done when it was done. The farm work was coming fast and he didn't have much time to do what they wanted. Rango made an implied threat that if Justin didn't do the work they would harm the family. Justin warned him to stay away from the family. Rango was a dangerous man but, then, so was Justin.

The next day dad and Tommy finished cutting grain in the afternoon. Then, with dad and Justin shocking they almost finished by supper time. There would only be a couple of hours of shocking for Justin the next day. In the morning we went out with dad to move the turkeys to clean ground.

After coming back from the turkeys Tommy and I went over to the swing. Tommy sat in the swing slowly swinging back and forth while I sat by one of the trees. We were really stuck.

"Why do those men want Justin to have the plates and why are they using the hollow tree as a kind of mailbox?" Tommy asked. "It would be simpler to send them by normal mail. We get stuff from Sears and Roebuck all the time. It works for us."

"Justin said Rango was a bad man that day after we had met him in the woods. Maybe he's afraid somebody will recognize him if he goes into the post office to mail it."

"Bet something illegal's going on."

"Justin is too nice a man to do something illegal," I retorted. "Maybe we should ask Justin about the plates."

"It's really his business and we shouldn't interfere."

"But we did interfere. We took the plates."

"Yeah, but it's our farm and I don't like those men sneaking around. I was really scared when they came into the woods when we were there. It's our woods, not theirs. They have no right coming in like they owned it."

This was tough. Finally Tommy said, "Dad is so happy to have such a good hired man and if we go stick our noses into his business he might leave. We have to put the plates and the note back in the tree."

Mom called for Tommy to come in the house to watch Mikey while she went to the garden.

With Tommy gone I got in the swing and only sat there hardly swinging at all thinking about the plates when I head a foot scrape on the gravel on the driveway. Justin was walking toward me having finished shocking the oats. He was not just happening by, he was coming toward me, or, maybe it only seemed that way because I didn't want to talk with him.

"Hi Jamie," he said in a pleasant voice. "Will you come to the shop in the barn and help me with something?"

"Sure," I said.

It was a good thing he asked me to help him because I was afraid he'd want to talk to me about the plates. We walked along and he didn't say anything which wasn't strange, but that I wasn't talking would have seemed strange if he had been paying attention. When we were in the shop he squatted down and looked right into my eyes.

"I want to ask you something." Before I had time to think he got right to the point. "Have you seen that man Rango we met in the woods in the last couple of days?"

I looked down and fidgeted but didn't answer.

"It's important that you tell me. I told you he was a bad man and he came to see me last night here in the barn. He thinks I have something that I don't have. This is very important. What can you tell me?"

I didn't look at him and didn't say a word. He could tell I knew something. With Tommy it might have been different.

"Come on, Jamie. You have to tell me or I might have to leave. Your dad wouldn't like that, would he?"

I shook my head. He waited as I stood there. I knew there was no way I could out wait Justin. Finally I said, "You want the plates, don't you?"

As I said it I looked at him for an instant. There was a slight shock in his expression like he had not expected me to say that, only that maybe I might have seen Rango, or heard his motorcycle in the woods.

"Yes. I must have the plates. Can you give them to me?"

I turned and he followed me out of the shop into the machinery room. I knelt down and pulled the package out from under the straw and gave it to him. "Tommy still has the note they wrote and put with it. But, all it says is that the last ones were worthless and you have to do it again and you have ten days."

Justin took the package, sat down on the straw, leaned his back against the silo and opened it. He studied the sheet of paper between the two plates and then put it with the plates back in the paper package, tied it with the string and laid it beside him. He let his out-stretched arms lay on the tops of his knees and thought.

"How did you and Tommy manage to get these?"

It was obvious that even though he was one of what I thought of as big people, he could not figure this out.

Cody

It was simple to me. "We were down in the woods when Rango and the other man came roaring into the woods on their motorcycle. We hid behind a big tree and didn't move or make any noise. It was hard because the mosquitoes were eating us alive. We saw them put it in the hollow tree and even watched Rango write the note. The next day we went back and took it out of the tree."

When someone didn't know what to say we would say he was speechless. Since Justin normally didn't say much it should not have been out of the ordinary that he didn't replay. But, it seemed to me he really didn't know what to say. He was thorough in whatever he did so it surprised me that he didn't ask what brought Tommy and me to the woods that day because it seemed like that was the next thing he'd ask.

He didn't ask that. Instead he said, "This is hard to say, and you might not understand it, but you must do as I say. I know you obey your parents and I'm not one of them. That doesn't matter. If I am to stay and help your dad there must be nothing said about this. Nobody besides you and Tommy know about the plates, is that right?"

I nodded.

"Fine. We have to keep it that way."

There was something in me that made it impossible to let the situation end at that. "What are the plates for?"

"It's the best that you don't know."

"What do they want you to do to the plates?"

Justin looked at me rather sternly. "Jamie, I won't tell you anything more. This must be between you, Tommy and me. There is no other way."

With that he grabbed the package and got up. "Now, I have to earn my keep. You go out and swing, play with the dog or whatever you want to do."

That evening when dad came in after evening chores—Justin never came back to the house in the evening—mom said, "I got a call from the hospital this afternoon. The woman said that the government is refusing to pay the bills for when they operated on Justin's leg and for the times the doctor came out to change the bandage. They think it's a mix-up but the war department said Justin Merchner, our Justin, is dead, that he died from wounds in the St. Cloud VA Hospital."

110

Dad was sitting in his favorite chair in the living room. During the week mom made him throw a blanket over it if he didn't change his field clothes which he seldom did. He had been reading the daily paper and only partly listening which was not uncommon. He lowered the paper and asked mom to repeat what she had said, which, with an exasperated voice, she did.

Dad said, "Of course it's a mix-up, he obviously isn't dead. He had his discharge papers with him when we went to the hospital. What about them?"

"The woman who called said she didn't see his papers, only that the War Department returned the request for payment stamped 'Denied' and a note that the subject died in St. Cloud in April. And, that the hospital has waited long enough—they want payment."

I could see that dad was irritated. "Oh, the government. If they can muddle something up, they will. Nothing ever works the way it should. There's no problem giving them money when we pay our taxes, but try to get some back and they'll make you pay for it a thousand times in grief. I'll have to stop at the hospital in the morning and see what I can do."

At dinner time the next day dad mentioned the payment problem to Justin who continued eating as the details of the morning's meeting at the hospital were relayed between bites of food. Justin sipped his coffee and replied, "There was a man in the room with me in the St. Cloud Army Hospital that was severely wounded and died shortly before I left. It's possible they mixed up our records. I have some money from when I was discharged from the Army and what you've paid me since I have been able to work. I'll give you what I have and ask that you take it in and pay for me. I think it best if I stay out of town whenever I can. Then, you'll have to tell me how much I still owe and I'll try to get it."

The way he spoke it didn't sound like he was bitter. There was more like caution in his voice. I wondered if it had anything to do with the plates and Rango.

"I sure hate to see you have to do that, Justin," dad replied, "the way you've been helping out. As a matter of fact, I was surprise at how demanding they were. They all know that farmers are stretched the thinnest as far a money goes this time of year. After the crops are in we settle up our debts, they all know that. That's the way it is in a farming community."

After dinner Tommy and I made ourselves scarce. We went to the haystack north of the barn. Tommy was excited. "So the plot thickens." That was a term we heard from time to time on radio programs. "I wonder why the government thinks Justin is dead? Maybe it has something to do with the plates. I've been thinking, maybe we should give them to Justin before more bad things happen."

I shook my head and he looked at me. "Why not give them to him?"

"That's not what I mean. He guessed that we had them and made me give them to him yesterday. He was worried because we stuck our noses into his business. The man, Rango, came into the barn after milking and asked Justin about the plates. Justin said that it's between you, me and him. If anybody else learns about any of it, he'll have to leave."

"Wow! This is really serious. We're just kids. How are we supposed to know what to do?"

I had never heard Tommy talk like that. He was my big brother. I was the kid.

At the end of July threshing started. It was the highlight of the summer other than the county fair that was held in mid-August, after threshing. But, this year there wasn't a fair. Dad said the war made it so people didn't have much money and didn't want to spend the gas to drive there. Besides nobody really felt like partying when so many men were dying or coming home wounded.

The canceled fair was a big disappointment to me. Dad was in charge of the fruit booth in the agriculture building. This was something he inherited from his father. This meant he was on the Fair Board and he'd go to a couple of meetings during the year so he knew well in advance there'd be no fair.

Other years he let me go with him the first morning of the fair which was the time for people to make entries. People would bring in all manner of fruit like apples, plumbs, raspberries, black walnuts, and stuff I didn't know the names of. It didn't matter if it was too early in the season for the fruit to be ripe because everybody else's was green, too. The person making the entry would write his name and address on a cardboard ticket and then arrange his entry on a paper plate the way he wanted it after which it was set out for exhibit. Dad would be picking things the day before the fair started, mostly apples because we had an apple orchard. He did this for two reasons. The first was so there would be more exhibits. During the fair people would wander through the various buildings to see what there was, and if they had made entries they wanted to see if they won anything. It was a kind of amusement. The fruit exhibit would look nice when it was all arranged properly, especially if there were a lot of exhibits.

The morning of the second day was judging time in the agriculture building where somebody who was considered a local expert would judge each category of items. If there were six entries of raspberries he'd judge which one was first, second, and third place. If none of it was very good, nobody got first prize. For things like this ribbons weren't used but colored cards—blue for first, red for second and white for third. There could be profit in it because first place was fifty cents, second a quarter and third fifteen cents. This was the second reason why dad brought in a lot of exhibits. A month or two after the fair checks would be sent out by the Fair Board for the prizes. When we got older, we'd pick things like black walnuts and could keep the prize money if we won anything.

The fair was like a fairy land to me with all the carnival rides and other attractions. The carousal spun around and its music filled the air. We had ridden the wooden horses that went up and down since we were three years old. Mom or dad would stand beside us so we wouldn't fall off. It must have made them feel young, too. There were booths of all kinds on the midway like the one where people could test their skill throwing baseballs to knock over milk bottles to win a teddy bear and other prizes. One was where men shot rifles to win prizes. With sufficient begging we always got mom or dad to buy us cotton candy. They hated that because our hands and faces would be sticky when we were done. But, it was good.

When I was four I wanted to ride on the Ferris wheel. It was set up right outside the agriculture building. I watched the men set it up in the morning. It looked like it was a mile high to a little kid like me. In the afternoon they had it running and I was enthralled with it. Mom was there for awhile with Mikey, too. I asked if I could ride on it but she didn't want to. Finally a friend of the family happened by and she asked if he would go with me for a ride.

When it came our turn to get in a seat, the man operating the machine was splashing water on the place where big people rested their feet. I didn't even wonder why he was doing that I was so excited about getting into the seat. After we were in the seat, the operator closed the bar in front of us and away we went, but only a little way. We had to stop for passengers to get loaded in the next seat. In this way we moved a little and then stopped until we made nearly a complete revolution of the wheel. When we stopped at the very top it was a great view. It was like flying with the birds. We could see down on the agriculture building, like the birds did. There were even some birds flying lower than we were.

The man with me pointed out mom on the ground watching us. She looked awfully small way down there holding Mikey. With all the seats loaded we finally got going. It was a thrill as we came over the top and started down—it tickled my tummy. Round and round we went. There were so many things to see from how the Ferris wheel worked to looking in all directions as we came over the top. I didn't want to miss anything. All too soon it was over.

When our turn came we got out. Mom was looking a little anxious as I ran over to her. Her first words were, "At least you didn't throw up like that other kid did before you got in."

Only then did I realize why the man was splashing water in the seat we had ridden in.

CHAPTER 15

Our threshing ring, as it was called, was made up of the farmers up the road from us going away from town a couple of miles. We were the last farm before town. There were eight or nine farms in the threshing ring. One of the farmers owned the threshing machine. He supplied the tractor that powered it and kept it running. He was also in charge of stuff like making the straw pile right so it would shed water and the straw wouldn't rot. The rest all sent at least one man with a hayrack and team of horses to the farm of the one being threshed on a particular day. Normally they could thresh a farm in one day, sometimes a little less, sometimes a little more.

The framer being threshed was in charge of the operation on his own farm which was mainly the handling and storage of the threshed grain. It also meant supplying food which was the wife's job. Mom and dad would plan for weeks beforehand what they would feed threshers. It was no small matter because there were twelve to eighteen men and they all worked hard. It wasn't like relatives coming over when half the people were kids or small women. They all had big appetites.

The tongue of the wagon with the rubber tires had been changed so the tractor could pull it rather than horses. So dad and Justin moved the hayrack over to the wagon with the iron wheels. It was hard because it was heavy which meant they both lifted on one end moving it a foot or two at a time, first front, then back, then front again. That left the tractor at home so dad didn't use so much gas and it was available for feeding the turkeys. We never used the horses for the turkeys.

The other advantage with horses for thrashing was that dad didn't need a driver, whereas if he had used the tractor Tommy would have had to go along to drive. With horses the farmer only had to say *giddyap*, which really sounded more like *geddap*, to go, and *whoa* to stop. To have them turn he's say *gee* for right and *haw* for left and the horses would obey. If it was a complicated turn he'd have to take the reigns and guide them.

Everybody pretty well knew all the farms so the farmer to be threshed the next day would tell everybody at supper time which field to start loading bundles in when they arrived the next morning. It was something of an art loading the hayracks with bundles so they wouldn't fall off when the wagon traversed uneven ground. And it seemed that there was a competition as to how high they could make the load.

The threshing machine had a conveyor trough extending from its inlet that was six or seven feet off the ground. One wagon would pull up to either side of it and the men would take turns throwing bundles on the conveyor. The bundles first encountered chopping knives that went up and down that cut the twine binding the bundles and cut the straw into manageable size. What went on inside I never knew but eventually the grain came out of a small elevator at the top into a hopper that dumped out with every quarter bushel. From there the grain fell into a screw conveyor where it went to what were called wagon boxes for transport to where the farmer wanted it. Wagon boxes were four-wheeled wagons with wooden sides about four feet high all around.

Weed seeds fell out on the ground under the threshing machine, and the straw was blown out of a large pipe on the end opposite to the input. The tube had a hood on it that the machine operator could adjust from time to time to form the straw pile. The straw was an important product too since it was used as bedding for the cattle.

Some days dad took Justin along for what was called a spike-pitcher. That was an extra man who stayed in the field and helped the others load bundles. When one wagon was loaded, he'd walk over to whoever was close by and help him. With the shortage of manpower, there was seldom a spike-pitcher so Justin was appreciated. Dad said they even talked to him now and then.

* * *

This year we happened to be the second to the last place threshed. How they determined the order in which the farms were threshed I never knew. As I always remembered from little on, threshing day was tense and busy. There were always last minute things to see to from food preparation to making ready for the threshing machine. Depending on where he wanted the straw pile dad might have to remove some fences so there was room for the wagons of bundles to move around.

The man who owned the threshing machine also owned a homemade elevator that was a real help in handling the grain. It was especially true for us because our granary was on the third floor of the barn. The wagon boxes would be driven into the barn the same way the hayrack was. The grain was scooped out of the wagon into the hopper of the elevator. It wasn't a particularly long elevator but long enough so the outlet was high enough to divert the grain into any of the bins. It still took someone in the bin to shovel the grain back away from where it fell just inside the bin.

The elevator had two wheels under the hopper so it could be towed behind a hayrack or other wagon. It had arrived minutes before and another man and dad were working on setting it up. I was in the granary fooling around like I usually was always in the middle of the action—under foot, really. Dad was in the granary too and the other man was below on the driveway where the wagons pulled in. They talked back and forth but it wasn't going well. Finally the other man said dad had to come down and help him. I saw dad rush to the door of the granary that looked down at the driveway. He grabbed for the 2x4 beside the door that we used as a pivot to step around to the third floor. In his haste he put his hand on the plank set up beside the door used to slide grain sacks down to the two wheeled trailer when we feed the turkeys.

As he attempted to pivot around the side of the doorway to the third floor the plank moved and he missed his step falling to the driveway nine feet below. I didn't see him fall because I was further back in the granary climbing into one of the empty grain bins. There were boards closing the entry to the bin up to about two feet off the floor. The plank fell so close behind me that I felt it brush my back an instant before it made a reverberating bang on the floor. If I had been six inches further back it would have hit me smack on my head and I would have been nothing but a grease spot. Another one of those times when my guardian angel was

117

there for me. As with the other times, I knew instantly that my life had been spared by a whisker.

Months later when we were all discussing the accident I told about the plank narrowly missing me as it fell. Mom and dad both moaned at the thought of what might have happened. Their looks were strange like they were looking at a resurrected grease spot.

I stepped away from the opining to the bin and went to the doorway to the granary. Dad was lying on the floor groaning. Luckily, he had not landed on any part of the elevator. The man who had been helping dad yelled for another man. The last thing I saw was the two men carrying dad out of the barn, one on each side, dad with one arm around the neck of each man. I assumed they put dad in our car and one of the men drove while the other stayed beside dad. The key was always left in the car so there was no problem starting it.

Threshing started that day without dad. Justin was nominally in charge though the rest of the men knew pretty well what to do having done the same thing before. But, there were always small changes from year to year. My grandfather had been an inventor, though he was never granted a patent that I ever heard. And dad took after him. He'd come up with a new idea of how to do something and when he showed it to us he'd say, "Here's my new patent." I didn't know if dad let Justin in on all the little secrets for how to do things easier this year but from time to time they'd have to ask about something and Justin was the man to ask. There was still the element of dislike for Indians among some of the men so I don't know how well it worked.

I stayed away from the house because I knew things would be frantic. Tommy was looking after Mikey and that was good enough for me. I think for most of the day mom didn't know dad's condition so there was nothing she could do but keep the food coming. At dinner they all knew that he had broken something in his leg or hip and wouldn't be home any time soon.

Threshing continued in a somber tone and they finished our place that day. One of the neighbor women came over to help with the food since mom had gone to the hospital immediately after dinner. It turned out that dad had multiple fractures of his hip and he would be in a hospital bed in traction until it healed.

That evening after chores, mom and Justin sat on the back porch. Mom was worried about dad, but she was also glad we had Justin. But, Justin was not being cooperative.

Mom asked if he would go to thresh the Klinder place, the last place, the next day. I could tell he didn't want to but agreed he would.

The next day it was late when Justin finished evening milking and since the threshers were always fed supper at the place where they threshed, Justin didn't come to the house at all after returning from threshing.

The next morning Justin ate breakfast on the porch. He said it wouldn't be fitting for him to come in the house anymore without Mr. Landon around. I didn't see what difference it would make if dad wasn't there but he insisted and mom didn't argue a bit. So, we all ate breakfast on the porch. Mom asked, "How did threshing go yesterday?"

Justin didn't answer.

Mom looked up, stopped eating her fried eggs and toast and looked at Justin. "Justin, please tell me how things went. I have to know what the feeling is with the people up the road."

Justin was uncomfortable I could see by the way he didn't look up. Usually when asked a direct question he'd answer.

"Come on, tell me." Mom wasn't insisting, more like pleading.

Justin flashed a glance at her. "Well, they made me eat outside. I hauled as many loads of bundles as anybody else, in fact, I had the last load."

Mom nodded, "I know, they're good folks, but they have their ideas about things, not always good ideas."

Mom told us to run along because they had business to discuss. Tommy and I ran out letting the screen door slam behind us. But, this was important so we ran around the house and quietly opened and closed the screen door on the front porch. The front door to the house stood open as it normally did during the day in the summer. Through the living room we tip-toed into the kitchen and listened.

"The thing is, Justin, you're a good man and we all like you, the kids too. It seems like it was the hand of God that sent you to us. You've been here long enough to know how things go and now we desperately need you. I hope we can count on you to stay on until Fred gets on his feet again."

"I don't think I can handle it all myself," Justin replied after a pause. "I'm no farmer. I have a strong back and I'm good for work, and I do appreciate how you cared for me when I was sick. But, I don't think I can do it."

"But, Justin, you're all we have." Mom was totally pleading now. "If one of the neighbors gets sick, the others pitch in and do the milking for a few days, but they have their own farms to run and that's a full time job as you by now can see. Besides, even if those bums wouldn't let you eat with them, and maybe the hospital staff won't even let you in to talk to Fred, I can bring home instructions as to what Fred had planned to do. And if you have questions I'll ask them. It'll be the same work you've been doing, and we'll increase your pay."

Again, Justin didn't say anything.

"The only thing you'll have to go to town for is to take the milk to the creamery. There shouldn't be a problem with that. If you don't help us we'll lose the farm. You see, after we were married Fred and I ran a resort for a couple of years. Then the war started and people weren't much into vacationing so we lost the place—couldn't meet the mortgage payment.

"Having no other options we came here. This farm is Fred's family's farm. He grew up here. His father was dead, but his mother was living here and renting out the land, but the place was deeply in debt. The bank was about ready to offer it for sale when Fred went in and said he wanted to start working it. It took some doing, but he managed to get the bank to give him some time.

"In addition, Fred's folks had standing charge accounts at most of the stores in town. He talked to the owners and got them to agree to give him a chance to pay off the bills. They all know, of course this being a farming community, that a farmer's main income comes in the fall when crops and stock are sold. The cream check for the milk we get each month pays for food and operating expenses. With nobody to finish the summer's work, we won't be able to make payments on the bills that will be due."

When mom fell silent, there was a long pause when neither spoke. Finally, Justin said, "I'll agree to stay on for awhile, but you must do all you can to find another man to work the farm."

With that, he got up and left ending further discussion.

Red Feather

Running Wolf did not want to take over running the Landon farm because he planned to leave after threshing. He knew Rango and his friends would not let him go since he did such a professional job of carving the type metal on the plates that they used to print counterfeit ration stamps.

He was torn by his duty to see the family through their tough time for having saved his life, and the danger he placed them in every day he stayed on. He had no doubt that those who were forcing him to carve the plates would harm members of the family to get him to do what they wanted. If he were to disappear completely, possibly even fake his own death, there would be no point in them harassing the family.

We learned that dad would be in traction for six weeks. That meant he had to lay on his back in bed with his leg pulled by cables that went over pulleys on a frame attached to his bed. Weights hung from the cables to keep a constant force on his leg. All of this was to insure the broken bones remained lined up so they would heal together in the right place. We learned much later that he nearly died, but mom didn't let us know that at the time. We all prayed for him a lot.

Tommy and I talked about what the plates were about almost every day if there were time. We all had more jobs to do with dad in the hospital. My memory of that time is indistinct with regard to dad. Mom went to visit him every day but we didn't because kids weren't allowed in the hospital no matter what. My entire life that seemed like an unreasonable policy. It was such a small town and small hospital there were seldom more than one or two other people in it. It seemed they could ask the others if they minded. Dad was in a room on the back of the hospital on the second floor which was the top floor. A couple of times mom took us with her and we waited outside and talked to dad through the window. He couldn't come to the window, of course, so we couldn't see him.

At Justin's insistence mom made inquiries to find another man but nothing came of it. Justin stayed on keeping up with the work. He made the second cutting of hay nearly by himself. Tommy drove the tractor for loading in the field. As usual Tommy drove the tractor backward to pull the rope to lift the hay off the hayrack into the haymow. I was on station to give my arm signals. It all went along as if dad were there with no hired man. Dad would write instructions about how he had intended to do things this year and sometimes Justin and mom would discuss them at breakfast.

Tommy and I had our secret and that was hard to carry around all the time. Things were subtly different between Justin and Tommy and me, or at least I felt it in his attitude toward me. Before I had been nothing but an inquisitive, talkative kid. Now, though I wouldn't have thought of it that way, I was a coconspirator. He had a secret, we knew the secret, or at lest that a secret existed, and he knew that we knew.

We had decided that Justin had special tools in his leather bag and he used them to do some work on the plates. Tommy had figured out that if Justin had really made his intricately carved silver belt buckle with the wolf on it, he was very talented. Since we had not touched his bag Justin didn't know we knew his new hiding place under the workbench in the barn. We also figured that the plates had to involve something illegal. For one thing, Rango did not seem like a nice man. Then there was the secrecy of it all.

We were watching for anything unusual. Every couple of days when Justin was in the field or taking the milk to the creamery we'd sneak into the woods and see if anybody had been there recently. After awhile, though, Tommy lost interest. He said it was probably the best if we stayed out of the way and let Justin take care of the business of the plates. If we stuck our noses into it any further than we already had, we could mess things up. That was Tommy. I was different.

CHAPTER 16

A big elm tree stood at the southeast corner of the back porch. It was so close that as it got a little larger each year it had grown onto the edge of the porch roof. The steps going into the porch were up against the house which left an area about six feet wide between the steps and the tree. Dad had hauled up a load of sand and shoveled it into that space for a sand pile for us kids to play in. This day I had been pressed into service to play with Mikey in the sand. Normally baby sitting Mikey seemed awful close to work and I avoided it whenever possible. But, he liked playing in the sand and so did I. Besides, sometimes he'd do funny stuff that made me laugh. And, after all, he was my brother, in fact I was his big brother, something I tried not to think about.

A black car drove into the yard. Chips, always on duty, barked at it. A man in a dark suit and wearing a felt hat stepped out a little cautiously, and seeing that the dog was not about to attack him proceeded to the house with a small suitcase in his hand. He knocked at the screen door and waited since he could see that the door to the kitchen was open and would not venture further under the circumstances. In the winter with the kitchen door closed a visitor had to go into the porch and knock on the main door or nobody would hear him.

I watched the man as he came to the house. He was a city man with his suit and about the same age as dad. His skin was light so he didn't work outside. While waiting for mom to come to the door he looked down at us and smiled but it was forced like he wished we hadn't been there. Chips had come near us and paced back and forth growling now and then. He looked like a salesman so after my first impression of him I mostly avoided looking up. Dealing with people like this was what big people did.

Mom came and looked at him through the closed screen door.

Before she could say anything the man said, "Please, let me introduce myself. I'm Leonard Haas. I work for the government, the Federal Bureau of Investigation, to be exact. We're commonly called the FBI as you probably know. You must be Mrs. Landon, is that right?"

"Yes," mom said guardedly.

As soon as the man had mentioned FBI, mom started to look worried and I was all ears.

Seeing mom's alarm he immediately said, "Nothing to worry about. I'm here to follow up on the strange set of circumstances about some charges at the local hospital involving a man who the records say passed away this spring, a man named Justin Merchner. I was told you have a man working for you by that name. Is that correct?"

"Yes we do," she answered. "He's been our hired man all summer and much needed."

The man interrupted, "Yes I'm aware of that. I hope your husband recovers rapidly from his injuries."

"Thank you. We do too." There she paused and the man didn't immediately say anything.

Finally he said, "You are aware, of course, of the charges at the hospital concerning Mr. Merchner?"

"Yes," mom replied. "As you said, the government seems to think Justin is dead, and clearly he is not. We all agree there was a mix-up of the records. In any event, Justin has already paid half of the bill and will pay the rest as soon as he has the money. The hospital agreed to give him time to come up with the rest of the payment. So that matter is settled for the time being. What interest does the government still have other than to tell us that Justin isn't dead? It's a rather obvious fact."

Once again, the man didn't speak right away. "Yes. I guess that is one way of putting it."

Mom was getting a little more worried all the time it seemed to me, or maybe a little mad. "What other way is there of putting it?"

"There's no reason to become belligerent, ma'am."

"I'm not becoming belligerent. From the way you said that, I assume your purpose is not simply to clear up mistakes made by the government. Now, I am asking you to show me some identification or I'm ordering you off our place. If you want to consider that belligerent, that's your business. The identification, if you please."

Wow! The only time I ever heard mom get riled up like that was when she and dad disagreed on something.

The man reached into his suit coat breast pocket and pulled up a leather thing that folded in the middle. He held it up to the screen door. Mom looked at it closely.

"Okay, Mr. Haas. I guess you are who you say you are. But, your business is with Justin and he's out cutting the meadow hay, probably be back in an hour or so. You can wait here on the porch if you like. But, I am not inviting you into the house, is that understood?"

"Yes, and that's kind of you ma'am. I'd like to take a look around your place if I may. That round barn is certainly interesting."

"No, sir. You may not wander around the farm. You will stay here where I can see you, or you will leave and come back at supper time, at six o'clock. I didn't like your tone of voice earlier. Besides, your business is with Justin, not with us or our barn."

That was not like mom. It was not uncommon for strangers to drop in and ask to look at the barn and nobody was ever refused. Something was wrong and I didn't like it so I got Mikey up and brushed the sand off him. He didn't complain having tired of the sand pile, anyway. Mr. Haas opened the screen door and proceeded to sit at the nearest chair by the table lowering his case to the floor beside his leg. I helped Mikey up the steps and led him into the kitchen. Mom crouched down by me and quietly told me to go through the living room and out the front door and dump the sand out of our shoes and then stay in the house, and to tell Tommy to do the same. From her voice I could tell she was afraid.

Tommy was on the front porch reading a comic book. As soon as I had our shoes back on I told him about the man from the government and how upset mom was.

Tommy didn't say anything for awhile. "If there was really something wrong and Justin had to leave who'd do the farm work? I guess she would be upset." He leaned over and whispered, "Boy, I wonder if it has anything to do with those plates? No matter what happens don't say anything about them."

We tried to amuse Mikey the best we could but he was getting fussy so Tommy went to tell mom. She made Tommy wait in the kitchen and to tell her if the man left while she was taking care of Mikey. She was really worried.

Finally we heard the tractor coming and watched out of the kitchen window as Justin stopped it by the old barn where dad always did. The tractor had the hay mower carried on the back, the cutter bar in the vertical position for transport. Justin started for the barn when mom called to him. "Justin. Come to the house for a minute. There's a man here who wants to talk to you."

Justin started walking to the house looking at the black car as he passed. By this time Mikey was sleeping and Tommy and I were both in the kitchen. Justin opened the screen door and the man introduced himself and said he was from the FBI. He than asked Justin if he was Justin Merchner. Justin said he was.

"I'm here in the matter of the charges that were submitted to the War Department for your care in the Deep Woods Hospital. It seems you showed them papers that said you were Justin Marcher just as now you agreed you were. However, the War Department records show that a man of that same name died in the St. Cloud VA Hospital last spring. How do you account for that?"

Justin immediately answered which was uncommon for him so he must have thought that sooner or later that question would be asked. "First of all, I find it odd that someone from the FBI would be here to inquire about such a simple administrative mistake."

"Don't be concerned about that. The War Department is there to fight wars. The problem, on the surface at least, is one of fraud against the government, and the FBI investigates things like that. In any case I still wonder if you can account for the situation?"

"I don't account for it. There was obviously a mistake." He paused but before the man could reply Justin continued. "It seemed like with the ever increasing number of wounded soldiers coming back they were a bit overwhelmed at that hospital as I suppose they were at all the VA hospitals and things were not as orderly as they should have been. There was a man, Jarvis Granston, if I recall correctly, that was in the other bed in the room I occupied. He was wounded severely. He knew he was dying and mentioned it to me a time or two when he was lucid. What I want to say is that sometimes the doctor would come in with a chart and address me with something like, 'How do you feel today, Jarvis?' You see, he had the wrong chart or didn't know who was who. I know the hospital personnel and the government are doing the best they can, but mistakes happen—a lot. I find it hard to think that it would be so bad as to get to the point where they bury the wrong person, administratively, that is, but that is obviously what happened."

Mr. Haas didn't interrupt Justin until he stopped talking. Then he said, "No matter how much the records were mixed up we have a foolproof way of determining who someone is, and that is fingerprints. As you know, in a war zone the Graves Registration Corps fingerprints all the dead soldiers before burial. The same procedure is followed here at home for the same reason, that being to make certain there is no doubt as to whom is being buried."

Justin replied, "They fingerprinted me when I went into the Army and again when I came to the VA Hospital in St. Cloud even though they said it was hardly necessary as I had nearly recovered from my wounds by then. So, fingerprint me again and compare them to the other two sets.

Tommy and I were in the kitchen looking out the window that faced the porch. The lower sash was up to let air circulate so we could hear and see everything. The man picked up his case and laid it on the table. Opening it he produced a small box-like thing and opened its lid. Then he placed a card about the size as a tablet from school on the table. He motioned Justin over to him. He took his right hand and rolled his thumb on the open box. After that he rolled the thumb on the card. Justin cooperated and not a word was exchanged since it seemed Justin knew what the man would do. He proceeded to do the same thing with each of Justin's fingers rolling a little black spool over the little case between each finger.

After the tools were replaced the man took a folder out of his little suitcase and looked at a similar card. "The prints I just took are clearly not the same as the ones I have for Justin Merchner," he announced.

"Do you have a description of the man to go with the prints you brought with you?" mom asked.

The man didn't immediately answer as one side of his mouth twitched. "Yes I do."

"Well?" mom said.

"The man from the folder I brought with me has brown hair and blue eyes."

Before he could say more mom asked, "What about the injuries he was being treated for in the St. Cloud VA Hospital?"

"Yes," he said slowly, "that also presents a problem. That man had abdominal wounds and would not be doing hard farm work this soon."

"Then, it seems clear," Justin broke in, "that in some way the entire contents of my file were exchanged with those in another." After a pause when nothing else was said, Justin continued, "I don't see the concern. I am willing to settle my hospital bills so that should end the government's involvement with me. Have you checked the file of the man in my room at the hospital, Jarvis Granston?"

He nodded. "While the staff remembers both you and him, as you say, there are a lot of wounded men coming through there and they aren't sure who was in your room."

"I do. At one time he was worried he was not being given the right treatments and he asked me to look at his chart. The name on it was Jarvis Granston. It showed when he was given medication, especially morphine since he was in a lot of pain. The first name, Jarvis, is not that common. That should give you something to go on. And, now that you have my prints from today, check them with those taken when I enlisted."

The man twitched the side of his mouth again, a nervous twitch it seemed, as if not wanting to answer. "Yes. I thought of that right off. But, you see, those records seem to have been mislaid. There is no record of you enlisting in the army."

"Well, I assure you I did, and served with honor." Now Justin seemed to be getting riled up. "I have my Report of Separation from when I was discharged. I used that when I was taken to the Deep Woods Hospital with the infected leg. Is the Army in the habit of filling them out for anyone at all?"

"I meant no offense," Haas said. "It would be most helpful if you could show me your Report of Separation. Do you have a copy of it handy?"

"That sounds like a good idea because my right thumb print is on the bottom of it. We can compare it to the one you just made. I keep it with my personal belongings which are in the barn. I'll go get it."

Justin had been glancing at Tommy and me standing by the window from time to time. Now he said, "Jamie, will you come with me? I may need a little help."

"Sure," I said.

Later Tommy told me what happened after we left the porch. Mr. Haas asked mom, "Aren't you concerned letting your young son go with that man under the circumstances?"

Mom was perplexed, "No. Why should I be? Justin wouldn't harm any one of us, he's practically one of the family. What did you mean by 'under the circumstances?'"

Haas leaned forward and said in a low voice, but loud enough for Tommy to hear, "I haven't mentioned it yet, so, of course, you couldn't have understood. It seems that the man belonging to the fingerprints I brought with me is a criminal. We aren't completely sure but he may have joined the Army to avoid prosecution and a prison sentence."

"Then, you're really barking up the wrong tree," mom retorted. "That's not Justin."

He nodded. "There's something that puzzles me. Why would he keep his personal belongings in the barn?"

Mom smiled a little. "He's full blood Indian and likes to be outside. Even when he nearly died from his leg wound he slept in the barn— never spent a single night in the hospital, or in our house for that matter. He mentioned he left the St. Cloud VA Hospital without being officially discharged. We assumed it was for the same reason. But, that doesn't detract from him being an honest and moral man."

When Justin and I arrived at the first floor of the barn we went in leaving the door open. "Keep an eye on the house and if that man comes out for any reason you let me know. I have to go upstairs for a few minutes. Stand back in the shadows so he can't see you."

"Your papers are in your leather case, aren't they? We found it, but don't worry we didn't look in it. Tommy saw that you had a thread on it that would tell if anyone had done that."

Justin had a strange look as he said, "How could you see it."

"We used a mirror and reflected sunlight under the workbench in the afternoon."

"Are you sure you kids aren't Indians?"

I watched as Justin made his way to the inside stairs that led to the second floor workshop. Then I looked toward the house and saw that no one had come outside. It didn't take long and Justin was back and we headed back to the house. As we walked he said to me in a low voice, "Be sure you guys don't say anything about anything."

Even I could figure out what he meant so I said, "Tommy already figured that out. We won't."

When we returned to the porch Justin carefully laid out the form on the table as he said, "You can see it lists my date of entry and date of honorable discharge, as well as my service number, physical description, and a lot more."

"Yes. I'm familiar with a Report of Separation Form," Haas replied a little tersely. He compared the thumbprints and nodded slightly.

"They match. Would you mind if I took this with me?"

"Yes. Very much. It's all I have, it seems, to say I served in the Army, and even to prove I'm alive as odd as that is."

Mom spoke up. "Deep Woods is the county seat. We can go in to the court house and have a certified true copy made and mail it to you."

"Yes," Haas said slowly, "I guess that will have to do."

Mom was looking at Mr. Haas as she said, "Justin, it seems that Mr. Haas is concerned about the man described on the papers he has because that man is or might have been a criminal. That's why he's here. It seems his visit doesn't have anything to do with the hospital charges."

Tommy and I both caught the small snap of the man's head when mom said that like he wasn't happy she had.

Justin was standing in a place where we couldn't see much of him but he answered, "My roommate had some unsavory visitors. A couple of times they told me to take a hike because they had business to discuss. I was doing pretty well by then, hardly needing my cane, so I left. But, it didn't seem as if they cared if I was able to leave or not—they wanted me out. It was crazy because when the morphine had taken effect he went to asleep or if awake he was lethargic. When the morphine wore off he was in such pain he hissed through his teeth most of the time. They woke him up while the morphine was working. It was no concern of mine what they wanted from him so I let it alone. He could have told them things he imagined about me the same way he imagined the doctors were treating him with the wrong medicine. Maybe you should find some of his known associates and see what they've been up to. By the way, wouldn't it be possible to exhume the dead man's body and fingerprint it. I think that should still be possible."

"Not possible," was the curt reply. "The body was immediately cremated."

Justin continued, "We have established that I am who I say I am, and that I'm not dead. I have work to do." He looked at mom then at Haas. "Is there anything else?"

"Just this," replied Mr. Haas. "With your permanent files missing, and the mix-up of our files at the VA Hospital, it would imply a wider plot that involves you. After all, as you admit, you were the roommate of this Jarvis Granston. Have you ever seen any of the men who visited him around town?"

Tommy and I both knew that was a tough question. But the way he had asked it saying "around town" left Justin open.

"No, can't say I have."

"How about you, Mrs. Landon? Have you had any unusual visitors?"

"Not until you arrived," she said.

After a short pause as he took the barb in stride he said, "Then, that does it. Here's a card with my name, address and phone number on it. If you should think of something or if anything out of the ordinary happens please call. You can reverse the charges and they will be readily accepted." Looking at Justin he continued, "Please don't forget to have a copy made of your Separation Record. Send it to the address on the card."

"Wait a minute," mom said. "What kind of crimes was the Granston accused of?"

"I'm not at liberty to discuss that, ma'am."

With everything replaced in his small suitcase, Mr. Haas left the house and went to his car. When he was gone, mom looked at Justin. "I hope this doesn't change anything. It seems strange all this can be happening. We are in such trouble and now it seems the darned government has it's records all confused regarding you."

"Nothing to worry about, Mrs. Landon. It'll sort itself out."

131

But, Tommy and I knew there was something to worry about. The FBI had actually been here. They knew there was something going on, and we were pretty sure it had to do with the plates.

Mom was in the kitchen and we were on the front porch when Tommy asked, "Why would those guys bringing the plates mix up Justin's records? It doesn't make sense. By doing that they brought the FBI out here."

"They didn't expect Justin to get sick. If he hadn't been in the hospital they would never know about the records."

"That's it," Tommy said. "That man Jarvis is dead and cremated."

"What's cremated?"

"That's when they burn up the body so they don't have to buy a cemetery plot." After a pause he continued, "By switching the records the police and the FBI would think Granston was still alive and would keep looking for him. If he was a really bad criminal, they'd go crazy trying to find him but never would because there was nobody to find. His friends could say they saw him someplace and away the cops would go leaving them alone."

That was all we could think of so I left by the screen door on the front porch and went to the barn. I wondered what Justin would be doing, and anyway it would be time to get the cows soon. I'd go get Tommy because we always did that together. I walked through the first floor of the barn and didn't find him. Going out I went around the south side of the barn to see if Justin was going to get the cows himself. I saw movement. In the barnyard were two large elm trees. Justin was standing about twenty feet away and throwing his knife at one of them. His face was set like he was mad, like he was working off steam.

He'd stand in all orientations to the tree, draw his knife and throw it. He was really quick. Most of the time it would stick in the tree straight out. He'd walk to it, work the knife up and down to pull it out and then do it again. A few times it didn't hit right and glanced off to the side. After about twenty times he put it in its sheath and went to the back door of the barn. I was crouched behind some tall grass so he didn't see me. As soon as he went into the barn, I ran toward the house and at the driveway stooped down like I was playing with the ants. Justin called to me. "Jamie, will you and Tommy go get the cows?"

CHAPTER 17

It was over a week later in the last half of August when something really bad happened. I knew that August was winding down because mom was checking to see if we had clothes to wear for school. It wasn't hard for me because I always got Tommy's clothes he had grown out of. But, finding clothes for Tommy that we could afford was hard as well as worrying about the ration stamps. Of course if the school year started with shirts that were a little too large it didn't matter because it was the same with most of the other kids. In fact, it was almost stylish to start school in the fall with a new pair of blue jeans with the cuffs turned up. The clothes had to be large enough so those worn in the fall would still fit when the weather got warm again in the spring. Normally we wore fall clothes until Christmas because some of the presents under the Christmas tree that Santa Clause brought were new corduroy pants, heavy flannel shirts, wool socks, mittens and stuff like that. Don't think we minded that because we looked forward to those gifts.

It was one of those beautiful end of summer days, if a little windy, when the sun was bright and warm. The goldenrod was blooming, and here and there a milkweed pod was opening sending its fuzzy yield flying away on the wings of the air currents. There were never more than one or two milkweed plants in one place because bigger kids were always out picking the pods. They could sell them to the government that in turn used the fuzzy stuff to fill life jackets for naval flyers in the Pacific.

It was a Sunday morning and we had returned from early Mass. Tommy was sitting at the dining room table reading the funnies from the

Sunday paper. If I were lucky mom would read them to me later. I quickly changed my clothes and took off in search of something to do. Chips came along like he always did.

It had been a few days since I had gone to the woods north of the barn to see if the motorcycle had been back. As usual I walked around the west end of the potato patch and then followed the north edge of the field to the place where I went into the woods. Where the field ended and the woods started was a wall of tall grass and brush that grew thick since it was in full sunlight. As a result I had my place where I'd crawl through a little tunnel I had made. Once in the woods where only filtered light penetrated to the ground there were brush and plants but not nearly as thick. After crawling a few yards I stopped short as the sound of voices reached me. I stopped, Chips didn't. He ran ahead and I crawled further into the woods.

I sat up leaning back on my heels. Justin was there talking to the man Rango and they were arguing about something. I heard Rango say, "You have *it*, I know you do. You were in the same room with him and there is no other way it could have disappeared."

Justin was firm, "You don't know what you're talking about. Now, get out of here!"

The next thing Rango said was, "There's that stupid looking dog again. Doesn't he ever stay home? I've a mind to plug him."

Chips was growling as he moved around behind Rango. Justin stood with his back to the west. The wind in the tree tops was making it hard to hear clearly what was said. I didn't know what to do. What if he really did shoot Chips? It would be my fault for leading him here. I tried to see if Rango had a gun in his hand but leaves were in the way and I was afraid to move lest I be seen. I'd have to wait where I was until they all left and then I could go back to the house.

I'd catch some words and then the wind would rustle the trees and what followed would be lost. It seemed like Justin was pleading with Rango for something which was strange because Justin was not a man who was in the habit of groveling before anyone. Now Justin had his hands on his hips being emphatic. I heard the words, "This is it! It's all over, there will be no more of this from me! I'm giving you good advice. The FBI was here and they know something is going on. The agent left, but don't think he'll stay away. Those guys know, and it's only a matter of time before they figure things out, so break it off."

Moving a little to my right I got a pretty clear view of both men. Rango was shaking his fist at Justin and Chips was growling more all the time. My attention was so riveted on the two men that the noise to my left front almost didn't register. I glanced in the direction subconsciously and caught movement. Now and then, Tommy and I had startled deer in these woods. But, once alarmed they dashed off at full speed. Finally it registered. There was a second man moving slowly up behind Justin now only twenty feet away. He carried a six-shooter in his hand. I recognized it because it looked like those the cowboys used in the movies. With the wind and Justin's reduced hearing Justin was completely unaware of what was happening.

I had to warn Justin but that would give my position away. I had to do it so I yelled out at the top of my voice. The piercing sound of my young voice was clearly audible above the background noise. "Justin, behind you!"

In a blink Justin swiveled his head around, saw the man and drew his knife. It was like he had been practicing in the barnyard. It was a hard throw, too, because I heard the thump as the knife hit though there were too many leaves to see if it had hit on the point like when Justin practiced with the tree. As a spastic reaction the man's arm flung out and hurled the gun through the air. I heard the leaves crunch as it landed further to the west.

At the sound of my voice warning Justin Chips attacked the ankle of Rango and was locked on. Rango let out a subdued scream and seemed to be reaching for a gun but it was too late. Justin was on him. I ran to them and tried to get Chips to let go lest he bite Justin in his furry.

"Get back," Justin said to me. Then to Rango, "Lay still like you are dead or the dog will chew you to pieces." Justin rolled off, crawled away and laid still, too.

Rango stopped all movement and Chips let go. "Jamie," Justin said in a firm voice, "move away from the dog, get down and be still. He's in a killing mood and might lash out at anyone. His mind is messed up right about now. I've seen it happen."

Chips was pacing back and forth, foam dripping from his mouth, growling and snarling. He was really mad.

"It's okay, Chips," Justin said softly. "It's okay."

Rango wasn't moving a finger, neither was Justin. The lower part of Rango's pants leg was in shreds and blood oozed from everywhere. Still Chips snarled. Finally he came toward me and I didn't move. He sniffed me and turned back to the two men on the ground. Sniffing Justin he seemed to be trying to figure out who was friend and who was foe. Then he came to Rango, his hair bristled and the snarl came back. "It's okay," Justin said again.

We stayed that way for ten minutes with nobody moving. Chips slowly regained his normal personality if you could call his life of barking and sniffing a personality. When Justin saw him sniffing trees and lifting his leg he must have thought things were normal enough to talk. Rango had been forced flat on his stomach with his face in the leaves. Now he turned and sat up grimacing as he tried to assess the damage to his leg.

"He could have killed you," Justin said. "And, I'm not sure why I stopped him."

"Where's Murphy?" Rango asked. "What happened?"

"If by Murphy you mean the man coming up behind me with a drawn gun, he's dead. Now I'll say it one last time. It's over. I'll see what I can find in your saddle bags to bind up your leg and then you will leave and never come back. Before you leave I will take the saddle bags off your bike. Those are the rules and there will be no discussion. Now, empty your pockets—very slowly. Try anything fancy and I'll sic the dog on you again. Understand?"

Rango's face was a picture of pain, rage and caution. I'd never forget it as long as I lived. He did as he was told. Among the things he took out of his pockets was a large roll of cash. For good measure, Justin went over him himself looking for a hidden knife or something like that. Justin went to the motorcycle leaning against a tree and found a T-shirt in one of the saddle bags. Using it he wrapped Rango's leg tying it with a belt he had found with the shirt. Justin helped him up and with Rango hopping on one foot they went to the motorcycle.

"Walk to the edge of the woods in front of me. I'll push the bike behind you to the road and start it. Then you get on and ride off. That's the way it'll be."

136

Rango did as he was told. I was still not sure what had happened. It had all happened so fast and violently. I sat down my back to a tree. Chips came, sniffed my shoes and sat on his haunches beside me. I talked to him in a low voice like Justin had done. I petted him and said "Good dog," and stuff like that. He still shuddered from time to time so I knew he wasn't completely settled down.

It took quite awhile for the men to get to the road with Rango hopping on one foot most of the time. Finally the motorcycle started and soon the sound disappeared in the distance to the east, away from town. It seemed like Chips knew from the sound that the other man was gone. He licked my face. I hated dog spit especially on my face and always tried to stop him when he tried to do that. This time I didn't stop him and it seemed to help. He seemed to be okay again, I was glad of that. He walked over to where Rango had lain on the ground, sniffed, growled a little and trashed up leaves and dirt with his back legs like he was covering up the spot. Then, he came back to me.

Justin returned and got down on his knees in front of me. He held out his hand and Chips sniffed it. He was okay. "How are you doing, Jamie?"

"Okay, I guess," I said in a low voice. "Is the other man really dead?"

Justin nodded.

"What are we going to do?"

"We need time for the summer farm work to get done and your dad to get back on his feet. Eventually this will all be known, but we need time. I'll take the man to the west end of the woods where the ground is soft and the digging easy and bury him."

I noticed he did not say body or dead man. I supposed he was trying to keep me from thinking about what had happened.

"For a few weeks you will have to say nothing about this, not even to Tommy. I'll work extra hard and get as much of the summer and fall jobs taken care of as I can. Then I will tell your mom what happened and leave. I can disappear so nobody will find me. Those guys won't come back. Come on. I'll take you and Chips back to the house. Try to think of something that you like to do so you don't let your mind dwell on this.

As we walked, I couldn't forget how Justin drew and threw his knife so I said, "You threw your knife so fast I could hardly see you move. How did you know it would fly straight and hit Murphy with the point

137

forward?" When he didn't answer I continued, "I saw you one day in the barnyard practicing and sometimes you'd throw it wrong and it would bounce off the tree. What if that had happened?"

By that time we were behind the shed by one of the huge elm trees. He stopped and squatted down so he was at my eye level. When he spoke I could tell he was picking his words carefully. "At a time like that, in a deadly situation like that, there are a lot of things going on. First of all, throwing the knife with the proper form is important. I couldn't throw it like you would a rock. All of my muscles had to be coordinated so my hand grasped the handle of the knife just right, and my hand and arm had to make exactly the right arc through the air to get the knife thrown in the right direction without it turning while it was in flight.

"That part of it a person could practice and practice for years until it was perfect every time and still in the moment of need do it wrong. What separates the man who wins in a contest like that from the one who loses is what goes on in the minds of the two men. The cases where it is no more than a contest to see which of the two combatants is the least clumsy is not what I'm talking about. For my knife to hit perfectly it was necessary for me to *know* it would. That is something that is hard to explain and impossible to teach. In a sense I had to *will* that the knife fly and hit perfectly. When you saw me practicing I wasn't training my coordination between my eye and how I moved my hand and arm. I was training my concentration, my will, to cause the knife to do as I intended. I was training myself to *know* I could do it. When the knife failed to hit its mark and stick in the tree it was not that the knife failed in its mission, I had failed in my will. Do you understand any of that?"

"Nope."

He smiled. "Don't feel bad. If you can remember what I said, one day it will make sense."

By this time he was on his knees leaning back on his heels. "When I was in the Army and bullets were flying all over I could see the men who would survive and those who wouldn't. In order to advance on the enemy some men provided covering fire while others had to get up and run ahead. Then, when they were under cover, they would provide covering fire as the others advanced. Some men would get up knowing they'd get hit, or at least hoping they wouldn't but leaving the possibility in their mind that they might. They usually got hit. Others would bowl ahead like the bullets were so many drops of rain. They'd come out of battle after battle still alive. Most thought it was nothing more than extremely good luck. But it wasn't. It was what went on in their minds."

He didn't say anything but watched me for over a minute. "Those situations are different from the angel stories you told me. In those cases you didn't suspect what was about to happen but were protected. What I'm talking about is where a man knows what he's getting into and uses his mind more or less well to control things. It doesn't always work but it isn't a matter of luck, either."

As little as I was I was getting an idea of what he was saying. "You're telling me this so I can deal with all that back in the woods without telling anybody, aren't you?"

He broke into a strange grin, "You're a smart kid. Now, go find a squirrel to bother or see how high you can swing so you don't think too much. I have a job to do."

At dinner I picked at my food, my thoughts on other things. Justin wasn't there which was normal for Sundays.

"What's wrong, Jamie," mom asked.

"I'm just not hungry, that's all."

"Well, try to eat some more. I made apple pie and you won't get any if you don't eat the rest of your food."

That helped some so I forced food down trying not to gag on it.

CHAPTER 18

The next day was Monday of the last week before school started. That all in itself didn't make me feel good on top of the rest of the stuff that had been happening. In spite of what Justin had told me under the elm tree, I was bursting to tell what had happened in the woods to someone but the only one I could talk to was the dog and he wasn't much help. By Tuesday I got up enough courage to go back to the woods. I wanted to see if anything had been left behind. Justin would have cleaned up everything he could find and the stuff he didn't want he would have buried with Murphy. The mosquitoes weren't bad this time of year, especially since it hadn't been raining much.

I wasn't too sure how Chips would take to being back at the scene of the crime, as it were, but there was no way I could leave him behind. Sure enough, as we came to the place where it had happened he started a low growl in his throat. I looked around brushing away leaves with my foot where Justin had taken Rango down. There was nothing that I saw. I walked to where Murphy had fallen and the leaves were hardly disturbed. Then I saw Chips stop and paw and growl at something in the leaves. There it was, Murphy's six-shooter that he had tossed in the air when Justin's knife hit him.

Wow! A real six-shooter, just like the cowboys had. Chips was uncertain about it, but I wasn't about to leave it there. He fretted as I picked it up. It was heavy but I didn't care. Laden with my booty we headed back to the barn. In the machinery room I found a tattered feed sack and wrapped the gun in it. I had no idea what I'd ever do with it, but I had it.

The following day I went to the other end of the woods in the area where I looked for the first mayflowers in spring. I knew that was what Justin meant when he said where he would bury the man. Not far from the big tree that marked the big May flower plant it became soft. Across the fence was a slough with a corner of it on our land. I could see where the tall grass had been padded down and soon Chips was sniffing in the area. After a rain or two the grass would come back and nobody would know anything had been disturbed. But now, even though Justin had carefully put all the clods of sod back in place, there was no mistaking where he had dug the hole. That settled it, I knew where the guy was. I wished he weren't on our property, but that was the way it was. There was a nursery rhyme that started with *If wishes were horses, beggars would ride*. Well, wishing him gone wouldn't make it happen.

Justin was working extra hard. One of the big fall jobs was to haul wood in from the woods for fire wood. Normally this was fill-in work during the next couple of months, but he was doing it now before he had to leave. Apparently he had asked mom to find out from dad where he should get it. In those days the wood was hauled in from the woods in pieces as big as could be lifted onto a wagon. These were hauled and stacked where you wanted the wood pile to be, all with the big end facing one way. Then when it was all hauled, a man with a power saw would be called to cut it up into chunks short enough to fit into the stove. The saw man usually had a couple of men to help him lift the logs and branches up on the saw. They'd place the end of the log on a platform and slide it forward into the saw blade to cut a piece off and then slide the log back and advance it for the next cut. The motor that ran the saw had one cylinder and dad called it a one-lunger.

After the sawing gang was gone the larger pieces of wood had to be split and then loaded on a wagon to be hauled to the house to be thrown through the trap door into the basement. Then they were stacked in the basement so the maximum amount of wood could be put up for winter. That was a lot of work that normally went on until early December. Justin was trying to get it all done in a few weeks besides doing the other farm work. He had the logs hauled from the woods but they hadn't been sawed yet. There was, of course, still a small pile of sawed wood left from last year since wood was needed through the summer for cooking and heating water.

*   *   *

School started and I supposed it wasn't so bad because it gave me something to occupy my mind so I wouldn't think about the fight in the woods. We were in a real classroom this year and each of us had his own desk. The school was a parish school so the teachers were all sisters. Our teacher was named Sister Mary Paulette and was she strict.

The first day of class Sister Mary Paulette opened with, "On this inauspicious occasion I have the duty to begin disciplining your unruly minds so you can dedicate yourselves to learning and virtue." None of us knew what inauspicious meant even though it was one of her favorite words. It didn't take long for us boys at recess to rename our teacher Sister Mary Pontius. We were in agreement that before coming here she had been an Army drill sergeant, but seeing as she was too severe for the soldiers, she was reassigned to teach first grade.

To start with she said the boys always wanted to talk in class to other boys and the same with the girls. So, she used an alternated seating pattern which was really yucky. I had a girl on either side, as well as one in front and one in back. The girl I had in front of me was Debbie Dinkle. The only small advantage the seating arrangement presented was that I could drop small objects down the back of Debbie's dress. I had nothing personally against her but she just happened to be there. She, of course, always tattled and I'd get my fingers slapped by a wooden ruler. That really stung. Didn't help because I kept doing it.

It was the third week of school when, coming in from recess, I saw a wooly caterpillar on the ground. I scooped it up, carried it in and placed it on my desk when we were seated. It lay there like a little orange and black doughnut until it finally uncurled itself and started exploring. I put my pencil in front of it and it climbed on. As soon as it did I picked up the pencil and it headed toward the eraser end in the funny way caterpillars crawled. As it approached the end I carefully extended the pencil until it was a fraction of an inch from Debbie's dress. The little guy got to the end and started waving its head and front legs around looking for something to climb onto. It found the fabric and quickly transferred itself.

We were having arithmetic class. In this the teacher would say, "Three plus two equals. . . ."

And we were supposed to answer, "Five."

I watched the progress of the caterpillar up the dress. "Three plus three equals . . . ."

"Six," everyone answered but I was always a little late because I wasn't paying attention.

He kept at it, almost to the collar of the dress now. "Three plus four equals . . . ."

"Seven . . . Seven." Up the collar now almost to the top.

"Three plus five equals . . . ."

"Eight . . . Eight."

At the top of the collar. She was leaning forward leaving a gap between the collar of her dress and her neck. Come on, lean back before he turns around. There, she sat back. He had his little front legs waving about looking for something, "Three plus six equals . . . ."

"Eeeeek!"

Everybody turned to look at Debbie. "What on earth!"

"Something's crawling on me!"

She frantically brushed the back of her neck and my little coconspirator landed in the aisle. The drill sergeant stood by Debbie and looked down. "Here. It must have been this caterpillar. There's no need to be so frightened. He wouldn't bite you."

Like a dummy I bent down and picked it up and placed it on my desk. The drill sergeant was doing arithmetic in her head like two plus two equals Landon. "How did it get in here?" she asked looking at me with a stare that could crack a block of granite.

I shrugged.

She knew I had done it by my ambivalent response but had no proof. She was about to turn away and I could see I was going to get off Scott free when the girl across the aisle, Carolyn Kramer, said, "He put it on her dress. I saw him!"

I hated girls!

By this time the furry thing was crawling across the fingers as my hands were palm dawn on my desk. In an instant the dreaded weapon of vengeance appeared and whap, whap, whap, whap on my fingers. Not only did my fingers sting but they were covered with the gooey remains of the caterpillar. "Jamie, behave!" She turned on her heel and went back to the front of the classroom.

I scraped the main parts of my partner in crime off on the edge of the top of my desk and wiped what was left on my pants. Maybe Sister Mary Pontius thought the little critter had given its life in the pursuit of a more civilized future generation. I, on the other hand, was pretty sure the poor bugger had died in vain.

Things went along as they normally do, that is, until the Saturday after the third week of school. Justin was still working for us and dad was due to come home from the hospital in a few days and we were all excited about that. Mom told us he would be weak and we'd have to be good so he could continue getting well. On this morning mom got a call from the hospital. After she hung up the phone she said. "Kids, somebody from the hospital called saying I should come in to make arrangements for the release of your father from the hospital, and he said I could bring all you kids." After a pause, she said, "That's a little strange. In the past they always said to leave the children home. Tommy, I think Justin's in the barn. Will you go ask him to come to the house?"

"Sure," and Tommy was off.

Mom looked at me. "I don't have time to get you kids cleaned up. I'll take Mikey and you can stay here. I'll tell Justin to keep an eye on you."

When Justin arrived mom was waiting on the porch. "Justin, the hospital called and they want me to come in. It has something to do with releasing Fred from the hospital. Will you stay around the buildings and keep an eye on the two older ones? I'll take Mikey with me. It shouldn't take long."

Justin nodded and said, "Come on guys. Let's go to the barn and I'll put you to work."

This was Saturday and I still hated to work even though stuff Justin had us do wasn't usually much like work. Mom put Mikey on the front seat of the car beside her, backed out the car and was off to town. In the barn Justin was in the workshop watching through the window as she left. He put an axe in the vice and started filing on it but he spent more time looking out the window than filing. Tommy was with him in the workshop and I was running around where we pulled the hay wagon into the barn. The haymow was full of hay by now so I asked Justin if I could slide down the hay toward the drive-in. He agreed but said I had to stay

144

within sight of him. That was kind of odd because we always had the run of the place.

Mom wasn't gone a few minutes when Justin stopped filing and stepped out of the workshop and stood at the side of the large doorway looking toward the house. "Do you hear that?" he asked. I had just slid down the hay and Justin said, "Jamie, stand still. Does that sound like a motorcycle coming?"

Tommy was standing beside Justin and I was on the other side of the large doorway a few feet back into the haymow. The throb of a motorcycle was evident and it was coming in the driveway from the gravel road that led to town. "Tommy!" He said. "Go to the first floor and stay by the wall behind the calf pens. Go on now, hurry. Jamie stay over there and move up by the wall and cover yourself with hay!"

The alarm in Justin's voice was obvious. I did the best I could which was pretty good because there was sort of a pocket where the hay had been pitched up against the wall that made a small tunnel. Tommy and I had crawled into it a few times. That meant I could see across the driveway in the barn into the workshop. Justin had his leather bag out from under the workbench and was throwing stuff out of it. Near the bottom he pulled out a round tubular thing that looked like dad's grease gun that the used to grease the machinery. He grabbed a couple of other things and stood up. I could hear snaps and clicks as he was putting parts together.

By this time I knew the motorcycle had stopped from the sound of the motor so I crept out of my place and peeked at ground level around the door frame. As I looked a car pulled to a stop a little behind the motorcycle. Chips was barking frantically because I think the man on the motorcycle was Rango.

"Kill the dog first!" Rango yelled. He gunned the motorcycle and drove up on the grass toward the house to avoid the dog. As he was turning back toward the car a man got out of the backseat of the car and walked toward the front of it. Chips directed his attention to this man. The dog was advancing and retreating snapping and snarling. It seemed he could sense he couldn't take on all of them so he was trying to retain them. The man on foot had a big gun and started shooting at Chips. It sounded like a machine gun. Chips dodged and the man fired again and I heard Chips yelping as he limped away.

"Finish him off!" Rango yelled. The man fired again, Chips fell and didn't move. I saw the gun clearly now. It was a Tommy gun like we had seen in a gangster movie.

Now Rango was off his motorcycle with a revolver in his hand and he walked toward the man with the Tommy gun. The driver stayed in the car. "Now, we find the Indian."

I was startled to hear Justin's voice because he had stepped out and said, "I'm right here."

His arm hung at his side with the grease gun thing in it. But, he was turned so the other men couldn't clearly see it.

Both men advanced toward the barn as Rango said, "Nice of you to be so obliging. It saves us the trouble of hunting you dawn. We want *it* and we'll kill you if we don't get *it*."

"You won't get *it*," Justin said as he raised the grease gun thing and started shooting. It fired bullets as fast as the Tommy gun did. The man with the Tommy gun was mowed down as he jerked first one way and then the other as the bullets hit him. Rango got off a couple of shots before Justin's bullets found him. I saw his right leg collapse under him like he had been hit in the knee. Parts of his boot flew off. He jerked a couple of times as he went down, like the other man. Justin stopped momentarily and then shot a steam of bullets into the car. The driver by this time had ducked down. I could hear and see glass flying in all directions.

"Get out of the car with your hands up!" Justin yelled. The driver obeyed. Rango was moaning, the other man was not. Justin slowly walked down to the car. "Turn around and put your hands on the car." The man did. Justin walked up behind him and pulled a revolver out of a pocket under his arm.

"Load these two in the car and get out of here. Move, do it fast!" The man hustled. "I only shot at the top parts of the car so it should still be drivable." As the man worked Justin took the Tommy gun, removed the drum of ammunition and leaned it up against the bumper of the car. He pushed hard on it with his foot and I saw it bend.

The man was panting by the time he finished putting the Tommy-gun-man in the back seat. Then he went to where Rango was still moaning. He looked at Justin and said in a seething voice, "You're a dead man, Indian. There'll be backup men coming before you can get away. And, they'll get *it* if they have to cut you up into fish food one little piece at a time."

"Get him in the car!" Justin snapped, "before I decide to kill both of you.

The man complied with Rango complaining the whole time.

Justin told him to take the bent gun with him, and leave by the field road and keep going south. The driver seemed to be glad to be alive and did as he was told.

It seemed like only minutes and all we had was a dead dog, and a motorcycle. Justin yelled, more like commanded, "Tommy, Jamie, come here quickly!"

We did. "You guys have to listen to me. When your mom comes back she must call that FBI guy, Haas. She shouldn't call the police. I have to leave and I'm sorry but I won't be back. I'll take Rango's motorcycle. It's dark blue. If anyone asks say it was silver, do you understand? I need time to get away. My family on the reservation needs me."

"Will other men be coming looking for you like that man said?" I asked.

"I don't think so. That was only a threat. But, we don't have time to lose in any case."

Justin ran to the barn—I had never seen him run before. In seconds he was back with his leather bag. He emptied it into the new saddle bags on the motorcycle after which he folded up the leather bag and stuffed it in. His big gun was hanging by a strap over his shoulder and he snapped and twisted some parts and soon it was small enough to fit in the other saddle bag. He asked Tommy if he would go to the house and get one of the kerchiefs that mom wore on her head sometimes. He left at a run. Turning to me he unbuckled his belt and slid the scabbard of his bone-handled knife off it. "This is for you, Little Manknife. Take it to the barn and hide it before Tommy comes back. Tell no one that you have it, not even Tommy. This is for Little Manknife, and must remain between you and me. Leave it alone until you are more grown. Go now."

I ran for the barn and as I reached it I heard the screen door slam as Tommy was returning from his mission. I came back as Justin picked up Rango's revolver and the one from the driver of the car. He put one in his saddle bag and the other behind his belt in the front. He pulled two cards from his front pocket and handed them to Tommy. "Give these to Mr.

Haas. One more thing," he reached into his back pocket, "here's some money to pay the rest of my hospital bill. If there's any left your mom and dad can keep it."

Then Justin sat astride the motorcycle. When he lifted his arm to put the kerchief on his head we saw blood on his shirt. One of Rango's shots must have hit him though he didn't seem to notice it. After tying the kerchief in the back of his head he put on Rango's goggles that had been left hanging from the handlebar of the motorcycle. He turned to us, "I'll drive out the field road to leave motorcycle tracks going that way. But, I will then turn toward town. If anyone asks, say I went south in pursuit of the car. Can you remember that?"

We nodded.

"I've enjoyed you guys and I'll never forget you. Good bye, now."

He stood up with some effort and winced as he pumped the starter with his foot. The motor roared to life and he was gone. We watched as he turned toward town on the gravel road and soon was lost from sight. We went to where Chips was lying and could see he was all shot up, stone dead. "Did you see any of it," I asked Tommy.

"Yeah. I climbed up on the boards of the calf stall and looked out the window. The window was dirty, but I saw the two men go down. So that's what Justin had in his bag, that big gun. I wonder where he got it? Maybe he knew something like this would happen."

"Don't know," I said. "That first day when we met Rango he told him to stay away. He didn't want any of this."

CHAPTER 19

The sound of a car made us both run for the barn. As we peeked out we saw it was mom. She drove into the shed, switched off the car. As she came from the shed carrying Mikey we ran toward her. She looked at us and saw something was wrong. "What happened? You both look scared to death."

"That's because we are scared. You have to call the FBI man, Haas. There was a shoot-out here. Justin's gone for good and Chips was shot by a man with a Tommy gun."

"Wait a minute. You've been playing too hard. Start again."

"Come over here."

Tommy motioned to where Chips was. She looked at him and drew in a sharp breath.

I said, "Come and look here. This is where the man with the Tommy gun was. See all the brass shells on the ground. And that's his blood."

"Why were they here in the first place? We haven't done anything.

I said, "They came to kill Justin. I heard them say that."

"What did Justin do when he heard that?"

Tommy started telling it. "He shot back. You know that heavy leather bag he had when he came, there was a gun in it, not a Tommy gun, but one that was just as good. He shot a ton of bullets and mowed down two of the men. Then he shot up the car pretty good, but didn't hit the motor or the wheels so they could leave. He had the driver get out, took his gun away and made him load the two other men in the back seat and then made him drive away that way," Tommy said pointing to the south.

"Where did Justin go?"

"When they came one man was on a motorcycle and two in the car. Justin took the motorcycle. He said his family needed him, but he had been shot and I think he didn't want to talk to the FBI."

"Why wouldn't we call the police?"

"Justin said not to. There's more to this and we don't have time to waste. Call Mr. Haas!"

Mom wasn't sure at first as we walked to the house. Then she said almost to herself. "It was strange because when I got to the hospital they said that no one had called to tell me to come in. I insisted that someone most certainly did. It took time to find everyone to be sure there wasn't a mix-up. But, no one had called. They must have called to get me away from the house. Oh! That's why they said to bring the kids. That must be it."

We were in the house now. "If I call the police, the whole town will be scolding us for hiring an Indian, but what choice did we have? Yes, I'll call Mr. Haas."

She found the little card he had left and called. It took quite awhile going thought the operator to make a long distance call and then reversing the charges. Finally, "Mr. Haas, Mrs. Landon. You said to call if anything happened. You had better get here as soon as you can. I need to talk to you."

She listened for a little bit and then said, "When you've heard me out, I'll let you decide. Can you come? It's important."

Another pause, "Yes, today, now."

More pause, "Okay, see you then."

We knew that the telephone operators in town would listen in on anybody's call if they thought there might be some gossip. That's why mom didn't say much.

She hung up the phone. "He's in Minneapolis. He said he'd leave within ten minutes and will be here in three or four hours."

Then I thought about the money Justin had given me. I pulled it out of my pocket and said, "Justin gave this to me so you could pay the rest of his hospital bill. He said if there is any left you and dad can keep it."

It was a big roll of money that looked a lot like the one from Rango when Justin had him empty his pockets in the woods. Mom simply took it and put it on the top shelf of the cupboard. "We'll worry about that later. Don't tell Mr. Haas about it."

We were sitting around the kitchen table. Tommy and I were at least partially prepared for this. It was all new to mom. I expected we'd start getting the third degree about what else we knew and scolded for not saying anything but she said, "What if they come back?"

I said, "One of the men said others were coming, but after the car left Justin said that was just a bluff."

"What if it's not? We're here all alone, no hired man, not even a dog to warn us. I wish we had something like a gun."

That was my cue. I was out the door as Tommy was saying, "There's always dad's shotgun."

I didn't hear any more. I went to the barn and found the old feed sack with Murphy's gun in it and ran back to the house. I laid the dusty old sack on the kitchen table. Mom was about to stop me, "Jamie, what's this all about?"

Then she saw the gun. She was surprised as I expected she would be. There was a real six-shooter on the kitchen table. It had brown wood on each side of the handle and the rest was dark gray. "Where on earth did you get that?"

I had to tell her. "That's Murphy's gun. He's buried back in the woods. Justin had to kill him with his knife before he shot Justin in the back with this gun. Like Tommy said, there's a lot more. Justin said that if anyone found out about any of it, he'd have to leave and we needed Justin to run the farm while dad was in the hospital."

Mom leaned back. "Oh, my. I suppose there *is* more."

"A lot more," Tommy said. "But, we might as well wait for Mr. Haas to get here. Who's going to do the milking tonight?"

Mom was pretty good at coping when things weren't going good and she was immediately at the phone. She called the place where Hank Cooper was working and pleaded with them saying Justin's father was dying and he had to leave. It was a sob story as the tough guys in the movies would say, but it worked.

"Hank will come and do the milking. Now let me see that gun. Pa was in the Spanish-American war and had one that looked like this. I'd better take it outside. You stay in here."

We stayed in the house but were at the kitchen window. Mom held the gun with both hands and pulled the hammer back. Then she turned the cylinder and bullets started dropping out on the ground. Then she spun the cylinder like the cowboys did. After picking up the bullets she came back in.

"It's awful dirty. It'll have to be cleaned but it'll do."

Tommy and I were awed and Tommy asked, "How do you know about six-shooters?"

"Even though I never shot it, pa showed us how it worked. This is what I think they call a single action. I'll explain later. It's after noon so I'll cut some bread and you make yourselves peanut butter sandwiches."

Mom put wood in the stove and put water on to heat. We made a sandwich for Mikey too and he was up on his knees on a chair munching away. In between bites he'd say, "Mama's gum."

"No, Mikey it's a *gun.*"

"Mama's gum."

When the water was hot mom started to clean the gun as it seemed she would. She put the water in the dish pan in the sink and added soap. Then in went the gun. She sloshed it around, worked the hammer and spun the cylinder. When she was satisfied she took the pan out and dumped the water on the flowers by the house like she always did. By now the water on the stove was boiling. With the gun in the pan she poured the boiling water on it. Then she got a meat fork and lifted it out by the trigger guard and laid it on a towel on the table.

She picked it up using the towel and shook it. Finally she spoke. "You see, boys, by putting it in boiling water, the metal gets hot. Now, that heat in the metal will completely dry it in a few minutes. When it's cool I'll put a few drops of my sewing machine oil in the action."

While it was cooling she carefully wiped off each bullet. "He wasn't too smart. He carried this around with a six-load."

"Of course," Tommy said, "it's a six-shooter."

"I'll explain later. But, that isn't many bullets. We have to go to town. Finish your dinner and lets go."

She went outside and we watched as she put the bullets in the gun but she only put in five and the sixth one went into the pocket on her dress. Then she wrapped it in the towel. She put Mikey in the back with us and the gun on the floor beside her. As she went to back out she ground the gears more than normal. Then as she shifted to get going she ground them more. That happened when she was upset.

Main street had angle parking and she pulled into a space in front of the hardware store. "Come on everybody. I'm not leaving you in the car alone."

That was fine with us. We always hated it when we had to wait in the car. Being Saturday there was a big kid helping out in the store. Mom, said, "Do you have any bullets like this?" as she pulled the one from the pocket.

The kid looked at it. "Yeah, I think so. Let me look." There were a few boxes of shotgun shells stacked behind the counter. "Not many people ask for that kind," he said. He dug around in the space below the counter and came up with two boxes. Opening one, mom said, "No. They're too small."

"Yeah," he said, "looks like it. They're thirty-twos."

He opened the other box. Mom picked one out and compared it to the one she had. "That's it."

"Yeah," the kid said. "Those are thirty-eights, heavy load. They're a lot longer than the one you have, probably more powerful than you need but it's the only box we have in that size. Fifty in a box."

"I'll take it."

Mom opened her purse and took out some money and paid. When she had her change she dropped the box of shells in her purse and snapped it closed.

Mikey took that moment to say, "Mama's gum."

Tommy retorted, "Mikey, shut up."

"Let's go," mom said.

As we got moving mom was grinding the gears again.

At home mom was intent on providing for our safety by all means possible and that included by gun fight. In the kitchen she said, "Tommy, take Mikey's stool out by the woodpile so I have a place to put the box of bullets when I reload." We had a stool higher than a chair that the smallest kid sat on at meal time. Tommy did as he was told. When he returned she said, "I have to see if this thing works so stay in the house. Is that clear? If the phone rings you come to the door and yell at me."

She grabbed the gun and the box of shells and left. The davenport sat along the north wall of the living room with a large double window behind it. We all ran to the window to watch. There was room behind it to stand and we pulled the curtains back. Mom held the gun in front of her with both hands and "Boom." A chink of wood went cart wheeling through the air.

"Wow!" we both said.

Mikey was standing on the davenport looking over our shoulders. "Mama's gum go Poom!"

"No Mikey, "*Boom!*"

It went off again and chips flew. "Poom!" Mikey said. Every time she shot Mikey said, "Poom!"

"I don't know if she's hitting what she's shooting at but she sure can make the wood fly," Tommy said.

After a few more shots she stopped to reload. We watched as she shot them too. Then she came back to the house.

"It works well enough," she said.

Tommy and I looked at each other as he said, "Good enough! It's a cannon!"

"Okay," she said. "I have to have something to eat. How about you guys, want any more? How about going out on the porch and getting an apple. But, stay in the house."

When mom had eaten she put Mikey down for a nap. Back to the kitchen she said, "I called him after eleven and it's not two yet. It'll probably be another half hour before he gets here. While we wait, I'll show you about the gun like pa did me. Go out where I was shooting and find some empties."

Boy, this was going to be great. We dashed out and mom came as far as the back steps. We returned with four or five each. She had the gun unloaded laying and on the porch table.

She started. "This is what is called a single-action. I'm not sure why, but you have to pull the hammer all the way back with your thumb and then when you pull the trigger it releases it so the hammer falls on the firing pin that hits the cap on the back of the bullet. See the little round thing in the middle of the back, that's the cap, it's what sets off the gun powder inside."

We were fully captivated. "To load it you pull the hammer halfway back," she showed us. "That's called the half-cock. The trigger won't release it but you can rotate the cylinder.

"Now, this is what I think pa called the loading gate." She flipped a little door aside on the right behind the cylinder and you could see an

154

empty hole. She pushed an empty shell in and then rotated the cylinder to the next space. "A smart person leaves the next chamber empty, and I'll show you why in a minute. Then you put shells in the next four chambers. That brings the first one you loaded under the hammer. Now the cylinder is loaded."

"But, one of the holes is still empty," Tommy said.

"Yes," mom said. "But, watch what happens. Now you pull the hammer full back and it rotates the cylinder one position. Then to 'safe' the gun you must hold the hammer back with you thumb while you pull the trigger and gently let it come forward. This leaves an empty chamber under the hammer. In case you accidentally snag the hammer on something and it is pulled part way back and snaps forward it will fall on the empty chamber. Even if you give the lowered hammer a hard push it might be enough to set off a cartridge. That's why it's important to have an empty chamber under the hammer."

"But, then the first time you shoot it won't go off," I said.

"No," mom said. "Now watch again. When I pull the hammer back to full cock the cylinder rotates to the next chamber that has a bullet in it. That's called a five load, or a safe load. In the old days the cowboys would roll up a dollar bill and stuff it in the second chamber. That meant they couldn't inadvertently put a bullet in it. When they were loading they'd start at the hole before the one with the dollar in it and then have to pass that hole with the 'buck' before they could load the remaining four bullets. That's where the term 'passing the buck' comes from.

"Okay. I've shown you how it works and you are never to touch the gun, do you understand? Safe load or not, guns are still dangerous. Now, go in the kitchen because I'm going to load it with real bullets."

CHAPTER 20

There was nothing to do but wait. Mom had the revolver wrapped in the towel and laying on the far side of the porch table. I hated to wait, but it wasn't long before a black car came past the house. We could see that Mr. Haas was driving. He stopped where he did the time before. He looked quickly around and seemed he noticed there was no dog. A second man emerged from the passenger side.

As they walked to the house mom was waiting on the step. "We got here as fast as we could, what's happened? Excuse me, this is Mac Adams, my assistant."

"We might as well start out here," mom said. The three of us came out, too. "First, there's our dog, shot to pieces. I got a call to come to the hospital with the kids. I didn't have time to clean up the two older boys so I left them with Justin so they saw what happened."

Tommy said, "Over here is where the man with the Tommy gun was when he shot Chips. See all the bullet casings on the ground?"

Mac picked up a couple. "Yeah, it looks like these came from a Thompson submachine gun all right. That looks like blood soaked in the ground. Where'd that come from?"

"The man with the Tommy gun," I said.

Before either of the men could say anything Tommy said, "Up here on the driveway leading into the barn is where Justin was. He had a machine gun too but it was different than the other man's." Both men picked up samples of the shinny brass on the ground.

"These are forty-fives," Mac said. "He must have been using an M3 grease gun."

"It did kind of look like the grease gun dad uses for the machinery," I said.

"How many men?" Haas asked.

Tommy answered, "Three. One was Rango on his motorcycle. He was shot down over here. That's his blood. When he drove in and saw Chips he started driving around the yard yelling at the other man to shoot the dog. After the man shot Chips Justin came out. They said mean things to each other. Justin was holding his gun down beside his leg so they couldn't see what he had. Finally he raised it and shot down the man with the Tommy gun and then Rango. Finally, he shot up the car. The driver had gotten down in the front seat and didn't seem to be hit. Justin made him get out of the car and load the other two in. The driver said there were others that were coming that would get *it* from Justin and then they'd kill him. He left going that way," he pointed to the south.

"Where's Justin now?"

"Gone for good. He headed that way too and said he couldn't come back and nobody would ever find him. He took Rango's motorcycle. He was bleeding but didn't seem to be slowed down by it."

"How badly were the two men hurt that Justin shot?"

Tommy and I looked at each other, and I said, "The man with the Tommy gun got hit a lot of times and I think he was dead. Rango was moaning, but when the driver was loading him in the car he didn't move. He might have died, too."

Mr. Haas shook his head and said, "Can we go to the house? We'll need all the information you can give us." Haas went to the car and got his little suitcase. There were four chairs, three on the side away from the door. Mom had told us to stay on her side of the table. She got another chair from the kitchen for Mac. So, they were on the east side of the table and we were all on the west side. When we were all seated, mom by her towel with the gun wrapped in it, Haas started, "It's good you didn't call the local police because there is more to this than you know, you don't see the bigger picture. What else do you know about this?" he asked.

I said, "A lot."

He jerked his head back. "Well please tell us what you can."

"Last spring when Justin and I were coming back from blasting stumps we met a man in the woods behind the barn. It was Rango. He and Justin knew each other. Rango said they had unfinished business. Justin said no they didn't, that he should leave and never come back. Rango said he'd give Justin time to think about it.

"A few weeks later I heard a motorcycle along the road north of our place and suddenly the motor stopped. That's what caught my attention. A few days later I told Tommy and for something to do we went into the woods and found where people had been crushing down the weeds."

Here Tommy took over. "While we were there we heard a motorcycle and we ran back further in the woods and hid behind a big tree. It drove right into the woods with two men on it. Jamie said one was Rango. There's a hollow tree there with a hole in it about the height of a man's head. Rango took a package out of it. There was some confusion because something was wrong with it. So, they left another package with a note for Justin. As soon as they left we ran out of the woods scared to death.

"Well, the next day we decided to see what was in the tree. We each carried a chunk of wood from the wood pile. We stacked them end on end so I could stand on them to reach in the hole. We got the package and carried our chunks of wood further back in the woods so nobody would see them. When we got back it was supper time so we hid it in the barn. The next day we started cutting grain so we were all busy."

I said, "The second day I had a little time before supper so I opened the package. It contained two gray metal plates, almost square. One had a big 'A' in the corner and then a lot of small writing. I know my alphabet, but these were mostly wrong."

"Wait a minute" Mr. Haas said. He opened his small suit case and took out a sheet of ration stamps. "Did it look like this?"

"Sort of but the 'A' was on the other corner."

He nodded.

"What does that mean?" mom asked.

"Those were probably plates used to print counterfeit gas ration stamps. You see, the top part is always the same, but the individual stamps change every couple of months to prevent counterfeiting. Someone in Washington who knew what next month's stamps would look like could sell that information to organized crime or others and make a lot of money."

"But, could Justin do any of that?" mom asked.

"Sure," I said. "Do you remember his belt buckle with the picture of the wolf on it? He said he had made that. He was a silver smith before he went into the Army."

Mac, who had been silent so far, lifted his hand as if he wanted to say something. "Go ahead," Haas said.

"Justin was the room mate of a dying man in the VA Hospital, I read your report," he said looking at Haas. "The dying man had some unsavory visitors. What if they saw Justin doing silver work to break the monotony. Silver and type metal are both soft metals and would work about the same. First they take a casual interest in his work and then force him to work for them. They even mixed up the medical files so Justin was supposed to be dead. He left the VA Hospital before being discharged and he probably did that to get away from them. But, they found him working here on the farm and threatened to harm the family if he didn't continue working for them. How does that sound?"

I said, "Justin said Rango came to see him in the barn after milking one night. He wanted to be sure Justin had found the plates and Justin played along as if he had. He guessed we knew something about it and the next day he made me give them to him. By then dad was in the hospital and we really needed Justin on the farm. Justin told us that if anybody found out about any of this he'd have to leave so we kept our mouths shut."

"And, that's why they came today, is that it? To get some plates?"

I shook my head. "I don't think so. They said they wanted *it* not *them*. And after they had *it* even if they had to torture Justin to get it, they'd kill him."

"Do you have any idea what they meant by *it*?"

Tommy and I looked at each other and we both shook our heads. I said, "It must have been something between them from before Justin came here. We knew about the plates but nothing else was ever mentioned."

At that moment Mikey came padding out of the house and ran to mom. She picked him up and put him on her lap. He saw the towel and said, "Mama's gum, go Poom! Mama's gum."

Mac said, "What's in the towel, ma'am?"

Mom slowly unwrapped it and laid her right hand on the gun with her finger near the trigger and her thumb on the hammer. "Mama's gum!" she replied.

"Where'd you get it?"

"Jamie gave it to me."

There was consternation on both men's faces.

Haas asked, "Where did you get it, Jamie?"

"It's Murphy's gun."

The expressions were intense now, like they were watching the end of a mystery movie. "And, who is Murphy?" he asked like he didn't want to hear the answer.

"He's the man that's buried in the woods behind the house."

Both men took deep breaths and Mac said. "In that case you have to give the gun to us because it appears to be evidence in a crime."

"No!" mom snapped. "Now, listen to me! My husband is in the hospital, my hired man was driven off, my dog has been brutally shot while my children watched. My yard was used for a machine gun battle, there are killers out there and the big bad FBI can't seem to catch them!"

Mac was about to reply when mom continued, "You are dangerously close to getting between a grizzly bear and her cubs. That's as big a picture as you have to worry about right now!"

Mr. Haas, a little shaken opened his mouth to speak when Tommy said, "And she can shoot it, too. After dinner we went into town and she bought a box of bullets, the only one they had. The kid in the store said they were thirty-eight heavy load. When we got home she blasted away at the wood pile. Boy, you should have seen those chunks of wood fly."

Mikey put in his two cents, "Poom!"

Haas said, "Okay, you can keep the gun."

But that wasn't the end of it, "I don't need your permission to keep the gun because there was no way you were going to take it away from me. Mac, put your hands on the table where I can see them!"

Jerking his hands up from his lap so fast he rapped his knuckles on the edge of the table he said, "Oh, sure."

Mom was riled, they both could see it, she had her hand on a gun that must have started looking bigger with each exchange in the conversation.

Mr. Haas was looking nervous. In a soft, non-threatening tone he said, "When you were shooting at the wood pile you wisely used two hands."

"How did you know?"

"That model of revolver is not commonly seen. It is heavily built and has an extra long cylinder so it can use the special cartridges you bought. The reason it was the only box they had left was most thirty-eights can't use those powerful rounds. Had you used only one hand to shoot you would probably have sprained your wrist if not broken it. That gun and ammunition is what you would use to stop a charging elephant. I ask you to please look at us as friendly because a man doesn't get up after being hit with one of those."

"Fine. Then be nice."

"Yes, we will." After a pause, "Now, will you please tell us the details of how you came to possess your gun, Mrs. Landon?"

"Like I said, Jamie gave it to me."

He swallowed, "Jamie, can you tell us how did you came to have Murphy's gun?"

"Since I'm the only one left who knows what happened, I'll tell you." It kind of made me feel good being the center of attention, and at long last I'd be able to tell what happened in the woods. "After Tommy and I found the plates in the hollow tree, and Justin made me give them to him, we wondered how often the hollow tree was being used as a mailbox. So, every few days we'd go back there and look around for fresh tracks, or freshly broken down weeds. But we never saw anything. Tommy decided we should let well enough alone, but I kept going back.

"Let me think, it was Sunday, not the one just before school started, the one before that. After Mass I changed my clothes and went to the woods. I'd walk along the edge of the potato patch where the tall grass and brush were thick along the woods. Tommy said it was that way because it got full sunlight. There was a place where I could crawl through that thick wall of brush into the woods without getting scratched. As I crawled in I heard men's voices. Normally I would have stood up once past the brush but this day I kept crawling. Chips, of course, was with me and way ahead. He was growling now and then, something that he normally didn't do. As I got closer I could tell Justin's voice. He was arguing with Rango. It was windy that day so when the wind blew on the tree tops I couldn't hear, but sometimes I did. Justin would say 'I'm done with this, no more!' Rango would say, 'No, you're not!' Stuff like that.

"I kept crawling and getting closer. All at once I saw a man coming up behind Justin with a gun in his hand. With Justin not hearing well and the wind blowing Justin didn't know he was there. I knew he'd shoot Justin so I yelled as loud as I could, 'Justin, behind you!' He snapped his head around, saw the man, drew and threw his knife at him. I heard the thud as it hit, and right away the man fell. But his arm with the gun flew up and the gun went flying through the air. There were too many leaves in the way to see him on the ground but there was no rustling around."

Mr. Haas interrupted me, "Was Justin that good at throwing his knife?"

"Oh, yeah," I said. "I saw him practicing with it a couple of times when he didn't see me. He'd stand in any position, and would draw and throw it in one motion. It almost always stuck in the tree he threw it at. And, it stuck hard because he'd have to work it up and down to get it out of the tree. Once while he was sick he let me hold it and it was awful heavy for a knife, lots heavier than the knives in the kitchen. He said it had to be heavy because it was a fighting knife."

"Okay, then what happened?"

"When I yelled it seemed to set off Chips because he grabbed Rango's leg and he started chewing on it. Rango was reaching for a gun but Justin jumped on him. They landed with Rango's face in the leaves. Chips was snarling and kept chewing, Rango kept struggling and yelling. Justin said, 'Lay still and make no sound so the dog thinks you're dead.'

"Before long Chips let go but he kept snarling, jumping forward, then pulling back. There was foam dripping from his mouth and it was like he was crazy. Justin rolled slowly away from Rango. I think he had Rango's gun by then. Nobody moved for a long time. Finally Chips calmed down and Justin sat up. Chips came by me and sniffed my shoes and then licked my face and sat down beside me. Justin went to the motorcycle and got a shirt out of the saddle bag and wrapped it on Rango's leg. Rango asked about Murphy and Justin said he was dead. Then Justin had him limp in front of him as he pushed the motorcycle to the road. When they got there Justin started the motor and told Rango to go and not come back. Oh, yeah, Justin had Rango empty his pockets, too. Tommy, do you have those cards Justin gave you before he left?"

He pulled the two cards out of his pocket and pushed them across the table.

Mr. Haas took them and said, "This might be some help, driver's licenses for Rango Smyth and Franworth Murphy. That's probably why he was called by his last name. What man would want to be called Franny. Then what happened?"

"I asked if Murphy was really dead and Justin said yes. He said we'd go back to the house and he'd get a shovel and bury him to the west where a slough comes near our property and the ground was softer. He said this would all come out before long and when it did he'd have to leave and not come back. But, if I could keep quiet for awhile he would get most of the fall work done on the farm before he had to leave.

"The next day I went back to see if there was anything left. Chips found the gun and I took it to the barn. A few days after that I went to see if I could find where he had buried Murphy. Justin did a good job of it but since it hadn't rained it was pretty easy to find. That's it."

Everyone was silent for quite awhile and then Mac spoke, "I'm very sorry that they killed your dog but it had to be done sometime. You see, when a dog gets in a killing frenzy like what you describe, and you described it in vivid detail, he'd never be the same again. From then on you could never completely trust him. There might come a time when someone drove into the yard and he confused their smell with that of Rango and he'd attack him. I'm sorry, but he would've had to be shot anyway."

After thinking about it Haas said, "Those are some terrible happenings. I'm sorry it had to happen this way, Mrs. Landon. I understand your motives, wanting to keep the bank from repossessing the family farm and all that."

Then he asked, "I wonder, would you let Jamie show us where the man is buried?"

"We'll all go. Jamie will lead the way, you follow him and I'll come behind with 'mama's gum.' Don't worry, it's a safe load."

Mac said, "I assume by that you mean there isn't a cartridge under the hammer?"

"What else would it mean!" mom snapped.

There was a funny look on both men's faces . . . like respect.

When we left the house we were all together at first. As we passed the wood pile, Mac stooped to pick up a piece of wood. It had a gray groove part way through it crosswise to the gain. The piece of wood had been split exactly in half. He might have thought mom was a good shot or had been lucky. But either way, it wouldn't be good to cross a grizzly bear, especially one packing a thirty-eight heavy load. He threw it on the wood pile.

After Mr. Haas and Mac had driven away, mom told Tommy and me to pick up all the brass casings we could find while she raked up the broken glass and using the dustpan from the kitchen dumped it in an old bucket. She also raked loose sand over the blood. Then she dragged Chips into the tall grass to the north of the barn. Nobody would take the time to bury him. She said she didn't want Hank Cooper to see any of it, and that if he asked about Chips we had to say he was hit by a car on the road. It was important that we say nothing about any of this.

A half hour later Hank Cooper drove into the yard in his Model T Ford. As he usually did when he worked for dad, he backed it up into the haymow in case it rained. The car's roof leaked.

A week later I went back to where Murphy had been buried, and it was obvious he had been dug up. Maybe they came to the house while we were at school, or else they had stopped on the road that ran north of the farm. The grave was only ten yards from the road. We didn't talk about this except when we told dad the story.

Dad was very weak when he got home not getting around any too well even on crutches. It wasn't until after Christmas that he could help with the milking again. But, he made a full recovery and ran the farm for the rest of his life—without the help of a full time hired man.

In the years that followed we often spoke among ourselves about these events. Whenever the revolver was mentioned it was always called "mama's gum."

CHAPTER 21

After the shootout on the farm life returned to normal. Other than when we reminisced about it, it was as if it hadn't happened. The war ended and so did rationing. We, at least in the United States, were prosperous even though the countries of Europe took many years to rebuild. England still had some commodities rationed five years after the war.

Things changed rapidly for us. Replacing the dog was first. The following spring we ordered a for real border collie from an ad in one of the farm magazines. Mom wanted a black and white one but when the crate arrived at the train depot we found it was light brown, the color of sand, so mom decided to name him Sandy. He was half grown so could stay outside from the start. Border collies are natural herding dogs and having him with us made driving the cows to the barn in the evening a lot easier. He never got the hang of herding turkeys, though. Other than helping with the cows he barked at cars that came in the driveway, sniffed the shoes of new arrivals and chased cats. In other words, he pretty much fell into what most farm dogs did and had a full life.

When I say we were prosperous I mean it sure seemed like we were because there were a lot of things that continually got better. Shortly after the war dad became intent on getting a well on the farm. Even though it had been a profitable place for over a half century it had never had a good well. To start with, the services of a water witcher were obtained. One could say that was dumb but there were hundreds of people who swore by them. In addition, since the earliest times several attempts were made to find water and all had failed. The spot to drill turned out to be between the house and the shed where we kept the car, not the best location, but better there than no well at all.

Well drillers showed up with a large well drilling rig. It wasn't really drilling because they used a steel rod about twelve feel long and five inches across that the drilling machine repeatedly lifted and dropped. So in effect it pounded the hole in the ground. There was enough moisture in the soil to keep the mud sloppy and every now and then they'd pull the drilling bit up and drop a cylindrical sluice bucked down and hoist out the mud. After about fifteen feet deep it all turned to blue clay. That was the soil type above the bed rock in our neck of the woods.

The first try went smoothly until they were about 150 feet deep. They struck water but it was muddy with blue clay in the water so they drove the five inch casing past it cutting it off and kept drilling. Somewhere about 320 feet they struck a good vein of water. There was only one problem with it and that was it wasn't very thick. When they went to drive the casing down the intent was to stop a little above the vein but they drove it too far cutting off the water.

There was consternation all around but not to worry. A few days later the drillers showed up with two very large hydraulic jacks. They screwed a collar on the top of the casing, set up the jacks on heavy wooden blocks and started pumping the jacks. It was done by hand and the mechanical advantage was huge because after twenty pumps on the jack handle you could hardly see that the main cylinder had moved. But, that was okay because it had to be done slowly. They knew that the 320 feet of casing would stretch so they'd lift the main cylinders a half inch and let it sit until the next day hoping the casing would let go of the dirt and clay in the ground and slide up.

The well drillers were good with that plan because they tended to imbibe the nectar of the gods a little too freely and that gave them the day to lounge around the municipal liquor store and tip a few. This plan was at work for a few days until one day there was a sharp bang and the top of the casing popped up a couple of inches. There was hope that the whole casing had released and would now permit itself to be jacked up. But, that was not to be. The casing had broken about half way down. They knew that had happened because with a mirror one could reflect sunlight down the casing as see an offset at the break.

The bottom part of the casing was lost for good. That being the case there were two options. The first was to pull the upper part of the pipe out and start over. The other was to pull it up far enough so the muddy water flowed in, put a pump on it and see if it were pumped for a few days it would clear up. They tried option two first. There was enough confidence in it that a well pit was dug, a small house built over it and a pump installed. They pumped it day and night but there was no improvement. That was it for the summer because I suppose dad only had so much money he could spend.

That method of drilling added up to a slow process. It took six weeks to get down the 320 feet. Of course the well drilling rig broke down at regular intervals and that meant the drillers had to go into town for parts and then they'd make a side trip to their favorite place that ended up taking the rest of the day. Since they were known as well experts they'd get calls for help with well problems all the time. That meant they were only on the job for us at most half the time.

The next summer a new water witcher found a better place behind the shed and the well drillers were called in again. First they pulled up the top 150 feet of casing from the first try and started drilling at the new location. There were more than the normal number of break downs but eventually they hit water at 280 feet. It was a good vein and the water was good. Dad dug another pit, installed a pump and pumped it. It was a little sandy at first but that cleared up. Then dad hired a man to dig a seven foot deep trench from the well to the house by hand. By the end of the summer we had running water in the house. We still didn't have a water heater, a flush toilet or a shower. They all came in the next year or two. This time the pump house was made larger so it was also a workshop with a wood stove in it so in winter we could do all-day projects in comfort.

As soon as we had a well dad built a new brooder house for the turkeys. It was located to the north of the shed and extended to the west from the pump house. It took the place of six individual brooder houses and incorporated many modern innovations such as wire mesh floors in the pens so the droppings from the birds would fall through to a space below.

Other exciting things were happening too. When I was eight Tommy and I both got Red Rider BB guns for Christmas. I had wanted one, oh, so bad, but had no hope of getting one. We kids would give small gifts to one another but those from mom and dad showed up under the tree Christmas morning. It helped with the Santa Claus fantasy for the younger ones. I was one delighted boy that Christmas morning. Tommy sort of wanted a BB gun and he was old enough, but dad must have known it would never work for Tommy to get one and not me. Mom said Santa Claus must have been crazy to leave one for me. In that first year dad took it away from me for a week or two a few times until I learned not to point it at things that I shouldn't, and once for general punishment.

In those days BB guns were a lot more powerful than ones of later years—you could kill a fully grown pigeon with one—and the guns were well built. The stock and hand rest were wood rather than cheap plastic. There were a lot of pigeons and English sparrows in the barn and I hunted them with abandon. They were like winged rodents and made a mess of everything so dad would have been glad to be rid of them. At first they were pretty tame since they had never been hunted except by cats when they were on the ground feeding. It didn't take long for them to recognize a small man carrying a stick-like thing. Tommy never hit much, but I did—eventually.

By the time I learned how to aim and shoot, the birds were educated. Their canniness didn't save them all, though, because I got a goodly number of them. I spent endless hours hunting sparrows and pigeons. In a couple of years the pigeons were gone except for a stray one that happened by once in awhile. It wasn't that I killed them all in our part of the state. It was that they seemed to smarten up and decided to live at neighboring farms where life wasn't so dangerous. The sparrows stayed because their population didn't suffer from my hunting them. They could reproduce faster than I could shoot them, and still most of them died of old age. Eventually I wore out my BB gun and then since Tommy was of a different sort and hardly used his, I wore out his BB gun too.

Immediately after the war model airplane kits became available. All kinds of entrepreneurs returning from the war were trying to make money anyway they could. The first ones we got for Christmas did not use balsa wood, but regular pine and it was hard to cut the parts out of the sheets of wood with a razor blade. In a year or two balsa became available and that was much better. The five and dime on main street carried a reasonable selection of kits. I bought the little ones for ten cents. All of these were stick and tissue planes powered by winding up a rubber band running the length of the inside of the plane. Mine never flew well mainly because I didn't understand aerodynamics so I wouldn't trim the control surfaces for proper flight. And, of course, there was no one to help me.

When I was ten I got a kit for a really big plane with a wing span of thirty inches. Though I can't remember who gave it to me it must have been a relative who lost interest in models after he got married or something like that. It would be a beautiful plane and was complicated to build with dozens of sticks bent to form the proper aerodynamic shape. I got it in the fall and by Christmas it wasn't done yet. Mom and dad must have seen me toiling away at it so I got a real gas motor for Christmas. It was a .049 Spitfire that used a five or six inch propeller. I also got a can of fuel and a few other accouterments. None of us knew anything about the sophisticated world of gas powered models. As a result the engine was much too small for the plane I was building.

Besides working on the plane I worked at starting the motor. I mounted it on a block of wood and flipped away. Never having seen anyone else do it made for a torturously long learning period. I had to learn everything the hard way. For example, the fuel was a mixture of a third oil and the rest was light hydrocarbons. I'd leave the cap off the can while I was trying to start the engine and before long the volatile components evaporated leaving mostly oil. No wonder it wouldn't start. Add to that a dozen other things I didn't know and it took until spring before I got it to run.

When the plane was done the last thing I did was mount the motor on it and was ready for the wild blue yonder. There was still a little snow on the ground when I took it out for my first trial. One of the old brooder houses was now located to the southeast of the barn. It had a flat roof with only a slight slope to it. I climbed up on it as a place to launch the plane. The first two times out the motor wouldn't start. On the third time I got it started and I adjusted the needle valve for maximum power. I hand launched it in great anticipation. It flew for about ten yards but the motor was too small and it continuously lost altitude until it crashed breaking off a wing. Eventually I would learn that free flight models had the two wings built all in one piece and held on the plane with rubber bands. That way if it crashed one wing tip would be shoved back and pop loose the rubber bands releasing the wing with no damage. Things like that were in the future.

Looking back the lack of reality in my thinking was amazing. With a rubber band powered model it had power for at most ten seconds if it didn't crash at launch. With a gas motor it had power for up to five minutes. Gas powered free flight models normally flew at about thirty miles per hour. If it flew straight away from me it would go two and a half miles under power and then maybe glide for another half mile. At that point it would be nearly impossible to find, though a few years later then that happened I did manage to locate it.

Undaunted, I decided to try a new approach. The Comet model company came out with what they called *Struct-O-Speed* models. These were rubber band powered models built entirely of sheets of balsa—no tissue paper. The biggest size cost a dollar which was a lot of money but I decided to try it. The one I bought was a high wing plane, a model of a light plane like a Cessna, with a span of about fifteen inches. I had to specially modify it, of course, to use the motor which was much too powerful for this size plane. By way of comparison, an .049 could fly a lightly built free flight with five times the wing area of these. As a result this would be a motor with a little balsa attached to it. I ended up mounting the fuel tank in the fuselage under the center of the wing since there was no place else to put it.

It was summer now as I mounted my trusty Spitfire motor to it. On nice days I'd give it a try still using the roof of the old brooder house as a launch platform. It would crash and after a try or two it was too damaged for further trials so it had to be taken to the house for repairs. Finally it had been crashed so many times that it was beyond repair but I learned a little more with each failure and felt I was getting close. As a result, I bought a second one identical to it. After a few crashes I had all the problems worked out and the day arrived when I had high hopes of a successful flight.

The thing to know about these little engines is that they are finicky. But, if everything is set just right they run very fast on a lean mixture so can run twice as long as they normally do.

It was a nice sunny afternoon and the wind was light from the southwest. The motor started easily and it almost crashed on launch but got itself righted and turned to the left headed for the fence. It cleared the fence by inches and came toward me. It passed in front of the brooder house and started another turn. In its third time around it almost hit the barn but it's circular path kept it clear of that obstacle. Flying in one hundred foot circles it cleared the barn roof in a stable pattern and it was on its way.

Tommy had been painting the north side of the old barn and had run to watch it go still carrying his paint brush in his hand. I climbed down from the roof, ran around between the barns and across the barn yard. I could still hear the motor and see it circling as it climbed ever higher drifting to the northeast. Running as fast as I could through the woods I arrived at the fence along the road that ran on the north side of our property. I could still see it but it was getting awfully small. I stayed there so I could keep it in sight. As it came around each time the faint hum of the motor could be heard. Finally, I could only see it each time it turned as the sun reflected from the underside of the wing. It was one of these perfect motor runs and I thought it would never stop.

But, it did. That was only evident when I failed to see the reflection of the wing as it came around and instead saw a relatively rapid flash as it spiraled to the ground. The plane was terribly nose heavy so it would never glide, something I had not planned on in any case. I tracked it with my eyes on its rapid descent to earth. As luck would have it, it came down right in line with the neighbor's silo over a quarter of a mile away. That meant I had a good land mark. If I walked straight toward the silo I was bound to find it.

Off I set. After awhile I was getting concerned that I had missed it because I had crossed an alfalfa field and was then in a corn field. Finally I emerged from the fields and the silo was only fifty yards from me. Still no plane. Then I saw it. It had crashed twenty yards from the silo, leaving a small debris field of balsa pieces. The grass and weeds were short in that area because it was a thoroughfare for farm machinery. After gathering up the motor and splinters of the plane I slipped away, the neighbor none the wiser. That, in case the reader didn't recognize it, was a massively successful model airplane flight.

CHAPTER 22

The winter of 1950 I turned twelve years old. The unemployment of the post war period was past us, the United States was a prosperous super-power and the general outlook was positive. It's probably impossible for people in succeeding generations to understand that feeling. It only happens maybe to one society in a thousand years. Everything kept getting better and better and, at least in our case, technology would solve all the problems.

Nothing in this world is perfect, though. We had our archenemy, the Soviet Union. That was a police state and we were free. It's hard to imagine two competing forces with such opposite points of view. We had no particular desire to impose our way of life on them, though it seemed that any rational person would accept our way over theirs. They, on the other hand, sincerely wanted to bring the entire world into their totalitarian system. The rivalry between our competing systems became known as the Cold War.

In February Senator Joe McCarthy made his famous speech where he stated there were 205 communists in the State Department. It caused a firestorm of protest from the liberals.

Being twelve years old meant I only partially grasped what was happening. It came up in conversation around the dinner table as dad always listened to the news at noon and read the daily paper in the evening. However, the rancor in the press caused by McCarthy died down in June when the communists in North Korea invaded free South Korea. In no time the U.S. was in a hot shooting war with communists.

However, McCarthy's attempt to wake up the population of the United States to the dangers of communism got him branded as a nut case. Eventually the forces arrayed against him proved to be too much and he died in 1957 having accomplished little.

As world events were unfolding, things for me kept plodding along. Tommy and I were able to help a lot on the farm. Work had come to be more satisfying to me as I could handle things better and see a job through. The sense of accomplishment was important to me. This isn't to say that I fell in love with work. There were still a zillion things I could think of to do that were more to my liking than work. Some kids liked farm work and I supposed they were born farmers. It wasn't that way for me.

To my great surprise and delight, that summer dad let me use the .22 rifle. He had bought it a few years before for what reason I didn't know other than to familiarize us with a real firearm. It was a Remington single shot bolt action. Once again I had to work on marksmanship. At first I couldn't hit anything mostly because the targets were further away than anything I shot at with a BB gun. It took a whole order of magnitude more precision and it was quite awhile before I got the hang of it. But in time I became an expert marksman. In my last years of high school I could hit a pigeon on the wing about one out of two times.

I would be in the seventh grade in the fall. Since the Catholic school was only to grade six in Deep Woods I'd be in the public school. The sisters ranted about how our parents should send us to a Catholic boarding school rather than go to the terrible public school where half the teachers were communists. Boarding school was out of the question for us so we'd have to deal with the commies the best we could.

That year the finances must have been good enough so we could afford a new car. In early summer of 1950 a new Pontiac appeared. We were told it had to be ordered from the factory and it took quite a while for it to come. It even had that new car smell in it. Various friends and relatives had purchased new cars in the years since the war and would drive out to see us to show it off. I supposed it was pride of ownership as much as to demonstrate they were doing better than we were.

That summer after the first cutting of hay was in, mom and dad decided to take a day trip in the new car so we went north to Itasca State

Park, in which was located the headwaters of the Mississippi River. The mighty river started as little more than a creek running out of Lake Itasca. You could walk across it on rocks that had been placed into it.

One of the attractions on the park was a big white teepee with a sign that said, "Visit Red Feather's lodge, have your picture taken with a real Indian—only fifty cents."

Sure enough there was an old weathered Indian wearing buckskins with a tomahawk in his belt and a full feather headdress. Mom and dad agreed it would make a memorable picture so they handed over the requisite fee. Tommy and I each stood at one side of the Indian and mom took the picture with her trusty box camera.

After the picture, and seeing there were no more tourists waiting, I asked, "Are you really Red Feather?"

He answered, "Red Feather, proud Ojibwe Indian."

Dad had walked over to the teepee to show the rest how it was constructed. I heard him say how cold it must have been living in a teepee in the winter. He didn't seem to notice that I was talking to the Indian.

"Oh," I replied. "Do you know an Indian named Running Wolf? He also called himself Justin Merchner when he was away from the reservation. He said he was from the Ojibwe tribe."

His expression changed from that of the picturesque tourist attraction to one of thoughtfulness as he looked me over. Finally, he spoke in a gravely voice a little reminiscent of the way Justin had sounded, "What caused you to ask about Running Wolf?"

He spoke in normal English, without a hint of the Indian accent. I asked in some surprise, "How come you sounded like an Indian out of the movies when we first arrived when you can talk just like us?"

"I man has to make a living and in this part of the state it's hard to turn a buck."

"Maybe if you had some scalps hanging on the teepee it would help business," I suggested.

"No good. The last real scalps were taken many years ago and are all gone. Two years ago I ordered wigs from Sears and Roebuck. I worked on them to make them look stringy and old. Didn't work. The women freaked out—had to throw them away."

I spoke before he could say any more, interrupting him I suppose. That was something I was scolded for frequently. "Do you live in that teepee?"

"Are you kidding. I live in a house with a table and chairs and R-12 insulation in the walls. What do you take me for, a savage?"

I laughed. "Of course not. From the way you're dressed I thought you might be a Boston lawyer."

There was a twinkle in his eye.

I continued, "It was the tomahawk that gave you away."

He chuckled deep in his chest. "You'll do, young man, you'll do."

It wasn't totally clear to me, but I took that as a compliment. Generally when I made a remark like that I was scolded. Yes, things like that were still the same. Even though I was six years older than when I knew Justin, I was still getting my ears pinned back at every occasion.

Then he turned serious again. "What do you know about Running Wolf?"

"When I was six he was our hired man for a summer. We became friends. After he left we never heard from him again. Do you know where he is?"

He asked, "What's your name?"

"Jamie Landon."

In a low voice Red Feather said, "Jamie Landon. Yes, I remember that. Do you have another name?"

"Yes," I said in a similarly conspiratorially low voice. "It's Little Manknife. Running Wolf and I are blood brothers."

Red Feather's eyes took on a gleam, "You're the one."

The rest of the family was standing at the entrance to the teepee. Red Feather waved his hand, the fringes on his buckskin flailing in the air and using his movie Indian speech said, "Enter teepee, look, no touch."

"What does that mean?" I asked.

"I don't want them to finger my means of making a living."

"No. When you said, 'You're the one.'"

"Oh that. Justin arrived at the reservation in the fall. He was wounded but of a stout constitution. He told me about you and the men that came to your farm. We talked for hours. Then, he went into the woods to be among the living things to heal. We didn't see him again and thought he had crossed the divide to be with the *pawáganak*."

"That means grandfathers," I interrupted. "He taught me a few Ojibwe words."

"Yes, that is a fairly close meaning. A few years later we learned he was alive. You saw what happened that last day on your farm?"

"Yeah. The day Justin left our farm, a man called Rango Smyth came with two other men to kill him. They said that when they talked to one another. I kind of think Rango might be dead because Justin shot him up pretty good."

Red Feather shook his head. "The next year we heard a man called Rango was looking for Justin. One of our men talked to him."

"Was he limping?"

The old Indian nodded. "He said he had lost his right leg in the war and had a mechanical one from the knee down."

"That was a lie. Justin nearly shot it off. He's a criminal. Did he ever come back?"

"No. We thought Justin was dead at that time and Rango was told that so what reason would there be for him to come back? Why was he looking for Justin, do you know?"

"Not really. The men who came to the farm that day seemed to think Justin had something and they wanted it. He never mentioned a secret or anything like that to me. We were pretty good friends and talked about all kinds of stuff. I think he would have mentioned it."

By this time the rest of the family was nearing us. I said, "Red Feather knows Justin who was our hired man when dad broke his hip."

"Is that so," dad said. "We wondered what happened to him. Is he around? Maybe we could say hello."

"No good," Red Feather said in his best Indian accent. "He work on reservation. Only few of us stay here to show Indian ways."

"Can you give me his address?" I asked. "I could write him a letter."

Red Feather solemnly looked at me as if thinking it might not be a good idea but finally nodded with a low grunt. He turned to the teepee but did not go inside. He stooped by a box on the ground, opened it, and withdrew a piece of paper. He handed it to me. "On top, post office of reservation. Write his name first on letter, then rest."

I smiled at the way he spoke with the rest of the family around. "Thanks."

CHAPTER 23

Writing letters was not big on my list of things to do. Mom always made me write a thank you letter whenever I got a Christmas present from a Baptismal sponsor or anyone like that. It was torture. She nagged me a hundred times before I finally did it. Partly it was because I was not learning much in school. The Dick and Jane method of teaching reading and spelling may have worked on other kids but not me. It didn't help that the teachers weren't much good either.

The fifth and sixth grades were combined. The teacher discovered we didn't know our multiplication tables so she set out to teach them to us. Taking both classes together she drilled us like this, "one six is six, two sixes are twelve, three sixes are eighteen . . . ." That worked because based on that class I remembered the multiplication tables my whole life.

When the same teacher had reading class it was a different story. We all opened our reading books to the same page and she would call on someone to stand and read aloud. The rest of us were to follow along silently and in some mysterious way that was supposed to teach us how to read. When my turn came I'd stumble on every other word so after reading a paragraph or two I'd be told to sit down. When a kid who could read perfectly, who didn't need reading class at all, stood up they'd read three pages. That I made no progress from the start of the year to the end didn't seem to concern either the teacher or my parents.

However, early in this summer after sixth grade I saw a book in the drug store written by a man who had been a fighter pilot in the Second World War. I bought it and that was the first book I ever read. Then I bought another. After that I discovered the public library in the public school and anybody could get a library card and check out books. With the kind help of the old lady who was the librarian I discovered science fiction books. Since I couldn't sound out words I always said science *friction*. She never corrected me, only carefully said science *fiction* whenever the term came up. Eventually I learned to say it correctly and was forever grateful to her for not putting me down by correcting me.

A couple of the science fiction books were written by Robert Heinlein. Particularly memorable was *Red Planet*. There was even a quasi history book about Galileo and his troubles with the Catholic Church. Since it was in a public library it was not sympathetic with The Church, but it was interesting. That started me reading and as I said in later life I taught myself how to read, and I wasn't a very good teacher. But, by the end of the summer I had improved a lot. I always had trouble pronouncing words because they didn't teach phonics and I never figured it out.

Back to my present situation. I had a bit more incentive to write a letter to Justin than I normally did so a few days after our trip to northern Minnesota I got started. My penmanship was bad and my spelling worse. I knew how to look up words in the dictionary if I had any idea of how to spell the word which frequently I didn't. As a result, I used short, simple words so my letters were not all that interesting. My purpose in writing was to reestablish contact with Justin. I'd write this letter and if there were no answer after a couple of months to try once more.

If truth be told, there was still the mystery of the knife that was also driving me to endure the pain of writing the letter. I still had it and had never told anyone about it, not even Tommy. Mikey was now nine and would be interested in it if I had shown it to him. He remembered small fragments of what had happened in 1944, and certainly heard us talk about Justin and the shoot-out at the farm enough times. But, he took after Tommy more than me. They both liked school because they had friends and most of all they seemed to really learn something. As much as I would have hated to admit it, Mikey at three years younger could read better than I could.

That left me alone with the knife and wondering why Justin had given it to me. He seemed to really like it the way he had always worn it. Yet, it probably wasn't so much that he liked it as saw it as a necessity, like a belt to hold up a guy's pants was a necessity. He had used it to save his life when Murphy would have shot him in the back. Maybe, he wore it because he had nothing else and gave it to me because he knew that after he left, he would find a better knife that he was more comfortable with.

Justin pulled out the knife and threw it in one motion while holding the handle and it didn't turn end over end. That had the advantage of being able to draw and throw quickly, but when we tried to throw a knife that way it didn't work at all. The fact that the blade of this knife was so heavy might have had something to do with how Justin was able to throw it. I wanted to try throwing Justin's knife, but thought I didn't dare. Sooner or later it would hit wrong and break the bone handle.

In movies when someone threw a knife they would grasp it by the tip of the blade. This I understood because Tommy and I had spent considerable time throwing knives at the south wall inside the haymow where we pulled in the hayrack. That method of throwing made the knife turn end over end as it traveled to that target. If the point of the blade was turned exactly right when it hit the wall it would stick. That was satisfying except for the fact that it didn't happen one out of ten throws.

I recalled Justin practicing with it in the barn yard, and how he was pretty good, but sometimes it wouldn't stick in the tree. He had told me about the concentration needed to make it do what a person wanted. I had tried the concentration thing a thousand times throwing knives at the wall in the barn but never got the hang of it.

Which way was the best for throwing a knife was beside the point. The question was why did he give it to me? When he was sick and he finally let me hold it for the first time, he said he had recently acquired it.

Many were the times that I took out the knife and looked at it. I made sure it always had a thin coating of oil on it so it wouldn't rust. I looked at it from every angle, pulled one way and another on the bone-handle. It wasn't loose at all. There were no marks on it that would identify a manufacturer. Lightly pulling my thumb crosswise to the blade it was clearly the sharpest knife I had ever seen. I could skin the side off a stalk of hay cleanly with no effort. None of the kitchen knives were sharp enough to do that.

The scabbard was nothing special. It was no more that two pieces of leather sewn together with a sewing machine like the leather in a pair of shoes. There was no possible way there could be a secret compartment in it. That left the enigma of the knife. There was one odd thing about it.

Normally the handle of a knife was made in two parts one that fit on either side of the shank and the shank was as wide as the two handle halves. The three parts were squeezed together like a sandwich by two or three rivets. With this knife the shank went into a one piece handle and the opening was perfectly matched to the shank of the knife as if they have been machined to fit together perfectly. Of course, I was no expert on knives, especially fighting knives as Justin had said this one was, so maybe it was common for certain types of knives to be made this way.

It was as if this were a piece of precision machinery rather than an ordinary knife. Or as Justin had said, the man who gave it to him said it was more than what a person normally thinks a knife is. I thought that maybe if it were taken apart either the shank or the handle would fit into something else like a key. That left the problem of how it could be taken apart. Somebody had put it together so it should come apart unless great force had been used to push the shank into the handle and it was jammed in. But, if that were true, the bone would simply have cracked. Darn it, still a mystery.

There was a table and chair in our bed room upstairs where I made model airplanes in the winter. Now it was piled with all kinds of stuff, so I made a clearing on it by making higher piles on one end. Oops. The dictionary was under the pile and for sure I'd need that. Finally, I had a space cleared, a piece of tablet paper—the only paper around—and a sharpened pencil. I started the letter.

Dear Running Wolf,

See. Already I have problems. First is how to spell Running, or is it Runing? That was one where I had a good start because I knew how to spell run so managed to find it in the dictionary. It was Running. There must be some rule about how to know if it were one or two n's but that was never mentioned in school. Then to say Dear when writing to a man seemed wrong so I erased it and wrote Hello. Still wrong. I changed it back to Dear.

Dear Running Wolf,
    Our family made a trip to Itasca State Park last Saturday. We stopped to have our pictures takes with an Indian called Red Feather.

You mentioned a grandfather called Red Feather so I asked if he knew you and he said he did and he gave me this address where you could get a letter. I hope you get it.

We still talk about you and how you helped us on the farm that summer in 1944. Thank you again. Dad was weak when he got home but by the next spring was completely well. Red Feather said that a man named Rango was around asking about you the summer after the one you worked for us but they thought you were dead and told him that. I thought Rango might be the one who was dead.

Your going away present is still safe. I think you mentioned there was something special about it. It's been a few years and I wonder if I remember that right. Is that true? And if it is, do you know what it is?

Let me know how you are.

Sincerely,

Jamie

Reading over the letter I was pretty proud of myself because it sounded like a good letter. I wanted to say more about the knife but wasn't sure who might read the letter, and I hoped my reference to the present would be enough for Justin to know what I meant.

I printed the address on the envelope to be sure the people in the post office would be able to read it. For the return address I put J. Landon, RFD 3, Deep Woods, Minn. I thought it looked more official with just a J. for my first name.

I folded the letter the way mom said letters were supposed to be folded, put it in the envelope and licked the flap and sealed it shut. Mom seemed happy to give me the three cent first class stamp because I had actually written the letter without being reminded a dozen times. She was not too happy that I had already sealed it. She liked to read my letters before I sent them so she was sure I had not said something to embarrass the family and if the spelling was too bad she made me do it again.

"Did you thank him for staying on when Fred was in the hospital?"

"Yep," I said. "I hope he answers."

"There's a good chance he will," mom replied.

First thing the next morning I walked out to the mailbox, put it in and put up the flag so the mailman would take it.

CHAPTER 24

The next week, if I didn't have other things to do, I was out at the end of the driveway waiting for the mailman. He always stopped at our mailbox because dad subscribed to the *Minneapolis Morning Tribune* and that came every day. We bought the Sunday paper from a high school boy who sold them on the front steps of church after Mass for fifteen cents. Most of the days I was waiting and there was no letter from Justin. The next week Monday and Tuesday I was helping shell peas so was busy. Mom got up early and picked them before the sun got hot and there was always a huge pile of them on the porch table waiting for us. It wasn't so bad. We sat on the porch listening to the radio as we shelled.

On Wednesday I was out there when the mailman came and there was a letter from Justin. I left the rest of the mail there because dad picked it up when he came home from taking the milk to the creamery unless the mailman was late that day. I stuck it in my pocket and when I got half way to the house I cut into the plumb orchard and walked around to the north of the house. I stopped behind the shed and took a good look at the envelope. There was no return address like mom always told us to do. I opened the envelope and started to read.

Dear Jamie,

He started his letter with "Dear" but he must still think of me as a six year old boy so that made sense. His writing was clear and easy to read.

Dear Jamie,

Your letter reached me yesterday. It was delayed because it had to be forwarded. I'm not at the reservation now. But, that's okay. If you write again use the address on the slip of paper in the envelope. I was happy to hear you still have the present. I know you were pleased to get it. You asked two questions. The answers are yes and no. Keep it safe and still between you and me.

You probably knew that when I left I was wounded. It took a long time for me to get better but I am now recovered. I was glad to hear your dad recovered, too. If people visit you, I don't mean relatives, please let me know.

Have a nice summer,
Justin

I read the letter three or four times. The address on the separate slip of paper was for a ranch in New Mexico. It was good that I had been out at the mailbox because if mom and dad knew I had gotten a letter from Justin they would have wanted to know what was in it. There had been times when I wondered if I had understood Justin correctly about not letting anyone else know about the knife. It was clear from the letter that he had been serious. But, what was so special about the knife? I was beginning to be obsessed with it.

What was special about it was one question—it seemed he didn't even know—the other was why he had given it to me at all. If it was so special why didn't he keep it? He could have hidden it someplace the same as I did. Suddenly, the obvious answer occurred to me. He didn't expect to live long enough to hide it. And, if he died after he hid it nobody would ever find it. That still wasn't right. It might have made sense six years ago but the secret would be getting old by now. Unless . . . it contained a map showing where a treasure was hidden.

As I thought about it his letter was full of information. Somebody else must know about the knife because it sounded like he thought that somebody would show up looking for it. Why was there interest now and not in the last six years? There could only be one reason. I had once again become connected with Justin. First, there was Red Feather. I thought his interest had been no more than our former association and it was a form of news about a member of the tribe. But, he did show genuine interest.

He could have told someone but that wouldn't have done any good because he didn't know where I lived. Oh, yes. He could have had someone at the reservation watching for a letter from me. They would have gotten my address from that. They might even have opened the envelope and read the letter before sending it along to Justin. At the very least, my letter had connected Justin with me.

I also had to take into consideration people on Justin's end. He might have told someone. Boy, this was getting serious. If there was something hidden in the knife, I had to find how to get it out.

When I came in for dinner mom had the mail lying on the cupboard where it normally was so dad could go through it in detail after he had eaten. She said, "I wonder if Justin will ever answer your letter. That Indian at the state park seemed confident he was on the reservation." She laughed a little. "Maybe he hates to write letters as much as you do."

I didn't want to get into discussing it so she wouldn't ask me if I had gotten one and she missed it so I said, "He might have a job for the summer away from the reservation."

"Yes, I suppose that could be."

Tommy came in and he started talking to mom which was good for me. I saw that I had to write a letter to Justin and have him send one to me with ordinary news in it so mom would be happy.

After dinner I went upstairs and wrote a short letter to Justin. I told him that if he had special information for me to put a second sheet in the envelope so I could show the regular letter to the family.

I had been an altar boy since the third grade and in the summer each of us was assigned a week when we came in each morning to serve at Mass. This was my week so I decided to take my letter to Justin in with me and mail it in the outside mailbox in front of the post office which was a half block from the church. Tommy and I each had a bike so we'd bike to town for things like that. I had to snitch a stamp for the letter but thought God would forgive me under the circumstances.

Riding a bicycle to town was hard on the gravel road and as the joke went it was up hill both ways. It was—in a way. When you came out of the driveway you were headed down hill. Then, the road was level for a quarter of a mile before going up a hill again as the road entered town. So, in a way, it was up hill both ways. The road was paved once it got into town and, even better, much of it had a sidewalk which was really smooth. That was fun because you could just fly along.

The next week we started cutting grain so as was normal during that time we were all busy. I drove the tractor to pull the binder and Tommy, now that he was fourteen, shocked alone until mom had the rest of her work done then she'd come out and work with Tommy. By this time we had my sister, Lucy, who was three. She seemed to take up more of mom's time that Mikey ever did. Anyway, it was Mikey's job to keep her amused but a boy had a hard time amusing a girl. What did a boy know about dolls?

We were nearly done cutting and dad was pleased because it looked like we'd get done without having it rain once. After the grain was shocked it dried quickly after a rain if the sun came out. If it kept raining we'd be threshing moldy bundles which happened some years. When dad came home from the creamery he had the mail and called to me.

"Jamie, you got a letter."

It was from Justin and I was surprised at his quick answer. There was no return address the same as last time but the post mark was in New Mexico. I knew someone would notice that. Anyway, I opened the envelope and saw the letter folded neatly in it and also a slip of paper beside it. I pulled the letter out being sure the slip stayed in. It was a short but newsy letter. He had traveled to the Southwest to visit another tribe and compare Indian culture with them. He had written the letter on the train and that was why it had a New Mexico postmark on it. I wasn't sure if all that was the truth but it answered all the questions everyone would have. I walked to the house and as I did I carefully put the slip of paper in my pocket.

When I entered the kitchen I could tell mom was dying to read it so I said she could. I didn't know what she expected but it seemed to satisfy her.

Dad was ready to go and we headed to the field, dad driving the tractor and Tommy and I riding on the back. Arriving at the binder we hooked the tractor to it and then had to put the canvases on it. They were taken off each night lest rain or the morning dew damage them. There were three all having strips of wood riveted crosswise to them at about one foot intervals. One long canvas went on the bed that the cut grain fell on. This conveyed the grain stalks from the bed to the main machine.

The other two were positioned at a steep angle and took the grain stalks between them up to the top of the binder. There they slid down a metal slide where the packer pressed them close together until there was enough grain stalks to make a bundle. Then the needle would quickly swing up and feed the twine to the knotter which would tie a knot, cut the twine and then arms would swing around and eject the bundle.

That was a pretty sophisticated machine for its day which was by now coming to an end. In a few years we'd go to combining and that was the end of the line for the grain binder and the threshing machine. It was those two machines, among a few others like the plough with the scouring moldboard, that had made it possible to open up the vast western wheat fields in the previous century.

After dinner before dad was ready to go back to the field I ran out to the pump house where I'd be alone so I could read the slip that was in the letter. It had only one line on it.

Expect visitors. Tell no one!

I knew he meant to tell no one about the knife and I wondered who might show up. It also made me almost crazy to find out what was special about the knife.

With the oats cut and shocked there was a little more time to fool around so I spent time studying the knife when I was sure I would not be interrupted and that took some planning. Finally I became curious about the bone-handle so in desperation I used a small file to see how hard it was. To my surprise it wasn't bone at all. It was metal with a coating on it to make it look like bone. It was harder than aluminum because I cut and filed aluminum now and then for one project or another. We had a toy magnet in the toy box in the house so I hid the knife in the back shadows under the workbench in the pump house and fetched the magnet from the house. It was not iron either since it was not magnetic. And, anyway it seemed it wasn't heavy enough for it to be steel. The blade was steel, of course. My conclusion was it was indeed a special knife.

In a week threshing started and after that the county fair was upon us. The fair was always fun. Mom and dad thought it was important for us to be in organizations so we were in 4-H. I didn't like it because it took away from my fooling around time. But, at fair time it was okay. We all had to have some project that ended up with something to exhibit at the fair. The girls took sewing, baking and projects like that. This year my project was a pig. Dad bought a piglet for me early in the spring and it was my job to feed and water it every day. By fair time it was pretty big. To show it at the fair it had to look its very best so I had to give it a bath before we set off with it. For the most part he didn't mind it because I used to scratch his back now and then and he liked that. We also were warned that the animals would refuse to eat at the fair with the noise, music, and all the commotion so we were instructed to play a radio near them for several hours a day in the week before the fair. Since my pig lived in a pen a long ways from the buildings the radio idea was impossible.

The year before Tommy's project had been a steer. By fair time it was several hundred pounds and almost as tall as he was but that didn't mat-ter—it too had to have a bath. One has to keep in mind that some kids really liked their project animals so spent a lot of time with them, so much so that they gave them names and made pets out of them. It wasn't that way with either of us. Tommy led the steer out of the barn and was about to tie it to a tree when the dog started barking as if trying to drive it back to the barn, I suppose. The animal took off with a bound with Tommy hanging on to the rope as best he could. Half way through the garden he tripped and was dragged through the peas and beans and two rows of tomatoes and then through the stubble that had recently been an oat field. Finally he had to let go. He was a mess with dirt and grass stains all over him.

I ran after him and he was getting up as I approached. Neither of us thought about Tommy, but only how mad dad would be if we didn't re-cover the animal. We sped off after it. The only thing that permitted us to outdo the beast was that we had more stamina than it did. Its first dash for freedom had completely winded it which meant we caught up with it a quarter mile from the barn. We didn't know what to make of it as it stood there glassy eyed, panting with its tongue hanging out. All we could think of is it could die. We talked to it in low voices and eventually it started to walk in the way we wanted to drive it. Luckily, the dog wasn't around because if it stampeded again it would probably run itself to death. That was it. Tommy refused to have anything to do with the dumb animal except to feed and water it. He refused to take it to the fair. It was one of the only times I could remember when one of us put his foot down with mom and dad and made it stick.

187

My pig ate like normal while it was at the fair, that is it ate, well, like a pig. I didn't have a name for him other than Pig. Each animal had its own pen so its owner got a pass to get into the fair grounds without paying to feed, water and tend to it. That didn't matter to us because if we walked across the fields the fair grounds were only a mile and a half from our house. It was closer to climb over the fence by the cattle barns than go around to the gate and it was more fun to sneak in, anyway. The livestock barns were pens with a roof over them and no sides so the air could freely blow though keeping the animals cool and the smell under control.

When it came time for judging I had my pig out in a show pen with a dozen others. How the judges could decide which one was the best with them all milling around was a mystery. I, as well as most others, had a plywood board to control my pig. It was about a foot wide and two feet long. The idea was if you put the board by the right eye the pig would go to the left, etc. That worked okay when there were no other pigs. This was a free-for-all. Eventually my pig went a little crazy and bit me in the leg. I limped around the pen trying to keep up with my soon-to-be-pork-chops.

After two or three eternities it was over and we were told to take our pigs back to their respective pens. After that I looked at my leg and it wasn't bleeding too badly anymore though my sock was soaked with blood. I could see the individual tooth marks in my leg. I went to the place we got water for the animals, took off my shoe and washed off the wound and wrung out my sock. It wasn't that I exactly put my foot down, but that was the last animal I had for a 4-H project.

For some crazy reason that I could never understand, I got a blue ribbon. Maybe the judges felt sorry for me. Maybe mine looked the best because it hadn't been subjected to the irritation of a radio for the week before the fair and hence hadn't eaten anything during that time. Or, as was most likely, they really couldn't tell what was going on with the chaos in the judging pen and I got the ribbon by mistake.

At home we soon ran out of Band Aids and when mom asked what happened to them I told her about the pig biting me and showed her my leg. She said, "Oh, that's too bad." I could have gotten rabies, tetanus, lock jaw, hoof and mouth disease (my hoof, the pig's mouth) or any of a dozen other diseases, but I was up and taking nourishment so nothing more was done about it. I didn't die.

CHAPTER 25

A week later, now beginning the second half of August, I was on the front porch reading comic books. Grape vines hung on the screens of this porch making it a cool pleasant place. This was the second porch and it attached to the west side of the house. It was entered from the living room, or from the front lawn. We had a relative who ran a drug store. Comic books came out every month like other magazines. When the new ones arrived they had to remove the previous month's unsold copies from the rack and were supposed to destroy them. Instead they tore off the upper half of the front page and gave them to us so we had a lot of Donald Duck and Bugs Bunny. Dad, Tommy and Mikey were out at the turkeys. I normally would have been with them but I had other chores to do and had finished them already. It seemed that I could work hard and fast when I knew I could goof-off when I was done. There were a couple of cots and one of our all-time favorite pastimes in the summer was to lay on the front porch and read comic books.

A car passed the house coming in the driveway. That should not have aroused my attention—it was common enough. For some reason I had an odd feeling about it so I went into the house and watched the car through the dining room window. It was a new black car that I could tell was a Ford because this year's model, the 1950, was unique in that looking from the side you couldn't tell the front from the back.

Sandy was barking at the car since it was his job to bark at any and all new arrivals. A man, uncertain of the dog, was slowly opening his door. Once out he closed the door and began walking toward the house while keeping an eye on the dog. Sandy kept his distance but didn't go away, giving a bark now and then. I suppose it made him feel important when he could intimidate someone. If a stranger ignored him or said, "Hi dog," in a friendly manner he'd walk away.

The man had dark brown hair carefully combed with a lot of hair oil in it, blue eyes set too far apart, a small mouth and a pointed nose. He wore a mustache and beard that were reasonably well clipped, at least not unkempt. His dark tan pants and lighter tan shirt were newly ironed as if he had put them on fresh this morning.

I could hear his knock on the screen door through the kitchen. Mom, unaware I was there, went to the porch. He spoke first. "Hello. Are you Mrs. Landon?"

"Yes."

"My name is Jarvis Granston."

The screen door was still closed because I hadn't heard the squeaky sound it made when it was opened.

Mom answered, "Yes, that name does sound familiar, though I don't recall the connection."

But, I remembered. It had something to do with the first time Mr. Haas from the FBI had visited us in 1944.

"Will the dog bite me?"

"If you behave yourself you'll be okay. But if you become aggressive he'll chew your face off."

It was not like mom to say something like that so I knew she made the connection, too.

"What can I do for you Mr. Granston?"

"Am I correct in that you had a man working for you called Justin Merchner a few years back?"

"Well," she said, "once we had a man called Justin working here for awhile but that was during the war. What's your interest?"

Mom was being guarded in her remarks.

"Yes, I was told he worked here in the past. I was wondering, is he still here?

"He was an Indian and as I recall when he left that fall he said he was going back to the reservation in northern Minnesota. There are several and I don't know which one. In fact we have been getting along without a hired man except for special jobs like sawing wood in the fall and things like that. So if you're looking for work I'm sorry but we can't help you."

"No. I'm not looking for a job. I'm trying to locate him."

"All I can say is you could try the Bureau of Indian affairs or contact the reservations up north directly."

"So, you've had no contact with him at all in the time since he left here, is that right?"

That pinned down mom. She wouldn't normally lie but the man was getting pushy.

Mom replied, "You never said why you wanted to find him."

"It's a personal matter."

Mom paused a few seconds and said, "I see. Justin was a good worker and followed instructions. That's all we asked. He kept to himself mostly but that was his business and we didn't pry. He left and hasn't been back. Sorry."

"I'm wondering, did he by any chance give you something, perhaps a present, while he was here or at the time he left? If not you, maybe to a member of the family?"

"Certainly not. We paid him the going rate at the time and he accepted it as a fair wage, though it was not lavish by any means. He would have no reason to give any of it back. Good bye, Mr. Granston." Mom turned and went back in the house.

He walked slowly to his car as if mulling things around in his head. It also seemed he was keeping an eye on the dog. It was like he was afraid to be here. He might have come a long way and was leaving with nothing so was trying to think of more questions to ask. He paused at his car and then slowly got in. He didn't start the motor immediately as if thinking about what he should do next.

When I walked into the kitchen mom was slipping cartridges into "mama's gum." I had a tinge of fear seeing mom upset like she was.

We both watched him through the kitchen window, standing back so he couldn't see us. Finally, he started the car and drove away. "I remember the name from the first time Mr. Haas was here," I said. "How did he fit in?"

"He was Justin's roommate in the St. Cloud VA Hospital and was the man whose records were mixed up with Justin's. Haas said he had died and was cremated. Looks like they didn't do a very good job."

She sat down by the table and laid the gun to the side. "Why on earth did he show up all of a sudden? I thought that business was long gone and forgotten."

I was pretty sure it had something to do with my first letter to Justin but didn't think I should mention that so I said, "What are we going to do?"

"I don't know. Maybe we should contact Mr. Haas."

She took a chair and stood on it so she could dig in the papers on the top shelf of the cupboard. It was strange but she came up with the little card he had given her all those years ago.

"I wonder if his phone number is the same, or if he even works at the same place anymore."

"Give it a try," I said.

Whereas the big cities were getting automatic dial phones we still had to call the operator who placed the call. It took awhile as it always did even though mom didn't ask to reverse the charges. Finally she said, "I'm calling for Mr. Leonard Haas. Is he there?"

She waited quite awhile and we both knew the charges were adding up. Then, "Mr. Haas. This is Mrs. Landon in Deep Woods. Do you remember me?"

There was a pause where he must have been replying to the question. "I'm calling because we just had a visitor, a man that you said was dead. I'm not very happy about this. That should have been all over, what happened?"

She waited as Haas was obviously talking. Then, "No, not really. He didn't seem dangerous, a little pushy maybe."

After a pause. "Yes, I have your old card right here. Yes, okay. Good bye."

Mom sat at the table and said, "He wants me to send him a letter with all the details, and the address is as shown on the card except that I should only use the address and not the FBI. I suppose that's so the nosey people in the post office won't start talking about the fact that we're writing to the FBI. We'll wait until your father comes in and see what he thinks."

Of course, it was a little surreal for dad because he had experienced none of it in 1944. He thought it would be a good idea to write the letter. He would, of course, because dad was the ultimate good citizen in that he did everything to help the government at all levels. He received letters from the Federal Government every month or two with a form to fill in about what crops he intended to plant, had planted, harvest results, etc. as well as all about his livestock. He never failed to fill out these forms and send them back. He was on the township election board and was an election judge. He was active in parish organizations, too. He thought the public schools were absolutely necessary because we had to have an educated citizenry and saw no other way to get that. In fact, he had talked about running for the school board for the public school this fall.

In the letter to Haas he told mom to describe the man and the car he was driving. It was too bad we didn't have his license plate number but we all knew nobody ever thought about license plates. Mom wrote the letter but she had Tommy print the address on the envelope so it looked like a kid writing for a free prize offer from breakfast cereal.

Something bothered me and I didn't know what to do about it. That was that Granston had asked if anyone in the family had received a present. He could have said gift, memento, or had anyone received something for safe keeping or anything like that. But, he had used the word present. I hated to even think about it but it seemed that he had read my first letter to Justin, or had talked to someone who had read it.

It wasn't until a couple of days later when I had time to examine the knife again. I took it back in the tall grass under the big oak tree north of the barn. For the hundredth time I examined it in every detail. I knew the bone-handle was not bone but metal and the outline of the shank was visible at the butt end of it. The metal of the shank was different from the handle so its rectangular shape was clearly visible at the back and was perfectly flush with the end of the handle. All at once I noticed something. It took a minute to verify what I saw. But, yes, it was really the case that the shank was thicker at the very back of the knife than at the base of the blade where it went into the handle—not much, but enough to see if a person looked carefully. Once I had verified the condition to my satisfaction it was clear that what I saw at the back of the handle was not part of the blade but a different piece of metal.

I wondered if the piece at the back would come out. I got up and went to the pump house. The machinist's vice had been moved from the workshop in the barn to the pump house. First I thought the suspected separate piece would fall out if it were jolted. I put a small block of wood in the vice and with a saw cut a shallow groove in it so when I hit the end of the knife handle on it the shank would be over the groove. After several attempts of slamming it down as hard as I could it still hadn't budged.

Running out of ideas I thought it might be possible to push it in a little and loosen it up. Maybe there was some corrosion or dirt making it stick. I placed the knife in the vice blade down with a piece of lath on each side so the jaws wouldn't scratch the blade. There was a short stump of a tree in the corner used for a stool. I moved that over so I could stand above the knife handle. Using a brass punch so I wouldn't damage the shank, I pressed down on the rectangular piece in the rear of the handle. Nothing. I leaned on it with most of my weight. Still nothing. Well I'd gone this far, might as well go to the last resort. I held the punch in place and whapped it with a hammer.

Wow! The rectangular piece popped out a quarter of an inch. I had unlocked the secret. It would not come out any further by pulling with my fingers but with a pair of pliers I was able to slide out a rectangular slip of metal. Sure enough it had a rectangular slot milled through its flat side. My hands were shaking a little because I was getting close to the mystery since there was what looked like a little rectangular metal can in the slot. I pushed on the under side of it with my finger to push it out the other side and had it out. I held it in my hand. Three-eights of an inch wide, a quarter of an inch thick and a couple of inches long. There was a notch at one end that looked like it was made for a person's fingernail. I tried and the lid came off.

In the light from the window there were glossy strips in it. From the negatives we got with the snap-shots from mom's camera I could see they were film. They had to be microfilm. From what I could tell there were at least a dozen two inch strips. Holding one up to the light I could see they were negatives of what appeared to be document pages with a clear line between them, six or eight to a strip. So that was the secret of the knife. It contained secret documents that had been microfilmed. But, I had no way of reading them.

The film would have to wait because I had more immediate concerns. Leaving out the odd little can of microfilm I pressed the rear shank back into the knife. It went in until there was a quarter of an inch still sticking out. I tapped it with the hammer. There was a strong spring that pushed back. With a harder rap it latched into it's original place. Oh, oh. There were scratches on the metal from the hammer. Dad had a selection of used pieces of sand paper in a small box so I selected first a medium grit one and rubbed until the scratches were gone. Then using a worn piece of the finest grit I worked away until the end of the knife looked like it originally did. After a half hour of worrying away at the end of the knife all signs of my tampering were erased.

I wrapped the little can in my handkerchief, put it in my pocket and returned the knife to its hiding place in the barn. Now if things got crazy, I could give the knife to anybody, though I liked it and would hate to part with it.

After supper when the chores were done I wandered around the yard thinking. Up until this day, all of the things that had happened were odd and scary but mostly behind us—except for our visitor a couple of days before. I could always imagine the knife was special only as a keepsake to someone. But now there was no avoiding the fact that men had died for that little can of film, and I had it.

This put me back to where I was when I couldn't tell anyone about the fight in the woods and I didn't like that at all. Maybe nothing else would happen and the film would be forgotten. After all, it was already at least six years old. But, if Granston was looking for it, it must still be valuable.

Would it be wise to write a letter to Justin and tell him I knew what was special about the knife? There was no question that I had to warn him that someone had read my first letter, though I didn't know how I could. I couldn't decide because in his last letter he said to expect visitors and to tell no one. If Granston came because he or someone else had read at least my first letter it might be dangerous to say anything about what I had found.

CHAPTER 26

I decided to write a letter to Justin and then figure out whether or not to sent it, or how to send it.

Dear Justin,

A couple of days ago a man calling himself Jarvis Granston come to the farm. He was looking for you. We think he was the one whose medical records were mixed up with yours at the VA Hospital. We also thought he was dead. From a question he asked I am almost positive he had read my first letter to you. I don't know if he read any of our other letters. Some relatives will visit this Sunday. I'll try to have one of them mail this from another town. If my letters are being intercepted on my end that will solve it. If they are being opened on your end, they'll know about this letter, too.

Sincerely,

Jamie

The relatives were cousins, actually, the father was my dad's first cousin and his son, a year older than me, was my second cousin, I think that's the way it worked. They didn't visit very often, but the second cousin and I got along well. We both made model airplanes and he had gotten gas motors before me and I wanted to have him tell me all he could about them. They were from The Cities, which for us were Minneapolis and St. Paul, but they were never referred to as anything but The Cities.

Regarding the letter, I'd try to convince him that the letter was to a pen pal, and I was trying to fool him into thinking I was in The Cities when I mailed it. I addressed the envelope and put a stamp on it. But before writing "Sincerely" I was trying to decide if I should say anything about the secret of the knife. This was Friday so I'd wait

By Sunday morning I had decided to say nothing to Justin about having solved the mystery of the knife so I finished the letter and sealed the envelope. A little before noon my cousin, Larry, and his family arrived. It was the four of them, his mom and dad, Larry and his sister Nettie a year or two older than Larry. She was pretty and always wore nice clothes. He and I had great technical discussions about model airplanes. One would have thought we were descended from the Wright Brothers.

It turned out that he had moved on to larger engines. The first ones were on the smaller end of the scale as those things went, and were hard to start, something I was well aware of. Since he had no place to fly free flights his were all U-Control and bigger engines were the fad of the day.

When I told Larry about the letter he was all too happy to be part of the conspiracy of deceiving my pen pal. He was that kind of guy. They lived in a well to do suburb to the west of Minneapolis and I always thought he suffered from having a little too much money.

During the last week of August a letter arrived for dad. The envelope looked like one of the regular Department of Agriculture letters. After dinner dad opened it by tearing off a narrow strip of the short end of the envelope like he always did and pulled out the contents.

"Oh! Look at this," he said in surprise. "The letter is from Leonard Haas. I wonder why he used a Department of Agriculture envelope."

As he unfolded the letter a small picture fell out. After reading the letter he looked at the picture and then handed it to mom. "He says that's what the guy, Jarvis Granston, looks like. What do you think?"

Mom took the picture and looked at it. She shook her head as she passed it to me.

"Nope. I don't think so," I said.

Mom continued, "It's a picture of a younger man like it was taken from a high school year book, but even so I'm sure that's not him."

Dad was staring at the end of the letter. "He says here that it appeared your letter had been opened and resealed. What do you suppose that's all about? And, that's why this letter came in an Agriculture Department envelope. There's even a similar postage paid envelope included for a reply."

Mom looked at the return envelope. "That's not the address where we sent the last letter to Haas."

We sat in silence for a bit. "Why would he come here and use a false name? What could he possibly accomplish by that?" Mom asked as if she were talking to herself and didn't expect an answer.

But, Tommy answered, "Because he wanted to see what we'd do. And you sent a letter to the FBI. That tells them you know someone at the FBI and that his visit was disturbing to you."

Dad was looking at the picture again when he said, "I wonder who opened the letter? Was in here in Deep Woods or in the FBI office."

"I'll bet it was here," I said. Of course, I knew, or at least strongly suspected, my letter to Justin had been opened so it had to be here in Deep Woods.

"Yeah," Tommy said. "The FBI has all kinds of stuff to do that's more important than us. And, all the people that work for them must have had all kinds of checks made on them to see that they're honest."

"Okay," dad said. "If it's in Deep Woods, who would it be?"

Tommy was good at sneaky stuff so I expected he'd have the best ideas. "It has to be our mailman. The mail he picks up he throws in a box in his car. I've seen him do it. When he gets to the post office I suppose the box gets dumped out and sorted by all kinds of people. So, once it gets to the post office there'd be no way any special person would be sure of seeing it. And then if he did spot it, he'd have to slip it in his pocket without anyone noticing. The mailman on our route is alone in his car so he could do anything he wanted. He could keep it over night and throw it in the box in his car the next day. So it gets delivered a day later than normal. Who'd know?"

Dad was shaking his head. "I don't know. We've had the same mailman for years and this seems like some kind of plot. I can't imagine he was spying on us for years to look for one letter that may never come."

"Wait a minute," mom said. "Remember a month or two ago we were wondering if we had a new mailman because we were getting some of the neighbors' mail and they were getting some of ours?"

"Yeah," I said. "Do you suppose it was about the time we went to Itasca State Park?" I thought I had to start them thinking some of these things were connected.

"Why would that make a difference?" dad asked.

"Remember the Indian, Red Feather, where we had our picture taken? The reason I talked to him was because Justin mentioned an Indian by that name. He said Red Feather was his grandfather. But, that didn't mean he was his real grandfather like we think of it. That's because they look at all old men as grandfathers. A few days after our trip I wrote a letter to Justin. Then before long a man shows up calling himself Jarvis Granston but that's not his real name. After all these years there has to be some connection to that Indian and Justin that got this all started."

"It even meant changing our mailman so they could be watching our mail," Tommy interjected. "And that means we can't mail any letters, even the return envelope that came in the letter today, in the mailbox. If they went to all the work of changing our mailman so they could watch our mail, he probably takes all of our mail home with him and makes sure it's not something he's looking for. That may look like a regular Department of Agriculture envelope to us, but being in the post office system he, or they, could find out if the address is really associated with agriculture."

Mom was looking worried when she spoke. "Tommy and Jamie, after the shootout you said the man, Rango, had yelled at Justin that he wanted *it*, like he knew Justin had some *thing*, something special. And, it seemed the thing was not the counterfeit plates Justin had been making for them. What if there really was something else, a thing Justin hid on the farm and they think it's still here? The man who was here calling himself Granston asked if Justin had given us a present or a similar word like that. I thought he was crazy because Justin worked so hard for what we could afford to pay him. And, besides it didn't seem like Justin's way to give us a gift."

I knew exactly what they were talking about and was a little scared that they had figured this much out. To stop everybody from talking about *it* I said, "Maybe to be sure we should mail the letter back to Mr. Haas from another town."

I was sure dad didn't want to spend that time and expense. He said, "They have a little mailbox in the office of the creamery as a service to the farmers. A lot of them who live on deserted country roads don't like to leave letters in their mailboxes. I could start mailing some of our letters there, but not all of them. The regular ones like the light bill have to go in the mailbox like always so the mailman doesn't realize we're on to him. If we're wrong and it's someone in the post office getting our letters, that won't help, though."

Dad leaned back. "I never realized what all of you went through when I was in the hospital. That must have been real hard. I wonder what Justin knows about all of this. We have no reason to suspect him of anything bad because he sure helped us, but he might know something. We'll answer Haas's letter saying the photo isn't the man who visited us using the name of Jarvis Granston. We'll have to see what happens next."

CHAPTER 27

After Labor Day school started and I was in the public school. It was different in that we changed rooms and teachers for each subject. I didn't mind that because it eased the boredom, and I had a mix of good and not so good teachers. I liked math class the best not because of the teacher or the subject matter but because of one of the other students. Her name was Emily LaNell. I sat in the row of chairs nearest the windows and she sat two rows further in and two seats further toward the front. As a result she was in my line of sight to the center of the blackboard. It was a few days before I realized that I spent far less time looking at the teacher and the backboard than I did looking at Emily. She was cute as a button. Her hair was very black and had a natural sheen to it. Her face was well proportioned with a hint of a turned up nose. When she smiled it lit up the room—anybody could see that.

If you think seventh grade boys don't notice girls, you're wrong, they do, some girls, anyway. It's just that for boys that age it was like a dog chasing a car, we wouldn't know what to do with it if we caught it.

Of my teachers, I liked Mr. Beecher the best. He taught a class that was a mixture of health, first aid, and science. The class was officially called Health, but I think he wanted to be a science teacher because he always went into a lot of detail about things like how the blood circulation system in the body worked. He added quite a bit of material that wasn't in our text book. He was interesting and the kids paid attention.

He even looked like a science teacher, or what I imagined a science teacher would look like. He was about thirty, average height, five foot, ten or so, but he was a little pudgy so he seemed shorter. He had a round face that always appeared slightly flushed, and he wore wire frame glasses. He spoke from his diaphragm so his voice was a deep baritone that you could hear a block away. His attire was standard in that he wore a white shirt and narrow dark necktie with either of two cardigan sweaters. One was brown with leather patches on the elbows and the other was blue with no patches. The most appealing thing about him was his good-naturedness. When he set up an experiment for class it seldom worked the way it should have, but in a dry humor way, he'd say it was through experiments that didn't work that we learned the most. I suppose it was true because years later the things I remembered most about junior high were his demonstrations that hadn't worked.

When he got to the subject of personal hygiene, diseases and micro-organisms, I was surprised at how many kids didn't understand germs and some didn't even think they existed. Mr. Beecher tried in many ways to convince the nonbelievers that germs were both good and bad. Some were beneficial to us and some made us sick. But, he could see he wasn't getting through to some of the hard cases. But, he was not about to let such a challenge go without a fight. The next day when we came into class we saw a microscope setting on the teacher's desk.

"Today," he began, "I will prove to you that germs exist. Here is a beaker of water and here is some wilted lettuce from my garden. I will mash up the lettuce and put it in the water, see? And, then I'll stir it up. Now this is a microscope," he said pointing to the instrument on his desk. "It is used to magnify small things so we can see detail that our normal eyes can't make out." He went on to describe how it worked with diagrams on the black board, and pointing to parts on the microscope.

That microscope had a turret on it with three lenses for different magnifications. First he pulled a hair out of his head and laid it between two glass slides. Then he had the whole class, all twenty of us, come up and one by one look at the hair. There were amazed exclamations from many of the students. It was barbed on the edges and looked as big as an axe handle.

When everyone was seated again he continued. "The hair you looked at was using the smallest magnification. I did that to show you how much the microscope can magnify things. To see germs we'll need the largest magnification. So, let us begin." With an eye dropper he took some water from the beaker with the lettuce in it and put a drop on the slide and then put another small slide on top of it.

A hand in the back. "Why do you put a second slide on top?"

"If I didn't do that the drop would be too thick. The microscope only focuses on a very thin area. If the specimen is too thick the germs will swim up and down and be out of focus most of the time. When they are out of focus they will appears as fuzzy blobs. You'll see in a minute."

He rotated the turret to the highest magnification, looked through the microscope, adjusted the focus and the light that was shining up from below. When he was satisfied, he had the class come up again so each of us could take another look. This time everyone was impressed. He had to remind everyone that their time was up because nobody wanted to stop looking.

As we were taking our turns he said, "If you will notice there are more than one kind of microorganism that are easy to tell apart. Some swim around rather fast, others only wiggle a little."

As interesting as the germs were, what I saw was a means to read the secret microfilm. I needed to get private access to that instrument. I was sure the lowest magnification would be what I needed. As I was waiting for the rest of the class to take a look my mind was working on ways to get use of the microscope.

My concern was that the microscope was not part of the apparatus normally allocated to junior high and it would disappear when Mr. Beecher had us convinced there really were germs.

The next day it was still there because there was more to come. He began class. "Yesterday we saw some of the little bugs that live on plants. Now, I want to show you we have them in us as well." He held up a test tube and let some spit drop in it. "My saliva is in the test tube. I will add a small amount of distilled water to make it more fluid." This he did. Then with the eye dropper he put a drop on a slide like he had done the day before. After he was satisfied the microscope was focused prop-erly he had us come up again for a look.

This time there were expressions of "Ugh," and "That's awful." When it was my turn I saw why. Whereas the lettuce had two or three kinds of microorganisms that one could define, this specimen had many different kinds, some of which were rather disgusting.

After everyone was seated he continued the class. "Is there still any-one who doesn't believe in germs?" No one raised his hand. "There are hundreds of different kinds of these microscopic organisms in your body and the total number is in the billions. You could not digest your food without them. You would be dead without them. The thing from the health standpoint is there are also many kinds of them that will make you sick. That's why we wash our hands after we go to the bathroom and be-fore we eat."

The rest of the class went on as normal. What if the microscope were gone the next day as it most likely would be? I hadn't come up with a plan of how I could use the instrument so after class I decided on the di-rect approach as the only way.

At the bell I let the others leave ahead of me until I was the only one left in the room with the teacher. I looked at him as said. "Is there any way I could use the microscope? My uncle is a botanist and when he vis-its he tells us about the strange things he can see through a microscope. For example, he said a butterfly's wing was a marvel of natural engi-neering. And, that the eye of a fly is really a whole bunch of little eyes. If I brought in some things could I come in after school and use the micro-scope to look at them?"

I could see I had him hooked. A good teacher was always a soft touch for a kid who wanted to learn things. But, he was thinking. Finally he said, "I have to return this one to Mr. Thomson in the senior high biology lab today. And it has a little too much magnification for what you want, anyway. I'll see what I can do. Tomorrow bring in what you want to look at."

"Okay. Gee, thanks." I ran out so as not to be late for my next class.

After school I frantically looked for things that I could bring to school. The housefly was easy because all I had to do was swat a couple on the porch with the fly swatter. I also wanted a butterfly and a dragon-fly. We didn't have a butterfly net and I didn't have time to make one. Why hadn't I thought of this before? In the shed back in the junk was dad's minnow net that was made out of screen door screen. It would work. It took until suppertime but I finally had several samples of each. Among my treasures was a small metal box with a hinged lid that had held pills or something. I folded up a white rag and put two of the microfilm strips in the folds. On the top were the least damaged butterfly, dragonfly, and housefly. It looked like something a kid would do.

The next day was Friday. After health class Mr. Beecher motioned to me and I stayed behind. When the room was empty he opened the big drawer of the teacher's desk and pointed to what was in it. There was a smaller and clearly older microscope. I smiled and he seemed satisfied.

"After your last class stop in. Do you have some specimens?" I pulled the metal box from my pocket and opened it. "Fine. That will do for a start. I got behind on my lesson plans this week so have to stay to prepare some for next week. I'll get you started then leave you to do your scientific research." He winked.

I had to be off to my next class and as I made my way down the hall and up the stairs to the second floor I was both elated and in deep dread. This would be my chance to look at one of the pieces of microfilm to see if it was really what everybody was after. But, I had to hope I could do it without Mr. Beecher seeing what I was doing.

After classes I was back and he was there. "You're prompt and reliable, I like that."

There was a small table in the corner with textbooks on it. "So we don't get in each others way I'll let you work on that table," he said pointing. Together we stacked the books on the floor against the wall.

He set the microscope on the table and produced a tweezers and a small scissors from the desk drawer. "I'll show how to get started," he said. With the scissors he snipped off a part of the butterfly's wing and laid it on a slide with the tweezers.

"Now, watch how this is done. First you look from the side and lower the optics tube by turning this knob to where it's a little above your specimen. Then you look in the eyepiece and raise the tube until it comes into focus. If you start above the object, you might miss the focus point and keep lowering the tube until it rams into the slide and breaks it. It could damage the lens, too. Do you understand?"

"Yes," I said.

"Okay, let's see what we've got." He looked in the eyepiece and brought it to the focus point. "Oh, yes. That is beautiful. I'm always thrilled to see the beauty of the natural world." He raised and lowered the tube very slightly as he turned the little knobs to move the stage. I was beginning to think I'd never get a chance to look at my butterfly.

Finally, he stepped back and let me look. "Remember," he said. "Due to the way the optics work, everything is reversed. So if you move the stage to the right it will appear to be going to the left in the eyepiece."

That reversal of things took a bit of getting used to as I got started. "Yeah," I said. "There is detail I never thought was there. The wing isn't slick and smooth like I thought. It looks fuzzy. I wonder how that helps him fly?"

"The first of many wonders to come. Enjoy yourself. I'll be here for at least another hour so don't hurry." With that he went to the desk and started to work. By turning my head inconspicuously I could keep an eye on the clock.

There was a stool against the wall that was the right height for looking in the microscope so I moved it over and settled in. I was so engrossed by what I saw I hoped I wouldn't forget about the microfilm. The first half hour went fast as I carefully cut off pieces of each of the insects to look at. Mr. Beecher finally said, "How are you doing?"

"It seems to get better and better all the time. I'm going to ask for a microscope for Christmas." He chuckled a little and went back to work.

The moment of truth was upon me. I lifted up a fold of the cloth and with the tweezers took out one of the strips of microfilm and placed it on the slide. It was warped so I placed a second slide on top. After lowering the tube looking from the side I watched through the eyepiece until it came into focus. It was perfect with a half page visible and easily read-able. But it was wrong. Oh, yes. It was up-side-down. I slipped off both slides and turned them around. Now, it would be right.

No! Still wrong. The letters were right side up, but were backwards left to right. Wouldn't the microscope work after all? I couldn't read anything like this. Then I remembered the counterfeit stamp plates. It was like them. Oh! Now I had it. It was no longer up-side-down as in away from me and close to me, but up-side-down as in the under side and the top side had to be reversed. Now. Yes. It was right.

Now the reversal of the left to right motions of the stage made a difference. With the insects there really was no left or right. Here it was exacting. I moved the stage along the strip of film until it came to its stop. All of the documents looked official in one way or another. Then I went back and settled on one page and started reading.

CHAPTER 28

At the very top of the page was the presidential seal with some standard writing. The first real part of the document was the date.

Date: January 5, 1944
Subject: FBI Investigations
To: Chief of Staff

The FBI has been useful to us up until now but their investigations must be kept within the bounds we set. It would not do to have them stumble upon the revolution in American society that we have planned. And, the closer to fulfillment we get, the more important it will be to keep a rein on that agency. I will order Hoover to supply you a weekly list of the more important investigations he has on-going. If he appears to be getting close I'll have him stand-down on this or that project. It will be necessary, of course, to have him successfully apprehend and prosecute a communist now and then.

In this vein there is a man, Alger Hiss, in the State Department that is doing good work for us and I like him. However, he has this against him. In May of 1942 the FBI interviewed the defector Whittaker Chambers who named Hiss as a communist. For the present I want him kept on the team, but if his connection to our close collaboration with the Russians comes out we'll have to cut him loose.

Franklin D. Roosevelt
President
Original to addressee one file copy.

It seemed this document was real. I wouldn't know if the signature was the president's but everything else seemed right. I knew J. Edgar Hover was the head of the FBI—everybody knew that. The name Alger Hiss was on the radio news a lot last winter. From this memo it appeared that turning over the microfilm to the FBI wouldn't do any good. If they tried to do something with it, it seemed like the president would stop them.

Turning the knob the opposite direction I back tracked and stopped at a page with Top Secret stamped on it.

It was from Louis Howe whoever he was.

Date: March 4, 1944
Subject: Manhattan Project Back Door
Mr. President:

Our Back Door project is functioning well. On nearly a weekly basis reports about progress on the Manhattan Project are being forwarded to Raymond. As a result, the Soviets are getting information as soon as we generate it. The primary sources, Robert Oppenheimer, Enrico Fermi and a few others are transferring virtually everything.

We have opened a new channel, one we have been developing for several months. It involves Julius Rosenberg. His information is good but limited in volume due to his connection to the project. We use what we get from Rosenberg to corroborate our main sources. So far there have been no contradictions.

As we have discussed, there will come a time when Back Door will become known or at least highly suspected. The principles have such a high international reputation it would not be good to expose them. I suggest an unknown like Rosenberg be sacrificed if the need arises.

I will keep you appraised if difficulties develop on this project.
Louis Howe

I wasn't sure what I was reading but I had heard about the Manhattan Project where they developed the atomic bomb during the war. As I re-read this page a voice startled me.

"You must have discovered something real interesting."

It was Mr. Beecher. I had been so engrossed in the film that I had forgotten where I was.

"You haven't changed a specimen for fifteen minutes."

Without looking up I heard the scrape of his chair as he got up and could tell by his voice that he was coming toward me so I turned the knob to another page that I hoped would not be important because I knew he'd ask to have a look.

"Can I have a look?"

I had lain awake last night thinking something like this would happen so I was somewhat prepared.

"Sure, I suppose if you want to. It's not really very interesting."

"What is it?"

"It's a piece of microfilm. You see, I got a *Junior FBI Kit* for Christmas a couple of years ago. It had a booklet with it. In one section it showed how to take fingerprints off a door knob. That didn't work very well. In another it described this piece of microfilm that was included with the kit since microfilm is used by spies. The only problem was the little magnifier included wasn't much good. I was curious about what was on it so I put it under the microscope. It looks like they must have watched a spy movie the night before they made it."

He was standing beside me. "Can I see?"

"Sure I said," getting off the stool knowing I really had no choice since he had gone to the trouble of getting me the microscope.

He bent over the eyepiece and turned the knob to move the film along. At one place he stopped a long time. Finally. He looked me squarely in the eye with a very serious expression on his face. "Do you have more of these?"

I showed him the other piece and he placed it between the slides and moved it along by turning the knobs. He didn't dwell on this strip as long as the first one. He must have seen it was more of the same type of documents. He looked at me again and in a whisper asked, "Where did you get these? I mean really. They didn't come from a toy. I'm almost certain that document from Howe is authentic. And, it's stamped Top Secret." He said the last two words louder for emphasis.

"What's Top Secret," a voice from behind us said.

We both flinched and turned. It was Mr. Marshall, the junior high principal. "What's going on?"

I knew Mr. Marshall from the junior high assembly at the start of school. He was of slight build, not more than five feet six and at least fifty years old. His hair was thinning and streaked with gray. He wore horn rimmed glasses that helped hide his bushy eyebrows though there was no way to hide his over sized ears. His complexion was slightly dark, but not from being in the sun. He was wearing a brown slightly crumpled suit like he always did.

Mr. Beecher turned and sat on the stool with his back to the microscope as he explained and I didn't say anything. "A few days ago, in health class, I used a microscope to show the students what germs looked like. It was a good teaching aid. They were impressed. Well, Jamie here was the only one to grasp the idea that a microscope would be good to look at other things, too. He asked if he could bring in specimens of insects and use the microscope. The microscope we used to look at germs was too powerful for that so I borrowed this old one from the biology lab. I had lesson plans to put together today so I was here keeping an eye on him as he looked at butterfly wings and dragonfly eyes."

"Is that top secret?"

"I guess we got a little carried away. Jamie thought it would be neat if we discovered that dragonflies were powered by small gas motors. I suggested that if we did and wrote a report about it the Federal Government would stamp our report Top Secret and file it someplace where it would never be seen again."

Mr. Marshall looked at me, "If dragonflies had gas motors don't you think someone would have found a dragonfly gas station by now?"

Mr. Beecher said, "There you go. Try to have a serious scientific discussion and someone has to come and spoil it with common sense."

We all laughed.

Mr. Marshall started to the door of the room. "I have to leave early today and it seems like you two are the last ones. Leave by the west door and be sure it's locked."

"I'll see to it," Mr. Beecher said.

Mr. Marshall stopped at the door. "I don't want to find out you two have been fighting over whose turn it is to look."

Before either of us could reply he was gone.

"He's an all right guy," Mr. Beecher said.

His trusting manner bothered me. In little more than a whisper I said, "Mr. Marshall might be an okay guy, but finding us here using a microscope may make him suspicious if he's working for them. The door was open, and there was no reason it should have been closed, but we don't know how long he stood outside the door listening. If he had heard me mention microfilm he might have been curious until you said Top Secret. That's when he came in and wanted to know what was going on. You explained about saying Top Secret but nothing about microfilm."

Mr. Beecher didn't seem to have heard me because he asked, "Now, to a more serious matter, where did you get the microfilm?"

I didn't know what to say so I tried to change the subject a little. "Why would you care where I got it?"

"I'm sure you have heard about all the communists that are supposed to be in our government."

"Yeah. Dad talks about it sometimes."

"In February there was a famous case about Alger Hiss, who was mentioned on the document about the FBI. He was high up in the State Department in Washington during and after the war, was a communist spy and there was a big public trial where he was finally convicted of perjury. Have you heard about that?"

"Yeah. Dad said the radio and newspapers couldn't seem to talk about anything else."

"Did you see the document about the Manhattan Project, and do you know what that was about?"

"It's where they made the atomic bomb."

"Okay. Last summer Julius Rosenberg was arrested for giving secrets to the Russians about the atomic bomb project like the document from Howe says. And, it looks like he'll be tried for treason. That's one thing, but if Oppenheimer and Fermi were giving secrets to the Russians, too, that would be very damaging if everybody found out about it. They're national heroes. That memo mentions that, too.

"That memo was written by Louis Howe. Do you know who he was?"

"No."

"He was President Franklin Roosevelt's most trusted advisor."

He paused and looked at me for a long time. "The reason I care is this looks like serious stuff. So, where did you get it?"

"Last year the sister that taught us sixth grade told us there were a lot of communist teachers over here in the public school. Is that true?"

"Yes, and you didn't answer my question."

"Are you a communist?"

"No. You're avoiding my question. You asked to use the microscope to look at the microfilm didn't you?"

I took the slides off the microscope stage and retrieved the second strip of film from between them and replaced both in the metal box. With it safely in my pocket is said, "Yes. Now, you must never tell anyone you know about this. Do you know why?"

"No."

"You have children don't you?"

"Yes, three. What does that have to do with it?"

"If certain people find out you know about the film, they will not hesitate to harm your children to make you tell where it is."

His eyes looked a little strange. I continued before he could say anything, "Those people, I suppose they're communists, will do anything to get this. Several years ago I was given something and was told to hide it so not another single person knew I had it, not even my family. I didn't know why he told me that, but I wondered why it seemed so important. It took a long time before I figured out how to take it apart and find the film. The people who want that thing may not even know about the film, only that the thing is very important. Now we know why."

He was thinking about what I had said with his face screwed up. "Why would they care about it now? None of the documents on those two pieces of film are dated later than 1944. When did you get the thing?"

"In 1944."

He seemed to relax. "Well, then, as interesting as this is I see no reason anyone would care about them now. But, you appear worried. Why is that?"

"Because last August a man using a false name came to our farm looking for it. They still want it."

"How did you know he was using a false name?"

"Because the real man of that name died in 1944."

He spoke slowly as if to himself as he made the connection of the film dated in 1944 and the man dying in 1944, "There is obviously a lot that I don't know about this." Then he perked up, "Are there more pieces of film?"

"Some."

"We can only imagine what's on them. Those documents I looked at came right from the Oval Office of the President of the United States, I'm sure of it. Don't you think you should get them to the FBI?"

I shook my head remembering Justin's warning to tell no one. The document about the FBI being directed by the president to do what he wanted caused me to include the FBI in "no one." "I was warned to tell absolutely no one about this, but now you know. You're the only other person on earth besides me who knows." I thought that might be stretching the truth a little but I had to be sure he wouldn't tell anyone. "If you tell, you're dead and so am I."

"Who warned you? Doesn't he know about the film?"

"No. He gave me the thing and doesn't know what's special about it. I wrote him a letter last summer and I know for sure that they intercepted my letter, opened and read it before he got it."

"And, you assume by *they* we're talking about communists.?"

"I think so. But whoever they are they play rough to the point of killing people."

"How do you know that?"

"Won't tell." I started to leave.

"Wait," he said.

I stopped half way to the door.

"If you'll bring in other pieces of film I'll make the microscope available. What do you say? We should see what else there is."

"Maybe. I'll think about it."

"If you do decide to bring them in, find more bugs and stuff to look at. I'll keep the microscope here until Monday for sure."

"I gotta go; 'have chores to do when I get home."

CHAPTER 29

When I left the school I set off walking fast because I should have been home by now. At the Catholic school I could ride my bike on nice fall days but at the public school there was too great a danger it would be stolen. Not that something like a bicycle stayed stolen for long in such a small town. Stolen bicycles were more borrowed than stolen. Eventually they'd show up, possibly even back at school but they'd be the worse for wear. So, we were warned not to bring a bicycle to school.

I hadn't lied to Mr. Beecher about chores waiting for me at home. But, they weren't normal chores like feeding animals. In fact, there was only one chore, one big chore that I didn't like—picking apples. We still had a pretty big apple orchard, not by commercial standards, but by local standards. My grandfather was a great one for things like that so he had planted a hundred or so apple trees and made quite a business of it in the fall. He'd even load up a truck on Monday morning and go out to peddle apples. They wouldn't see him again until he came home with an empty truck. As a result our farm was known for miles around as a place where people could buy farm fresh apples in the fall. With twenty-five or thirty large trees left we had plenty of apples to sell if we could get them picked.

There was a saying that a person needed only to like to pick apples to be an good apple picker. Well, I didn't—didn't matter. It was my first introduction to a rule that I learned with considerable prejudice years later in the Army. It was a case of mind over matter—they didn't mind and I didn't matter.

As soon as I had my clothes changed I took off almost running to the apple orchard which was across the road that ran through our property to the south of the house, but the trees bordered on the road. Some days when I got there dad would already have twenty bushels picked. He'd haul them to the house and park the car outside. The whole shed was full of apples ready to sell. The best business came on weekends as one would guess. So, this being Friday it was important to have a good supply. Whether or not dad was picking there were always some empty bushel baskets left in the orchard for us.

Picking apples was a more exacting activity than most people realized. The apple had to be grasped and turned half-way up-side-down so the stem would bend and snap off where it connected to the tree. If the apple were pulled off the tree it would pull off the end of the little branch from which it grew. Those ends were where the apples next year would grow so if they were pulled off there would be no crop the following year. Then the apples had to be carefully place in the pail so as not to bruise them. A bruise would soon produce a rotten spot which would in a short time ruin the whole apple and those around it. It was a lot like handling eggs.

My problem with apple picking arose mostly because I was impatient when things didn't work right. Setting up the ladder was where that was most evident. There were always branches in the way and thwarted my attempts to get the ladder where I wanted it. I suppose if I were a full grown man like my father I'd have been strong enough to handle the ladder more easily and also would have learned how to maneuver it to avoid offending branches.

The previous fall this resulted in a situation that in later years I looked at as humorous though it was anything but that at the time. There was a limb hanging heavy with apples and that was good because I could expect to pick several pails full of apples without moving the ladder. The ladder I was using was the upper section of a wooden extension ladder so it was something I could handle but with difficulty. I got the ladder set up and the top of it was just long enough to reach the limb of my choice. It was easy to set up the ladder, too, because this particular limb hung out over empty space—there were no other branches to interfere. It looked like my lucky day. When we picked we had a hook made out of a heavy piece of wire attached to the pail's handle so we could hang the pail on the ladder or a nearby branch. That was so one hand was free to pick apples while we hung on to something with the other so you wouldn't fall.

With the ladder in place I climbed up and hung the pail on the limb. Filling the pail went fast because the apples were so plentiful and close at hand. However, when I lifted the hook of the full pail off the limb I noticed something disturbing. The branch started to rise up since some of its load had been transferred to the pail. And, if I let it rise as much as it was inclined to do, it would go high enough so it would be above the top of the ladder. With no branches under the ladder it had a clear path to fall all the way to the ground. I held the branch down with one hand so I could hang the pail back on the limb.

What to do? I saw few options. Being impatient I took the obvious route. I unhooked the pail while holding down the limb with my other hand. Then I backed down the ladder as far as I could. Letting my hand slide off the limb proper and letting it catch on a small branch I got another step down before the branch snapped off. Then I climbed down as fast as I could while the ladder was falling. I made it the ground, did the best I could to set the pail upright on the ground and rolled as I hit. About half the apples spilled out and were bruised. That's the way it was in the fast world of apple picking.

As one might assume picking apples was piece work. We got fifty cents a bushel for crabapples, and twenty-five cents a bushel for large apples. We were definitely not paid by the hour. My dad was more than happy to pay his sons for work, but there was no point in being dumb about it.

The other thing I didn't like about picking apples was it was boring. Fill up a pail, empty it in a bushel basket and fill it up again, and again. The Saturday before I was picking apples in a big tree close to the road. As cars came along I'd lob an apple out of the tree top at them. I hadn't gotten the hang of leading a moving target so the apples always fell behind the car which was a good thing, I suppose.

My attention was drawn to the telephone wires that ran right through the branches of the tree. Over time the tree had grown and the telephone company hadn't allocated the resources to trim trees. I thought at first I might get an electrical shock if I touched one of the wires. But, since the leaves and small branches were touching them with no apparent ill effect it seemed safe enough. So I cautiously touched the end of my finger to a wire for an instant. Nothing. Good. Taking a large apple I sawed it back and forth on the wire until the groove was a little past center. I knew I needed more weight under the wire or the apple would tip over and fall off.

After pushing the apple out as far as I could reach from the ladder it was hardly clear from the leaves of the tree. That wasn't good enough. I climbed down and searched around for the longest stick I could find. With it I climbed the ladder and using the stick pushed the apple out from the tree so it was clearly visible from the road. Immediately I did another one the same way pushing it out so the two were a foot apart. If I had done only one, a passersby might think it was a freak of nature. Two clearly, at least to me, indicated intelligent intent.

A few day later at supper dad said in a deadpan voice, "Even apples on the telephone wires." He didn't look at me and nothing else was ever said about it. I considered it a great compliment.

By Saturday I decided it would be a good idea to look at all the pieces of microfilm so on Sunday I chased around and caught several kinds of bugs, flies and moths. As I was leaving health class on Monday I mentioned off handedly to Mr. Beecher that I had some more bugs. He knew what I meant.

When I arrived after classes he was waiting. He, like a lot of people, had a 35mm camera and a slide projector. It was the slide projector that he had brought to school with him.

"Do you know what a slide projector is?" he asked.

"Yes," I said. "My uncle who told me about the insects has one. He travels a lot and when he comes he shows us slides of the places he's been and of relatives in other cities he has visited."

He nodded. "I thought we might try to read the things you have by projecting them. Since a normal slide is not as wide as the strips are long I made a special slide and we'll have to see how it works."

He had moved the table I had used the time before back from the wall about six feet. I opened my box of bugs and using the tweezers picked them out and placed them on a white sheet of paper. Then I opened the fold of the cloth and lifted out a strip of film and placed it on the paper, too. He took the tweezers and put the film in the modified slide letting the edge of the cardboard frame of the slide hold it in place.

"It looks like we won't see the page on each end," I said.

He nodded. "But, this will be good enough to see if the idea works at all. If it does we can slide the film to the left and right on my little invention to read what's on the ends of the strip of film." Before he put the slide with the strip of film attached into the projector he opened a box of slides, put one in the machine and turned it on. It was a picture of a butterfly. "I took some of these last summer to see how much detail I could capture on normal film," he said. "We'll always have one of these in the opposite side of the slide holder so if someone comes in unexpectedly I can quickly slide it over and we'll be looking at butterflies. That's a pretty good shot of a monarch, don't you think?"

I agreed it was and hadn't thought about someone breaking in on us and could see it was a good idea, and told him so.

Now, he put in the modified slide and slowly slid it in front of the lens. We were projecting onto a light yellow wall so it was okay since we were only looking at black and white, anyway.

It was surprising how clear the letters were in the documents. By walking up so I was a couple of feet from the wall we could read them clearly. "That is some very high resolution film they were using," he said.

We had to change places so one of us was near the projector at all times in case someone came in. "Can you make it any bigger, so we can read it from the projector?" I asked.

"Sure," he said. "I can make it bigger, but to do that I have to move the projector further away from the wall so standing at the projector they will look the same size. And the letters will become less sharp the more it's magnified. I'd say, what we have now is about as good as it gets."

"It's better than squinting through a microscope," I said.

I had brought in four different strips today and we looked at all of them. There was stuff about the conference at Tehran, Iran at the end of November 1943 that was attended by FDR, Churchill, and Stalin. It told about how FDR had passed information to Stalin about the atomic bomb and how he wanted Europe divided up after the war. Apparently, Churchill was left out of most of that. He thought he was an equal player, but wasn't because of all the stuff that was going on behind his back.

One memo was dated in February 1944 from FDR to Truman telling him how sick he was and how he hoped he could stay alive long enough to get reelected in the fall. But, if he didn't live to see the end of the war, there were instructions as what to do as far as Stalin and Europe were concerned.

"That's amazing," Mr. Beecher said. "It's only February and he's making plans as though he knew he'd be reelected in the fall."

He came back to where I was by the projector and slid the butterfly slide into view, pulled out the film slide and removed the film with the tweezers and replaced everything in my box. He had warned me not to touch them with my fingers because finger print oils would smudge them.

"What we have here is a complete rewrite of history for the last thirty years. It's too much. I can't see that anyone would believe it and as a result I don't know what we, or you, could do with it. It's all passed now anyway—history."

He was a believer in the authenticity of the documents, I could see that. "Maybe we have to look at the rest of them. There might be something on one of the documents that was planned but hasn't happened yet."

"I can't see how any plans they made back then could still be any good. Too much changes as time goes on and plans have to be changed to account for the things that really happen."

"Then, why are they still looking for the film?"

He shook his head. "I can't imagine other than the film reveals how deeply revolutionary elements have infiltrated the government. Clearly if these were made public people would want answers. Covering it over would take time and resources they would want to use for other purposes."

"We have to look at all of it," I said. "Who knows what we'll find."

"Okay," he said. "But, we can't do this every day. Now many strips are left?"

"We've looked at six so there are ten left. I'll bring in five next time. When?"

"This is Monday. I'd say next Monday but I have to leave right after classes that day so how about in two weeks, that okay? Mondays after classes work the best for me because that's the time I set aside to make lesson plans unless I get behind then I have to stay late other days as well."

"Yeah, unless something comes up."

CHAPTER 30

A week later at supper on Monday Tommy said, "We had a new English teacher today."

"You mean Mrs. Abbot was sick and you had a substitute?" mom asked.

"Nope. His name is Gregory Hindle and he said Mrs. Abbot had quit and he was the new teacher."

"Are you sure?" dad asked. "As far as I know the teachers sign a contract to teach for the whole year and they can't decide to quit any time they want."

"Well, he said he'd be our teacher for the rest of the year."

"I wanted to talk to Marty about the school board anyway. I'll call and see if he's home tonight and go over there for a little while. I'm curious about how those contracts work."

Marty and his wife had been friends of my parents for a long time. He ran a five and dime on main street. They went to dances with mom and dad sometimes. I knew them mainly because we had visited them for supper once. Being Italians, they had served a dozen kinds of spaghetti, macaroni and stuff like that. Of course they had fancier names for them. They had three daughters so I wasn't terribly interested in going to see them. It was boring. Mostly I saw Marty when I went into his store to buy model airplanes. But, he had been picked to be my confirmation sponsor last spring. That was nice but it wasn't as though I knew him.

The next day at supper dad told us what he had learned from Marty. He was intrigued by the story and I wasn't sure why he would be other than if he ran for the school board and won he'd have to deal with things like that, too.

Since he had talked to mom when he got home the night before he was mainly telling Tommy. "I was right in that normally Mrs. Abbot would not have been released from her contract. But there were an extremely odd set of circumstances that led up to it. To start with, her husband works for the County Extension Service here in town."

We all knew what the Extension Service was. The Department of Agriculture that's part of the federal government provided that service mainly to farmers. They were available to give free advice on how to rotate crops, what crops did well in what kind of soil, what breeds of cattle were best for our climate, how to handle insect pests, and all kinds of stuff like that. Normally each county had an office and since Deep Woods was the county seat the office was in town.

"Out of the blue her husband got an offer for a good promotion, but he had to leave immediately. He had only a week to decide if he wanted to take the job and if he did to be ready to start. The new job was in the southern part of the state and he would supervise a group of counties, a whole district.

"Normally his wife would not have been able to quit on a moment's notice like that. But, a couple of days before a resume landed on the superintendent's desk for a well qualified English teacher. He was available after the start of the school year because he had taken a leave of absence from his job in Mankato to care for his ailing father. As a result a replacement had been hired to fill in for him this year. His father unexpectedly died in late August so he was available.

"The superintendent made a bunch of phone calls and his story checked out. And, his references highly recommended him. The school board had an emergency meeting and decided under the circumstances it would be the compassionate thing to do to release Mrs. Abbot from her contract since a qualified replacement was at hand. That's why you have a new English teacher."

After he had been eating for awhile, dad shook his head, "Can you imagine how lucky that woman was, and the man, for that matter, too. She suddenly needs to leave, and he suddenly needs a job. Wow! Those two people must live right." So much for lucky people.

On Friday when we got home from school it appeared that sometimes people made their own luck. The county paper, *The Deep Woods Sentinel*, that was edited and printed in town, came out Thursday afternoon so our copy arrived in the mail Friday morning. Tommy and I had walked home together today as we some times did. Even though we had entirely different interests, we were brothers.

As we walked into the house this carefree sunny day in late September we let the screen door slam behind us. Mom had the latest issue of *The Sentinel* lying open on the kitchen table. "Tommy, come here."

She was pointing to a picture on the second page of the paper. "Is that your new English teacher?"

He glanced at it, "Yeah, that's him."

Then to me. "Jamie, come here. Do you recognize that face?"

I looked it at and for a moment couldn't speak. I looked at mom. She was thinking what I was thinking. Then I looked at the picture again. "That's Jarvis Granston who was here asking about Justin."

Dad had hardly stepped though the door when he came in for supper when mom said, "Look what we found!"

He paused on his way to the sink to wash his hands. "What?"

"Look at this picture in the paper. I noticed it a little while before the boys got home."

He looked at the picture and then at the headline. "So that's the mysterious and lucky new teacher."

"Yes, mysterious," mom said, "but maybe not so lucky. Tommy agrees that's his new teacher, but Jamie and I both recognize him as one Mr. Jarvis Granston. What's going on?"

Dad proceeded to wash his hands, then sat at the table and looked at the paper. After reading the article he said, "That's about what Marty said about him. Why would he be here asking about Justin? And all the way from Mankato. That was quite a drive. And, why use a false name that we might recognize?"

Tommy spoke. "He would have no way of knowing we would connect that name with Justin's dead roommate at the VA hospital."

"Then, why did he use it? He could have said he was John Jones."

Nobody had an answer until mom said, "He must have known Granston, known him well, so he could impersonate him and not get tripped up by hesitating about details if it came to that. But why did he come here and why now?"

"It has to be because of my letter to Justin," I said.

Tommy was ahead of everybody. "Whoever they are, they still want something that is connected to Justin, and they think he left something with our family or on our farm. They managed to get the County Extension Service man promoted so his wife would want to leave. And, they had Granston there ready to take her job. They really want it bad. I wonder what Granston, or I guess we have to call him Hindle, will do to us?" After a pause he added, "Or to me. He's my teacher. Maybe he'll make me fail so he can come out here to help me with my English lessons. But, that'll be hard because English is my easiest subject. I hardly ever get one of the answers on my tests wrong."

Lucky Tommy. None of my classes were easy for me. Of course while I was out shooting sparrows Tommy was in the house doing school work. Darn it, he actually liked that stuff.

After we ate dad said, "We should send the newspaper clipping and what we know to Haas. I'll write a letter tonight and like it or not I'll have to drive to another town to mail the letter. I hate to do it tomorrow because I want to be around to sell apples. But it seems we should do it as soon as possible. If I leave right after breakfast I'll be home before they start to come."

Mom said, "Stop in town and buy another paper so we can keep this one."

He nodded.

That evening I set to work writing a letter to Justin.

The next morning I was ready with my letter and as dad was getting ready to leave I asked if I could come along. He knew I was always jabbering and may have thought it would help to keep his mind off things so he agreed.

When we were on our way to town I told him I had a letter for Justin too, and wanted to send him a copy of the clipping to see if Hindle was the man who had been his roommate. Dad hadn't thought of that but it seemed to him like a good idea. He bought two papers.

As we started down main street I said, "We have to go to Deer Falls to mail the letters."

"That's twenty-five miles and Hansville is only eight. Why not there?"

"Because Deer Falls is a bigger town and I have to buy something. It's really important. I have some stuff to tell you while we're driving. It has to do with what Hindle is looking for."

"Do you know what that is?"

"Yes, because I have it."

Dad jerked the steering wheel a little he was so surprised.

"Please. It's really important," I pleaded.

He turned the wheel and we headed out of town by the other road going to Deer Falls. Mom had given me a scissors to cut out the article so I set about cutting it out of both papers.

"What is it that you have that seems so important?'

"It's some Top Secret microfilm, tiny pictures of documents that came right from President FDR." I continued. "Before he left the day of the shootout Justin gave me something while Tommy went to the house to get a kerchief for him to tie on his head as he rode the motorcycle. He told me to tell no one about it—ever. I hid it and didn't tell. I thought it must be important but I didn't tell because Justin was so insistent that I didn't. He was hurt and I thought he was afraid of losing it if he had to go to a hospital and that he'd come back for it. Well, he hasn't come back so I kept it to myself. After the man calling himself Granston came to the house I was worried."

"Why would that worry you?"

"Because in my first letter to Justin I told him I still had the present he gave me. Granston asked if Justin had given anyone a present. He didn't say gift or keepsake or anything like that. He said present. That's how I knew someone had opened my letter to Justin just like someone opened our letter to Haas. That meant what Justin had given me was really important and my letter to Justin had gotten them looking on our farm for it."

I wasn't sure why but I wasn't going to say anything about the knife, at least not now. "I felt I had to open the package. It might contain a treasure map or something like that. Or, I was wrong about the whole thing and it was something important to only him like a souvenir. When I opened it I found a little metal box two inches long and maybe a quarter of an inch wide and deep. It had a cover with a little catch on the end so it could be pulled off with your finger nail. It contained sixteen strips of microfilm.

"In health class my teacher, Mr. Beecher, used a microscope to show us what germs looked like. I asked if he would keep the microscope in the room for a few days so I could look at butterfly wings and stuff after classes. He did. But, after looking at bugs I looked at a piece of the film. He caught me at it and wanted to look. Now he knows too but I don't think he'll tell anyone. Anyway, the documents are from 1943 and 1944 before Justin came to work for us. They are stamped Top Secret. We looked at six of the pieces and he can't see why anyone would care about them now because they are so old. That means there must be something else on the strips that we didn't look at yet. I can't bring any more to school because it would be too risky. That's why we need to buy a magnifier."

By this time we were starting down the big hill. Along this road headed east you'd be climbing slowly but you wouldn't notice it. Then you'd go up a small hill and all at once you went down one three or four times as high as the hill preceding it. The hill ended in bottom land and then proceeded on its way. We always waited for the big hill when we took this road. Of course, it was only a big hill for flat-landers like us.

Dad didn't know what to say as he mulled it over. "Is that what the shootout was all about? When they mentioned *it*, that must have meant the film. Is that what you think?"

"Yeah. Now that I looked at some of the film it makes sense except that like Mr. Beecher said it seems old now. There must be something else."

As we drove we discussed it. "There is another thing about this," I said. "After Mr. Beecher had seen some of the documents we were talking in hushed voices even though the school was practically deserted. But, he raised his voice when he said Top Secret. It was stamped on some of the documents. At that moment, Mr. Marshall, the junior high principal, came in and asked what we were doing. Mr. Beecher made up a story that Mr. Marshall seemed to accept but he could have been listening at the open doorway for a long time and we didn't know it. It was one week later when Tommy got a new English teacher who is the same man who was out at our farm looking for a present that Justin may have given to us."

Glancing at dad I could see he was worried. "And, Marty, as well as the rest of the school board, thinks it was nothing but luck that caused Hindle to be the new English teacher." After driving in silence for a few miles dad said, "You need a magnifier to read the film. How powerful does it have to be?"

"At school we could read it good with the microscope that had thirty magnification. We could read most of the documents with twenty power, I think. The second time I brought some pieces of film in Mr. Beecher brought in his slide projector like Uncle Ben has. He attached a piece of film to a blank slide. That worked pretty good, too."

"Let's look for a magnifier first. We'd have no need for a projector after this is done."

"What kind of store would sell a magnifier?"

"We'll look for a stationery store. Stamp collectors would want good magnifiers and I think that's where they'd go. Or, we could try a hobby store. If neither of them have it maybe they could tell us who might."

CHAPTER 31

When we got to Deer Falls dad pulled to the side of the street and we put together the letters and sealed them. Then we found the post office and mailed them in the mailbox on the sidewalk. There was a stationery store but their magnifiers were only ten power.

The town had a hobby store that I had been hoping we could visit in any case so that's where we went next. We parked down the block from it and as we approached I saw model airplanes hanging in the windows. Inside more were hanging from the ceiling. There were some real beauties. Of course a lot of them were models of World War II planes but one was of a Piper Cub that was done to scale in minute detail, painted in Piper yellow, of course, with many coats of dope so it looked like a real plane in all respects. We saw them fly over the house quite often so I was familiar with the type. The gas motor was mounted inverted so only the glow plug protruded from the bottom of the cowling and the exhaust port came out the left side. Under the left wing tip was a swivel bar there the control lines attached so it was a U-control model. Other than that it could have been a real plane that I was looking at from a block away. Talk about a kid dropped into fantasy land, it was me.

At that time there were two types of flying models, U-Control and free flight. Radio control was not available for models yet. The U-Control planes were flown in a circle by means of two strings. The pilot held a stick six or eight inches long with one of the strings attached to each end. By how he tipped the stick it pulled on one or the other of the strings. In the plane the strings by means some simple levers made the elevator go up and down—up to increase altitude and down to go down. If the plane were properly powered it was possible to fly the plane in the complete half sphere above the ground. Centrifugal force kept the lines tight when it was overhead.

Free flight was just as the name implied. It would be launched and would fly freely wherever it wanted. Once launched the pilot, and all too often former owner, had no control over it. Of course, some precautions were used. The motor was offset a few degrees to one side so it would fly in a circle when under power, and the rudder was likewise offset so after the motor stopped it would circle back down. They were only flown in wide open spaces at times when there was little wind.

The Piper Cub model would be a U-Control plane because most modelers would not put so much work into a free flight that may disappear forever on the first flight.

Dad had gone to the counter and asked about magnifiers. He called to me and I visibly jerked I was so intent on the airplanes. The clerk had two magnifiers on the counter. One was hand held and intended for use in the field. It had fifteen magnification. The other was larger and had a clear glass skirt on the bottom that was placed over the specimen.

The man said, "This one is primarily used for examining documents. The magnification is adjustable from ten to thirty. It's normally used to determine if documents such as stock certificates or even currency are forgeries. By looking at the way the ink soaked into the paper at the edges of the letters experts can determine things like that. Of course it's perfect for looking at things like insects, parts of flowers and stuff like that. It even comes with a light that is attached so it shines through that hole in the side of the glass at the bottom."

"How much do you want for it?" dad asked.

"It's priced at fifty dollars, but I've had it on the shelf for a long time and want it off my inventory so I'd let you have it for forty."

It was clear this was what we needed so I said, "That's the one I want. It's perfect."

Dad stood back and said. "I don't know. That's an awful lot of money. Maybe we should look around."

"Okay, I'll go to thirty-five, but that's as low as I can go."

Dad looked at me. "If I bought it, Christmas would be very slim for you this year. Do you understand?"

"Yes, I do. But, I have to have it. It's got everything I want. The light and the adjustable magnification are perfect."

"Okay," dad said, "I guess we'll take it."

As we walked out of the store I looked longingly at the model planes swinging from their strings. For thirty-five dollars I could have bought half the models in the store.

As we started the drive back to Deep Woods I could see that if dad had been given to using bad words he would have been using them now. As it was it looked like he was thinking them. Finally he said, "I hope that was not for nothing. I must be crazy."

"You'll see," I said. "You've never seen letters from the president of the United Stated to Joseph Stalin in Russia. You'll see them now. You have no idea how many communists there are in the government. You talk about Joe McCarthy sometimes. Well, he's got nothing like what's on that film. It's terrible."

The rest of the trip home went fast even though we didn't say much. Coming through town I said, "Tommy and I know about this stuff but Mikey doesn't. We should keep him out of it if we can. He might say something at school."

"We can try," dad said, "but it'll be hard. How about this. After you go to bed mom and I'll look at the film."

"Okay. But be sure you use mom's eyebrow tweezers to handle the film so you don't get fingerprints on them. Fingerprints will cause smudges so you can't read them."

Dad nodded.

When we got home mom said we were gone a long time. Dad said we had driven to Deer Falls so I could do some window shopping at the hobby store. She looked at him a little funny but didn't object. We immediately changed clothes and went to feed the turkeys. They were big now and took a lot of feed. We were due to have the big trucks come from the turkey plucking plant in a week to take them away. The price of turkeys was a common topic at the supper table as it always was this time of year.

*　　*　　*

Sunday morning was like most Sunday mornings except as we drove to Mass mom and dad looked tired. Normally I wouldn't have paid any attention but I wondered how late they had stayed up looking at the film. I could tell they had stayed up pretty late.

When we got home dad usually sat in his easy chair and read the Sunday paper while Tommy read the funnies at the dining room table. After Tommy finished I got a turn. Today dad sat down and closed his eyes. Tommy and Mikey had gone outside and mom came in and motioned me over to where dad sat.

"The other two are outside," mom said.

Dad looked at me in an odd way. It wasn't that he was angry with me, it was something else, more like he wanted to accuse me of something. "We looked at all the strips of film. We didn't spend a lot of time on them, but read some of the documents and got the idea of what they were about. By the way, the magnifier worked good even though we both have eye strain. We think we found out why they are still important, though. One of the strips had nothing but lists of names and addresses on them."

"Was that the list of communists in the government?" I blurted out.

Dad shook his head. "It's different. They were called 'sleeper agents.' We couldn't find any place there that term was defined. Obviously it was assumed that the people that used the lists knew what it meant. Each entry included the names and addresses of a married couple, and the name and date of birth of one child. The child's name was always underlined as if it were what made the list important.

"The birth dates ranged from the early nineteen-twenties to the early forties. We didn't look at the complete list but we found none out of that range. The latter date makes sense because the list was dated in 1943 so there would be no birth dates after that. That means when the list was made those children would have been from babies to about twenty. Today they would be six or seven years older or from seven to twenty-seven. If these children are special for some reason it would be important to keep the list secret because most of them are still kids."

"We have to find out what sleeper agent means," mom said.

"Tell Tommy about it. He can go to the library at school during lunch hour. He's good at stuff like that. I'll bet a book about the FBI would have it."

"Or one about communism," dad said.

Monday evening after supper Mikey had wandered off into the living room but just in case Tommy said, "I'm doing a report for English class on sleeper agents. It's really interesting."

It didn't seem that Mikey was interested though at nine years old he might have to be told something about all of this at sometime.

"In the FBI book it talked about sleeper agents in general terms as if any country was doing it to any other country. It seemed like they meant Russia and the United States, though. There was another book about the communist revolution in Russia that had some stuff on this so I'm using some from each book.

"The Communist Revolution in Russia happened in 1917. But 1920 they were in complete control and planned to spread communism all over the world. They knew America would be the hardest and take a long time so they started making long range plans. One part of this was to place sleeper agents, sometimes called deep cover agents, into our country. What they did was give IQ tests to a lot of people. When they found a married man and woman who both scored high they made sure they had children. They took the first boy from them giving them some money in exchange. It's a police state so the people have no rights. If the government wants to take your child, they take it.

"Then they would sneak the child into the U.S. They managed to make a real birth certificate for the baby. That is done with the help of what is called fellow travelers. Fellow travelers are people who believe in communism but don't want to get deeply involved. But, they help out with the cause now and then. So, if a fellow traveler is someone who routinely types out birth certificates, they do a fraudulent one when asked to.

"Now a committed communist couple has a child. They move to a new town so nobody will know that the woman didn't go to the hospital to have a baby. They settle down and raise him like a normal American kid. When he's about twelve or thirteen a friendly uncle begins to stop by to visit quite often. From then on the child is trained—brainwashed—into living a double life. If he's intelligent, as most of them are, he magically gets a scholarship to go to a good college. If he needs tutoring to get though a hard class, he gets it. After graduation these guys normally get jobs in the federal government.

"They are used in two ways. One is to pass secrets on to the Russians. The other is to get into decision making positions and make policy that favors the communists. That's about it."

"That'll make a great paper for class," mom said, "except that you dare not use it. Mr. Hindle will want to know why you chose that topic."

"And," dad said in a whisper, "that's why the list is so valuable, and will remain valuable for as long as we and they live."

"What'll we do?" mom asked.

"One book I looked at," Tommy said, "went into that. One way is for our government to tell those people we know about them so their plan is thwarted. Or, we could keep track of those sleeper agents and make sure they never amount to anything. Another idea is to keep track of them, let them get into sensitive positions and feed them false information to be sent back to Russia. If they get into policy making positions we make sure someone else is there to countermand bad policies they make but let others go through. That way the Russians are not forced into making more deep cover agents that we don't know about."

"I see," dad said. "We, as a country, wouldn't want to tip our hand now. We want them to spend all that time and money thinking their secret is safe."

"I don't mean we as a country," Mom said, "I mean we as a family. We have to send a letter to Mr. Haas and tell him he must visit us, in the middle of the night if necessary. We'll give him the film and he can do whatever he wants with it."

"But," Tommy said, "my English teacher seems to think we have it. What do I do, walk up to his desk and say to get lost because we gave what he thinks we have to the FBI?"

Dad wasn't looking so good. Normally he had all he could handle with worrying about farm prices and not enough rain on top of doing all the work. But, he was in the game. "From what your research shows, Tommy, we should give the film to the FBI so they can make copies of it and then let the communists get it back in some way that they think their secret is still safe."

"What if there are fellow travelers in the FBI?" Tommy asked. "We could give it to Haas and he tells his superiors about it. They say, 'Good work. Sent the film to us.' When they get it they destroy it and nothing's gained."

Dad looked at the table as he spoke, "We wouldn't be in this mess if we could trust our government."

I said, "Yeah. Did you see that one where the guy working for FDR sent all of the atomic bomb secrets to the Russians as soon as we leaned them ourselves?"

"Hey," Tommy said, "when can I look at those things?"

Mom got up and started clearing the table. "Might as well look at them. Maybe you'll see something we missed that'll tell us what to do."

Tommy and I went up to our room. The two of us still slept in the same double bed and Mikey had his own. It was no picnic sleeping with Tommy and I was always surprised that I slept at all. Being young gave a person a certain resilience, I suppose.

I showed Tommy how to handle the film pieces with the tweezers so he wouldn't get fingerprints or dust on them. He was pretty good at things like that when he wanted to be. I was good at fine things because I was always making model airplanes. Tommy made a few airplanes but wasn't really interested enough to become good at it. I had a little homework to do and spent a half hour at the kitchen table.

When I came up to go to bed, Tommy was still looking at the film. He had a tablet beside the magnifier and was writing down the names and addresses of the sleeper agents. He was more tenacious than I was with things like that and it was likely he'd work at it a little each day until he had them all. He said that if they were not exposed we'd hear about them in fifty years. To me fifty years in the future was like saying forever.

CHAPTER 32

The next day was Tuesday. The time we looked at film with Mr. Beecher's slide projector he had said to bring in more pieces on Monday, yesterday, but he had changed it to today. However, I brought no film, only bugs. When I arrived at Mr. Beecher's classroom in the afternoon after classes, he was there.

He smiled at me as I came in. "Here to look at some more insects?" he said in a cheery voice. He was wearing his sweater with the patches on the elbows today.

I nodded. "Is the microscope still here?"

"Yes it is, but we were doing pretty good with the projector last time."

"We have to talk in lower voices. Can we close the door?"

"We could," he said in a whisper, "but it would call attention to this room because all the classroom doors are kept open when no class is going on except when a teacher is reprimanding a student."

"Okay. But, I have only bugs this time. Things have happened so it wouldn't be safe to look at the film."

He looked at me askance but said nothing as he took the microscope out of the desk drawer and went to the table. I opened my little metal pillbox. This time I had mostly ants of various sizes.

"Have you met the new ninth grade English teacher?" I asked.

"Sure. Seems like a nice guy."

"Well, he's a communist and was sent here to keep track of me and my family. They want the . . . ah . . . you know what."

As I spoke I used the tweezers to place a little red ant on the microscope slide. Looking at it I said, "He really has some mean looking pinchers."

"Those are called mandibles. Can I have a look?"

The building was old, and while the exterior was made of brick, the interior was all wood. The floors were two inch wide boards that had been varnished every year for fifty years. I mention that because the floor in the hall outside the room creaked. It might have been the old building shifting as it heated and cooled. However, it might have been caused by someone standing outside the door, just out of sight

"I wonder if the government would classify mandibles as Top Secret?" I said the last words louder than the rest of the sentence.

Mr. Beecher looked up from the eyepiece. "Why would you say . . . ."

"Hold it right there!" a loud voice behind us said. "Don't touch a thing and move away from the microscope."

We both turned to see Mr. Hindle striding across the room toward us. "Stand back. I want to see what you two are so interested in."

Glancing at us to be sure we meant no hostile move, he peered into the microscope. "What's this?" he said incredulously.

"It's the mandibles of an ant. What did you expect it to be?" Mr. Beecher spat back in disdain.

"What else do you have here?" He spied my metal pillbox and lifted out the white cloth spilling my bugs on the table and floor. He unfolded the cloth expecting to find film. When there was nothing but more folds of soft cloth he glared at Mr. Beecher.

Mr. Beecher was struck by what had happened and must have been thinking about what I had said when I first came in the room. But, he had to maintain the part of the injured party, "What gives you the right to barge in here acting like you own the place?"

Hindle was grasping, "There have been some thefts in the school and everyone had been told to keep his eyes open."

Mr. Beecher, still indigent shot back, "It can't be worth much if it's so small it takes a microscope to see it!"

"A couple of weeks ago you were looking at film in here with this kid. Where is it?"

"Wait a minute. Mr. Marshall came in one of the times we were here and we told him what we were doing and he certainly didn't disapprove, he was even encouraging. We're looking at insects. This young man is interested in entomology and as a mater of fact so am I."

"What about the film?"

"The only thing you can be referring to is some 35mm slides we looked at. I took pictures of butterflies over the summer to test my new camera. I brought some of them in to show Jamie, not that it's any of your business."

Hindle drew himself up and said, "Well, make sure that microscope gets back to where it belongs. I doubt you own that, too."

With that he turned and stalked out of the room.

When we were alone Mr. Beecher's mouth dropped open. "Wow! This is serious. He's serious. What happened?"

"As far as we can figure when Mr. Marshall came in that first time he heard you say 'Top Secret.' Even though he was congenial it must have set off all kinds of alarm bells for him. So they got Mr. Hindle in here to find the film."

"How could that be? Mrs. Abbot quit and Hindle was available."

"Yes, but she could not have walked out any time she wanted, she had a contract for the year the same as you do. Her husband received an offer for a promotion but he had to leave at once if he wanted it. So, she asked to be relieved from her contract. She normally would not have been, but Mr. Hindle happened to be available with good references and all that stuff. Do you see?"

He nodded, "They manage to promote the husband so she'll want to leave, and Hindle is ready to take her job."

"I've heard the superintendent checked his references and said he came highly recommended."

"Unless the superintendent is in on it, too." Mr. Beecher stood thinking for a minute. "Hmmm . . . , I wonder if he's even an English teacher."

"Wouldn't know. Seems to me ninth grade English wouldn't be too hard to teach. He could read up on the next day's class at night and go by the book. You know a lot of stuff that you add to make the classes interesting. You wouldn't have to do that."

Mr. Beecher's demeanor changed as he smiled, "You really think my classes are interesting?"

"Yeah, most of the time."

"That's nice to hear. A guy never knows if the extra work is worth it."

"That still leaves the question about why they would want the film. Those documents are historically interesting, but not of any real value now."

"We bought a magnifier and read the rest of the film. There is a reason why it's still important, but you don't want to know that. It's safer for you."

I picked up my bugs, the ones we hadn't stepped on, and put them back in my pillbox. "You can bring the microscope back to the chemistry lab. That magnifier we bought is adjustable up to thirty power and works good for looking at bugs. I brought these in today to see what would happen and now we know for sure."

Mr. Beecher had seated himself in the chair behind his desk and was leaning back thinking. After a bit he said, "That was crazy the way he stomped in here ordering us to stand back from the microscope. Are you sure he isn't working for the FBI or something?"

"I don't know about the 'or something,' but we're in regular contact with the FBI and he's not them."

"You are? You're in contact with the FBI?"

"Of course. Remember that first time you saw the film I said they played rough? Well, that got the FBI involved and they didn't want the local police to know about it. This is a federal matter. I suppose the FBI will visit you sometime. My advice is to answer the questions but don't volunteer information. And, don't tell anybody else about what just happened. What Hindle did would have been okay if he had found the film because in that case he would have been gone tomorrow, and too bad about no ninth grade English teacher. Since he didn't get it he has to stay so don't make it any harder on him than you have to. Act like it didn't happen."

"You're acting awfully grown up about this."

"Yeah. It's been going on for awhile. I have to go now."

A couple days later on Thursday a little before six in the evening a black car drove in the yard. Sandy barked to let us know someone had arrived, but being a warm late September day the kitchen door was open and we heard it. We thought it might be someone wanting to buy apples. I went out to wait on the customer but I recognized the man who got out. It was Mr. Haas. He was wearing a crumpled suit with no tie. It might have been the same one from six years ago, but it seems that one was nearly worn out then, and this one was on its way to the rag bag, too.

"Hello," he said. "And, which one are you?"

"Jamie."

"Yes I remember you. You've grown. I hope things are going well with you."

"Mostly. Except that there are a million commies after us."

He smiled. "Few Americans have had such a time with that crowd as you people."

By this time we were at the house and we went in.

"It's Mr. Haas," I said.

Mom turned, "We expected that you might show up. Fred should be in soon. Have a chair. Have you eaten?"

"I don't want to impose, Mrs. Landon. The reason I arrived at this time of day is I wanted to meet with all of you—both you and your husband and the boys. This seems to be getting serious again and I want to do what is necessary to prevent overt hostility."

"You mean blood shed," mom said.

He nodded. "That, of course."

Dad was walking to the house and glanced at the car and must have noticed that there was no one looking at apples. In the house introductions were made and dad went to the sink to wash up. Mom set a place for Mr. Haas with his back to the window, the place reserved for guests.

Dad sat and immediately asked, "Have you identified our new English teacher, Gregory Hindle?"

"No we haven't, though his story that he taught in Mankato doesn't check out. Without having his resume and the references he listed we can't go any further. We suspect his references are bogus. We are leaving it to your school administration to assess his qualifications as an English teacher. He might actually be one. And at this point, we in the FBI don't want to approach your superintendent for a copy of the resume. Once alerted of our interest, people disappear, change stories or suddenly become afflicted with memory loss. We want things to go along as normally as possible so we learn as much as we can before making arrests."

We had said our before meal prayer without our guest joining us. That was always the dead giveaway as to whether or not a new arrival was Catholic. Mr. Haas ate with enthusiasm since it was roast beef with boiled potatoes and gravy. It was late in the year for garden vegetables but since it hadn't frozen yet we had fresh sliced tomatoes.

"Would you make arrests?" dad asked.

"Certainly, in time. The ruckus Senator McCarthy is making about communists is making the American public anxious for us to do something about the problem."

There was silence as we ate until mom said, "What you said sounds a little funny. Are you saying that if Senator McCarthy were not stirring things up you would not be interested in finding communists?"

Haas knew he had been caught in what seemed like a political statement and he immediately responded, "Not at all. Please understand, that often investigations take a long time and if we are forced to make arrests based on political pressure we may jeopardize long running operations before we have enough evidence to get convictions."

All I could think of was his reply was nicely done. An excellent statement that sounded good without saying anything. But, it made me wonder ever so little about where his loyalties lay.

He accepted a second cup of coffee after supper. We were all wondering why he had come so all eyes were on him.

He began, "I suppose you're wondering why I made the trip up here. As you recall the first time I came my main reason was to sort out why hospital charges were being made on behalf of a dead man. But, just as important was to discover why medical records had been mixed up, deliberately as it appeared, and who was the man who received the medical care. We established it was Justin Merchner as stated on the billing and he wasn't dead as the records showed.

"After all the time, you, Mrs., Landon called me and said a Mr. Granston visited you asking about Justin Merchner. His name came up six years ago and he seems to be the man who died rather than Merchner. You verified that the man posing as Granston did not match the picture I sent you which, by the way, was a picture of Granston. Then you sent the newspaper clipping showing the Granston who had visited you and who also presenting himself locally as a teacher under the name of Gregory

Hindle. That man is unknown to the FBI. Obviously you know something about why this is happening and I want you to fill me in."

Dad spoke. "We made a trip to Itasca State Park as a family outing. They had a display of authentic Indian culture. We asked an old Indian there about Justin and it turned out that he knew him. He gave Jamie an address and Jamie sent him a letter. We are pretty sure the letter was intercepted and opened. Shortly after that Granston showed up here."

Haas nodded. "We have been unable to locate Mr. Merchner. Where is he now?"

I ignored the question and said, "Probably the reason you couldn't find him is because you would have to have asked about him under his Indian name which is Running Wolf."

Drawing in a deep breath Haas said, "All of that is well and good. What I want to know is what are they after. After the shootout you told me about the counterfeit ration stamp plates. They would by useless now. Reviewing the report I made at the time, I saw that both at the altercation in the woods and the shootout here near the house, you, Jamie, said they asked for *it* as if they were after a specific thing, not 'things.' What is *it* they want?"

CHAPTER 33

We sat in silence until dad said, "We might know what they want but the situation is very complicated. Tommy get the list."

As I had expected, Tommy had worked away at the list of sleeper agents until he had copied all of them. Expecting someone from the FBI would show up, dad had told Tommy to make a list of only the fathers of the sleeper agents.

No one said anything while Tommy was gone. When dad had the list and said, "I am asking you to trust us for a few minutes here. We are the ones in danger, not you. Are you agreeable with that?"

Haas appeared bewildered. "What do you have in mind?"

"I have a list of names. As I read them off I want you to tell me if you recognize any of them. Will you do that for us?"

Haas didn't seem to like that but what else could he do without pushing us around and that wouldn't help anyone.

He shrugged. "That seems all right."

Dad started reading the list. There were about a hundred. After ten he said, "Mac Adams." That was the name of his assistant who had been along at the time of the shootout.

He said no. Then, after the next name, Haas said, "Wait. Mac Adams was the name of the man who was with me the second time I came here. Why is he on the list?"

"He's not on the list," dad said. "I put his name in to see if you were paying attention."

Haas had a wry smile. "Nice. Continue."

After that dad waited longer between the names to give Haas a chance to think. When he came to Wendell Mitler, Haas said. "That's the name of an agent I worked with on a case in Iowa. How would you get that name?"

"You wouldn't happen to know if he has a family?" dad asked.

Haas thought. "As I recall he mentioned a son about twelve."

Dad nodded and continued with the names. He was stopped one more time at the name Harry Fies. Haas said he was part of an ongoing investigation and he was not at liberty to say any more about him.

At the end of the list, dad said, "That's it. Now, I suppose you would like to know what this is all about?"

"An understatement, if anything."

Dad folded the list, pushed back his plate and laid his hands on the table while he thought. I knew dad was good at figuring things out but he had to work at it. He even said now and then that he thought his mind worked while he slept because problems with no apparent solution one day had an answer the next morning.

Haas was beginning to fidget when dad finally answered. "I'm afraid I can't say anything more right now. I have to think about it for a few days. The fact that you identified one of the names on the list as an FBI agent is very troubling. Other than that let me repeat, we are the ones in danger and it doesn't seem the FBI has made any progress on this case in six years. Either this is simply too trifling a matter for you to spend your time on, or there are internal problems in The Bureau that cause you to deliberately not pursue it. If either is the case I would not expect you to admit it."

Now Haas openly bristled, "I for sure can't help you if you won't tell me what you know especially where you got that list of names?"

Dad shot back, "You said you found nothing on Hindle. If this case was at all important to you, you would have found something. You didn't even try! Tell me I'm wrong! You walk in here and flash a fancy federal government badge and we are supposed to swoon at your omnipotence!"

All of us, including Haas, sat in stunned awe. But he didn't know that no one on earth had ever heard dad get riled up. Wow! And he was well spoken when he did, I had to give him that.

Dad continued in a more conciliatory tone. "The time will come when we will need help, there is no question about that. What you have to ask yourself is whether you want us to go to the local police and the Minneapolis newspapers for help. If we do the FBI will be made to look as bad as we can make it look. Things are bad here, for us, and it seems you people are not taking it seriously at all. The simple fact is, we don't trust you personally, the FBI or the federal government. It's a sad day and I hate to say it, but it's true."

Haas twitched his cheek as he took what dad had to give. After some silence he said, "I gather that the list you read to me didn't come out of thin air, that there's a lot more involved. And, it is apparent you think at least part of the problem is the federal government itself."

"The thing is, there has been overt hostility toward us."

I had mentioned at home the incident where Hindle had barged in on Mr. Beecher and me demanding the film.

"We need help especially in the form of information. Who is Hindle? You see, we don't know who to trust. Is Hindle really such a good under cover communist, or are you protecting him—is he in fact working for you? Do you understand our dilemma? You came here with nothing other than Hindle hadn't been working for the Mankato school system. I could have picked up the phone and found out that. If that's the best you can do we don't need J. Edgar Hoover and his boys. We don't even know if the superintendent made any calls at all to check Hindle's credentials. Maybe he's a communist, too."

"If you'd tell me where you got the list, maybe I could help you a lot.

"Right now I can't. Suffice it to say the names on the list are truly bad men. You have the two names you recognized. If you really dig you can find out what put them on the list. If you do that we'll know we can trust you and you'll also know where we got the list. Remember this, if the shooting starts again, we won't be calling you—there won't be time."

Haas got up to leave. "One more thing, don't go stirring up a hornets nest in town. We have to live here, you don't. You can do a careful investigation if you want to. And, the real information you want isn't here." As an afterthought dad said, "If either of us has to call the other due to an emergency the message will be that Aunt Bertha is very sick. It will mean that you will be here as soon as you can. We want to trust you."

* * *

The next day on Friday as I was leaving Health Class Mr. Beecher caught my eye and motioned with a movement of his head to the side of his desk. Hanging back I fiddled with my books until the room was cleared. He smiled slightly and said, "Have you looked at any interesting insects lately?"

As he said it he flipped up the cover of my book a couple of inches and slipped a folded paper under it. "Haven't had much time." I said. "I've been picking apples with most of my spare time." In a hushed tone I continued, "Come out sometime and buy apples—maybe tomorrow morning. I have something to show you. It's the greatest bug you've ever seen."

At supper that evening Tommy wasn't looking very good. Mom asked him what was wrong.

"I failed an English test."

"What happened?" mom asked. I could hear that tone in her voice as in "What will people say?"

"Let's see the paper," dad said. "We can find out what you did wrong."

"Can't do that. Mr. Hindle didn't give them back. He just read off the grades. Most of the kids were mad about that."

I knew what was happening because of the note I had gotten from Mr. Beecher. But, I didn't know if I should say anything because I didn't want to get him into trouble. He was the only person in the whole school I thought I could trust. The note said he had heard that the word was around that some of the teachers would be treating the Landon boys severely because they were trouble makers.

Dad looked dismayed. "Since it's Hindle, it has to be about the film."

Tommy said, "We have to get the film back to them in such a way that they don't know that we've looked at it. Then maybe they'll leave us alone."

"Eventually, yes," dad said. "It would be a shame if responsible people in the government didn't have a chance to see it first, though. Let's see what happens. Maybe things will lighten up. If not, I'll mention it to Marty. I wonder if anything as been mentioned along main street."

CHAPTER 34

The next morning, Saturday, an older model car drove in. It was Mr. Beecher. I had been staying around the buildings in case he came. It didn't surprise me that he did because of the film. He would suspect I had something other than a strange bug to show him.

He was wearing a subdued plaid shirt, worn jeans, scuffed brown boots and a light denim jacket. It was almost shocking for me because I had only seen him dressed professionally. It was like seeing a doctor in street clothes when you had only seen him in his office wearing a white lab coat.

I waved and said, "Hi, Mr. Beecher," as I came from the hay mow of the barn. "A good day to buy apples."

He smiled as we both noted the reversal. Normally he was the one in charge, the seller, so to speak, and I was the customer. Now I was the seller—we were on my turf. "The apples are here in the shed," I continued pointing that way.

"Beautiful place you have here," he commented. It looked nice. The trees were still mostly green and a few late summer flowers were blooming. The grass was neatly mowed as it always was. That was Tommy's and my job. Dad insisted on the place looking nice especially during apple season.

In the building I pointed out the varieties as I walked to the wall on the left that was in semi-darkness. "These are eating, or what are called table apples," I said. "These others are for cooking."

I had hidden the knife along the west wall and now retrieved it. Looking out I made sure no one was coming. "This is what I wanted to show you," I said pulling the knife out of the sheath. "It's a very unusual and valuable knife." In a whisper I said, "The micro film was hidden in the handle. The reason I wanted you to see it is because at some time I may want you to mention to Hindle what a strange knife I have. Other than that don't mention it to anyone." Then I added, "It's really sharp."

I picked an eating apple off the top of a bushel and with a swipe cut it in half letting the cut off part fall. It was an impressive demonstration because no ordinary knife would have done that. I handed the half in my hand to him. "They're good. Here, try a bite."

While he was chewing I wiped the blade on my shirt sleeve. When he finished his apple half I handed him the knife. It's heavy, isn't it? That's because it's a fighting knife. The odd shade of the blade means it was made from a special steel."

He handled it and cautiously drew his thumb across the blade and then handed it back to me. I re-sheathed it and returned it to its hiding place.

"These are good," he said. But a whole basket full is too many for me."

"That's okay," I said. "They're three dollars a bushel and a dollar fifty for half a bushel. Is that okay?"

"Sure." When we had the half bushel of apples in his car trunk he asked if I would show him the barn. That was not an uncommon request for someone new to the farm so we went on a tour. In the hay mow he could see the bales piled high. "All ready for winter, I see."

"Yeah," I said. "Farming's a lot of work. Did you grow up on a farm?"

"No. I was bred, born and raised a city kid."

I didn't take him up to the third floor because it might not be safe for him. We went through the first floor, though. Being the middle of a fall day there were no cattle in the barn. We walked between the silo and the front of the feed troughs. When he saw how the stanchions for the cows faced the center of the barn he said. "I see. This makes sense. A cow takes up more room in the back than in the front so the round barn is a good idea."

He stopped and looked around. In an apprehensive voice he asked, "What will happen, I mean with the film?"

Not knowing how much to say I knew he wanted more than I had given him. "The best we can figure out is we have to let them get the knife back with the film in it without them knowing we found the film. I don't want to say much more. As I mentioned, at some time we might want you to casually mention the strange knife I have, but only when I tell you to. When you do, don't only mention the knife, but that I got it from an Indian during the war. Then they'll know. As soon as possible after you have told him you have to tell me because we'll have to be ready in case something happens which it most likely will."

He nodded. "Why doesn't the FBI settle the matter? What are they for, anyway?"

"The last guy that was here from the FBI said they couldn't move too fast or they wouldn't have enough evidence to get convictions. Remember in the Alger Hiss trial they only got him on perjury, and they almost didn't get that."

"But you said they played rough. I assume that means you are in some danger. Isn't the right?"

"Yeah. We're in danger."

"There you are. Who cares about convictions. If they're dangerous people they could be scared away or something else could be done."

"Sure, but they keep coming back. What we have is really important to them so they won't stop."

He shook his head like not knowing what to believe. Then he said, "You said I was to let Hindle know an Indian gave you the knife, is that right?"

"Yeah, in 1944."

"That's an expensive looking knife. Why would an Indian give it to you?"

"He didn't say why exactly, and he only gave it to me as he was leaving, but I think it was a token for my having saved his life."

He looked at me a little surprised. "You were how old then?"

"Six."

"How could a six year old save the life of a grown man?"

"It'll sound a little strange but here is how it was. It was during the war and dad needed a man to help on the farm but all the able bodied men were in uniform. One day Justin came walking in here and asked for a job. Dad really had no choice but to give him a try so he did. When he arrived he was limping a little but it was hardly noticeable. He was a good man and dad liked him because he worked hard and followed instructions. And he was smart so he could suggest how to do things. But, the limp kept getting worse and finally we found out his leg was badly infected so dad took him to the hospital. They operated on his leg to remove a piece of shrapnel he had gotten in the war. A shell had exploded near him and he got several shrapnel balls in him and the small piece of jagged metal. The doctors missed the small piece. He got out of the Army because the shell had effected his hearing and he couldn't hear much out of one ear.

"He always slept on the hay in the barn. That was his way so that's where he wanted to go when they brought him home from the hospital. He had a high fever but there wasn't much anybody could do about it. Dad left him a big jar of water before he went to bed.

"During the night I was suddenly awakened thinking about Justin. I don't know why I woke up or why I decided I had to go out to see how he was. I took the flashlight and snuck out of the house. It was bright moonlight and the grass was wet. When I got to the barn Justin was delirious. He had tipped over the jar of water in the dark and was burning up. I called mom and dad and after seeing how bad he was they called the doctor. The doctor wet his clothing and covered him with wet towels to bring down the fever and eventually he got well. Anyway, the doctor said I had saved his life by coming out to check on him because he would have been dead by morning."

He smiled a little and said, "That's really something." Then I saw his brow scrunch up and drawing out the first word said, "Yes. Then, the knife would have been a gift and not something of vital importance to the country that you were given, so to speak, for safe keeping."

Mr. Beecher was good at figuring things out so I was forced to reveal a little more. "First of all, I think he really wanted me to have the knife because I had been so impressed with it from the first time I saw it. Secondly, it isn't a real practical knife for the normal things you do with a knife. It's awful heavy. But, and this is also between you and me, he was injured when he left and I think he was afraid that if he ended up in a hospital it would be stolen from him. I always thought it was possible he would show up sometime and want it back but so far he hasn't."

He nodded as if accepting what I had said. I had previously said there was more to all of this than he knew and he may have began to see that more information was not necessarily good for him.

"Well," I said, "that's about it for the tour unless you want to get the feel of what it's like to be a farmer by pitching in. You could help clean the gutter behind where the cows stand."

"No," he said with a smile. "This has been enough for me."

It was hard for me to imagine, but I sensed that this was a totally alien world to him. He knew his food came from farms, that beef roasts came from cut up cows and things like that, but only in an abstract way. The actual places it happened, the calluses on the hands, the strong backs, the physical labor, the dirt, the cobwebs hanging from the ceiling, the untidiness of it all was outside of his existance.

When we were back at his car, dad was there and I made introductions. After a little small talk Mr. Beecher left.

The rest of the weekend things should have been forgotten except they weren't. The problem of Tommy's failed English test came up several times. Finally at supper on Sunday I said, "Dad, why don't you talk to Marty. Mr. Haas said Hindle hadn't been a teacher at Mankato. You could say the coincidence about the woman wanting to quit and Hindle being available bothers you. And, someone you know told you Hindle hadn't taught there. You don't have to say who it was that told you that. Then ask Marty to go to the superintendent and ask to see the man's papers. We know Hindle must be a communist because he's looking for the film. Maybe the superintendent is, too, and didn't really check the references because there aren't any."

There was silence. I could see dad was working on it. Then he said, "I could say the kids don't like him and he isn't a good teacher. If he pressed me I could tell about Tommy's test paper. Not giving it back so a student can see what he's doing wrong is unforgivable."

Later that evening I heard dad on the phone with Marty.

Monday afternoon I got home before Tommy. He got home later because he had band practice. Being in the ninth grade mom and dad had bought him a trombone and he liked to play it. He wasn't the athletic type and they wanted him to be in a social group at school. He liked to play the horn and drove me crazy as he was practicing all the time. But he got good enough to be in junior band in only a few weeks.

When he arrived home a half hour before supper he was all smiles as he walked in. "Mr. Hindle decided to give the English tests back and this is really dumb. Look at the paper. He had written an 'F' on it. Then he made a line along the right side of it so it looks like an 'A' with a flat top. I've seem him write on the blackboard and that is not the way he normally makes his 'A's. He makes then with a pointed top like you'd expect. And, there are none of my answers marked wrong, anyway."

"Did he apologize for saying you had failed when you really had gotten none of them wrong?"

Mom was as always worried what people would think.

"No. But, I said in a loud whisper that everyone could hear that I had gotten an 'A' after all. Everybody knows."

After supper the phone rang and it was Marty. Dad listened and didn't say much. He thanked him and hung up.

"That was Marty. He had received a complaint from another parent about Hindle not giving the test papers back so he called the superintendent this morning. He mentioned the test papers and then that he had heard that Hindle had not been a teacher at Mankato. The superintendent said he'd check on the test papers, but that the information was wrong about Mankato because he had personally called there to check. Marty asked if he could see the credentials and he said he didn't see why not. When the superintendent called back he said there had been a misunderstanding about the test papers and that they had been returned to the students. But, he said he seemed to have mislaid Hindle's resume and try as he might he couldn't find it."

That was one more reason not to trust Hindle or the superintendent. But, since they knew people were watching what was going on in the school, maybe they'd change their minds about harassing Tommy and me.

CHAPTER 35

Things were normal and Tommy didn't have more problems in English class. The seventh grade math teacher was sharper with me than the other kids but nobody really noticed other than they seemed to be getting the idea that I was a general screw-off. It didn't matter to me because I never had any real friends in the Catholic school so that I didn't have any here was nothing new. Occasionally when I was reprimanded there'd be a few snickers, but I was used to that, too.

The first Saturday of October we were all delighted to see Justin ride into the yard on a motorcycle. He had left on Rango's motorcycle and this was a different one. I especially was glad he had come thinking he'd have some way to solve the problem of the microfilm in the bone-handled knife.

Mom insisted he come in the house and sit down. It was a gossipy town and mom could hold her own in that department. But, she was careful not to repeat things that should not be told. Some place she had learned about the sin of detraction. That was knowing something damaging but true about someone and telling it when there is no reason for the greater good to do so. We all make mistakes and it's common charity to let people leave their mistakes behind and move on.

That didn't mean that she didn't want to know everything that had happened to Justin since the day he left. He obviously understood this would be the case and was able to provide answers that satisfied mom without telling much. It seemed to me that there were a lot of things he didn't mention that I thought would have helped figure out what we could do about the film. But, then maybe he didn't know either.

He, of course, would not dare be on his way without having dinner with us. This he also understood, I'm sure. If he had made other arrangements for dinner he was out of luck—he was staying. Dad was genuinely glade to seem him, too. After all, Justin had almost single handedly saved our farm. It wasn't mentioned but the deep gratitude was evident in the things dad said.

After dinner Justin said, "Hey, Jamie, why don't you show me what's new with the farm?"

"Sure, let's go."

Out of the house we tuned north. "I saw when I walked to the house a new building where the little brooder houses were."

"Yeah, that's the new brooder house. It has six pens in it so it's all in one."

We entered from the west end. "The first part is the feed storage room. From here through the door is an aisle the runs along all the pens so we can bring feed and water to the birds."

"The pens don't have a floor."

"Those frames stacked along the side of each pen are the floor. They have wire screen on them so the droppings fall through. When the turkeys are hauled out to range the frames are lifted up so the manure can be shoveled out. Boy, it really smells bad when you're doing that but it goes pretty fast."

We came to the east end of the building and out that door. That brought us behind the pump house. I took him around to the front and showed him the shop as I told him about all the problems we had finding water. He said, "We should talk about the knife. Where can we go?"

I took him to the oak tree north of the barn. It stood a short distance to the west of the stack of bales beside the manger ready for the winter.

"I see you're baling hay now. Does you dad have a baler?"

"No. We hire a guy who comes and does it for ten cents a bale. It seems to work better than loose hay."

We sat with our backs against the tree so we each faced out in a little different direction. I had made a point to sit on his side with his good ear so we could talk normally. It was a warm clear October day. Some of the leaves had fallen from the white oak tree. Those still hanging on were dark green. Since we had not had a hard frost yet, they were not changing color. "In the summer with all the green leaves on the tree the tall grass reaches nearly to the lowest branches. This is one of my favorite places to sit and think."

Justin nodded. The sun shone through the branches on his face as he leaned his head back against the rough bark. "This is nice, so peaceful."

"This is where Tommy and I smoked some of your tobacco. We stole it, I suppose we shouldn't have done that."

He smiled. "I knew you had done that. How did you smoke, did you roll cigarettes like you dad?"

"Nope. Tommy had read a story called *Huckleberry Finn* where the boy had a corncob pipe. So, he made one for both of us. They worked real good."

Justin was still smiling a little. "Did you enjoy your smoke?"

"Heck no. We both got sick and barfed our guts out. I'm surprised there isn't still a pile of barf here six years later."

He laughed like I had seldom seen him do. "I remember when you two came in for supper that evening. You were still green. Tommy could come up with stories to cover up stuff you guys had done and he did a pretty good job of it that day."

After a minute he said, "What's the point of being young and dumb if you can't be dumb once in a while?"

"Is that an old Indian saying?"

"No. I just made it up."

"Well it should be an old Indian saying. Maybe you should go back to the reservation and find a grandfather, a *pawágan*, who is old and couldn't remember too well any more. You could tell him he had told you that when you were a boy and you thought it was a good old saying. He might think he was smarter than he thought he was and would start telling it to everybody."

"But, that wouldn't be entirely honest."

"Where else are old sayings supposed to come from? If they don't start sometime they don't have a chance to get old. And, I don't so much mind being young, but when does a guy stop being dumb?"

He shook his head and I noticed a shadow come over his face. "All I can say is learn from the mistakes of others because you won't live long enough to make them all yourself."

"Now, that sounds like a genuine old saying."

"Nope, made that one up, too."

"You're an old sayings factory today, aren't you? Have you ever stopped doing dumb things?"

"God help me, no; doubt I ever will."

"Did you mean the Indian God that you called *Atahocan*, or the Catholic God?"

He was thinking like he used to and I didn't know how long it would take for him to answer, but I knew I'd have to wait. It didn't take long.

"I was referring to the Catholic God. *Atahocan* is remote and almost never spoken of. The rest of the spirit world is all about nature because my ancestors lived so close to the earth. They relied on the sun and the rain and those tools each man could make with his own hands. They lived directly from the abundance of the land and if it failed they starved.

"The power of metamorphosis among living things and even between living and natural objects like rocks makes us cautious and suspicious of interpersonal relations of all kinds. You might meet a man who is a bear that has metamorphosed into a man and could without warning attack you. I've come to see that life is hard if you can't accept a man as he is."

We sat in silence. It was good to sit with someone you liked and talk about nothing, though it was about something. It was beyond the mundane of our lives and spoke of friendship, closeness, common feelings, and the spiritual.

Finally, I said, "Do you remember the day when you said you were my guardian angel, and when I asked if that was so why couldn't I see your wings? You said I was a kid and kids couldn't see them. Well, I still can't."

"Of course not. You're still a kid."

I reached over and pinched his arm hard so it would hurt.

"Ouch. Why'd you do that?"

"Testing to see if you're an angel and you're not or you wouldn't have felt that. But, that's okay. I like you as a friend better."

He had that stony look on his face like he didn't want me to know what he was thinking, and as usual I didn't. "You know what they say about friends?"

"No, what?"

"Good friends are like boogers; once you pick 'em they stick around."

He couldn't stop a short burst of laughter. "Is that an old saying?"

"Nope. I made it up."

"Now who's the old sayings factory? Have you ever said it around your mother?"

"Yeah, once. She said it was terrible and she didn't ever want to hear me say it again. But, she laughed, too."

He couldn't stifle more laughter as he said, "I believe she would. Your father is one of the most honest, decent men I have known, but he's reserved. I think you get your lively, half-wild side from your mother." After he thought awhile he continued. "And, as far as you're concerned you're glad she said it that way, aren't you? Because she can't hear you say it out here so you're free to say it."

I was chuckling as I said, "Nobody's prefect."

He nudged me with his elbow. I nudged him back.

We sat in silence again enjoying that warm feeling inside. Why couldn't life always be like this? Why did I have to worry about tests in school, or about that darned knife.

I think Justin knew what I was thinking because he said, "We've been avoiding what we came out here to discuss. What are we going to do about the knife?"

"I was hoping you'd have some ideas. We see that the only thing to do is to let them get it back without them knowing we discovered the secret. How are we going to do that? Right now they don't even know for sure any of us has it?"

"So, you know why it's still important—even after all this time?"

I nodded my head. "Yeah, we do. I forgot that you and I have only been talking to each other in coded letters and you don't know what I found. In my first letter to you I said I still had the present you gave me when you left. The guy that showed up at the house last summer calling himself Jarvis Granston asked about any 'present' you might have given us. You see, he used the same word. He had intercepted my first letter to you and knew what was in it. We remembered the name Granston so knew it was all connected. Mr. Haas sent us a picture of the real Granston and the man who came here calling himself Granston wasn't him. Haas told us our letter to him had been opened, too, so they're now watching all our mail.

"All of those years after you left I had been wondering about the knife. Frequently I took it out to look at it and I kept it oiled so it wouldn't rust. But, after the guy calling himself Granston showed up at the house last summer, I really started to look at it. I had decided that eventually if nothing else worked, I'd saw into the handle with a hacksaw.

"I kept looking at it because I had to find out the secret and finally I did. It turns out that if you press in real hard on the end of the shank where it's even with the back of the bone-handle—by the way, it's some sort of metal, not bone at all—you compress a strong spring and a part of the shank pops out. In it was a small rectangular tin can containing strips of microfilm. All of the film was made of Top Secret White House documents from about six months before you showed up at our farm.

"They tell about how the government let the atomic bomb secrets go to the Russians and stuff like that. But all of that is old now except for several documents. They contain a long list of sleeper agents. Those are Russian babies that are brought over here and raised by communist parents to be normal Americans. Except that they are like sleeping time bombs. The kids are from eight to about twenty by now. So you see, the list will be important as long as we live."

He nodded slowly as I spoke. When I paused he said, "That helps to make sense out of a lot of things. As far as them not knowing if you even have it goes, they know for sure that I had it while I was working here. Rango saw me wearing the knife that first time he met us in the woods when we were coming back from blasting stumps. I suppose you didn't notice how his eyes were riveted on the knife. And, of course, before the fight in the woods he said he wanted *it*, and a few seconds later I used *it* to kill Murphy."

"What were the plates all about? We thought that was why he was here."

"It started while I was in the hospital. One of the men who came to see Granston saw me tooling silver. It was so boring that I did that to kill time. The communists use anything they can to bring down the target country, which in this case is the United States. Counterfeiting ration stamps was a good way to help that along. I suppose that's what got their plan off course. When Rango finally found me here on the farm they could have sent in two or three men some night and simply killed me and taken the knife. They'd be further ahead now if they had. Of course, it wouldn't have done anything to improve my health. As it was they needed me for the plates so had to wait for the knife. But, since they knew I had it and where I was, they could bide their time.

"After the shootout, I went to the reservation and told Red Feather some of what had happened. I was severely wounded and would not likely survive so he put together some gear and a canoe and drove me to where I could enter the wilderness. It was less than fifty miles. I was weak but if I took it slow I had a chance. Eventually I arrived at a small cabin across the border in Canada that's never used in the winter. I lived mostly on animals I could snare. By spring I was doing pretty well.

"I disappeared and with me all traces of the knife. At the reservation Rango and his buddies learned I had gone into the wilderness. That wasn't so odd given the Indian culture that developed entirely without modern medicine. A severely wounded man, especially a warrior, knew he was going to die and rather than waste away while burdening the tribe he went to the forest to meet his end. And, in our thinking, the life force of the wild without a lot of humans to disrupt it was thought to be thera-peutic. Often it was. When I didn't come back they assumed I was dead. But, since no one had actually seen me die Rango and his comrades kept looking.

"Before I buried Murphy, I cleaned out his pockets. There was quite a bit of money on him so I could get by. I didn't know why the knife was important, but I figured they might still be after me because I was the last man to have it. If they thought I had died in the wilderness they could think it went with me and it was gone for good. I decided to keep it that way. When I came out of the wilderness the spring of 1945 I went to the southwest. In 1948 I ran across a man from my reservation. He reported back that I was alive, Rango found out and started dogging me. That told me it was really important because after all that time they were still des-perate to get it."

"Who was the real Granston," I asked, "and where did he get the mi-crofilm and the knife? The knife seems like a strange place to hide mi-crofilm. And, what was he doing in the St. Cloud hospital?"

"I don't know the answers to all of those questions. But, once when he was in pain between doses of morphine he told me in a rambling way that he was a major in the army working under cover for the OSS. Ap-parently, the story that he was a criminal was a cover. This is where my knowing about the microfilm helps. Once he managed to get it, and presumably knowing what was on it, he would have known there was nothing that could be done with it during the war. So, he wanted to get away from the centers of power as fast as he could. However, they were after him and nearly got him as his wounds showed. When he got out of the Washington D.C. area, though, they lost him. He headed for Central Minnesota which is about as far away as a person could get.

"What he hadn't counted on was the extremely liberal mentality of Minnesotans. There were, and are, a lot of communists in this state, as many per capita as any place in the country. The iron range was a hotbed of them. In fact in 1932 a card carrying communist by the name of Karl Nygard was elected mayor of Crosby, the first in the whole country. In the late thirties the Teamsters Union in Minnesota was completely under their control. Anyway, his pursuers started a silent man hunt. Do you know what fellow travelers are?"

"Yeah. That came up with regard to the film. They're communist sympathizers."

"Okay. They put out the word to all their sympathizers, and there were a lot of them, to be looking for a man of a certain description who may or may not be in the military. That accounted for all the people that happened by to 'visit' Granston. The first was a fellow traveler who after seeing him passed the word along that Granston might be the man. Then, an undercover communist visited, then others came until finally they thought they had him. About that time he gave me the knife. Some of his visitors were a tough looking lot. They must have tried to make him talk, got too rough and killed him. My guess is one of the early visitors saw the knife. Later, after he was dead, they realized the knife was gone and put it together that the knife was important. Either it contained the film or had directions to where it was. I was his roommate, and I left before being officially discharged to get out of that business about the counterfeit stamp plates. But, they must have figured it was to get away with the microfilm. Hence, they came after me for both reasons."

"And, like you said, at that first meeting Rango saw you wearing the *it*. So, they know about the knife, that it's important and that it's either here or you have it. Why did they always call the knife *it*?"

"My guess, knowing what I know now, is because they did not dare mention the word microfilm because everybody knows only spies use that. It might also have been because they didn't know for sure where the microfilm was hidden. By saying *it* they didn't get sidetracked to looking for a single thing. The knife was circumstantial, but as time went on it remained the only clue they had so now they want it at any cost. As far as why a knife was used, I bet Leonard Haas could tell you that.

"Anyway, why don't you let this guy posing as Granston, or Hindle the English teacher, know indirectly that you have a knife for sale to the highest bidder, or something like that? If they want it so badly let them buy it. This is America where everything is for sale for the right price. As communists they seem to hate that, but they would for sure understand it—the old profit motive."

"That's a good idea. It would sure be better to sell it to them than to have them take it off our dead bodies. There's another problem, though. Dad is the biggest believer in the American system of government there ever was. He thinks it would be wrong to give it back with the microfilm in it without letting the FBI or other responsible Federal officials know what's on the film. After all, it's their job to keep us safe."

"So, why not give the film to the FBI, have them make copies of it and then put it back in the knife and let the communists get it back?"

"That's the second problem. When the man posing as Granston showed up as the new English teacher we notified Haas. Tommy had made a list of all the parents of the sleeper agents on the film so when Haas was here dad read the list of names to him to see if he recognized any of them. He knew two, and one was an FBI agent. If there is at least one agent who is actually the parent of a sleeper agent there must be many more undercover communists in the FBI to say nothing of a ton of fellow travelers. So if we gave them the microfilm to copy it's very possible we'd never get it back and then we'd have nothing to give to the communists to get them off our backs."

"Does Haas know about the film?"

"No. Dad only read him the names to see if he recognized any."

"What does your dad plan to do, then?"

"Right now we're waiting to see what happens. Shortly after Hindle took the job of English teacher I was warned that the word was out that some of the teachers were told to be hard on the Landon boys. Hindle started to get funny by giving Tommy an 'F' on a test when he should have gotten an 'A'. He didn't give the test papers back and other parents complained, too. So he fixed it up and things have been okay since then with Tommy. So far my math and American History teachers have been kind of rude to me, but I'm always doing things I shouldn't so it isn't too unusual."

"Is there anything I can do?"

"I don't know. If they got you nobody would know. If something happens to any of us, there would be an investigation. That's something they can't afford to have. They did get Alger Hiss and now they're after the Rosenbergs. That Senator McCarthy is really after the communists."

"Maybe you should send the film to McCarthy."

"Yeah, we could but you don't know who you can trust. Oh," I said, "I almost forgot to ask, did you recognize the man in the newspaper clipping I sent you?"

Justin nodded. "I assumed you knew. He was the driver of the car the day they shot your dog."

It had all happened so fast that neither Tommy nor I had paid much attention to the driver.

Justin said, "The paper said he's an English teacher. I can't believe he'd make a good teacher."

"Tommy says he's not. By the way, is there a phone number where we could call you?"

Justin gave me a number and a new address that I could also use. Our beautiful day of earlier had become clouded with the worries of life.

CHAPTER 36

After the start of January, 1951, things became more uncomfortable for me at school. It built up slowly in both the math class and American History, but Mr. Russo the math teacher, was the worst. He was about six feet tall, not over weight but with a little paunch showing. His round face with black hair was punctuated by dark eyes. His ears were over large and his nose was kind of flat. The strange thing was he seemed to like teaching math and took to it with an affable attitude. Other than that, he had a mean side to the point where he seemed to delight in tormenting me.

Under the best of conditions I seemed to have tried the patience of every teacher I ever had. A few of them like Mr. Beecher recognize the fact that I bored easily. Sometimes his class would bog down on some question that the students don't understand and keep asking it to be explained ten times. That's when I'd loose interest and start fidgeting around and eventually annoy even him. Mr. Beecher would say something, like, "Hang in there, Jamie, we'll get through this." The other students knew what was going on and some of them would laugh, but not meanly.

Math class was my trial. For example, one day he was teaching proportions. As one application he said, what if you wanted to know how tall a tree was, how would you do it? After taking a few ideas from the class, most of them dumb, he explained how it was done. The example was a spruce tree with a nice pointed top on flat ground so it was easy. He drew a diagram on the backboard to illustrate it. First you measure the length of the tree's shadow. Then, take a yard stick, hold it up vertically, and measure the length of its shadow. Knowing the length of the yard stick and the length of the two shadows, you can calculate the height of the tree.

To me it made perfect sense the first time he said it. But, the questions kept coming until I lost interest started playing with my pencil, dropped it on the floor, the kid across from me nudged it under his chair with his foot and I had to scramble for it. Mr. Russo snapped at me that I was disrupting the class and made me stand in the back of the room for the rest of the period. The back of the room was nothing new to me. Some of the kids snickered as I took my place. The snickering was nothing new, either. Of course, it was all my fault and would not have happened if I had left the pencil alone.

At first I think he thought I was dumb so he'd have me go to the blackboard and work out a problem. There were smarter kids than me, but I could usually do it easily so he tried other things. One time as I approached the board I said in a subdued voice, "Gee, these blackboards get lower every year." A few of the kids heard it and laughed. I stood in the back of the room.

Ever since Mr. Beecher had slipped me the note saying that some of the teachers would be after the Landon boys I had been on the lookout. Clearly Mr. Hindle was in on it because of his showing up at the farm and then the thing where he charged into the room when we were using the microscope to look at ants, to say nothing about trying to give Tommy an "F" when he had gotten and "A". Mr. Marshall the junior high principal was in on it because he had been listening at the door that first time I used the microscope. I suspected the superintendent because of the way he simply could not find the credentials of Mr. Hindle. Then there was my history teacher, Mrs. LaBeta and, of course, Mr. Russo. How many more there were I didn't know but these were the ones in a position to affect me.

Through January and February I stood in the back of the math room about once a week. I wondered if any of the kids were noticing that something was wrong because not another single student had ever been made to do that. Once in a while two kids would say a couple of words across the aisle. He'd see it and say something like, "Stan and Mike, pay attention." If I were involved, I'd go to the back of the room but the other kid wouldn't.

There were basically three categories of kids in the seventh grade. Those who had gone to public school from the beginning, the Catholic school kids, and the country school kids. At that time there were still numerous small country schools. Usually they had all six grades, sometimes eight, in one room. It was surprising how much they learned. There was no noticeable difference in how well any of the groups were prepared for seventh grade. The Catholic school and public school kids knew the others in their group. The country school kids didn't since there were only one or two others from their grade in the small schools. As a result, some of the country kids were a little more open to Catholic school students because they seemed to feel that we were all outsiders together.

I mention this because of two country school kids. The first is Emily LaNell who I have already mentioned. I could tell her father was not the last of the great land barons, and was probably a small farmer eking out a living. I knew how it was from the war years for us. The difference being that it had gotten better for us and not so much for others. She had two dresses that she changed off wearing like my two shirts and pants. She was always neatly pressed and either she or her mother cared about how she looked.

To me she seemed small and alone. She always talked to other girls around her though she didn't seem to have any real friends. And, she wasn't tiny, it's just that she seemed small to me. She was even about my height having grown pretty fast as girls of that age frequently did. My mother, for example, said she had reached her full adult height by the time she was in the eighth grade. It seemed Emily might still have some growing to do, though, because I had seen her older brother who was taller than most. I wanted to talk to her but couldn't get up the nerve, and there never seemed to be the right time. It took until February before I managed it.

"Is this place taken?" It was dinner time in the school cafeteria and Emily was seated on the end of the table and the chair across from her was vacant.

Glancing up she said, "It's a public school and I suppose that makes this a public table."

I pulled out the metal folding chair and sat down. "What I meant was I thought you might be waiting for a friend."

We had chili that day and she was focused on eating like it would be her best meal of the day. I understood that. Some of the kids complained about the school food but I never thought it was so bad.

She glanced at me again. "I don't have many friends. That's the way it is when you come from a country school. Did you go to country school?"

"Nope, the Catholic school. Are you a Catholic?"

"There's some amount of discussion between my parents about that. I guess I'm more Catholic than anything else."

I was eating and mentioned that the chili was pretty good.

"They put too much chili powder in it to suit me."

"What's chili powder?"

"It's what makes it taste like chili."

"Oh." Here I was talking to a girl and stepping on my tongue. I always did that.

She was nearing the end of her bowl of chili and I didn't want her to get up and leave when she said, "Mr. Russo in math class is hard on you, why is that?"

That was the first time it had come home to me that there was something going on that was obvious enough so other kids could see it. That bothered me because it would sooner or later get home to mom and dad and I didn't want that in the worst way. I had been going with the flow and living with it. Since being scolded had been a big part of my whole life, and since Mr. Beecher had warned me of what might be coming my brain added the two together and I adjusted to taking it as normal.

"Teacher's pet, I guess." There, stepped on my tongue again.

"You're a nut."

"Thank you, 'thought no one noticed." Again.

She looked at me intensely and it felt kind of good.

"Something bad is going to happen if that doesn't change. I can feel it."

It took a second to register, but her eyes were beautiful. I swallowed hard feeling my tongue getting even thicker than it already was. Without thinking I said, "Oh," as I pulled in a breath.

"What?"

"Your eyes are so pretty. They're the color of wild violets."

She smiled holding my eyes intently by her gaze, "Do you really think so?"

She seemed genuinely pleased. Had I actually done something right? "Oh yes. Don't you have wild violets where you live?"

She nodded and immediately looked down at her plate. "I should go so somebody else will have a place to sit down."

When she was gone I felt good. Inadvertently I had complimented her and she liked it. Maybe she'd talk to me again. And, she did.

A week later I had gotten to the lunchroom earlier than normal. The grade school kids ate first, then the junior high followed by the senior high. The smaller kids were filtering out and I found a table mostly empty near the back of the room. I sat facing the back wall. We had baked beans with a wiener thrown in it—not the best meal they made, in fact, close to the worst. It was beat out for bottom place by salmon loaf.

Without warning a voice that was oddly familiar said, "Is this place taken?"

It was Emily! She had placed her tray opposite mine and was sitting down. I could hardly speak it was so unexpected. "Well, of course it's taken, I mean no it's not except that now you've taken it. Ah, please sit down . . . sure, that would be nice. Wow, this is a surprise, a pretty girl asking to sit across from me." It was getting worse with every word I said so I shut up.

She smiled and it made me feel good, though things were confusing. The only thing I could think of was, why was this happening?

"You gave me that nice compliment about my eyes the other day and I forgot to say thank you, so I thought I should or you might think I was rude or something. So, thank you for the nice compliment."

"Ah . . . you're welcome, but a thank you wasn't necessary. I mean, sure it's nice and I'm glad you did . . . but you didn't have to bother."

She started to eat and I stuffed a chunk of wiener in my mouth not knowing what to say next.

"You're kind of nervous around girls, aren't you?"

It took me some time to swallow the food. Then I said, "I don't know. It's that I always seem to get into trouble when they're around. I mean, more trouble than I normally get into."

"Girls don't bite, you know."

"Oh, yes they do." Then, like a dummy I put another chunk of wiener in my mouth.

She gave me a mischievous look that could only portend something bad. "Well, I may want to kiss you sometime, but I promise I'll never bite you."

What she said took a moment to register until all at the same time I almost gagged on the food and started to blush.

She saw it and immediately said, "Oh, I'm sorry. I embarrassed you. I'm so sorry. Why did I have to say that. Hurry up and think about something else before anybody notices. Think about something terrible, think about something disgusting, think about the food, think . . . ."

The connection between disgusting and the food struck me as terribly funny and now, in spite of my other problems, I started to laugh. Putting my hand in front of my mouth lest I burst out and splatter food across the room I tried to hold it all together.

She immediately caught what was so funny and started to laugh too, partly at the joke and as I suspected mostly at me and my uncomfortable condition.

To add to everything I heard a skirt swish as it passed behind me. It was Ruth Meyer, a town girl. She immediately saw me laughing, blushing, and trying to swallow my mouth full of food.

"Are you blushing, Jamie?"

Emily was still laughing and finally I managed to swallow and said, "Emily said something funny about the food."

"Well, it must really have been good, mind telling me?"

By this time I was getting things under control and said, "It's something only farm kids would think was funny."

"Well! Fine." Rather than sitting close to us she moved down a few chairs.

Emily and I could hardly glance at one another lest we start laughing again. I made sure to take small bites of food. We said a few things but mostly ate, giggled and glanced.

She was getting up and it dawned on me why I was always in trouble. It was because I was prone to saying things that I really shouldn't. "Wait a minute."

She looked at me strangely.

Just loud enough so she'd hear I said, "What about that kiss?" I didn't know why I said it or even what I meant by it. It had the effect of producing a strange combination of expressions on her face that ended in a smile. She didn't say anything, but as she left I thought I saw a tinge of pink in her complexion.

Now, after becoming sidetracked, I'll mention the second country kid. This dealt with an event in early March. As we left class this boy said to me, "What did you ever do to Mr. Russo so he hates you so much?"

This second mention of it started me worrying more than I normally worried about stuff. Being naive about how people, including kids, gossiped, I didn't realize that most of the school had begun to quietly talk about it. But as I thought of it, the snickering had died down over the past weeks when I got my punishment. This country kid's name was Ray Brinks and he wasn't a kid. Some of the country kids didn't go to their little schools on days when they were needed on the farm and sometimes it took them a year longer to get through. This meant he was probably a year older than the rest of us and had grown up fast. He was a full grown man and a strong man. He was pretty smart, too. He never asked questions in class and got good marks on his tests.

I didn't know what to say, but I didn't want to let it go since he had taken any interest in the situation. So I stammered, "I get bored and can't seem to keep from making a nuisance of myself."

"Nah. It's more than that. Look at Roger Atkins who sits behind you. He's always cutting up in class and nothing's ever said to him."

He was headed to the second floor and I was going down the hall so I said, "See ya."

Of course, I knew what it was all about. They suspected we had *it* and they wanted *it*. How do you walk into the principal's office and say the communists are out to get you, especially since the principal was probably a communist himself. That was another thing. Mr. Russo had warned me that he'd send me to the principal's office a few times, but never had. But, two days before he even mentioned getting me expelled. They must be getting desperate because the school year was wearing on and they had no more of a lead to *it* than the mention of "Top Secret" by Mr. Beecher last fall. Sooner or later someone would stumble on the fact that

Mr. Hindle wasn't a teacher, he'd be forced to leave and they'd have to start over.

By this time I had arrived at my second worst class, American History. Happily it was the last class period of the day. The teacher, Mrs. LaBeta, had been a teacher, married a farmer, been a farm wife, and now was a widow of about fifty-five. From time to time she mentioned how hard things were in the dust bowl years and depression of the nineteen-thirties, and how the Federal Government didn't do anything to help them. If the opportunity arose she would point out how unfair the government was in its treatment of the Indians and anything else to disparage the country. It was easy to see that she didn't like the United States and was probably a communist. As far as her attitude toward me went, she'd scold me but never made me stand in back of class. Today, I hunkered down and made a real effort to pay attention and not fidget.

Walking home it was cold and windy. We always wore long underwear and corduroy pants to school just for the walk home. Dad always arranged to take the milk to the creamery at the time to coincide with getting us to school on time. As I walked I thought about what Ray Brinks had said. No, that's not right. It wasn't about what he said, it was that he had said anything at all. That was bothering me.

It was then that the unimaginable horror of all horrors dawned on me. Debbie Dinkle was in my math class. What would happen if she had noticed that something was wrong, too, and told her mother. Ever since the caterpillar incident the third week of first grade, I had been gun-shy of that girl. That act of malfeasance hadn't ended with me getting my knuckles whapped with a ruler and left with caterpillar guts slopped on my fingers.

After school that day Debbie Dinkle went home and told mama bear Dinkle. It wasn't a couple of days later that mama bear Dinkle happened to run into mama bear Landon in a store and proceeded to unload a large piece of her mind on mama bear Landon. How could anyone have such a mean son, compared to him Adolph Hitler was a boy scout, blah, blah, blah. After school mama bear Landon proceeded to unload most of her mind on me. I was made to stand in the corner until supper time, and didn't get dessert for three days.

I was even made to apologize to Debbie in class with everybody watching. My humiliation was beyond measure. Everybody laughed and the teacher watched with a smug satisfied look on her face that I can still see to this day. After that the girls called me worm boy and stuff like that.

And, it didn't end at home, either. For years after that whenever I was discovered to be less than perfect—which was quite often—I not only took a berating for the current offense, but was reminded about the caterpillar and Debbie Dinkle. Poor girl must have been warped for life. Worms have that effect on some people, I guess.

To add to the unimaginable horror of all horrors that Debbie Dinkle was in my math class was the fact that she had become one of the most popular girls in school. And, she was beautiful. This was partly because her dad was a successful business man in town so she always wore great looking clothes.

Debbie had darkish blond hair that was always nicely done. Sometimes she wore cute clips in her hair with bright colored butterflies on them and butterfly earrings to match. On other days it was bright colored ribbons. She had the biggest light blue eyes in the world with long eye lashes that could knock a guy dead. She could smile at any boy and he'd be stepping on his tongue as he drooled all over himself. It was terrible except I never paid any attention to her.

But, that wasn't my problem at the moment. She might have noticed what was happening to me. If it was obvious enough so Emily and Ray from country school to see it, the town girls would certainly have been talking about it. They always talked about stuff like that.

CHAPTER 37

By the time I got home I was really worried. Why had Ray said anything to me today. Couldn't he have let it alone? If mom talked to me she'd guess something was wrong and start to pump me for information. As a result, as soon as I got in the house I took off my coat and boots and went upstairs to change. I decided I'd go out to the barn since dad would be in the brooder house getting things ready for the turkey chicks that would arrive in a week or two.

I almost made it with boots on and buckled, and my barn coat on, all I had was my cap and mittens when mom came up from the basement.

"Hi Jamie."

The tone of voice was a little off, like something wasn't quite right.

"I ran into Debbie Dinkle's mother in the store today."

Armageddon had finally lashed out upon the earth. I could only muster a spastic instinctive reaction like a dying animal gasping its last breath. I rolled my eyes. That always irritated mom. "Ah, gee, mom. The caterpillar thing happened the third week of first grade. I've paid for that. Give me a break."

By this time I had my cap on with the ear flappers down and was working with my mittens and it wasn't going so well.

"I'm not talking about that. Are you having problems in school?"

There it was, the girls were snitching like I knew they always did. I hated girls. Trying to act normal as I struggled with my second mitten, I thought I might be pulling off because I was completely ensconced in winter clothing and kept moving around so she couldn't get a good look at my face. I said, "Nothing out of the ordinary. I get scolded for not paying attention now and then, but that has always been my problem. We've talked about that."

"Why are you going out so early? It's so cold and blustery. Don't you want to work on your model airplane?"

"I need to get some fresh air. Might start chores a little early."

I had just walked home from school in a blinding snow storm so why would I need fresh air? Well, it had started snowing a little as I was coming in the driveway, but a guy can exaggerate to himself, can't he? Then I was outside. Whew, I made it. Mom would dig away again once I came in but this gave me time to think.

As I walked to the barn I could see that Debbie Dinkle had really gotten even with me this time. Of course, my troubles in math class weren't all my fault but I didn't want to tell mom and dad about Mr. Beecher's note or he might get in trouble. I'd need him on my side to drop the word about my having the strange knife if the need should arise.

Everybody had scolded me so much in my life that if the principal called mom or dad in to tell them how bad I was, they'd believe him. Especially dad would. To him the public school system was the all perfect thing that made America, America. Even though Mr. Haas had said Hindle had lied about teaching at Mankato, dad automatically believed the superintendent when he said he had verified that he had taught there. The school could do no wrong.

It was cold with a strong gusty wind. Snow was falling horizontally. In the barn I walked around and stopped to pet a couple of cats. It didn't help. I kept worrying about school. There was no way out with nothing I could do but let things go the way they wanted to go. Finally I decided to throw down silage. It was my night to do that, anyway. Tommy and I took turns. One of us would throw down and distribute silage in the feed troughs and the other would put down straw bedding for the cattle.

The irritation was still with me. First Emily had mentioned it—oops. When I mentioned before that I hated girls I didn't mean to include Emily. Something had gone wrong with her upbringing because she had turned out nice. Well, accidents did happen. Then Ray had mentioned it and now mama bear Dinkle. Oh, wow, another thing occurred to me. If Debbie's mother mentioned it on a chance meeting with mom in town today, Debbie had mentioned it some days earlier to her mother, maybe even weeks before. This was even worse than I had thought.

The howling wind was rattling the back barn door where the cattle came in and that irritated me. I looked that way and saw the ten-tine fork had fallen down and was lying with the curved tines angled up. It had been leaned up against a post between the chute that ran up alongside the silo that was used for both silage and hay, and the back door. We used a ten-tine fork to distribute the silage to the feed troughs. It had ten curved tines like a pitchfork but it had a handle like a scoop shovel. We were always warned never to leave a fork lying down like that because someone could come along and ram his leg into the tines.

In my irritation, I thought I'd pick it up after I threw down silage. After all, I was the only one in the barn and nobody could get hurt. And, it was subconsciously as act of rebellion against all the troubles that were being dumped on me. I climbed up the steps inside the chute to the window in the thick concrete wall at the level of the silage.

The inside of the silo was dimly lite from openings above, but there was a bare bulb hanging from an extension chord from an upper window. I turned it on. We always left a five tined fork in the silo so we didn't have to carry it up every day. This fork had a long straight handle. I had to pitch out a half layer of silage eight inches thick. That was enough for the evening feeding. I got to work and it felt good.

I always remember how on holidays, especially Christmas, we'd be in the nice warm house fooling around with things we had gotten as gifts and nibbling on Christmas candy all day. When it came chore time we hated the thought of putting on our old clothes and going out into the cold to work. But, after loafing around all day and eating too much the exercise felt good.

Even though I didn't mind the physical work, my mind was not at peace. When I had enough silage thrown down I was still agitated. I climbed down and stepped on the pile of silage and then into the lower barn. At that moment a strong gust of wind ripped around the barn and the back door swung open. The cattle were all grouped around the door waiting to be let in to their evening meal and the warmth and shelter of the barn.

Instantly I yelled at them and sprang for the door. As I ran I impaled my shin bone on one of the tines of the ten-tine fork lying on the floor.

Ow! Did that hurt! But the cattle were about to charge into the barn. The fork was stuck in my leg so I kicked the fork off and grabbed it up using the back side of the tines to thump the nose of the first cow trying to come in. I yelled and banged away with the fork and finally got them backed off so I was even with the threshold of the door. But if I stepped to the left to grab the handle of the door I had to leave the doorway unguarded. It was a test of wills but eventually I managed to pull the door halfway closed and kicking at the cow's noses got the door shut.

I was hardly rational for a minute as I stood there with my hand on the door handle lest it be sucked open again. Ten feet away was a pile of baler twine. When a bale of hay was burst open you were left with two loops of twine. These were deposited in a convenient place and periodically taken outside and burned. If they were left lying around they could eventually become caught in a machine or tangled in an animal's feet.

After carefully setting the fork against the barn wall I waited for the wind to momentarily let up and sprang for the pile of twine. Grabbing a handful I raced back to the door catching it in the nick of time as it was opening again. With one hand I shook a loop of twine loose and looped it through the handle of the door. There was a post eight feet from the door so I looped pieces of twine together until I had enough to wrap it around the post and tie it.

All this time I had hardly noticed my shin where I had stabbed it with the fork. Now it started to hurt. Sitting down on some hay I leaned my back against the silo, unbuckled my boot and pulled it off. I pulled up my pants leg and my underwear to see a seeping round hole in my skin. It wasn't bleeding much and that was bad. In health class Mr. Beecher had spent quite a bit of time on first aid. He told us that puncture wounds were bad in that the object that made the wound normally poked dirt into the wound with it. This could cause an infection so it was important to make the wound bleed to cleanse it. Since the tine had gone through the top of my boot, my pants and my underwear it had plenty of time to pick up dirt on its way in.

Squeezing the wound on the sides didn't help and it hurt when I did that. The rest of my problems were forgotten as I decided what to do. One thing was certain. I couldn't sit there all night so I pulled down my underwear and pants, put my boot back on and stood up. Nothing was broken or anything like that and it didn't hurt bad when I walked so I finished my job by carrying the silage to the six-inch high feed troughs like I normally did.

I had planned to start on the straw if Tommy hadn't come out by the time I was done with the silage, but decided it would be a good idea to go in and at least put some iodine on the hole in my leg.

In the house I told mom what had happened and she looked at the wound. It wasn't a very big hole but it had started to get blue around it. We had a disinfectant called *Lysol* that we used for just about everything. She put some in a pan of warm water and made me hold a rag soaked in it on my shin.

To keep the discussion about school from coming up, I said, "When Tommy goes out he has to tell dad that there's something wrong with the latch on the back door." I blabbered about how the cows would have gotten in and been running all around inside the barn if I hadn't managed to get the door closed again.

After five minutes mom wiped off my leg and put a Band-Aid over the hole. I went upstairs and said I'd sit on the bed with my leg up. Most days we had some homework problems to do for math class so I decided to do that. Nothing was said the rest of the evening about school. That was good.

The next day was Tuesday. That wouldn't normally have meant anything to me and it didn't except that the line up of days this week would be important. My leg hurt a little more today but I didn't say anything. The day went on like normal. I walked with a little limp and if anyone mentioned it I said I had injured my ankle. Things were going okay until math class. Debbie Dinkle was there, of course. She had on a blue corduroy jumper the color of her eyes with a light rose colored blouse. Her hair was in a ponytail, not stringy, but all carefully curled. It was tied with satin ribbons, one matching the jumper and the other the blouse. Earrings were small roses the same shade as her blouse. She even wore blue shoes that matched the rest. I hardly noticed her.

My leg was hurting a little worse at times, a throbbing ache, really. It didn't matter if I walked on it or not. I thought it might be my imagination, that it only hurt when I thought about it.

The class inched along like it always did, but I couldn't get comfortable. I tried putting the heel of my hurt foot up on the toe of the other one so it would be raised up but it slipped off. Of course Mr. Russo noticed it and made me stand in the back of the room. I limped back to my customary spot. Now I was feeling sorry for myself and it hurt all the more so I sat on the floor.

"I didn't say you could sit down. Get up!"

A barely perceptible groan could be heard from the collective class. By this time most of the kids knew I had a sore foot. With school so boring, any news was welcome so they had something to keep their minds off the mental drivel dished out in class. Word spread fast. And, I was getting mad. "I hurt my foot last night and it's hard to stand on it."

He took this as a direct affront and started back toward me. "I doubt that, let me see your foot."

This was terrible. First of all the stab wound didn't look like anything that would cause much pain. And, as I thought about it I was horrified. If he pulled up my pants leg all the girls would see my long underwear. There was no choice. I stood up keeping my weight on my good leg.

"Just as I thought, malingering. Any more of that back talk and you're getting expelled." He stopped and returned to the front of the classroom savoring his victory.

It was now apparent that the intent was to get me expelled, and in exchange for them getting *it* the harassment would stop.

The class ended and I waited for the aisle to be cleared so I could go to my assigned desk and pick up my books. Somehow, my foot didn't hurt so bad anymore. Maybe it was panic that was over-riding it.

Leaving the room I headed down the hall to history class, my next to the worst one. Gulp! There was Debbie Dinkle looking my way while talking to another girl. There were kids coming and going and the stream of traffic forced me so I'd have to pass close to her. But I'd slip past. After all, for someone like her I didn't exist. Looking straight ahead I moved on dreading my close encounter. The stars were aligned in a crooked way today because completely against my will I glanced at her and she was looking at me. Eye contact! The other girl had vanished into thin air.

She smiled and said, "Hi Jamie."

Something was wrong with her tone of voice. It sounded odd, really odd . . . nice!

"Ah . . . ah, hi Deb."

She held out her hand as if to stop me so I did but only when I was partly past her. I turned being at a loss of what to say. She had grown fast and was about as tall as she would get while I still had a lot of growing left to do. This made her taller than me and all the more intimidating. I had my books in my left hand so in a reflexive gesture I held out my right hand palm toward her with my fingers spread. "See. No caterpillars."

She had the strangest look like I had said something totally inane, which I suppose I had. In something of a bewildered tone she said, "It's the middle of winter. There are no caterpillars. Don't be silly."

I replied, "You said silly but I think you meant stupid. Gotta go."

With that I turned and started walking while the foot hurt more than it ever had. Behind me I heard her say the oddest thing, "Jamie, nooooo."

I did it. I really did it, I stepped on my tongue. Near the end of the hall was the door to history class. I hoped I could get to my desk without doing anything else that was dumb. At least we didn't share American History so here I was safe from the Debbie monster.

Walking home today the wind wasn't so bad as yesterday but it was colder. It didn't matter. My leg was uncertain as to whether it really wanted to ache or give it up as a bad job because I kept walking on it no matter what. At home I had the same problem as the day before. I had to get out to the barn before Debbie got home and told her mother about our almost encounter. It seemed she had something in mind but it couldn't be good. By this time, as irrational as it seemed, I began to think mom and Debbie's mother were phoning each other. Alexander Graham Bell's invention sure wasn't helping me.

I was changed and nearly suited up again when mom said, "Did you talk to Debbie today?"

I almost dropped down dead on the spot but managed to answer. "Yeah. She said I was stupid."

Opening the door I was hit in the face by a puff of cold air as I heard mom say, "Jamie, nooooo," and the door was closed.

I had the feeling of a delayed echo. But, that did it. My remotest ink-
ling near the farthest edge of possibilities was true. Mom had been talking
on the phone with Debbie's mother. Probably did it while I was in the
barn last night. That was no chance meeting in the hall at school today. I
was being driven like a wild animal into a killing zone.

It was my night to do the straw and I was glad of that. I wasn't sure
I'd make it up the steps in the chute by the silo. The bales of straw were
piled along the north side of the barn. One of the first floor windows
swung in on hinges along the top. A stick was used to prop it open so we
could throw in bales. I grabbed bales and started heaving them in. By
that time Tommy was out and started on the silage. I should have helped
him by carrying the silage to the feed troughs but after the straw was
spread out my leg was hurting worse than it ever had.

On the way to school that morning dad said the hasp on the back door
had rattled loose in the wind and that's why the door had blown open. He
had driven in new nails so it wouldn't happen again.

I waited for Tommy to finish and we walked to the house together. I
asked him how Mr. Hindle had been acting. He seemed a little surprised
that I asked. "Now that you mention it, he has been kind of nasty to me
the last couple of weeks. I say the slightest word out of place and he
snaps at me. Everybody makes a comment now and then or asks a question without raising his hand. That's the way the class goes. But if I say a
word, boy it's the end of the world."

"Yeah," I said. "I have two of them, Mr. Russo in math and Mrs. La-
Beta it history, but Russo is the worst."

"Oh, that's it. There's been talk about how the seventh grade is getting rowdy and that one of the kids is always in trouble. It's you. Why
are they doing that?"

"The school year is moving on and they want the film. I guess they've
decided we have it. Dad and mom don't want any trouble plus dad thinks
the FBI should make copies of the film before we give it back to the
communists. Seems like a long time since Haas was here. If the FBI
wants it, what's taking them so long?"

After supper when we were still sitting around the table and the two
smaller ones had left mom asked, "What's going on in school? And, I
don't want any evasive answers. It sounds to me like you were rude to
Debbie today."

"Mom! Debbie Dinkle is the most popular girl in our class and I don't exist. You and her mother might be friends but that doesn't mean we are. You set it up so she would stop me in the hall and I was so shocked I almost died and said something dumb. You're not in school, you don't know how it is."

"It's not that she's poison, you know."

"Yes she is."

"We'll forget about that for now. What is this about you having to stand in the back of class all the time, and even being threatened with being expelled. We won't allow that. What would people say?"

Tommy took this point to intrude on my interrogation. "Mr. Hindle has started snapping at me every time I move. And the other kids are starting to notice that, too. They're all in on it together, they're communists. They must have decided we have the film and they want it."

I started talking, "They will get one or both of us expelled and when we give them the film everything will be fine again. We have to figure out how to give it back to them or our lives will be miserable. And I don't need Debbie Dinkle to worry about. After all the years of scolding I got about that caterpillar in first grade we are never going to be friends so forget about it."

"Jamie, don't you sass me!"

"Okay," dad said. "Jamie, settle down."

I did but started talking again. "Dad, this won't magically go away. One of the boys from country school even asked what I had done so Mr. Russo hated me so much. Everybody knows something is wrong. No matter how much you liked going to school and playing football and stuff like that it's different now. The school is full of communists and they're mean. Call Haas and find out if he has learned anything. I'll bet he won't even remember us. He doesn't care about where you got that list of names you read to him. He doesn't even know what it means. Have him come back and we'll let him look at the film. Then he can decide if he wants to do something."

"I hate to call him from here with those women at the exchange listening."

"Who cares? Maybe if they know we're calling the FBI Mr. Russo and Mr. Hindle will stop being so hard on us."

Dad agreed to call Mr. Haas as soon as he got home from the creamery the next day.

CHAPTER 38

Wednesday dawned cloudy and windy but it was March and that was normal. School went along as well as it ever did. My leg was hurting but what else was new. Then came math class. It seemed like before class the kids were in small knots talking about something. And, there was no laughing. The bell rang and I was in my seat but most of the other kids weren't. Mr. Russo had to firmly say. "Class, take your seats."

It plodded on but wasn't so bad because we were covering new material and it was interesting to me. With about ten minutes left in class Roger Atkins, in the seat behind me, pinched me on the arm. I shook my arm. He did it again and once again I pulled free. This was insane. He had never done anything like that. He kept at it until he dug in his finger nails and it really hurt. I turned around and said, "Roger, stop pinching me! Who do you think you are!"

Almost as if Mr. Russo had been waiting for me to say that he said, "That's it Landon. You've disrupted this class for the last time. I'm marching you to the principal's office and you are going to be expelled from this school. See how you like that."

It was like someone had punched me in the stomach. The whole class was in on it. No wonder they were all whispering before class.

I got up and the pain was back but who cared now? He grabbed me by the shirt behind my neck and we walked out of the room, me in front. As we did, there seemed to be a commotion in the room like when the bell rang to end class. When we emerged into the hall, the rest of the class flooded out behind us and soon was all around. They were saying, "We're all going to be expelled." And things like that.

Mr. Russo paused and released my shirt as he looked around. I turned to look at him as he was caught by surprise. Not wasting any time I decided to get behind him. No sooner had I made it when another boy punched him in the back, his fist flying over my shoulder. That forced Russo forward. He spun his head around, and assumed I had been the one who had hit him. He made a fist of his right hand where he wore a big ring and swung it around backhand planning to do some real damage to me. I saw it coming and ducked but the girl standing next to me didn't and the fist landed on her face with a smack. It was Emily! I had no idea she was there. At that instant a flash bulb went off.

It was all like a crazy play. The photographer must have been waiting for us to come out of the room. What had been meant to be nothing more than a stunt had become deadly serious. Emily took the blow and flew against one of the other girls and they both fell down. As I ducked I twisted my leg and a stabbing pain sent me to the floor. Kids were swirling around, a shout here, a scream there. It was pandemonium. As fast as the photographer could feed flashbulbs into the camera he was taking pictures.

Three offices were against the west wall of the building raised three steps. One was the junior high principal's and I didn't know who used the others. They had windows facing the inside so people in the offices could watch the hallway as classes changed. The flashing camera along with the growing commotion drew the occupants of the offices out.

One of the girls yelled, "Call a doctor!"

Someone else yelled, "Call the police!"

Mr. Russo was walking away when Ray Brinks grabbed him from behind holding his upper arms in his fists. "Where do you think you're going?"

A woman from the offices ran to where Emily was sitting against the wall. The milling around hadn't stopped. I saw the woman pull back a handkerchief that Emily was holding to a cut above her right eye. The woman stood up. "Don't call the doctor, I'll take her."

When she had Emily standing up, Mr. Marshall ran down the steps with the woman's coat and purse. He threw a man's coat over Emily, maybe his, and they made for the door. As they were going out a policeman came in. A town boy was standing beside Ray who was still holding Mr. Russo. As the policeman arrived the town boy said, "Arrest this man for felonious assault on a minor. We all saw it."

Then I remembered. That boy's father was one of the town's lawyers.

As the policeman was taking Mr. Russo out they chanted, "Lock him up and throw the key away. Lock him up and throw the key away."

The bell rang for the end of class and the hall flooded with even more kids each one wanting to know what all the ruckus was about.

My leg was hurting more then ever so I decided to go home. There wouldn't be much teaching for the rest of the day, anyway. At my locker I pulled on my overshoes and buckled them. One thing was good. The math class had ended early so Mr. Russo hadn't had time to pass out the homework papers.

It was windy but warmer than it had been. My leg was hurting more with each step and I hoped I'd make it home. I couldn't stop thinking about Emily so I prayed one prayer after another for her. If I only hadn't fidgeted in class, Mr. Russo could not have made me stand in the back and this couldn't have happened. If I hadn't tried to get away by stepping behind him. I kept praying.

About half way, when I was past the last city street, I had to stop. It dawned on me that I wasn't going to make it. Standing on my good leg I looked around. Any cars coming this far would be farmers so I might be able to flag one down.

Sure enough here one came. I waved, it went past and then stopped and backed up. I was lucky. It was Mr. Segal. Their land was across the road to the north of us. When the car stopped I hopped over to it.

Opening the door I asked, "Can you give me a ride home? I hurt my foot a couple of days ago and I can't make it any further."

"Sure, hop in."

When we were moving he asked like I knew he would, "What happened?"

"It's really dumb, but I got stabbed in the shin bone with a pitchfork."

He glanced over at me. "Saw it laying there and didn't bother to pick it up, eh? Then forgot about it and wham it was stuck in your shin."

Looking straight ahead I said, "Yeah."

"Pick it up next time, I bet."

"Yeah."

It was only a half mile so it didn't take long. I got out and said, "Thanks really a lot. I don't think I would of made it."

"Sure, any time."

I hopped to the house and sat on one of the kitchen chairs. Mom was in the kitchen and looked at me as I came in. "You're home early."

"My foot hurt so much I had to come home. Half way I couldn't walk on it anymore. Luckily Mr. Segal came by and gave me a lift or I'd still be sitting out there beside the road." I said the last part to garner a little sympathy.

"Is it bleeding?"

"No. Just hurts like it's falling apart or something."

"You can't walk on it at all?"

I shook my head, she frowned. "Mikey, come here."

He was in the other room and appeared at once. "Go out and tell Fred I have to take Jamie to the doctor before the Doc. goes home for the day. Then come in and watch that Lucy doesn't get into mischief."

For things like this at this time of day we went to the doctor's office rather than the hospital because the doctor would be in his office. We normally went to Dr. Henderson if we could. The other doctor was good, too, but mom and dad preferred Henderson who was a school board member. If that had any bearing on the preference I didn't know.

As we entered the waiting room it was empty except for a small girl sitting alone near the corner. Mom told the nurse why we were there and we sat down diagonally across the room from the girl. It hit me in a flash that the girl was Emily. "Stay here," I said to mom and I hopped over to her.

"Emily," I said in a soft voice.

She looked up, the saddest face I had ever seen. There was blood on her dress and a big bandage over her right eye that left only enough room so she could see out.

"Jamie."

The tone of her voice was different than I expected, like she was glad to see me. "Emily, how could this have happened? Oh, your eye must really hurt. I'm so sorry this happened."

I couldn't keep standing on one foot so I sat on the chair to her left and took her left hand in both of mine.

"I got seven stitches and the doctor thinks my eye will be all right, but isn't sure. My dad is in talking to him now."

"I'm so sorry, it's all my fault. You look like you're going to die. Are you sure you're going to be all right?"

Then I notice I was holding her hand and said, "Oh, I'm sorry. I didn't mean to grab your hand."

"That's okay, I don't mind," she said in such a quiet voice I could hardly hear it but I didn't let it go. She squeezed some of my fingers.

"I prayed for you all the way home and I'll pray that God sends His angel to watch over you so you get better."

She looked at me. I saw her good eye and the right one that was starting to swell shut. "And I won't ask God to send any ordinary angel, I'll ask for the prettiest one He has because you are the prettiest girl He ever made. Who else has eyes the color of wild violets?"

As I spoke her face was turned to me and seemed totally intent on what I was saying. After the last word she smiled the brightest smile in the world, and in a soft voice said, "Thank you, Jamie."

The door to the doctor's office began to open and I dropped her hand like a hot potato. Her father came out and said, "Come on, princess, I'll take you home. The rest of this can wait."

"Daddy," she said in a pleasant almost happy voice, "I'm going to be all right, my eye will be just like new."

"We sure hope so, but the doctor isn't sure."

"But, I know it'll be okay."

"Whose next?" the doctor asked.

Mom got up and I slipped off the chair favoring my leg as I mostly hopped. When he had me up on the examining table he removed my boot and mom told him why we were there. The hole was a little above the ankle joint. He gripped my foot in one hand and the leg above the hole with the other and started gently bending and twisting it each time asking if it hurt. No matter what he did it hurt. He nodded his head.

"Was the fork stuck in you leg, or did it only poke it enough to break the skin?"

"It was stuck in. I had to kick it off."

He nodded again and looked at my mother. "The fork tine injured the bone and with continued use the bone started to crack. Don't feel bad because it would have been hard to tell how bad the original injury was even if you came right in that day. But, and this is important, the bone is ready to break." He paused, "Hang on a moment."

He got up and opened the office door, Elmira, see if you can find a pair of small adult crutches."

"Coming up."

Returning he said, "I will have to put the leg in a cast but I don't have what I need here in the office. Therefore, I'll give you a pair of crutches and send you home. Come to the hospital about nine in the morning. Meanwhile, Jamie, you are not under any circumstances to put any weight on that leg. Do you understand?"

I nodded.

"The way it is, you'll wear a cast for two or three weeks. If it breaks, not only will it hurt a lot worse than anything you've felt so far, but you'll wear a cast for six to eight weeks. You don't realize how important that is, but after two weeks with the cast you will."

"Has he ever had a tetanus shot?" he asked mom.

"I think he had one when he got cut with the corn knife, but that was about eight years ago.

He nodded. "He's due for a booster shot anyway. It'll only take a minute."

I hated those needles but it wasn't like I had a choice so I took off my coat and rolled up my sleeve.

There was a knock and the door opened. The nurse handed a pair of wooden crutches to the doctor. He had me stand up and I tried them. He made an adjustment and then had me walk with them. After some instructions we were on our way.

As we left the nurse said to the doctor, "The phone won't stop wringing. It all seems to be about what happened at school."

When we were on the way home mom asked, "Do you know the girl that was in the office?'

"Yeah. That's Emily LaNell. She's in my class. She came from a country school."

"What did you say to her? When we came in I have to say I never saw a more forlorn little girl in my life and when she left her spirits were way up. As she was leaving she seemed, well, happy. And from that bandage on her face, that's the last thing a person would expect."

I shrugged.

"Come on, what did you tell her?"

"I said I'd say a prayer for her."

I had never heard my mother in such a cajoling, playful mood. "Hey, guy, you're holding out on me, you said more than that. As you talked to her, her attention was transfixed on you and then she gave you the sweetest smile I've ever seen. When she spoke to her father you could hear it in her voice, she sounded almost cheerful."

I shrugged. It had gotten awful hot in the car.

When I didn't say any more she replied, "Well, whatever you said it was very kind. I was afraid at first that she was so down that she'd never get well. You perked up her more than I would have thought possible. You know, it's important for a person who's sick or injured to want to get better. She'll get well now, that's for sure."

CHAPTER 39

When we got home there was a red and white Buick parked where we backed out of the shed to turn around. It was Marty's. Dad was in the house with him and it seemed like they were waiting for us to get home. When I fumbled my way through the door on the crutches, Marty said, "Not another one!"

I stood on one foot as mom helped me out of my coat. She looked at Marty as he stared at me and finally put it together. "Jamie hurt his leg in the barn a couple of days ago and it wasn't getting better so I took him in. His shin bone is cracked and the doctor will put a cast on it tomorrow."

"But, you were there, weren't you?" he said looking at me. "I mean at school this afternoon."

"Yeah. Boy, that was something. The math teacher was almost dragging me out of the room taking me to the principal to get me expelled and there was somebody waiting in the hallway with a flash camera. Then, all the rest of the kids flooded out of the room like it was the end of class. They were all around us. Mr. Russo had let go of my shirt so I eased myself behind him. Just then a boy punched him in the back. His fist came right over my shoulder. Mr. Russo turned his head around and seeing me thought I had done it and took a backhanded swing at me. I ducked and he hit Emily in the face instead."

"Oh!" mom said. "That was the Emily in the doctor's office!"

"Yeah," I said, "of course."

"You saw her?" Marty almost demanded. "How is she?"

"She had a big bandage on her . . . ."

"Seven stitches," I interrupted. "He always wore a big ring on that hand and he had his hand in a tight fist. It cut her face real bad."

"The bandage was above her right eye," mom continued, "and the eye was almost swollen shut. But as I overheard, apparently the doctor thought she'd be all right, but couldn't be sure. She really looked down hearted when we came in but Jamie talked to her and cheered her up. I actually think it was good that we happened to be there."

Oh man. Did she have to say that. Now everybody would know. But it wouldn't have mattered because the doctor's combination receptionist and nurse had seen the whole thing, too. I don't know if I mentioned this before, but this was a small town. Yeah, I guess I have. Anyway, Mrs. Elmira Hamilton was a good citizen, one of the best. That is to say, she wasn't stingy about spreading gossip. Being in a doctor's office gave her access to a lot of people's troubles, and what else but people's troubles was the engine of gossip. In her humble way she could put any railroad locomotive to shame. By the time I got back to school everybody knew that she had said that if she ever got sick she wanted me to hold *her* hand and whisper sweet nothings in *her* ear. It was terrible.

Marty was rubbing his hand across his chin in agitation. "This is really a mess . . . . Wait a minute, that teacher was taking you to the principal's office to get you expelled, as in expelled from school? Did I hear that right?"

"Yeah."

He looked at mom and dad in bewilderment apparently thinking we were closet werewolves or something.

Dad appeared about to say something but I interrupted again, "Did you call Mr. Haas?"

"Yes. He said he'd try to get up here tomorrow. It's a pretty long drive in the winter." Looking at Marty he said. "This is a complicated matter and there is a limit to how much I can tell you. But, what I do tell you should not be repeated. I can't force you not to talk, but if you do it could cause you a lot of trouble."

Marty still had that look like he wasn't sure we weren't werewolves.

"Mr. Haas is an FBI agent and we have met with him several times about this. This is a matter of national security. So far we haven't told Mr. Haas the whole story because the FBI is infiltrated by foreign agents. We have proof of that."

Marty was incredulous.

"It started with *us* some years ago but it started at school last fall. Do you remember when the ninth grade English teacher wanted to leave and it happened Gregory Hindle was available?"

"Yes. That was all straight forward."

"Not really. There are communists in the school and they think we have something they want very badly. Last fall Mr. Marshall, the junior high principal, thought he had proof we had what they wanted. Exactly a week later Mr. Hindle started teaching ninth grade English. You recall it all happened quickly. Hindle is a communist, we know that."

"How would you know?"

"In August he was here at the farm using a different name asking indirectly about what they want. Ann and Jamie are both certain he's the same man. And he also connects to more events some years before. The FBI confirmed that. Anyway, Hindle was brought in to get what they want and he almost did. He expected to get it and if he had he would have disappeared leaving you to scramble for another English teacher."

"But the superintendent verified Handle's credentials."

"No he didn't. He's a communist, too. He didn't call anyone and saw no reason to. If things went according to plan they'd have it in a few weeks and we would all be sitting around talking about that rat of a teacher who took off with no warning.

"Remember the first week Hindle was teaching and he didn't give the test papers back? And, parents were calling complaining?"

Marty nodded.

"He had never taught a class before and didn't know how it worked."

"This all sounds like a spy movie. But, let's say I believe you. All I have to do is demand that Hindle appear at a school board meeting and give us his resume. Then the board members can verify his references."

"It's too late," Tommy chimed in.

"Why?"

"There are a couple of books in the library at school about communism and I've read them. By now they've backstopped his story."

"What does that mean?"

"When Hindle arrived he gave the superintendent what basically would appear in the *Sentinel*. It gave the college where he graduated, that

288

he last taught at Mankato, and stuff like that. There were no records at those places but that didn't matter."

"Well, what if someone had checked?"

"That's the point. If you had done it *then* you could have exposed him as a fraud. But those places listed are where the communists have helpers, what they call fellow travelers, in the records offices. Seeing that it was going to take longer than they thought, they backstopped, that is, manufactured files on Hindle so if you check *now* the records are there. The FBI checked at Mankato right away and Mankato had no knowledge of him. Haas said they didn't want to do more checking because it might have exposed other on-going investigations."

Marty was a good businessman and was trying hard to cope. Finally he asked, "How does what happened in school today connect with that spy story you just told me?"

I spoke up. "It looks like they were first going to get me expelled from school and if that didn't work they'd get Tommy expelled, too. That would be the incentive to get us to give them what they think we have. Mr. Russo was singling me out for punishment since January. It seems like they thought the school year was moving on and they had to step up the pressure.

"I always tend to fidget around when classes get boring. In addition to that I was warned last fall that some of the teachers were going to single out Tommy and me for harassment."

"You never told us that," mom said. "Who was it?"

"Can't say," I said. "It was something people were taking about. You know how that goes." I lied a little because I realized I should not have mentioned it.

"As a result of being bored I have always gotten scolded by teachers so it wasn't so bad. I was used to it. But, in the last few weeks three kids from math class mentioned to me how Mr. Russo seemed to have singled me out for bad treatment."

Tommy said, "Wait. I want to say that Mr. Hindle has been getting hard on me, and kids are noticing that, too. He had never threatened to expel me, though. And, Jamie's situation was even being mentioned among the ninth graders."

"Then what?" Marty asked.

"Today before math class started the kids seemed to all be standing around in small groups whispering but I didn't think much about it. Maybe there was a big party Friday night or something. With about ten minutes left in the class, Roger Atkins, who sits behind me, started pinching my arm. He kept at it until I turned around and told him to stop it. When I said that Mr. Russo said I had disrupted the class for the last time and that he was going to get me expelled. When we were out in the hall the flash camera started like I told you."

"So, it seems it was planed, is that it?"

"I don't know but that's what happened. Yesterday when I had my sore leg he made me stand in the back of the room for almost the whole class time. Some of the kids even groaned when he made me do it. They might have gotten fed up and decided to do something about it. Now that I think about it, one of the girls in that class has an aunt who works for the paper. The photographer might have been from the *Sentinel*."

Marty looked worried. "That wouldn't be good. What do we do?"

I spoke again. "One of the kids said that Russo had committed a felonious assault on a minor by hitting Emily. His dad is a lawyer. Throw Mr. Russo in jail."

"But, won't the communists retaliate?"

"Not likely," Tommy said. "At least not directly or right away. They are ruthless. In the early thirties when Joseph Stalin finally consolidated power in Russia, he had tens of thousands of other communists killed because they had a little different idea about what communism should be. They think nothing of sacrificing their own."

Dad finally spoke. "It looks like all you can do is punish the teacher for the obvious crime he has committed. The town will be hopping mad but handle it like it's an isolated case."

"What about this Mr. Hindle, and are there more?"

"There's Mrs. LaBeta the seventh grade American History teacher," I said. "It sounds like she's treating me like Hindle is treating Tommy. The harassment must stop or the paper will start snooping. In fact there was someone there interviewing the kids after Emily was hit. She might have been a reporter for the paper who came with the photographer."

"I can see the midnight oil being burned at the *Sentinel*," Marty said wistfully. Then he said, "Oh! Today's Wednesday! That's why it was set up for today. It'll be in the paper tomorrow while the news is still hot."

WILD VIOLETS

The next day I managed to get to the hospital without breaking my leg. Maybe it was my imagination again, but it seemed like the bone was ready to break every time I moved my foot. The cast felt heavy on my leg, but it kept me from putting sideways pressure on it so it hurt less. They left a hole in the cast so the puncture wound could be seen in case it became infected. Mom and dad decided to have me stay home Friday, too, so I had time to get used to the crutches.

By the time mom brought me home from the hospital Mr. Haas was there. Dad was in the house and had asked him if he had found out anything about the two names he had recognized from the list. Haas said he hadn't which dismayed dad, but maybe dad was starting to see the government wasn't all perfect. He then told Haas about the microfilm and the list of sleeper agents. But nothing could be done until I got home because only I knew where the film was. Before long we had Mr. Haas set up at the dining room table with the magnifier so he could look at the film. Dad and mom made sure he understood that there was no way he would be permitted to leave with even one piece of film. It was our only way to get our lives back.

Tommy, Lucy and Mikey were in school so it was the four of us for dinner. As we ate, Mr. Haas said, "The film is important, and in spite of there being one agent on the list it doesn't mean The Bureau is completely useless. I'd like to take the film back with me and copy it. Then I'll return it and we'll do all we can to help you get it back to them in such a way that they won't think it's been compromised."

Dad shook his head. "It takes only one rotten apple and it'll disappear. You didn't know about the agent on the list. Even if there's only one in a hundred FBI employees who is a fellow traveler, it could be one who handles the film. If you want a copy bring some equipment here and we'll do it on the dining room table. We give you one strip of film, you photograph it and give it back. We look at it with the magnifier to see that it isn't in any way damaged or even marked. One little mark and no more film. And everyone who enters the house will be searched and be carrying no arms, not even a fountain pen. I've been thinking about this and with what has happened at school. I'm not very happy. Take it or leave it."

Haas shrugged. "I'll take it. I think it's important to know how it was packaged when you got it. Will you show me?"

Dad looked at me. "I hate to say it but only Jamie knows that. What do you say?" he said looking at me.

I figured the time had come so I told dad where it was. While dad went to get it, mom cleared the table. Dad laid the rolled up old feed sack on the table and unrolled it.

"It's Justin's knife!" dad said.

Mr. Haas picked up the scabbard, pulled out the knife and examined it carefully. "They're all different in some way but the basic design is standard." Looking at me he asked, "How did you ever figure out how to get the film out with no damage to the knife?"

"I had six years to look at that thing. After Granston's visit in August I got serious and figured if there were no other way I'd use the hacksaw on it. That handle isn't bone, it's metal."

He nodded.

"The shank at the back of the knife is a little thicker than the base of the blade where it goes into the handle so I thought they might be separate pieces. Eventually I discovered that if you press in real hard on the back of the shank a stiff spring is released and the back part pokes out."

"Bravo. That's excellent work. When you get through school, would you consider working for The Bureau?"

What could I say, I was only in the seventh grade.

"There'll be time," he said.

It was about one o'clock. "If I start now I can get back before dark. The roads aren't good after that freezing rain you had a few days ago. I'll come back with another man and some equipment. When's a good time?"

"I'm scheduled to get the turkeys next Tuesday so it should be before that. Tomorrow or Saturday would be best."

"Let's make it Saturday, then."

After Mr. Haas left, dad went out to the brooder house again. And I went to the living room. It was hard getting up stairs. I had slept in the spare bed on the first floor last night but wanted to get upstairs tonight. The crutches would take practice but already I was getting better at using them.

When I had settled down on the living room sofa, mom came in. "I don't want to pry, but did you know Emily was beside you when she was hit?"

292

"Oh, no. Everybody was moving around. Some of the kids were saying, 'We're all going to get expelled' and stuff like that. It was like a party. They were going to play a joke on the teacher, I guess. Mr. Russo was surprised and I think pretty mad. His class was out of control. Nobody goes into the hall during class periods unless they're sick or something."

"But, you think Emily's getting hit was your fault?"

I was wringing my hands. "If I didn't fidget in class so much it couldn't have happened. She's the only girl I like even a little. I only talked to her in the lunch room. When she's not all bandaged up she's real pretty, and she's nice. I feel so bad."

From mom's expression I could tell some wheels were turning in her head and that was never good. But, she was being nice like she sometimes was. "When other people get hurt, even those we don't know real well, we feel bad and suffer for them. That's the way life is. I can't see it was you fault at all. We know why the teacher was after you and if you didn't fidget he'd have thought of something else. Don't worry, I think Emily will be all right. It was nice of you to cheer her up yesterday, though. I bet she appreciated that."

Mom brought me one of my airplane books and I started to read it in places. A couple of hours later the phone rang.

"He's all right. His leg will be in a cast a few weeks but, that's all." She listened for a while. "Emily is one of the girls in the class . . . ." Another pause, "I've talked to him and she happened to be in the wrong place—could have been anyone." More waiting. "None of us know anything about the teacher. We're as surprised as everyone else. Yeah. Good bye."

She hung up. "That was Mary Fergerson." She was the mother of one of the Catholic school kids. "The paper is out in town and the front page had nothing but the school story."

The phone rang again. It went about the same. She hung up. It rang again. After she said good bye she let the receiver hang beside the phone.

"I don't know what to do."

CHAPTER 40

The next morning when dad came home from the creamery he said the whole town was steaming. He had picked up the mail on the way in the driveway as usual and we had our copy of the *Deep Woods Sentinel*. Above the fold was the picture of Mr. Russo's fist hitting Emily. I was in the process of falling down and was a blur toward the bottom of the picture. At the top was the headline "Junior High Class in Rebellion." Mom and dad were reading aloud some of the news story. "The students were chanting, 'Lock him up and throw the key away,'" and stuff like that. Jamie Landon was prominently mentioned in the lead article as was Emily. It seemed Emily LaNell might lose an eye and Jamie Landon was made to stand in the back of the room with a broken leg. We all heard a touch of Elmira Hamilton in that.

Before the paper went to press the editor had called the president of the school board and got him to commit to an emergency board meeting in the gym on Friday night at seven o'clock. Marty and dad had talked on the phone a couple of times and it seemed like they would set up a way any student could directly call any or all of the school board members if they thought someone were being harassed. I understood that and thought it was good but it would force the communists to do something else.

On Saturday Mr. Haas arrived about eleven since it took about four hours to drive up. It went okay with them photographing the film as we all took turns looking at each strip as they finished. The man operating the equipment was exceptionally careful like he had to do sensitive things like that all the time.

Before they left Mr. Haas asked what we intended to do.

I told him Justin's idea of selling the knife to them.

"That might work," he said. "However, they would know or at least assume that you had it for a long time and might get suspicious that you had found out exactly what you did find out. That could make them want to clean up loose ends."

"We're open to any other ideas you have," dad said. "Don't do anything right away and give us a chance to work on it. I'll be in touch."

I was dreading going back to school Monday. It wasn't that I couldn't handle the crutches, because I could. It was unsettling was all. On the other hand I was dying to find out how Emily was, without, of course, letting anyone know how desperately I wanted to know.

When I got to school the reception was mixed with most of it positive. They said things like, "It looks like the teacher got expelled."

Emily and I only had math class together so it wasn't until then that I had any assurance of seeing her. I got there a minute before the bell because I wasn't very fast, and saw her place was empty. Some of the girls must have been waiting to see what I'd do because one of them said to me, "Wondering where Emily is?"

Boy, they were like vultures. "Well, yes. I heard the smack when Mr. Russo hit her. She was bleeding pretty bad."

"You're dodging the question. We know you were sitting with her in the doctor's office and holding her hand. Did you kiss her?"

It was getting worse. The bell rang. As they say, "Saved by the bell."

Everywhere I looked it seemed there was a girl smirking at me. Our teacher was a woman who did substitute teaching when a regular teacher got sick.

The first thing she said was, "Emily is in Minneapolis. The school decided to pay to have her taken to an eye specialist. I think we'll see her tomorrow. We can hope and pray that she'll be all right. Now to work. Open your books to page. . . ."

After class, before I could get mobilized on my crutches there were several of them, girls, that is, around me. "What did you say to her in the doctor's office? It must have been pretty good for her to be smiling so much after having her face smashed up."

"I said I'd say a prayer for her. Come on, let me get up, you're in the way." There were teasing comments about my lady love and that stuff like girls always talk about, but I ignored them.

The next day Emily was in class when I hobbled in. There were girls around her but when they saw me they stopped talking wanting to see what would happen.

I worked my way to my seat which was two rows from her. She was looking at me, smiling. Did she have to do that? Already the bandage was smaller. She had a real shiner, though. Her eye was mostly open so she could see with two eyes. I said, "Hi Emily. How's your eye?" I was smiling, too. Darn it I couldn't help it. Everybody saw it.

"It'll be okay. How's your leg?"

There was music in her voice which thrilled me and I smiled even more. Dang it. "It'll be okay." I don't know why I said it like all the other dumb things I've said, "That must have been some fight. How does the other guy look?"

"I broke his leg."

The room exploded in laughter, and seeing I had set myself up once again for humiliation I blushed. She saw it and there was a look of horror on her face as the laughter grew ever more intense. At that moment the teacher called the class to order.

As far as the harassment went, it stopped for both Tommy and me instantly. The new plan where any student or parent could call any school board member if there was a complaint was like it hadn't happened. There were no calls. The town worked its way into thinking that Mr. Russo was nothing but a bad egg. The fact that he had been a good math teacher that most students and people in the community liked was lost sight of. People here like everywhere wanted to get back to a routine that was comfortable.

Tommy said that was the modus operandi for the communists. Once an operation went sour, they dug in, regrouped and thought of something else to try. Those caught out in the open like Mr. Russo are left to twist in the breeze. The rest of them, the superintendent, Mr. Hindle, Mr. Marshall, and Mrs. LaBeta were forgotten and free to attack from a new quarter.

* * *

Time passed. Blustery March became April and still nothing happened. It was almost like they were deliberately letting the tension build so we would be forced to make the next move. We had discussed it and I had told mom, dad and Tommy that I had shown the knife to Mr. Beecher last fall. We wanted it over with so I wrote a letter to Mr. Beecher that I'd deliver to him personally. We all read it and agreed on what it said.

The next day after health class I hung back until the room was empty except for Mr. Beecher and myself. I handed him the letter and smiled. He nodded.

The letter said he was to let it be known in the presence of Mr. Hindle but not directly to him if possible that he, Mr. Beecher, had heard one of his students talking about how much he wanted a certain model airplane and gas motor. He'd seen the odd knife while buying apples last fall and even though the boy seemed to like the knife he'd bet the boy would sell it to get the airplane. After all, boys and model airplanes. The boy lived at that place with the round barn.

Mr. Beecher was told he could add as much detail as the situation warranted, but the less said the better as long as the basic facts were passed on. The important thing was that Hindle was to think he had gotten vital information by accident and that Beecher didn't know its value so Hindle would act on it.

We also gave Mr. Beecher a code by which he would inform me if he had managed to pass on the information. Before or after class each day he was to say something to me about homework, a test or class. If it was a negative comment it would mean he had not yet passed on the information; if positive he had succeeded. That was on Monday.

Now that the plan was started, in the evening dad placed a call to the number Justin had given me. When we had talked about the situation under the oak tree last fall I had given him the code of Aunt Bertha being ill the same as for Mr. Haas. Dad told him that Aunt Bertha was ailing and it would be good for him to come if he could. Justin said he would leave the next day. Depending upon how ill Aunt Bertha was said to be indicated the urgency of the situation.

Justin had been insistent that we call him if trouble started. We hated to inconvenience him, but we felt the need for another man, a fighting man.

The negative comments came all week until Friday I got a positive comment. The plan was set in motion and we'd have to see what would happen. It worked out perfectly because Justin arrived about noon. He put his motorcycle back in the shed where it was out of sight. We didn't even know if Hindle would be the one to show up. Maybe when they knew where the knife actually was, they'd come and take it at gunpoint. We had "mama's gum" loaded and ready at hand. I kept the .22 loaded behind the door. Dad has his twelve gauge out of the case and in the coat room off the kitchen where the steps went to the basement. It wasn't loaded, but shells were handy.

We worked on the story we, or mostly I, would use. I was the one selling the knife. I did want a certain model airplane and had a model magazine with an advertisement for it. But I planned to ask for a lot more money than the model cost. We had worked on that, too. Dad was a pretty good businessman. He said if I only asked for, say twenty-five dollars, Hindle would think it was too easy, that something was wrong. I had to really cherish the knife and appear truly torn to part with it. I was pretty good at stuff like that.

Shortly after lunch on Saturday we were still all in the kitchen. It was good having Justin around and we were all getting caught up on the news. He was working on a ranch in the Southwest and since they had recently finished branding it wasn't hard for him to get free for awhile.

A car pulled into the yard, a 1950 black Ford. It was Mr. Hindle. Justin turned and glanced out the window behind him, "Speaking of the devil."

Even though he had worn a beard and mustache the time he was here the previous August, he had to believe mom would recognize him. But, as far as he knew, she was the only one who had seen him.

Since we had no idea what their response would be there was little we could do by way of preparation except keep loaded guns handy. Justin said he had a revolver in a saddle bag on his motorcycle.

As soon as we knew who it was, Justin had everyone but dad and me wait in the living room because Hindle would for sure recognize Tommy and Justin. And it was good to keep the two younger ones out of the way. This way we, as well as he, could pretend we were strangers. It was thin because I had seen him charge into the room when Mr. Beecher and I were looking at bugs with the microscope.

Justin told me to make sure I took him to the barn. The knife was hidden in the machinery room so that would work. When we were out of

298

sight in the barn, Justin and Tommy would leave by the front door. Justin would make for the shed and get his gun. Tommy would work around behind the brooder house. His job was to watch for anyone sneaking up to the buildings from the road that ran to the north of the farm.

Hindle knocked on the screen door since the kitchen door was open. Dad went out and said, "Hello."

He got right to the point. "Hello. I heard that someone here might have a quite unusual knife. It's a rather big knife with a bone-handle. I'm something of a knife collector and it sounded like this is one I've been looking for. Of course I can't be sure unless I see it."

When dad didn't reply, he continued, "Am I correct in that you have such a knife?"

Dad replied slowly, "Well, my son has a knife that some might say was unusual, but I doubt that he'd sell it."

"Maybe he would if the price is right, you know what I mean."

"Sorry, didn't catch your name."

"Granston, Jarvis Granston."

Dad hadn't opened the door so they still stood with the screen door between them. Dad said, "Just a minute I'll get my son."

We had decided not to give any names, and since he was using the name of Granston that was all the more important. "Son, this here feller wants to buy your hunting knife."

Dad was speaking with less than perfect English and in a slow drawl to give the impression he was nothing but another farmer, something town people tended to look down on.

Hindle wasn't dressed anything like a teacher. I had seen him at school quite a few times. Today he wore worn jeans, and an old button shirt with the sleeves turned up part way. A leather vest hung open. His scuffed brown boots had seen better days. He looked like a bum. The commies must have bought him two sets of clothes for the teaching job and on his time off he wore his normal duds.

"Young man, it's possible I'm interested in purchasing your knife. If it's the type of knife that I'm looking for I'd give you a good price."

"I don't want to sell it because it was given to me by my best friend."

"May I ask who your friend was?"

"He was an Indian that worked for us one summer during the war."

We had hoped he'd ask these questions because this would help convince him he had found the right knife.

"Where do you suppose he got it?"

"Don't know. I always thought he got it in Italy where he fought in the war. He was wounded by shrapnel when a shell blew up near him. That also caused him to lose his hearing in one ear so when he got out of the VA Hospital they let him out of the Army."

"What hospital?"

"He was from a tribe in Minnesota so they put him in the one in St. Cloud."

He was hooked. The questions came too fast for anyone to think this was a normal inquiry. Each answer narrowed his search until he knew he had it.

"Could I see the knife?"

We had him where we wanted him, now it was our move.

"Sure, I'll go get it, I keep it in the barn. Ever seen the inside of a round barn? Might as well come along."

I headed for the barn, he followed me and dad followed Granston by ten steps. We feared that when he saw it, he'd grab it and dare us to do anything about it. Without Justin dad might have put the .38 behind his belt in the back but with mom in the house with the two younger ones she had to have "mama's gum" in case there was someone near the house for Granston's backup. We'd have to rely on Justin getting to his gun in case anything happened.

Entering the second floor of the barn I pointed out where the granary was and that having the silo in the center of the barn kept the silage from freezing in the winter. The hay was mostly gone but he could see where it was stored. None of this seemed to interest him in the least.

In the machinery room it was dusty and dimly lit as was normal. We had an old hand crank corn sheller mounted in there. It wasn't used much anymore but it still worked. A man would drop a cob of corn in the top small end down and turn the crank. The crank was attached to a round iron plate with barbs on the opposite side. As the barbs came around they'd rub the corn kernels off the cob. The corn would fall out the bottom. Normally a burlap bag would be attached to the bottom of the sheller. But with the sheller at a convenient height the bag wasn't long enough to reach the floor. As a result an eight inch platform had been built to set the bag on. It was under this platform that I hid the knife.

I knelt down and stuck my hand under the end of the platform.

"Aren't you afraid a rat might bite you when you do that?"

"Nah. We've got a dozen cats and they're always hungry. Don't have any rats."

Anticipating what we would do, I had only wrapped it in a small piece of feed bag.

Dad had walked to the entry to the machinery room and said, "Might as well bring it out in the light, son, so he can get a good look at it."

Out at the large door to the haymow I handed it to him. He pulled it out of the scabbard and studied it closely especially the butt end where the film came out. "I'll be darned," He said slowly. "That looks like the kind of knife I'm looking for. Why does it have so many scratches on it?"

"The hired man wore it all the time and used it for a lot of things. It was a working tool for him so I suppose it would get a few scratches."

He nodded as he slipped the knife back into the scabbard. "How much would you be asking for it?"

"Well," I said, "I looked in the Sears and Roebuck and they don't have anything like it. But, the closest one was pretty expensive. And, it's sort of personal to me, because I kind of liked that Indian." I paused as if thinking and then said, "Two hundred and fifty dollars."

"Whoa. That's too much. I'll give you a hundred dollars for it."

"Three hundred."

"Hey! That's not how it's done. Okay, one-fifty."

"Three-fifty."

He didn't say a word. He held his hand out toward me, palm first, like he wanted to stop the bidding before it got even worse. Suddenly he said, "Three-fifty"

"Okay."

"I didn't come prepared to pay that much."

Dad reached over and took the knife from him before he had a chance to think saying, "Then come back when you have the money. We'd be expecting cash. We'll be here tomorrow but we all go to church together at seven o'clock so nobody will be here before about eight-thirty. How about then?"

He nodded. "Yeah, that sounds okay."

Dad handed the knife to me and said, "Might as well put it back for now."

I took it and disappeared into the machinery room. When I returned dad stood and watched Granston get in his car and drive away.

We were all together in the yard where dad and I told the rest what had been said.

Justin nodded and said, "That was about as good a job as you could have done. If they intend to steal the knife, it'll be between seven and eight in the morning."

Dad said, "Ann, you'll have to take Mikey and Lucy to Mass so you'll be out of the way and the car will be gone. In fact, we'll all have to go to the shed as if we were getting in the car in case they're watching from the south. You'll have to wear my hat until near town."

We decided Justin would wait in the machinery room to stop whomever went in there. The knife was elsewhere, of course. In its place we had prepared a little surprise. There had always been a large double spring trap hanging in the workshop. Dad said it was a wolf trap. We would set it in the space under the corn sheller platform with a hair trigger. If he stuck his hand in there expecting to fine the knife, he'd stay put until someone decided to let him go.

Since it was spring the fields were bare and open to the south. If the man or men came in a car, a backup man would have to come from the north or northwest to remain under cover. Tommy would hunker down in the woods beyond the yard to the north of the house and I'd do the same among the crabapple trees fifty yards to the north of the barn. I'd have the .22 because I was by far the best shot of Tommy and me. If Tommy saw somebody he'd wait until the car arrived and then yell a warning. If I saw somebody and he was carrying a gun in the open I'd shoot him in the shoulder of the arm carrying the gun. Otherwise I'd yell, too. Dad would be in the shed with "mama's gum."

CHAPTER 41

Sunday morning with milking done we were ready. Justin stayed in the barn because he never went to church with us. Dad wore his tie, suit coat and hat to the shed. He told mom to try not to grind the gears like she did when she was upset. With the car gone Tommy and I crawled out and carefully made our way to the places we had selected. We had to be careful because someone might have snuck up on the place earlier.

The morning was quiet and overcast, but not dark like it might rain. I still had not reached my selected spot when I heard the unmistakable sound of a Harley Davidson motorcycle coming from town on the road to the north. Sure enough, the motor stopped and it coasted to a stop at the approach to the woods. It would be Rango, I knew it.

Reaching my spot in the trees I laid down and covered myself with dead grass. The grass was flat on the ground from the snow so concealing myself was hard. Tommy decided to lay beside a rotting log in the woods so it was easier for him. The ground while thawed felt cold on my belly and legs.

I had a .22 long-rife cartridge loaded. That had the heaviest bullet of the common .22 shells. Even though I shot sparrows and gophers all the time, the thought of shooting a man was unsettling. The thing was, someone would be coming past me in minutes and I'd have to decide.

I waited. Being naturally fidgety made staying still agony. It was only the danger of the situation that made it possible. Then . . . the snap of a twig behind me and to my right. I was left handed so that was my good side to shoot to. More crunching of dried grass by cautious steps. He was expecting someone might be waiting. Otherwise he could walk up to the buildings with hardly a care. We were all supposed to be at Mass.

I didn't move, I hardly breathed. Justin has told dad and me, it was one thing to shoot a bird or an animal that couldn't shoot back. Combat was entirely different. It was. I wasn't sure I'd be able to move let alone shoot accurately. Suddenly there was movement out of the corner of my eye. It raced through my mind how vital peripheral vision was for survival. Slowly I turned my head. He was a little past me already. While I saw movement through small woody shoots I couldn't see him clearly. Then, he was in the open. He was wearing a gun in a holster on his right hip. Now what? He was carrying a gun but not in his hand. Did that count?

The dog barked which meant a car was coming in the yard. We knew Sandy would have to be in evidence and not tied up or it would look strange. If it were Granston in the car, Sandy wouldn't likely be shot because Granston had been here twice before and Sandy would recognize his scent.

My man had stopped behind the large oak tree where Justin and I had spent the afternoon the fall before. He was perhaps ten yards from me. I could easily have shot his ear off at that range. I knew I could kill him because when I was in the third grade one of the boys from the Catholic school was shot in the head with a .22 by his friend. They were out target shooting and got careless. He had been an alter boy and since I was an alter boy we all went to the mortuary to say a rosary for him.

I didn't move. The sound of a car door slamming was heard, and then a second. There were two men in the car. Mine advanced to behind the pump house. Now it would be harder for me to get a good shot especially if he were moving. I caught a glimpse of movement as a man walked into the barn. The man behind the pump house turned around and through sprigs of dead grass I was pretty sure it was Rango. He sensed I was there, but he couldn't spot me. He edged around to the west side of the pump house where the grass was mowed and he could move silently. He was lost from sight.

Waiting a few seconds I was about to move closer when his head came around the corner—almost gave myself away.

At that moment there was a yell from Tommy, "West side of the pump house." Apparently he had seen Rango. Now we were given away so I sprang up and dashed to the oak tree. Nothing moved. Moving as silently as possible I came up on the east side of the pump house. Here the grass was never mowed and it crunched under my feet. Rango appeared headed to the small corn crib between the shed and the barn with his gun out.

I raised the rifle and flipped off the safety. It was an easy shot and I heard the thump as the bullet hit. I crouched and scooted behind the pump house to reload as two shots from a revolver erupted behind me. Whatever happened he missed. I was fast at reloading and in three seconds was ready to move, but where?

More shots from the yard. One was the bark of "mama's gum" the other less loud a second later. Dread seized me. What if dad had been shot? Then, shots from the barn. Justin's voice, "Fred, stay behind the tree." There was a large elm tree to the west of the entry to the shed and three feet to the south that you narrowly missed as you drove the car in.

I edged around to the southwest corner of the pump house. I saw the man and he saw me. It was Rango. I jerked back as a bullet chipped wood off the building. "Behind the corn crib," I yelled.

Edging around to the east side of the pump house again I saw Justin coming down the incline from the barn on the east end of the corn crib. The corn crib was mostly empty so his movements could be seen through the slats. Rango had moved forward to the south and was mostly covered by a small bushy elm tree. All I could see clearly through the bare branches were his legs. He was looking east so his left side was toward me. Rather than take a chance of my bullet being deflected by a branch, I shot for his knee which was his good one. The right was mechanical. An instant later Rango shot but he was in the process of falling. His gun was in his left hand because of my first shot and it was angled down from the center of mass of Justin. Justin shot and rolled down. They both came up on their knees and Justin shot twice. Rango never got off another shot.

Justin struggled up and advanced on Rango, paused for an instant and yelled, "Clear."

"Clear," dad replied.

I had reloaded and stood ready with my gun angled up. Justin was standing over Rango shaking his head. Justin looked up and waved me in. Without looking Rango's way I walked a little behind Justin to the yard. He was bleeding from his leg.

The third man was laying beside the car not moving. "How about the man in the barn?" dad asked.

"Caught in the trap. Good idea."

Justin sagged to the ground beside the elm tree near the shed. Tommy was cautiously coming from the woods. Dad said, "Tommy, get some bandages from the drawer in the house," and he was off.

"How bad?" dad asked.

"Not real bad. Missed the bone and any main arteries the way it looks." It seemed the bullet had gone behind the bone in the thigh, an angle shot from his left front.

"What about him?" Justin said, pointing to the man on the ground near the car.

"When Tommy yelled the warning, he must have seen him because he slowly leveled his gun to take a careful shot. I said, 'Drop the gun.' He turned his gun toward me and that's when I shot. This thing packs a punch, I'll say that. His gun went off skyward as he was flying back."

They wrapped Justin up good and he carefully got to his feet. "Now for Granston in the barn."

Dad and Justin started walking that way with Justin limping. Inside they were hardly visible in the darkened space. I heard Justin yell, "There are two of us, both armed. You can't get us both so I want to see an arm raised with fingers spread."

A few minutes later Granston appeared holding his right hand in his left with dad and Justin behind. He had to have broken fingers because that was a powerful trap.

They marched him to the car. Dad said, "Son, get it."

It was in the shed so I ran and got it. As I walked up with it dad rammed his gun into Granston's gut and he doubled over. Then he turned him around and emptied his pockets. Among other things was a roll of bills.

Dad took off the rubber band binding them and said, "See ya brought payment."

Granston was holding his hand and his stomach. "Hey, there's nearly five hundred dollars there."

"Price just went up. Here's that darned knife!" Dad opened the car door and threw it on the front seat. "Must be a treasure map or somethin'. What's so important as to die for, crazy mutts."

"What about the other two?"

"Both dead, jerk!"

"What are you going to do?"

"Bury 'em deep, wa-da-ya 'spose. Don't know what this is about, but the cops are in the habit of blaming whoever happens to be handy—that's us." After a pause he continued. "Now ya got your treasure map or whatever—you leave. Never show round here or in town again, got it?

"Next time we'll shoot with no warning even if we have to shoot through the door." Dad pealed off a bill from the roll. "Here's twenty." He stuffed it his shirt pocket. "Drive 'til that's gone and don't look back." He pushed him in the car and slammed the door. Through it all, Justin stood to the side with his gun leveled at Granston. He started the car and shifting with his left hand drove out of the yard.

We had two bodies on our hands. Dad dragged the one in the yard back beside Rango and we all went to the house.

"Call Haas," Tommy said.

"Yes. There seems no way around that."

He found the small card and went to the phone. When he had the connection to The Cities he said, "I need to talk to Leonard."

After a few seconds he said, "Fred. Fred Landon. Tell him Aunt Bertha took a turn for the worse. He has to come right away. Can you get that to him? It's urgent."

Then he hung up. "He'll be given the message and hopefully call back in a few minutes."

We waited ten minutes and the phone rang. Dad waited for the third ring and picked up. "Hello."

"Yes. It's urgent—like the last time but worse. It would be good if you were here now." Pause. "Wish we had a better doctor, but it's a small town. Yeah. That's good." Pause. "Well, it's been a little dry. Could use some rain." Another pause. "Good. That's good. Bye."

He came into the kitchen. "They're coming as fast as they can. He said they'd take the tan car because it's a lot faster. Wonder why he asked about the rain."

"Bet they're coming in a plane and plan to land in the field," Tommy said. "He wanted to know how soft the ground was."

We waited around the kitchen table. Justin said, "It wouldn't be a bad idea to collect up their guns. The FBI will want them, but you may need them. It seems like the communists wouldn't be back because they got what they were after. But, you never know. It was good you had the .38 today."

307

Dad got up and Justin said, "Wait a minute. I'll go with you, there should be two of us. It's possible two came on the motorcycle."

That done, we waited. Tommy and I started breakfast. We'd have fried eggs and toast. A pop-up toaster was still in our future but we had one of those that toasted on one side and when it was done you had to turn it over to toast on the other side. The slight disadvantage with that is we always forgot about it and the smell of burning toast reminded us it was time to turn it. We'd take a table knife and scrape off the burned part in the wood box—always had scraped toast.

Before long mom drove into the yard. Dad went out to meet her while we stayed inside. In the house she counted noses being sure everyone was there. After changing clothes she took over the cooking.

Tommy and I went outside. "I wonder how long it would take to fly from The Cities?" Tommy asked.

"Depends on how fast the airplane can go. But, they all go at least a hundred miles an hour and it's a hundred and twenty miles by the road."

It wasn't long before we heard the faint droning of an airplane. In seconds we saw it coming from the southeast right for us. It passed over the house real low and swung to the east. It was a tan low wing with a V-tail. "A Beachcraft Bonanza," I said. I had built a model of it a year ago.

Tommy ran into the house while I tried to follow the plane with my eye. Faintly over the horizon it had turned to the west and headed back. I saw the wheels come down. In the house Tommy was saying, "Dad, we have to drive out to the field to pick them up!"

We hurried to the car and drove to the field. There was no way we weren't going along because we wanted to see the plane. It was settling on the alfalfa field with the wheels and flaps down.

By the time we arrived at where the plane had stopped, there were three men standing by it each with a bag. When dad stopped we jumped out and walked to the plane. The pilot waved at us.

Haas was one of the men, and since the engine was still running he made sure we didn't get too close. "We have cars coming so he'll leave so as not to draw attention."

Raising his hand Haas motioned to the east. The pilot nodded and the engine revved enough to get the plane turned around and then the engine burst into power as he opened the throttle. The plane bumped along the field until it lifted clear. Hardly ten feet off the ground the wheels folded into the underside and the flaps went up. It was gone.

We all squeezed into the car and dad drove back. "Is the farm secure?" Haas asked.

"As far as we know."

"How many injured?"

"One, with a leg wound. Not too bad, I guess. He can still walk a little."

"The attackers?"

"Two dead, the other gone. He has what they were after."

Dad parked the car outside so it would be easy for everyone to get out. Haas said, "Joe, make a sweep through the woods around the north and west of the buildings, and then keep an eye on the driveway and stop anybody coming in." To dad, "Clem is a doctor and he'll take a look at the wound."

Clem had Justin lay on the rug on the porch where the light was good. I normally hated things like that but couldn't tear myself away. He seemed to know about bullet wounds. He set out some things from his bag. "Now, this is going to hurt you a lot more than it'll hurt me," he said in a dry humor. "Since the bullet went all the way through, I'm going to poke a strip of silk fabric though the hole. That will clean out most of the bits of clothing and other debris that the bullet dragged in with it. There is also an antiseptic on the fabric to help prevent infection."

Justin clenched his teeth but said nothing. That done the doctor sutured both wounds and wrapped gauze around his leg. "Best to walk as little as possible for a few days and keep the leg elevated when possible." After that he gave Justin a shot of penicillin.

By this time Haas and dad were back from taking an inspection tour of what had happened. The sun had come out and it was warmer than normal for April so we sat around the porch table with Haas taking notes as we all told our stories. Justin sat on a chair with his leg on the wash bench that was kept in the porch except in summer.

When my turn came I told what had happened and the two times I shot Rango. When I told about shooting him in the knee, Justin said, "I wondered what happened there. When I came around the end of the corn crib he had his gun up and leveled and I thought he had me. But as he shot he seemed to stumble. But it was your shot that made his gun go down and only hit my leg—perfect timing, perfect shot."

"Luck," I said.

When the issue of the guns came up, dad wouldn't budge. After a few terse comments about all of the help the FBI *hadn't* given us it was settled, we'd keep them.

Dad told Haas to keep the roll of money from Granston because it was blood money as far as he was concerned. He also asked if they could find where Granston/Hindle lived in town and clean out his apartment so it looked like he had left town rather than mysteriously disappeared. They agreed to that.

Two cars arrived an hour and a half after the plane with one man each. They loaded up the cadavers. They shoved Rango's motorcycle in the back seat of one of the cars. After some wandering around they all left.

Justin had come into the kitchen and mom was putting on a late dinner. She was saying, "Justin, you saved us again. We'll never be able to thank you."

He was looking embarrassed so I said, "Good friends are like . . . ."

"Jamie!"

Justin looked like he'd explode trying to stifle laughter. Then he said, "Good friends stick around!" He then folded his arms across his chest and in a guttural voice said, "Ancient Ojibwe saying. Good saying. Ugh."

Mom looked sidewise at him with a hint of a smile before she turned away.

Justin, of course, refused to sleep in the house so after sunset—which wasn't so late with no daylight savings time—he and I walked to the barn. A full moon was coming over the horizon. "Moon of the deep water," I said.

He stopped to look at it. "That was a time, wasn't it? It'll be tugging at both of us tonight." After a pause, "It's funny how life is. You never know what's around the next bend in the trail."

He started walking again, more of a shuffle. In the barn I twisted the light switch to turn on the bare one-hundred watt bulb so Justin could get bedded down. Mom had brought out some quilts for him. When he was settled I twisted the switch again. To the darkness I said, "Good night, Justin."

The darkness replied, "Good night, Jamie."

CHAPTER 42

The next day, Monday, after the final accounting at our farm, everyone was surprised that the ninth grade English teacher didn't show up at school without leaving a message with anyone that he wouldn't be in. When someone finally checked his apartment which was located above one of the stores on Main Street they found he was completely moved out. Seeing as it was April and the school year was nearing its end they used a substitute teacher rather than try to fine a full time replacement.

I saw Emily at school in math class each day and now and then said a few words in the hall as we changed classes. I wanted to talk to her about the doctor's office, but I wasn't sure if she wanted to talk to me. It didn't matter because the opportunity never presented itself until unexpectedly it did.

Emily's family almost always came to the Catholic Church on Sundays now. Maybe it was at her insistence but I didn't know. We'd see each other after Mass sometimes but we only had a chance to say "Hi" to each other. The parish had what was call the bazaar both spring and fall. It was both a fund raiser and a means of bring the people of the parish together socially. The women would work all day getting things ready for what would be a fried chicken dinner. When enough people had finished eating they started Bingo as others kept coming for the meal. There were a few things for the children but mostly the little ones chased around. Most of the kids who were old enough were kept occupied playing Bingo. It wasn't terribly expensive and you even won now and then. The adults played Bingo, too, but a lot of them visited with friends.

Mom had been at church working the whole afternoon and when chores were done dad took us in to eat. And it was a good meal with a big selection of pies for dessert. Sometimes mom would be waiting tables and sometimes working in the kitchen. If she were waiting tables we'd manage to get seated at one of her tables so we'd get extra good care.

In the church basement dad had paid for our meal and we were waiting to be seated. It seemed that many of the farmers did as we did so they arrived at about the same time. Most of the crowd was made up of men and children because the women were working. I was getting taller each year but still couldn't see over most of the heads. It was my hope that Emily would come tonight and I was looking everywhere for her. I had stepped to the side of the waiting crowd and looked over as many of the tables as I could see and didn't spot her. Then I turned to the back and saw more people waiting on the steps to the basement. The basement was half in the ground and half out.

At first I wasn't sure and then I was. She had a pretty pink bow in her hair and was wearing her school coat. She was with her dad and older brother who was in the tenth grade. Her two younger brothers must have been with them but were too short to see over the big people. The good thing I noticed was her mother was not with them which meant she was probably working and would be eating last with the other women. That meant Emily would be around until it was over—please God! I had so hoped we could sit together to eat but that seemed impossible.

We were getting close to the head of the line to be seated. God, do something! The woman who was seating people came up and said hello to dad and he did likewise. They addressed each other by first names as most of the people did.

"There are some places opening up over here at one of Ann's tables. She said it would be nice if you could sit there."

When we were about to be seated the woman said, "Oh, it seems like we're a place short. Maybe we can squeeze in another chair."

Mom had come over and said, "Hi everybody. Who do you suppose this fine looking bunch belongs to?"

She was looking a little tired but it seemed to lift her spirits to spend the day with other women and get caught up on what was going on. It got kind of lonely for her on the farm.

I stepped back next to her and said, "Mom, it's okay if the table is a place short. I saw Emily's family come in. I'll wait if you can manage to get me to sit next to her."

She looked at me kind of oddly and then smiled. "So that's it."

"Please . . . . I'll never do anything bad again if you do this for me. I haven't had a chance to talk to her since the doctor's office and have to find out how she is. Please."

She had the look in her eye like wheels were turning in her head. "Okay. My coat will be in the car. There's a lipstick in the pocket. Go get that for me and that will delay you and I'll see what I can do. No promises, though."

I slipped away and knew she'd come though. I was excited as I worked my way thought the crowd being careful not to terribly offend anyone. As I went past Emily we made eye contact and I smiled. She was a little behind her father who was mostly occupied with keeping track of her younger brothers. I nudged past a man and came up beside her.

"I think I have it arranged so we can sit together to eat. Is that okay with you?"

She gave me one of her bright smiles and nodded enthusiastically. I was right! She did like me.

When I got back I worked my way down the steps since the people were still coming. It was always surprising to me but even some Protestants came. After all it was a good meal and they were acquainted with most of the Catholics, anyway. Emily's family was at the head of the line, and I walked along a little behind them as they went to their table. What do you know, that table was a place short, too, and there just happened to be two places open on the next table. How did she do it!

Mom was there. She spoke to Emily's dad, "We have such a good crowd tonight that it's getting kind of hectic. Would you mind if Emily sat at this table? My son was running an errand for me and lost his place. Maybe they could sit together to keep each other company."

"Sure, seems okay. He's a nice boy."

I pulled the lipstick tube out of my pocket and handed it to her. She took it and put it in her apron pocket. She turned to Emily. "Hello, Emily. You're looking nice tonight."

"Thank you, Mrs. Landon."

Mom said, "Let's see. Left hand. Jamie, you had better sit on her left." When we were seated mom said. "I'll bring your plates in a minute."

It all happened so fast I hardly had time to look at Emily—no that's wrong. I had a chance to look at her, but not enough time to take her in. She had on the prettiest pink dress I had ever seen with violet accents. The violet collar and sash matched her eyes.

Emily looked at me her eyes wide. "Jamie, this has worked out perfectly. I was hoping more than anything I'd see you here and now we're sitting by each other. I can't believe how lucky I am. What was that about the left hand?"

"I'm left handed and you're right handed. That way we can both eat without bumping elbows."

The people across the table weren't taking any notice of us so I leaned over to her and whispered, "And we can hold hands under the table."

I couldn't believe I had actually said that! This was the prettiest girl in town and I was sitting beside her. What more could a guy want?

"Jamie," she looked at me and whispered, "I would really like that." It wasn't five seconds before I felt fingers on my shirt sleeve and then our hands found each other.

She looked at me, "And, the lipstick?"

I saw her expression. "We came before you and I told mom I wanted to sit by you so she needed an excuse for me to get delayed so she sent me out to the car to get her lipstick."

"Remind me to thank your mom."

"Emily, that's the prettiest dress I've ever seen."

"Thank you. My mom made it."

"I see. She makes dresses for the Queen of England and took time off to make that one for you. That was nice of her because she must be awful busy."

"I'll tell her you said that because I know she'll be pleased."

Everyone got a prepared plate with chicken, mashed potatoes and gravy and green peas. That's the way it always was. Then, extra bowls of food were place on the table. Farm people worked hard and had good appetites.

Mom brought our plates and set them down. "Okay, you two. Enjoy your food and no holding hands under the table."

314

Emily giggled as she put her right hand in front of her mouth. A dead give away. No problem. Mom knew.

We started to eat. There was no holding hands as we were cutting chicken. It seemed we were both hungry. Between bites she said, "Jamie, how did this happen, I mean that we got to sit together?"

"I bribed my mom. When she wants people to do something, she has a way about her that you wouldn't believe. She can get anybody to do just about anything."

"How can anybody bribe his mother? I couldn't even begin to do that with mine."

"I told her I'd never do anything bad again."

It took her a little bit to think about that. "First of all, how could you ever promise something like that, and secondly why on earth would she believe you?" She wasn't quite giggling but I could see the mischief in her eyes.

"You really think I'm that bad?" I nudged her with my elbow. She nudged back.

When she didn't immediately answer I said, "You know when you go to confession you have to make a firm purpose of amendment which means you promise God you won't sin again. But, we all know that we'll have to go to confession again. It's like that. I really meant it. But, I never said I was a saint."

She giggled and so did I. Her feet didn't quite reach the floor when she sat back on her chair and I could hear her shoes scrape the floor as she swung them back and forth. I knew how it was. My feet did that too when they were happy. I was happy, too, except my legs were an inch longer than hers and they couldn't swing. We had finished eating and were holding hands again when mom came to take our plates.

"What kind of pie would you like?"

"Cherry, please" Emily said.

"Lemon for me, please."

When mom was gone I said, "Emily, look at me so I can see how your eye is doing."

She turned her head.

"That seems to be healing perfectly. Does it hurt?"

"No, not at all."

"I prayed for you every day and God must have been listening."

"Jamie," she said as she moved her eyes far to the right indicating the other people at the table. In a glance I could see they were watching us.

Mom set our plates of pie in front of each of us. "How are you two getting along? No fighting I hope."

Emily said, "Thank you for doing this Mrs. Landon."

"For what?"

"You know."

"You're welcome, little lady," and mom walked away.

People were still watching so we talked about teachers in school, and anything that came to mind. Whatever we said seemed to be funny in one way or other. I hadn't know it was possible to have such a good time talking to someone. When she had finished most of her pie she said, "That's as much as I can eat."

I had finished mine and got up and backed out her chair for her. Boy, were people watching.

She said, "Thank you, Jamie."

"You're welcome, Miss Emily."

We both laughed, but from the amused looks we were getting, it was like we were on a stage.

"Let's go over here for a minute," I said as I pointed to where the coats were hung and piled. There was a bench along the wall and after we moved a few coats we had room to sit down. "I really would like to talk to you about *you* in the doctor's waiting room. I can guess that any girl likes to be told she's pretty, but that wasn't what did it."

"You mean what made me so happy?"

"Yeah. Would you tell me about it? If it's something personal I don't want to pry."

"Of all people I'll tell you, Jamie, but I don't know if I can find the words."

"I'll be happy if you try. How about we go out on the schoolyard. I have to make a stop in the, you know, the men's room. It'll be chilly outside so I left my coat in the car. Do you think you can find yours?"

"Sure."

"Okay. If we miss each other in here I'll meet you out by the merry-go-round. Is that okay?"

She nodded. "I have to make a stop, too."

I took my time since women always seemed to make men wait. When I arrived back where the coats were stacked she was frantically trying to pull her coat from under a pile of others. With my help we managed it. Outside I took her hand and we ran to our car where I had left my coat. I slipped into it and we went to the far side of the merry-go-round and sat on the outside board. I couldn't help noticing she sat real close to me.

"Jamie, would you mind if we held hands?"

It was a dark moonless night with only the stars and I had a funny feeling inside, more of a new feeling. I said, "Not at all."

She took my right hand in both of hers and it felt good. "I don't know why you're being nice to me but I'm glad you are. I made you blush in the lunch room and then in math class. I was horrified at what I had done. Please forgive me. Please?"

This was so unexpected I didn't know what to say. When I didn't respond she said, "Please, say something, Jamie."

"I can't think of what to say. None of that was you fault so there's nothing to forgive. If I hadn't said that about you're being in a fight you wouldn't have said what you did. It was all my fault. It's always been that way. I get humiliated and I have no one to blame but myself."

"Even the way Mr. Russo treated you?"

"Well, that was a special case, but yeah most of it was my fault. I remember in the fifth grade it would be my turn to read aloud in reading class. I couldn't read so would stumble over every other word. She'd tell me to sit down and then say something like, 'One of his ears is bigger than the other.' Everybody would be looking at me and then she'd say, 'Now, watch him blush.' I'd turn beet red and everybody laughed."

"Did she ever do that to anybody else?"

"No. Just me."

"So, Mr. Russo singling you out for bad treatment wasn't anything new to you."

"That's about it."

"But, that doesn't explain why you're being nice to me. Wait a minute. When I made you blush in the lunch room that was all my doing. If I hadn't said that about kissing you, you wouldn't have blushed."

"First of all, you had no idea I blushed so easily. And second, if I hadn't talked to you the first time you wouldn't have said anything to me."

"Now you're being hard on yourself and I won't let you do that. That was very nice that you talked to me the first time. I was feeling low that day and you made me feel good by the nice things you said. I won't let you take that away from me. Even now if I'm feeling bad I think of that day and it cheers me up. You still haven't said why you're being nice to me."

It was hard to answer. Finally I said, "I guess it's because you smile at me. Almost nobody does that. I'm lucky if they only frown. Whenever we see each other you smile. I like it so much that I can't wait to see you. I guess I don't smile back now that I think of it. I'm sorry I don't. But, it doesn't seem to matter because you always do."

"You may not know it, but you do smile, a real bright smile, and that makes me feel good, too."

We sat next to each other. She still held my hand and that was okay. Then I said, "Before you were asking me to forgive you, but I'm the one who should be asking you to forgive me. It was my fault that you got hit in the face."

"You said that in the doctor's waiting room and I still don't understand."

"I knew he wanted to hit me as I saw him start to swing his arm around with the clenched fist. At that moment he was really mad and would have killed me if he could. If he had hit me in the side of the head with that swing he would have. I ducked and he hit you. If I hadn't done that you wouldn't have been hurt. I wish I hadn't ducked."

She had turned and was holding my hand up under her chin. "Jamie, you would have wanted to be killed so I wouldn't have gotten seven stitches?"

Our eyes had adjusted to the dark so I could see her face dimly and her eyes blinking. Her expression seemed to be one of compassion if there were such an expression. This was all new to me. "When I saw you standing against the wall crying with blood running down your face onto you dress I thought I'd die right there. You were totally innocent, your only fault was accidentally being in the wrong place. And, that wrong place was near me."

She squeezed my hand and said, "That wasn't an accident. I was there because I wanted to be near you. I even had to nudge another girl out of the way."

I didn't know what to say other than, "Why?"

"Jamie, can I hug you?"

It seemed like the natural thing to do though I didn't know why it would be. "Sure, if I can hug you, too."

Her arms pulled tight around me and mine around her as she laid her head on my shoulder with her face against mine. Feeling her soft hair brushing my skin almost made me explode with delight. In a moment I felt wetness against my cheek. She was crying.

I didn't know why she would cry. I felt good, not bad. I put my hand on her soft hair and gently stroked it trying to soothe whatever was causing her distress.

Finally I said, "Don't cry, Emily. I don't know what I did or said to hurt you. Tell me so I won't do it again."

She lifted her head and I could see a smile. She sniffed and said, "Jamie, I'm crying for happy, not for sad. I was beside you because I was crazy about you."

"Sure, I knew that. In twenty years I might even know what's going on."

She laughed in a low pleasant way. "You say those cute things and I can't help laughing. You always make me happy."

CHAPTER 43

There were no kids running around outside. It must have been too chilly for it to be fun. After what seemed like a long time but was probably only a minute of two I said, "Can you tell me about the doctor's waiting room?"

"Jamie, what happened is you saved my life. I'll try to tell you but it might not make sense. To start with there were no girls my age in country school, I have only brothers, and I couldn't seem to make any friends in public school. I became very lonely. Then, you sat down across from me in the lunch room. I was almost rude to you but you kept coming back with funny little remarks until you said that about my eyes. It was so unexpected and so nice that I had to leave before I started to blubber. I hope you weren't offended."

"No, no. I was delighted you would even let me sit down."

"After our lunch I really started to notice you and felt bad because of the way that Mr. Russo treated you. I knew what the other kids planned to do in math class that day so when the class emptied out into the hallway I moved as fast as I could to get beside you. I wanted to tell you I felt bad for you and maybe even take your hand for a moment. Then, I got hit in the face. When I got up you were gone. I thought you had been expelled and you, my only friend, would not be back.

"In the doctor's office my father knew the doctor was on the school board and after the doctor was done bandaging me up they were really going at it so daddy had me sit in the waiting room. It seemed like nobody cared about *me*. I was left and forgotten and was so blue I could actually feel my life slipping away. All along I thought about you when I could get any thoughts together at all.

"Then, you said my name. It was like the sun bursting out in the middle of the night. And then you touched me—you took my hand. I could hardly understand what you were saying other than that you were worried about me, that you cared about me. You were so concerned that I remember feeling bad for you, and I really wanted you to be better more than I wanted me to be better.

"When you said you'd ask God to send his prettiest angel to watch over me, He did it, right then. This is the hard part."

She was looking at me, our faces only inches apart. "All I can say is I thought my heart would burst with joy. But, that doesn't come close to describing it. God touched me and He made sure I knew He had. It leaves a beautiful mark on you when He does something like that so you never forget. The thing is, God came to me in a special way, but he did it because *you* asked Him to. You said the prayer. Thank you, Jamie."

"That's the nicest thing I ever heard."

She had her arms around me again and squeezed me hard, "I've been dying to tell about it, but thought I had to tell you before anyone else. And, I didn't think I'd ever get the chance."

Once again she laid her head against me and we sat for a long time. She'd move a little and I'd squeeze a little after which she'd squeeze me. It seemed as if we had to reassure ourselves the other was still there. It was nice to hug and be hugged.

It was a clear moonless night and the stars had never been so bright. "Look how bright the stars are," I said.

She looked up and I looked at her. I could see the stars reflected in her eyes.

Then Emily looked right at me and said, "Jamie, if I asked you to do something for me would you do it?"

"Sure. Anything."

"Kiss me."

"Almost anything."

"Come on, you said . . . ."

Our lips were only inches apart. I swallowed. "I don't know how to kiss . . . . I never kissed a girl before."

321

"I've never kissed a boy either, but how hard can it be? And, what about our second lunch, haven't you ever thought about kissing me?"

Actually I hadn't because that's not the way seventh grade boys think. They like to look at pretty girls and wonder about things. And it's nice if one will talk to you without being rude. But, kissing?

I said, "Well, I suppose, but that doesn't mean . . . ."

We moved toward each other until our lips touched and we kissed.

"That wasn't so bad, was it?"

"No. But, we should try again just to be sure we got it right."

"Good idea."

Then, looking at the stars again she said, "What will happen to us?"

"I sure hope we can see each other now and then."

"So do I, but, I don't think we'll be allowed to do that."

It took me some time to think about that and I knew she was right. "Yeah, once our parents learn we were out here hugging in the dark they won't let it happen again—and they'll find out. At school the teachers and other kids were watching us all the time as it was. Everybody'll hear about our eating together. And somebody must have noticed us as we left. Are you going to tell anyone else about the waiting room?"

"I don't know. Maybe not all of it."

"I won't tell and if you tell that's up to you. Don't forget, people already think we're pretty odd."

She nodded and then said, "We'll never forget this evening will we—as long as we live?"

Then she said the sweetest thing, "Jamie, I love you and you love me in the only way our young hearts can love. It's a simple love not like adult love where they talk about babies and payments to the bank."

What she said took me by surprise but it seemed about right so I said, "That's how it is but I didn't think of it like that."

We both knew it had to end and it did. Some kids had come out and were out running around in the dark.

As we walked back to the church basement we were holding hands. It wasn't just fun now, it was a bond. We arrived in the basement as they announced the quilt Bingo. Several women of the parish spent a lot of time hand sewing quilts. They were a club of sorts. They made nice looking quilts, too. Special cards for the quilt Bingo were sold and almost everybody had at least one. This was a pretty big deal because the quilt Bingo was the biggest money maker after the meal. We found a place to sit and didn't say anything so the numbers could be heard by everyone.

When it was finished everyone collected their families together and the church basement emptied pretty fast. On the way home mom and dad talked about people they had run into that evening. The four of us were in the back seat nudging and pushing each other like we always did. Emily was not mentioned.

It was late enough so we all went immediately to bed. A half-hour later I still hadn't gone to sleep and that didn't surprise me. All I could think about was Emily as we hugged each other and then kissing her. It was like any boy's wildest fantasy and it had happened to me. It was like a dream and I was sure I'd wake up. The only problem was, as far as I could tell, I was awake, and that was the problem, I couldn't sleep.

I wondered if the stars were still so bright. It was silly, why wouldn't they be? They were only stars. But, I wasn't sleeping so I decided to go downstairs and check. I slipped out of bed and put on a shirt over my pajamas. Very quietly I went down the steps and opened the door at the bottom without a sound. In the living room I heard voices from the kitchen. Mom and dad were still up. About to go back upstairs I heard Emily mentioned so I tiptoed close to the doorway to the kitchen.

". . . and I quickly went back to the kitchen to get Angie, Emily's mother. She had been working so hard and now was washing dishes. I said she had to take a break, that I had something to show her. She was a little puzzled but was glad to get away for a minute. Out along the wall between the kitchen and the first table in the dining room I pointed to Emily and Jamie eating their pie. She was almost transfixed at the sight. Both were laughing, even people around them were laughing. She said, 'What can be so funny?' 'They're enjoying each other's company,' I said. She watched for a little longer. 'Yes, they are, aren't they.' Then I said, 'If you notice you only see one boy hand and one girl hand.' She watched awhile longer. 'The little stinkers are holding hands under the table. When we get time to eat will you sit with me? We have to talk about this.'

"Angie said that it had started a few months before. Emily all at once seemed to be happier than normal. When asked about it Emily said she had found a friend. When Angie asked the girl's name she was evasive and wouldn't tell. She could see now that it hadn't been a girl, it had been Jamie."

I knew it was wrong to eavesdrop so I went back to the stair door twisted the knob making a lot of noise and closed it pretty hard. I came into the kitchen. "I didn't think you'd still be up. I came down to get a drink of water."

Proceeding to the sink I ran water in a glass. Mom said, "You seemed to have a good time eating with Emily and she seemed to be having a good time, too."

"Yeah, we're friends. It was nice to see her because we don't have a chance to talk in school. There's always someone around listening."

"After you ate I saw you leave. Where'd you go?"

This was interrogation time. I knew it would come so might as well get it over with. "We went out and sat on the merry-go-round and talked."

"It was pretty cold to be sitting outside."

"We didn't notice it was cold."

"Was that because you had your arms around each other?"

I could only stare at the floor and say, "Yeah, sometimes. She didn't seem to mind."

"I bet she didn't." The comment dripped with sarcasm.

"Mom. I've been dying to know what happened to her in the waiting room. You saw it and so did I and so did Mrs. Hamilton. When she smiled it wasn't because of something I said. It had to be special."

I told them the story—about our chili lunch, math class, and the waiting room. I saw no reason to mention our second lunch so didn't. First I told what I knew and then I told what Emily had told me except at the part where I talked to her in the doctor's waiting room I said, "I told her I'd say a prayer so she'd feel better and God seemed to answer it right then. She perked up. She said she could feel God doing it and it was nice. So, it wasn't something fancy that I said. It made me feel good, too, like God was telling me he had come through for me."

I was scratching my head as I said. "This is not something either of us planned, but it is what happened and it was kind of special for both of us. I suppose if we had known we could make it happen we would have because we sure like each other. Emily even said out there under the stars— they were so bright tonight—she said, 'What will happen to us?' It's like we're a freak show."

Then mom said, "Did you kiss her?"

I knew sooner or later that would come up, too. I looked at the floor and nodded. Then without looking at her I said. "She said, 'If I asked you to do something for me would you do it?' I said of course I would. Then she said, 'Kiss me.' Girls are so tricky."

"You're learning," dad said.

"Well," mom said, "one little kiss, I guess, isn't so bad. It was one, wasn't it?"

"Well," I said drawing out the word, "she had never kissed a boy before and I had never kissed a girl so we sorta had to practice at first."

"I'm going to bed," dad said as he got up.

Mom didn't say anything as she sat leaning her forearms on the kitchen table looking at me. Finally she said, "Emily's mother and I ate supper together. I had taken her out where she could see you two eating your pie. You were really having a good time. Later she said how Emily had not been able to make friends in public school and was lonely. She's not against you two having become friends. She wishes Emily could find a girl friend and I'd be happy if you could find a boy to be friends with. It would be nice to have someone to fly model airplanes with, wouldn't it?"

I nodded but that wasn't the point. There was no other boy in school who flew model airplanes that I knew of, and anyway, my friend was Emily.

"But this is kind of a problem, she's a girl and you're a boy. And, being friends with a girl is complicated by the fact that, well, boys and girls are different. You wouldn't have been out on the merry-go-round hugging and kissing a boy friend, and neither would she with a girl friend. It's really complicated."

Sometimes parents were even right and I knew where this was going so I said, "We both know that we won't be able to see each other again. We talked about it. Tonight was a special night of our lives that we'll never forget. We're young, and her parents and you and dad wouldn't allow that to happen again even if she were the loneliest girl in the world and I were the loneliest boy. As it was, we could hardly say 'Hi' in the hall at school without someone kidding us. The whole town will know we ate supper together and now it'll be even worse. We'll suffer more from all the talk than you will." I got up. "I'm tired and I'm going to bed."

I thought about Emily until I fell asleep and dreamt about her all night.

CHAPTER 44

And, thus life became different. Before I was alone and lonely, now I had a friend who seemed to really like me as odd as that seemed. Before this in each of our chance meetings I got the feeling she was pleased to see me, but that was far from her liking me better than anyone else as now appeared to be the case. I thought about her a lot and whenever I did it gave me a thrill. There was no question that her being a girl was a large part of it. Prior to this I had no interest in girls and they certainly had none in me. The part about kissing still left me uneasy. I guessed it must be a girls way of telling a boy she liked him though I still wasn't sure it was right for kids.

The down side of this was when I hadn't seen her for some days I felt more lonely than before. On one of those dreary days I found myself walking down the long hallway to the math classroom. How long had it been? Lets see, this was Tuesday so it was three whole days since we had sat on the merry-go-round together. Suddenly I felt a gentle hand on my arm.

"Hi there, handsome."

I turned my head so fast the bones in my neck popped. It was Emily! "Hi yourself, beautiful," I whispered.

"Can't hear you."

"Ahem. Hi yourself."

"You didn't say it all—what you said the first time."

"Okay. Hi yourself, beautiful is that better everybody's watching."

"Much better. So, let them watch. They'll get over it."

It was that simple—who cared about what they thought or said. In a matter of steps we faced the math room. From a dull day to a bright day in seconds. I wondered if that was hard on one's health not that I'd have changed anything if it were.

I had to give Emily all the credit. She had the courage not to care about what people said. Either she was crazy or she was crazy about me. It may have been prideful on my part but I assumed it was the latter.

And, she was right. In a couple of weeks we'd walk together side by side talking and while some took notice, they were forced to accept us as a fact of life like hot days in the summer. When someone mentioned my girl friend I'd reply, "Emily's my friend who happens to be a pretty girl."

If they persisted and asked what the difference was, I'd say, "Darned if I know." At that, they'd either laugh or walk away mumbling to themselves.

Sundays after Mass it seemed my parents happened to run into Emily's parents quite often. They wouldn't talk long or it seemed like they didn't because I'd find Emily and we'd talk. Whenever I was with her time seemed to go so fast. Mom told me what Emily's mother had said to her at the bazaar—the part I had overheard in the kitchen that evening. She wished Emily had found a girl friend, but in so many words, I was better than nothing. Emily had been lonesome and moody and now was upbeat, cheerful and helped around the house like she never had before. I think my parents saw that in me, too. There was a continual barrage of parental guidance from my mother concerning association with the opposite sex. A lot of it had to do with something going wrong and how hurt a person could be when it ended. I didn't care because the simple fact was I liked Emily and she liked me. I'd deal with the future in the future. Being young was great but when you're young you don't know it.

That fall we were in the eighth grade and we were still friends. We sat together to eat at the church dinner, though we made a point of not holding hands under the table. Afterward we'd walk around the block and we'd hold hands. We'd sit together in the school cafeteria once in a while. Sometimes another guy would be sitting opposite Emily while I was headed for a place further down the table. He'd say, "Oh, oh. I got Jamie's place, better move." Of course he wouldn't and everybody would laugh. I'd say "Hi, Emily," and she'd say "Hi, Jamie," back. She was right. They did actually come to accept us as being friends, boy-girl friends or however they wanted to look at it.

The year passed and the next fall I was in the ninth grade and dad insisted I play basketball. I couldn't hit that basket worth a darn when I started and never seemed to improve. He set up a backboard and hoop in the driveway on the second floor of the barn. I practiced but my heart wasn't in it. Emily got prettier every day and had started to mature in the most delightful way.

Sophomore year went about the same as the one before. I still played basketball and still couldn't hit the basket. I was on the B Team, of course, which was the training ground for the varsity. In February I turned sixteen and a month later got my driver's license.

Many of the teachers still had it in for me as if I had been the one who smacked Emily in the face and by some odd quirk of fate an innocent teacher had landed in prison rather than me. A good example of this was what happened at the start of basketball season junior year. There were not many boys that would willingly put up with the indignity of having to run themselves to death while under the direction of a coach that was a moron. This year the surviving seniors left a thin bench. That meant that all the juniors were automatically on the varsity—except me. Even though I wasn't good at hitting the basket, I was good at getting rebounds but it didn't matter. I mentioned it to my father and he didn't say anything. The school and by association the teachers and coaches could do no wrong. From his attitude I assumed he thought it was because I wasn't any good, but still I had to keep playing.

In March I asked Emily to the prom but she turned me down. She said she didn't have anything to wear. I assumed she meant that figuratively. I knew Emily could sew well enough to make a lot of her school clothes that always looked nice but she said she was not good enough to make a formal. Her mother was a good seamstress but she was getting arthritis in her hands and wasn't up to it anymore.

When my mother learned Emily couldn't go she suddenly became all concerned that I be properly socialized vis-à-vis girls—other girls. She harangued by the hour about how I had to get a date to the prom. It was the old problem. I first had to pick out a girl I might like to go with. That was hard because most of the girls that would be at the top of my list were at the top of every other guy's list, too. Plus many of them were going steady. That was the social stratagem to ensure boys as well as girls had a date for the prom as much as anything.

Then, I had to get up enough nerve to ask the girl and what was even harder, find a time and a reasonably private place to ask her. I asked two girls other than Emily and they both turned me down, one because she didn't have a dress and one didn't give a reason. Since she showed up at the prom with someone else, I assumed it was because she was hoping he'd ask her.

One of my friends, Eddie Norbert, was a town kid, and he was more socially connected than I was. It turned out that a rather popular senior girl didn't have a date and Eddie told me if I asked her she'd say yes which I did and she did. It got us both to the prom even though I was out of place since she socialized with seniors.

Senior year came around. There hadn't been an incident of any kind associated with the events from the spring when I was in the seventh grade. We still kept a wary eye on any strange car that drove in the yard because we knew Granston was still out there someplace. But, with each passing year we felt more comfortable.

We weren't milking many cows anymore so we could put the two or three cans of milk in the trunk of the car. On days when nobody at home needed the car I'd drive in and drop off the milk at the creamery before going to school. It was one of those days in late September when Emily said she'd like to see our apple orchard and get a box of apples. That was fine with me.

She had been out to our farm once before so the round barn was nothing new. At home I removed the empty milk cans found a cardboard box for apples, and we drove up to the orchard. Only about one out of three of the original trees were still there, but since they were now mature trees, we still had a lot of apples. We both still had our school clothes on and it looked so nice to see her with the skirt fluffed out by a couple of petticoats walking among the trees.

Dad was there on a ladder picking and we waved as we walked by. She said, "Hello, Mr. Landon."

He smiled and said, "Hi, Emily." He knew why we were there. We'd fill the box I carried and I'd drive her home.

We started picking apples and as one would expect the best ones were high up on the tree, many beyond even the reach of a ladder. It wasn't long before we were having a good time throwing apples to dislodge the good ones. As always when we got going everything was funny and you could hear her silver laughter ringing off the hills.

She was intent on a group of three apples way up on the top and her arm was pretty good. She wound up and threw and as she did she went to step back but her heel caught on a root and she began to fall. I was a couple of steps behind and rushed in and caught her with my left arm around her waist. As she felt my arm around her she threw her right arm around my neck in a reflexive act to break her fall. I lifted her off the ground holding her only by the waist and started to spin her around backward. She let out a squeal of delight as she held fast to me. Around and around we went. I don't know why but it seemed like the thing to do. Finally I said, "Time for a landing," as I settled her on her feet.

"Jamie. I'm so dizzy I can't stand."

"That's why I'm here to hold you," I said as I wrapped my arms around her. She had her arms around my neck.

"Why did you do that?"

"I didn't have any choice."

"Why?"

"Because you're Emily."

"But, that doesn't make any . . . . Oh, yes . . . ."

I saw the look in her eyes and she in mine. We kissed long and hard holding each other tight like we'd never see each other again.

We stood there hugging for quite a while. Since seventh grade it was right to say we were friends. We were happy in one another's company but we didn't do a lot of necking—we never had the opportunity. A few times we managed a little hug and kiss, but not often.

Finally she asked, "Aren't you dizzy?"

"No. I fly those U-Control model airplanes on the two strings where you turn around all the time. After you do it a few time you get used to it and never get dizzy. I think it worked out perfectly."

She smiled, gave me a last kiss and we parted.

With the box full we walked to the car. I put it in the trunk and she said, "Do I owe you anything for the apples?"

"Yes you do—three kisses. Since you already gave me two you're still one short."

She threw her arms around me and seemed more than willing to pay in full. Then, I asked, "You wouldn't happen to need another of box of apples, would you?" Her laughter could have been heard for half a mile.

That evening after I had finished my homework I came downstairs and mom and dad were sitting at the kitchen table. Mom said, "We'd like to talk to you about Emily."

I sat down and said, "Good. If you hadn't brought it up I would have." I looked at dad. "You saw us in the apple orchard today." He nodded. "First of all, we made sure you knew we were there and that way let you knew that we also knew you were there. We weren't doing anything sneaky."

I told them exactly what had happened, how it wasn't planned and how rarely we were together where we could just have fun. "We say a few words as we walk down the hall at school or when we meet after Mass on Sunday. We aren't seventh graders anymore and I'll admit we aren't exactly adults, either. But, we aren't kids.

"After that church bazaar you said her mother told you how lonely Emily had been before she met me. Well, I was lonely, too, and after all that terrible stuff with the microfilm I was more depressed than you realized. When I asked her that night what had happened in the waiting room she said it was no exaggeration to say I shaved her life. At the moment I said her name she was literally slipping away. It wasn't so immediate for me, but she saved my life, too. She made sense of the world for me again. We were becoming friends before that but those events really brought us together." I looked at mom and continued, "You told me more than once how easy it was to get hurt when the break-up comes. Well, it's been five years and we're still crazy about each other."

I paused and mom said, "I probably shouldn't say this but about a year ago at church Angie told me that a few weeks before Emily was really blue. It was Saturday and she asked her what was wrong and Emily said, 'Jamie hasn't said "Hi" to me for a whole week.' Even though it was winter they lingered after Mass on Sunday until you and Emily saw each other. You said 'Hi Emily,' and Angie thought you'd hug and kiss each other right on the church yard. You said a few words and in seconds Emily was laughing. She was back to normal."

Looking at my hands on the table I said, "I remember the time. I didn't do it intentionally but I got busy. I have only one rule with Emily—I want her to be happy. I felt terrible about that."

There was silence and then dad looked at me and in one of his rare moments of genuine interest asked, "If you don't want to tell us it's okay, but what did you say to her at the car that made her laugh so hard?"

I smiled. "It was nothing. After I put the box of apples in the trunk she asked if she owed me anything for the apples. I said, yes, three kisses and since she had already given me two she was still one short. That's when she threw her arms around me and we kissed. Then I said, 'You wouldn't want another box of apples, would you?' It wasn't funny except we like each other so much that everything's funny when we're together."

They couldn't stifle the smiles.

"It makes you feel good just to hear about it, doesn't it? That's the way it is with Emily and me all the time."

"But," mom said, "this could get out of hand."

"That's the first time we really hugged and kissed since the seventh grade on the merry-go-round. That's hardly out of control.

"I can see that if at all possible I want to go to college. Being a machinist or electrician won't work for me. I get bored too easily and that makes me unhappy. If I'm unhappy anyone I'd be with would be unhappy. And, that leads back to my first rule of Emily.

"I may even have to go in the Army. Mom, you know the lady that runs the draft board. Since Tommy has his balance problem he won't have to go so that means me, right?"

She nodded. "Probably."

"More years. Emily needs to know all of this and the sooner the better. We've had so little time together we hardly know each other. You could say that today in the apple orchard was our first date. We have to talk about the future and it won't happen in a day. I don't want to lose her, but I can't hold her, either. You can see that, can't you?"

They were both stumped. Parenting wasn't supposed to be this hard. Mom said, "You're more serious about her than we guessed."

"The thing is, I can't understand what she sees in me. Maybe when she gets to know me she won't like me. I have to find out."

This year I was finally on the basketball varsity. Big deal, because it would have raised eyebrows all over town if I hadn't made it. I even was in the starting line-up now and then. We lost most of our games this year like we did every year.

January came around and I was planning which college I'd attend. I had grown up, at least physically, to six-three and slim but hard because I still did a lot of farm work. I wasn't good looking but not bad either. For ease of grooming I wore my hair in a buzz, not a flat top because my hair simply would not stand up.

Emily had grown up, too. She was tall, five feet seven or eight and had bloomed in the most womanly ways. After the apple orchard, our parents had finally relented and allowed us to double date a couple of times. Usually we'd go to a movie with Eddie and his date. Deer Falls was the best bet because it had three movie theaters and a better chance of a good movie. Deer Falls was twenty-five miles away which gave us more driving time. We all chatted having a good time as we drove. All four of us would sit in the front seat with the two girls in the middle. All cars had only bench seats and seatbelts were unheard of. It was a little snug— just enough to be cozy. Since everybody was slim it worked fine. After the movie we'd sometimes come to one of our houses for cake and ice-cream. The parents and siblings would be conveniently out of sight.

Mom was still concerned that I be properly socialized and generally I didn't like to socialize unless it was with Emily. Otherwise, I'd rather build a model airplane. Some weekends there'd be a sock hop. If I knew Emily would be there I'd reluctantly give in when mom badgered me to go even though wild horses couldn't have kept me away.

I'd always be looking for her and I think she was looking for me even though sometimes she made it hard for me to get a dance or two with her. There were times when I couldn't figure out if she liked me or not. If I were really lucky I'd get to her before someone else did for a slow dance. That was the best because I could hold her close to me, well, pretty close. There were chaperones all over the place as if the morals of society could become perverted at a sock hop.

By mid-January mom was already asking me if I had a date for the prom. Of course I wanted to go, it was the social event of the year. But, I wanted to go with Emily, and if neither she nor her mother were up to making a formal she would say no again this year. I knew her folks didn't have the money to buy a dress.

But, this year I had the hint on an idea of an outside chance I could level the playing field. Larry, my second cousin, the one with all the model airplanes, had visited with his family on the Sunday between Christmas and New Year's. His sister, Nettie, a year older then Larry was along. Larry's father showed us slides of their summer vacation to some exotic place as well as of relatives we seldom saw. It was a way of letting us know how everybody was. I hadn't been much interested in the vacation, but as an afterthought her father had shown a few pictures of Nettie in her senior prom dress. Her mother mentioned how her husband was still grousing about how much money they had paid for it. But I think he showed the slides because he was proud of how great she looked. Money aside, it was gorgeous. I immediately thought of Emily. She would be a knock-out wearing that dress.

Before they left I was so nervous I thought I'd die. I asked Nettie to come into the little spare bedroom off the living room so I could ask her about the dress. We sat on the edge of the bed.

"That was really a beautiful dress you wore to the prom. What do you do with something like that after the dance?"

"We had it cleaned and it's packed away in a big box. Why do you ask?"

I had nothing to lose like I was a fatally wounded soldier falling on a live grenade. Okay, that's an exaggeration, but I was desperate. "Ah . . . does a girl ever borrow another girl's dress to wear at a prom a few years later?"

I though I was being slyly circumspect.

"Who is she?"

"Who is she who?"

"The girl you have in mind to wear my dress."

"Dang it, girls are so tricky."

She laughed. "So, are you going to tell me?"

"Her name is Emily LaNell."

"What a pretty name. I like her already."

"I've known her since the seventh grade. Okay, I've liked her since the seventh grade. To be honest, I've been crazy nuts about her since the seventh grade."

"This sounds serious."

"Yeah, there was a real mess that year in math class. I hurt a leg and she got smacked in the face by a teacher but it healed okay. I already had a crush on her and that kind of brought us together. It's a long story."

"Is she pretty?"

"She's beautiful."

"Oh, yeah . . . crazy nuts . . . dumb question.

"Sooooo, I'm sold as far as that goes. Why my dress?"

"Her family is not well off. Her father works hard but they have a small farm and if I ask her to the prom she'd have to say no even if she wanted to go with me. They couldn't afford a formal for just a dance."

She was serious, now. "This would be a project, you know. A girl doesn't just step into a gown like that and look like a queen. I'm intrigued, though, I have to say that. She, and her parents, and your parents for that matter, would have to be agreeable to do what it takes. You can't do something like this half way. I'd have to come up a couple of times to fit it and get her ready. What size is she?"

"Stand up," I said. She stood and even turned around once. "Almost exactly the same size. And, I don't mean only her height."

She laughed. "You've been, shall we say, keeping an eye on Emily?"

We both laughed. Nettie was open and outgoing and I liked her.

"What I'd need is those slides of you in the dress so I could ask her what she thinks."

"Wait a minute. How does she feel about you?"

"We were in love in the seventh grade and our parents didn't exactly like that at first but they came around—a little. We're still good friends and she likes me, I know that. Not crazy about me like I am about her, though."

She gave me a wise look. "You never know. All the way back to the seventh grade? That's pretty long. Has she ever gone steady?"

I shook my head.

"Hmmm.

"If she wears that dress you can't wear any old thing. You'd have to rent a tux. Are you good with that? And what would the town say? I'd imagine there aren't many tuxedos at your prom."

"I'll talk to mom and dad about that before I ask her."

"One more thing. I'd really need some of her measurements. Her measured height and, you know, the other three."

I swallowed hard. "That's pretty personal, isn't it? Most girls don't want to let anybody know that."

She smiled. "That depends. If they're favorable dimensions she wouldn't mind and from what you said they are." Chuckling a little she said, "I think what I'm hearing is that you'd be embarrassed to ask.

"It's important because we have a mannequin that we could adjust to her size and first see if there was any hope. In spite of your keen eye you might be off the mark as far as the two of us being the same size. If it turns out to be possible we could make most of the alterations before I came up to fit it."

"You're right, this is complicated."

"Men have no idea what women go through to look beautiful for them. And, you're not worth it."

"No argument with that but we're glad you do."

She smiled. "I'll get the slides from daddy's box and you let me know." She was about to leave the room and stopped. "Almost forgot. There's more I have to tell you. It's more than the dress. There're some things that go underneath that are most important. Let me enlighten you so you're prepared for the inevitable questions."

Gulp! I almost wished I hadn't gotten into this.

CHAPTER 45

When mom and I were alone after school in the kitchen one day I said, "I'm going to ask Emily to the prom."

"Oh. That's nice."

She was being noncommittal which was the best I could hope for.

"It's good to ask her early before somebody else does because she's a pretty girl. And, I know you kind of like her."

Oh, come on. We're nuts about each other. Has everybody suddenly gone blind? "There's a problem though. I asked her last year and she said no because she didn't have a formal. One of the other girls that I asked turned me down using the same excuse. In Emily's case I'd believe it. She always looks nice, all pressed and stuff, but she doesn't even have many school clothes. The point is, if she didn't have one last year, it's likely she won't have one this year, either. But, I think I might have it figured out."

Mom looked at me in an odd way like how could I figure out a girl's prom dress?

"Do you remember over Christmas when Larry and Nettie's family were here and their dad showed vacation slides? Nettie's dad showed some of Nettie's prom dress, too."

"Yes. I remember the dress. It was really something—sleeveless, strapless—but she was stunning."

I could sense trouble coming but forged ahead. "I asked Nettie if she'd let Emily borrow her dress and she basically said yes. She thought it might be fun. What do you think?"

"Oh my." She sat down across the kitchen table from me. "I don't know. Even assuming it fit her, and come to think of it, it might, that dress is from a class above us and above Emily, too."

"Nettie said it has a shawl that could be worn with it to cover up her shoulders."

"Yes. But, you have to understand that would be to keep the cold off outside, not part of the dress to be worn at the actual dance."

"I borrowed the slides from Nettie. We still have the microfilm magnifier if you want to look at them."

"Okay. I'll do that but I still don't think so."

"Well, it was a thought. It was fun while it lasted."

"Don't give up totally. I'll have to think about it, and ask your father. What would you wear?"

"She said I'd have to rent a tuxedo or it wouldn't work. And, I know, I'd probably be the only one there wearing a tux. The town probably isn't ready for that."

"I hate to ask this because it seems you have your heart set on Emily, but if she says no would you ask someone else?"

"I'm not going through that again like last year. If Emily says no because of no dress I won't go to the prom. Maybe I'll ask her to go to a movie that night."

Mom was thinking. "You always double date, who would go with you?"

"On prom night? Are you kidding? Nobody. It would be just the two of us. That might be fun. We've never been out together alone."

When I said that I wasn't thinking of extortion. My mind didn't work that way. It was only some weeks later that I realized what must have been going through my mother's mind. She had a dilemma. Either she'd have to worry about what people would say because her son and his date arrived at the prom overdressed. On the other hand, we might spend some time alone underdressed. That is, would she have to worry about what people would say if Emily turned up pregnant. The latter situation was the furthest thing from my mind. But, it was not unheard of that high school kids had to get married. And, every parent worried about prom night.

A few days later mom told me I should ask Emily and see what she says. Maybe she could come up with a dress after all. And otherwise it was likely Nettie's dress wouldn't fit anyway, all of which came under the heading of grasping at straws.

There was more. "Mom, I've been thinking. If we go ahead with this there's something we have to discuss and that's secrecy."

"What do you mean?"

"I mean the talk around town. Remember when I saw Emily in the doctor's waiting room after she got socked in the face?"

"Yes."

"You probably didn't hear much about it, but the gossip was pretty bad. At school they had Emily and me smooching in the doctor's office. I'm not too worried about them finding out Emily and I are going to the prom together. But, if they learn that the boy is getting the dress for the girl, they'll have us married, or worse. You and dad will have to keep completely silent about this. I'll tell Emily, too, but she'll understand. If we show up at the prom, well, that will mean it all worked out and the deed is done. There are so many ways this could fall apart, and if it does I'd rather nobody knew that we tried.

"All my life you've been saying at every turn, 'What will people say?' That was so you and dad wouldn't be humiliated. Now, it's my turn not to be humiliated. And it's both of us. I don't want Emily to be hurt, either. So, promise me you will not mention this to anyone."

She nodded.

"Say it. Say you promise."

"I promise."

Now it was up to me, and it was tough. I needed at least a few minutes with Emily because it was not as simple as coming up beside her as she walked down the hall and saying, "Hi, Emily. Will you go to the prom with me?"

"Yes/no." Job done.

Then—bang—it happened in the lunch room. Practically the same place where I had first spoken to her. She sat at the end of the table and the place across from her was empty. And, there were other empty chairs that were next nearest.

"Hi, Emily, is this place taken?"

She looked up and smiled, "Hi, Jamie. It's a public school . . . . Have to stop there because no chili today."

She had remembered. I sat down and didn't waste time. "You remembered. That pleases me. But to business."

She smiled and cocked her head like she sometimes did when she was amused.

"Emily, will you go to the prom with me?"

"You asked last year and when I said no you went with someone else. I was hurt."

This was going to be tougher than I had thought. "And, two besides you turned me down. My mother was hounding me mercilessly. It's hard to pick out a girl who isn't going steady and get up enough courage to ask her and then find a time to do it only to have her say no."

I was floundering and had to get back on course. "Having you say no was the hardest, though."

That put her on the defensive. Man, love is war. "You turned me down because you didn't have a dress, but you have one this year, right?"

She shook her head sadly. "No I don't. Not this year either."

"No possibility?"

She shook her head.

Okay, now I could get into the plan I had figured out. "Let me ask you another completely different question. If you *had* a dress, would you go to the prom with me?"

She looked at me through slitted eyes. "You want to know if I'm using the dress as an excuse, is that what I'm hearing?"

I smiled and nodded enthusiastically.

Neither of us were eating much, though we ate a bite now and then. It was Friday and we had macaroni and cheese in deference to the Catholic kids. A third of the kids were Catholics so there was no meat on Friday. Nobody got in a snit about it. And, what's more, they did a reasonably good job of macaroni and cheese.

"Jamie, I would have hoped you knew that I'd go to the prom with you if there were any chance, that I'd never use 'no dress' as an excuse. It kind of hurts me that you'd even think that." She was looking at her macaroni and cheese messing around in it with her fork as she said, "I suppose you'll ask someone else."

340

I said, "Emily, look at me." She looked up. "No. I'm not going to ask someone else. And, I'm sorry I said it that way. That was thoughtless of me. But, I have an idea if you'll give me a chance."

She was smiling now and I liked it so much when she smiled. "I have some pictures to show you but they're 35mm slides. So, I'm going to ask Mr. Beecher to bring in his slide projector tomorrow, no Monday, since tomorrow's Saturday, and I'll show them to you in the chemistry lab over lunch break. Okay? Eat fast on Monday and get there as soon as you can. Don't worry, Mr. Beecher will be there, not that I'd mind getting you alone in the chemistry lab."

She giggled. She was puzzled but intrigued too, exactly like I had hoped.

She nodded.

CHAPTER 46

Mr. Beecher had been promoted to teaching senior high classes. He taught chemistry and physics on alternate years. Every year he taught a class of plane geometry and another that was a half year each of trigonometry and solid geometry.

I knew Mr. Beecher brown-bagged so he'd have no problem eating in the chemistry lab. I didn't have to ask him specifically to be our chaperone, nor did I suppose he thought it was necessarily required. When I said I had some slides to show to Emily, he was as intrigued as she was. He'd have the projector and I knew he'd be there—protect the morals of society, you know, as well as being the first to know what was going on.

The chemistry lab was seldom used since there was only a chemistry class every other year and then there were only a half dozen times when the students actually did experiments. On the wall was a large periodic chart of the elements that was flipped over and the white back used as a screen to show slides when needed.

When I arrived on Monday he had turned over the chart and was opening the slide projector box.

Emily walked in. "I hope this is worth it. I'll have indigestion all afternoon I ate so fast."

"It'll be worth it," I said.

Everything was set and I put the six slides in the feed tray.

"I've already eaten so I'll be over here at the end of the table correcting papers. Behave yourselves," Mr. Beecher said with a chuckle.

The big moment. I slid in the first slide—upside down, darn it. I slid it back and turned it over checking the others, too. Now, again.

Emily looked at it intently. "She's beautiful."

"Yes she is. But, she's not the point—the dress."

I heard her draw in a quick breath. Glancing at her she was looking at me.

"It's available, if you would want to wear it to the prom. Look." I slipped in the next slide, and then the next. One was from the right rear so you could see the back. One had her spinning so the skirt flared to the point you could see her knees. Another was a close-up to show the pattern of pearls sewn on the bodice. The dress itself was shades of violet to rose with what seemed like layer upon layer of gossamer lace and fabric.

Emily had her hand to her mouth and was giggling, almost keening. "Jamie! That's much too nice. I just couldn't."

I had envisioned this was one possible response so was prepared. "That's my second cousin, Nettie, and though we're related, their family and ours are more friends than relatives. You'd like her. Well, everybody likes her. She's two years older than me and that's her senior prom dress. She and her mother got carried away and her dad almost had a stroke when he saw how much they spent. She said it would be nice if someone else could use it."

"But, would it even fit?"

"There's a good chance it will. You're almost the same size she is—same height and in, ah . . . other . . . ah ways, too."

"Jamie! You've been stealing glances at me."

"Much more than glances, and enjoying every minute of it."

"Jamie, you shouldn't say things like that!" she said as she playfully whapped me on the head.

"Hey, hey, there. No fighting in the chemistry lab." We had forgotten about Mr. Beecher.

"But seriously, how would I know if it fit?"

"Now we get to the heart of it. She said it would be a project, and I've come to see that. First of all, Nettie's dad does whatever he does very well because they're well to do, as in what we'd call rich. As a result, she has an adjustable mannequin. You would have to measure your height in you stocking feet, or have someone else measure you. And you'd have to take your other measurements, you know the ones, as in the three main ones also in . . . ah . . . so to speak, your stocking feet."

She was looking at me as I got more uncomfortable with every word.

"Jamie, you're blushing."

"I know it, darn it."

A chuckle from across the room.

My mouth was dry. "Anyway, she could adjust the mannequin to your size and see if the dress would fit. Can we talk about something else?"

Another chuckle.

Emily said, "Not yet."

I could see she was thinking about how to broach the next subject. "A girl doesn't just step into a dress like that, you know, no straps."

"Those are the exact words Nettie used. You need foundations. It's all included if your size is close to hers. There's a corset that contains the, well you know the . . . the bra . . . well you know how that works—I hope—because if you don't I sure don't. Then there's a girdle that comes down over the hips. I'm not sure why you'd need that except it has the garters to hold up you socks . . . you know, your nylons. You'd have to supply nylons and shoes. See, made it all the way to the floor. How'm I doing?"

"You're still blushing."

"Dang it, this isn't easy." After a pause I continued, "There are 'bones' in the dress above the hips to keep it stiff so if it's fitted right and the corset keeps your size constant the dress will stay up. Sometimes a few stitches are made between the dress and the corset after you put it on to keep everything in its proper place."

She was smiling that sweet smile she has. "Boys aren't supposed to know stuff like that. How come you do?"

"I don't. I'm only repeating what I was told. For all I know I could be giving you coded instructions on how to build an atomic bomb. Come to think of it, what we're talking about could be more dangerous than an atomic bomb."

More chuckling.

I turned my head and said, "You're enjoying yourself, aren't you?"

"Immensely."

"And, you're not getting any papers corrected either, are you?"

"Not a one."

Mr. Beecher laughed as he walked over. "I love my job. Being around young people keeps me young. Could I see the pictures? I was too far away to see the details."

I went through them slowly again with Emily closely watching for some aspect she might have missed.

"If Emily's going to wear that gown to the prom, I'll have to find a date."

Emily frowned. "But, Mr. Beecher, you're married."

"Well, I expect I'll ask my wife first."

"You're a rat."

He boomed his baritone laugh.

I looked at her, "I didn't occur to me until now, but it's, well, you know, awfully open on the top."

She looked at me with a mischievous look like I had never quite seen before. "Jamie, you're concerned about my virtue. I'm touched."

"Well, virtue, that's true. But, there's the practical side. Anybody that dances with you will be drooling all over you, me included. That's pretty daring. Isn't there anything . . . ?"

She threw her arms around me and my arms responded without thinking. We were hugging. It was the first time since the apple orchard and it was, as always, a special occasion.

I heard her say, "I promise you if the size works I'll think of something."

"Okay. Break clean from the clinches. We don't want any broken ribs here." Mr. Beecher said laughing.

We parted and Emily looked from Mr. Beecher to me and back. "There's something here, isn't there. You two are sort of friends. I mean apart from school."

"You could say Mr. Beecher saved my life."

"Oh no. I had my little assignment and he did the rest."

"Wait a minute," she said looking at me, "you gave *him* an assignment?"

"And, it was no small thing. He had to pass on information to a very dangerous and cunning man. And he had to do it in such a way that the man overheard it so casually that he'd think only he knew the real meaning of what was said so he would act on it. He did it perfectly. If the man had suspected he were being set up it could have gone very badly for Mr. Beecher."

"I didn't sleep for a week."

She looked at me. "When was this?"

"Some weeks after you got hit in the face."

"Was that all connected?"

"Sure."

"You knew why that math teacher was being mean to you?"

I nodded. "We didn't want to do anything until they acted overtly and that incident with the math teacher really stalled things. Finally we were forced to act and that's where Mr. Beecher came in. It's over now, though. With the information Mr. Beecher gave the man, he acted and we finished it."

"What was it about?"

I thought a minute, "It was so people in this country could go to bed at night feeling safe."

"The whole country? It was that big?"

Too much was being said. "One could say that. Anyway, that's all I can say and you must never repeat what we've said about that subject.

"There's something else we must discuss and that's secrecy. The dress might not fit but if it does I want this to be a surprise for everyone."

She nodded.

"Tell your family not to mention it. If it works out and we show up at the prom with you looking like a movie star, well, good for us. But, there are so many things that could go wrong. I've already sworn my family to secrecy."

The bell rang. "You take your, ah, you-know-whats . . . ."

"My measurements."

"Yeah, and give them to me and I'll send them to Nettie. You can put them in a sealed envelope. It all hinges on that, I guess. By the way, I'd rent a tuxedo so I wouldn't look like a hayseed."

She smiled that cute Emily smile and she left for her class. I knew Mr. Beecher didn't have a class to teach next hour and I had study hall.

"How about you?" I asked Mr. Beecher. "You can't tell anyone either, not even your wife."

"That's going to be awfully hard."

"Come on. It might not even fit and if it does the word will get around that I'm supplying her dress. What will people say? You're a good teacher and I like to think of you as a friend. Please do this for us."

He shrugged. "Okay. I won't say anything, but you owe me."

"Any time, just let me know."

CHAPTER 47

The next day Emily surreptitiously handed me a small envelope. I slipped it under the cover of my physics book. When I had a chance to look at it unobserved, I saw it had not been sealed. Love is war! She was tempting me. I hated it when girls did things like that. I knew I'd give in sooner or later as she knew I would so I slipped the paper out of the envelope. She had cut the page out of the Sears and Roebuck that showed every dimension that could be made of the female body so mail-order clothing had a chance of fitting. She had written in her measurement for every one, including her bra cup size. I was more than a high school kid could take. It was beyond war, it was getting dangerous—that atomic bomb effect.

That evening I wrote a letter to Nettie telling her that if her family had any connection to Deep Woods beyond my family to say nothing. I told her about how we wanted it to be a surprise. I included the little envelope from Emily after sealing it—so there.

Every time we met in the hall Emily would smile at me, I'd smile back and shrug which meant I had heard nothing. Some weekends they had a sock hop. After the meeting with Emily in the chemistry lab I was keenly interested in not missing one even if I wasn't sure Emily would be there. This year it seemed her folks had decided to let her drive the car to the dances if the weather wasn't bad so she was at most of them.

For ninth, tenth and eleventh grade mom had to pry me out of the house to get me to go to a dance so when I started to go to all of them she knew it was because of Emily.

Tommy had been different. He didn't go to dances but went to all the things the band did and that was a lot—all winter and all summer. It was perfect, nice socializing but no boy-girl, at least as far as my parents knew. He always did the perfect son things. He rarely dated though he had no problem getting a prom date with a girl who had a dress to wear.

A couple of weeks after the chemistry lab meeting we were both at the sock hop. It was called a sock hop because it was held in the gym. It damaged the floor finish to walk on it with anything besides rubber soled shoes so we danced in our socks. The music was strictly from spinning forty-five rpm records complete with scratches. The kids would bring in their own records to play. We were dancing to *Mr. Sandman bring me a dream. Make him the cutest I've ever seen . . .* by the Chordettes. While we danced she said, "Can I talk to you after this dance?"

When the music stopped we sat on chairs along the side of the gym floor. She asked me what was taking so long to get a reply from Nettie. "Are you sure you included my you-know-whats," breaking into a giggle as she said it, "to Nettie."

"Maybe it's taking longer to get an answer because you sent so may measurements."

"You looked?"

"Of course, it wasn't sealed."

"You didn't have to look."

"If you ever find a man who you honestly think wouldn't have looked under similar circumstances, walk away. He isn't human."

"That bad."

I nodded.

"You thought I was teasing you?"

"It crossed my mind."

"Jamie, I'm sorry. I would never tease about something like that."

"Thank you. I'm glad you said that, and I'll never tease you about stuff like that, either. I'm getting deeper into this that I should. A guy normally says he'll pick up the girl at seven and she appears all decked out. That's all he knows. What we're doing is fun but how do I say it, it's too much like playing with fire."

Then I added, "I hope it's not wrong to pray for something like this because I'm praying that it'll work."

She smiled and said, "So am I."

The next dance was *Rock Around The Clock* by Bill Haley and His Comets and I danced this one with her, too. She was a better dancer than I was but I was coming along.

A few days later I saw Emily in the lunch room. If the adults had only known it, the lunch room was where the morals of the young were going to the dogs. But, they never figured it out. I sat beside her, not across the table. As soon as I sat down I said I had gotten an answer. Her chair magically took it into its head to shift my way.

One of the chairs across from us was vacant, but the other was wearing ears. But the ears were nearly done eating. We waited for them to leave. When they did I said, "Nettie said it will work fine. It looks like my eye is better than you girls gave me credit for." I started to giggle.

"Stop that. I know what you're thinking."

Because of my left-handedness I was sitting on her left as usual. Meanwhile under the table her hand found mine, or was it the other way around? Palm to palm our fingers laced together; she squeezed my hand and I squeezed back. This was nothing new, but it was still fun.

I said, "This food is no better than it normally is so why am I enjoying lunch so much today?"

She squeezed my hand, I returned it and added a little nudge on her shoulder.

There was a saying at the time that went, "Soak a sinny in the passion pit," which meant to take a girl to a "B" movie at the outdoor drive-in theater. That was nothing compared to eating lunch in the school cafeteria. The adults never figured it out.

I can't remember what we had for lunch that day, I only remember realizing my plate was empty and so was hers. We walked to the table where we deposited our plates, silverware and trays, and exited the lunchroom into the gym where there were a few kids shooting baskets. We walked around the edge to the far wall. Even though we weren't going steady like other kids did, it had long ago been accepted that we were together.

"Nettie sent some things for you. There are some ads from the Sunday paper that show what type of shoes you might want to get."

"I expected that. I can manage the shoes. What else?"

"There's a booklet about how to walk, sit down, stand up and things like that while wearing heels and a fancy dress. It makes sense. I always wondered how girls could get around in high heels without falling. It takes practice."

"When can I see it?"

Her voice had urgency in it like I had never heard before. "Now. Lets go, I have it in my locker."

The hall was mostly empty as she leaned against the lockers paging through the booklet. "This is really kind of Nettie. It shows how to curtsey, bow, twirl around, move my arms and hands, all that stuff.

"Look at this, it shows walking with a book on your head so you learn how to walk gracefully. In a movie once I saw some rich girls in a finishing school walking around with books on their heads. I thought that was so dumb but now I'll do it. I never thought of it, but I could have been wearing that gown and come in walking like a plow-horse."

She studied another page. "It says it's important to have comfortable shoes which means as much as anything developing the leg muscles that are needed for heels. I'll get the shoes as soon as I can so I can practice walking in them. I'm determined to get this right."

In that vein I was doing my part by letting my hair grow out. If anyone asked I'd say I had to be in a wedding in the spring and the bride-to-be wanted all the men to have the same hair style. "Can you imagine anything as crazy as that?" They bought it.

"Secrecy is still important," I said. "After you left the chemistry lab that day, Mr. Beecher was ready to blab everything to the whole town. I got him to stuff a sock in his mouth, though. This has to be a total surprise."

She nodded. "I'm so excited I could burst, but I know you're right." She looked directly at me—those eyes; not only were they that seductive color but they were sparkling. "Oh, Jamie, we're going to the prom, and I'm going to be pretty!"

CHAPTER 48

Time went along and finally March flowed into April. Emily and Nettie were writing letters and calling each other. It was a project all right and Emily's parents seemed to be agreeable to it. I was never sure what all the motivations were. It was possible they thought that if I had relatives that rich maybe some of it filtered down to me and therefore I was a good marriage bet for their daughter.

I had, of course, thought about life married to Emily and it was not at all unappealing. There were many problems, not the least of which was I had to get an education so I could support a family. And, Emily was at her prime husband snagging age right now. The dress project was to a point that there was nothing I could do to change the course of things even if I had wanted to, which I didn't. Right now the prom was the goal and we'd have to talk about other things later.

Nettie visited two weeks before the dance to finalize the fitting of the dress. The day before the prom Nettie arrived for serious preparations. That evening Nettie stayed with us. She talked about how much fun they had doing Emily's hair and practicing a lot of things. She even made me back the car out and with Nettie taking Emily's place I had to practice helping Emily get out of the car with high heels and a full dress with several petticoats. She swiveled on the car seat and set her feet on the ground. I was to take her extended left hand and a moment before she pulled on it, she squeeze my fingers. The squeeze was to warn me what was coming so I wouldn't be pulled off balance. There were several little things like that which would have seemed crazy only a few days before, but now were all important. It was an education for both Emily and me.

The next day, the day of the prom, Nettie went to Emily's place to help get her ready. The prom officially started at 7:30 and we planned to be there about 7:45 so Nettie arrived at our place with Emily at 7:15. Of course, my mom and dad wanted to see her and take pictures. Nettie's mother, Martha, had gotten caught up in the undertaking and had driven up during the afternoon in her big Cadillac. It was a 1952 Cadillac Coupe DeVille hardtop, baby blue with a white top. It had to be one of the longest two-door cars ever made to that time.

I had struggled into my tuxedo and carefully combed my hair, and combed my hair, and combed my hair. It was not well behaved like me. When Nettie and Emily arrived I helped Emily out of the car as practice. She was lovely, no that's not right. She took my breath away. Her black hair was done up in loose curls and extended to her shoulders. The waves on top made her look an inch taller. On the sides the wave was rolled back enough to reveal her earrings. It was the nicest I had ever seen her look. It was the nicest I had seen any girl look.

We went into the house and on the dining room table was box covered in blue velvet with *Tiffany's* on it in an ornate script. Martha said, "Emily, I have a few things to complete your ensemble." She opened a box and laying on a bed of black silk was a gleaming single strand diamond necklace.

"Oh!" she exclaimed. "Are they real?"

"Yes, they are."

Her mouth trembled, "I don't know if I can . . . ."

"We've gone this far so why stop now? You'd do me a favor if you'd wear them. Nettie has told me how hard you've worked at all this. You have heart, girl, so let us girls do it right."

Emily let Martha put it on. It was constructed so all one saw was a row of diamonds coming around from the back of her neck until near the center four inches below her throat it expanded into three joined clusters of diamonds with the largest in the center.

Then came the earrings which, of course, weren't rings but roses set with many pearls on the petals and a cluster of diamonds in the center. My mom had a hand held mirror and handed it to her. Her expression showed she was pleased.

Then the pictures flashed. As expected they wanted one of the two of us, but there were many with only Emily, and why not? She was the beautiful one.

When we had arrived Nettie had gone upstairs to change and about this time she appeared in a red dress with a full skirt. If she had twirled around it would have gone straight out. It had short sleeves that extended up over the shoulders a couple of inches. The neckline was a little low but not so much as to show anything. The shoes, of course, were red to match. She wore a small sparkly necklace with matching earrings. What can I say, she always looked great.

As we got into the car I opened a paper bag and pulled out two corsages, one for each of the girls. Nettie's was a standard cluster of flowers with a carnation in the center. But Emily's was an orchid. When Nettie saw it she said, "Oh Emily, an orchid. Look how delicate it is."

"I thought about getting you violets, but the florist said they didn't work for a corsage because the wilted too soon. Since, there is no top or even straps for your dress he suggested an elastic band so you could wear it on her wrist."

"And," Nettie said, "it's perfect with your dress."

And then we were off to the prom. Martha insisted that since we had gone that far already we must take her car. I drove and Nettie was in the backseat. She'd park the car and be around to keep an eye on Emily in case anything went wrong. Besides, she said she wanted to see a genuine small town prom.

As we drove to town Emily fanned her face with her hand and said, "It certainly has gotten warm. I must be excited."

"Jamie," Nettie said, "press that button labeled A/C and we'll see if we can make Emily more comfortable."

A fan immediately came on blowing air over our heads from the corners of the rear window. In seconds it became noticeably cooler.

"What did you do?" Emily asked.

Nettie answered, "Turned on the air conditioning. After all, this is a Cadillac."

"Emily," I said, "it's remotely possible that you will be very popular tonight. Please don't forget to have a few dances with me or I'll go crazy, especially the last dance."

"You worry too much, or are you jealous already?"

"Jealous? Of course," I said looking at her. "I don't want to share you with anyone, but I know I'll have to."

There were hazards to what we were doing and to pull it off would require a lot of finesse on our parts, especially Emily's. She had a pleasant expression on her face as I glanced her way—determination, too.

Emily was looking at the flower. "Jamie, this is so sweet of you. It's the one thing from you to me. Thank you. This is all I need."

"Let me suggest that you need a few other things besides the flower even if they are borrowed."

"Nettie, was that a risqué comment?"

"Sounded like it could have been."

"What I meant," I emphasized, "is keep your entire ensemble together until you get home, okay?"

"Oh . . . . But, somehow I liked it better the way you said it the first time. It left the way open for interesting interpretations."

"You're hopeless."

"I know."

"But, I wouldn't want you any other way."

"I know that, too."

Nettie said, "You kids really get along, you know that?"

To enter the first floor of the school you had to go up eight cement steps, then cross twenty feet of broad concrete to the school. Once inside there was a long staircase down to the basement which was the level of the gym floor. There were a half dozen couples outside chatting. The long awaited moment had arrived. I pulled the big Caddy to a stop where the sidewalk came all the way to the curb. Heads turned. I heard Nettie say from the shadows in the back seat, "Graceful and gracious."

I opened my door and let it swing part way closed but not latched so it would be easier for Nettie to get out from the back seat. Someone said, "Who's that?"

Then, "Jamie?"

"The one and only."

"Where'd ya get the great car, and why the zuit-suit?"

I held up my index finger, "Just watch, you'll see."

I took my time getting to the passenger side of the car so they could gather around. With that car it was a long walk in any case. That was when outdoor lighting had gone to mercury vapor lights which gave off a brilliant white light (orange high pressure sodium vapor lights were still in the future.) There was one on the top of the school aimed down to where I had stopped the car.

I opened the door and Emily pivoted herself ninety degrees. One by one she gracefully placed each leg out. Her white shoes had straps around the back, a buckled strap over the instep with open toes, and three inch spike heels. She was mostly still in shadow due to the angle of the light. She slid forward and the light hit her necklace. It was as if there were a ring of white fire around her neck. Next came her smiling face. She extended her left arm covered to the elbow with a white silk glove and I took it. She squeezed my hand and I braced myself so she could use me to pull herself forward off the seat to a standing position. As soon as she was clear of the car her right arm gracefully swung out and down.

As she arose from the car seat her strapless gown came into full view. The bright white light made the subtle shades of rose to violet in the layers of the formal stand out vibrantly. Covering the bust were layers of folded silk satin in graduated shades of pale pink at the top to dark rose that matched the bodice. The bodice was dark rose satin covered with pale pink chantilly lace re-embroidered in palest pink with pearl accents highlighting a petite rosebud pattern.

The deep rose satin skirt hung in lush folds from Emily's trim waist. Overlaying the satin was the same lace, this time re-embroidered in multi-colors giving a three dimensional appearance to the flowers. The pattern on the lace progressed from baby rosebuds at the waist matching the bodice, to large, full roses at the hem. The color of the roses progressed from pink at the waist to deep rose mingled with violet at the bottom. Several full, flouncy crinoline petticoats caused the skirt to billow so the sheen of the satin skirt produced subtly shifting hues in the flowered lace as she moved.

The diamonds in her necklace and earrings glistened and sparkled with each movement. As she walked, the swishing rustle of her petticoats drew the attention of all nearby to the beauty of the classic feminine form graced with the finest adornments.

Emily greeted those standing nearby, some with gaping mouths. It wasn't until they heard her voice that they realized it was she. I was smiling and she was smiling. It was getting dark and the sky was clear.

The school was to the west of us so the sunset was obscured. She said, "A beautiful evening, isn't it?"

Phase one done, she was out of the car.

She took my arm as we walked to the steps, that is, I walked, she floated. At the top of the steps we met none other than Debbie Dinkle and her steady. Emily stopped and extended her hands which Debbie took. "Debbie, you look like a million dollars every day of the year, and are positively stunning tonight. I had a chance to look nice for one evening and I took it. Please don't be angry with me."

The look of consternation on Debbie's face softened to a smile.

Emily leaned toward her and in a soft voice said, "The dress is from a friend and it was the only one she had that would fit. It's all borrowed, even the things underneath. Only the shoes and socks are mine." She giggled. "Oh, and my flower from Jamie. Isn't it pretty?"

"It's an orchid, you lucky girl. Let me help you down the stairs so you don't snag your gown."

I could see the relief in Emily's eyes. "Oh, thank you. Could you run a little interference for me, too? I don't know what others will say."

I took up the rear with Debbie's date, Tom Bolen who was a Catholic school kid, too. I said, "It was either that dress or nothing. The second option, while interesting, was decided against."

With a snicker he said, "Careful about sinful thoughts there ol' buddy."

"Yeah. But, sometimes it hard."

And then we were in the gym. It was the junior class's job to decorate and they had done a fine job. There was a six piece orchestra and they were playing *Smoke Gets In Your Eyes*, the favorite from the thirties. We all had our names on the tables where we were to sit, but before we found our table I took Emily and started to dance.

"Magnificent entrance. We're off to a good start."

She was smiling at me and glancing around. With the heels she was only a couple of inches shorter than me and I liked that because I could look almost directly into her eyes.

The music stopped. I had gotten the first dance with Emily. I was ahead of the game. We found our table and we were matched with Eddie Norbert and his date. We were asked beforehand if we had preferences for table partners and if possible people's wishes were granted. They were returning from the dance floor, too. "Is that really you Emily?" his date, Kathy, asked?

She nodded.

I said, "Her dad struck oil on their farm."

Stares. They were waiting for the real answer.

"What can I say," she said. "I borrowed the gown from a rich relative." She left it there, leaving them to assume it was her relative.

As I pulled out her chair to seat her, I said, "She's my princess tonight."

When we were all seated she said, "When I was small my dad called me his princess."

"I know."

She cocked her heard smiling at me.

"When you left the doctor's office with a bandaged face he said, 'Come on, princess, I'll take you home.'"

"You remember that?"

"Every word."

"Oh," Kathy said, "would you tell us what he said to you that day? In fact everybody would like to know."

Emily answered, "I doubt there are many people who would care. But, maybe, only not right now."

The music started and a handsome young man, who of course I knew, took her away. It was Hank Jeffery, captain of the football team and class president, the all around he-man of the class.

I was concerned that others would take offense at us and in retaliation would make sure I didn't get another dance with Emily. I watched them and after the tune ended he brought her back and thanked her. I was surprised no one had cut in on him.

I hadn't seen Mr. Beecher yet and wondered if he'd come.

The next song was *Autumn Leaves* which was very popular and was one of my favorites. I had Emily on the dance floor before anyone else could ask her. I held her close and she didn't seem to mind. "Are you going to tell about the doctor's waiting room?" I asked.

"What do you think? I've always cherished that but maybe it would smooth things out in this town."

"If you want to, it's all right with me."

CHAPTER 49

Things went well. Not too many guys asked Emily to dance and I was beginning to wonder about that. I think she knew what I was thinking. "You're wondering why more guys aren't asking me to dance, aren't you? With my heels and the way my hair is done I'm taller than most of the boys and a guy doesn't like to look up to the girl he's dancing with."

I guess I worried too much, but it wasn't over yet. There was still the announcement of the prom king and queen to get passed. It came and I was sitting on the edge of my chair as the chairman and chairwoman of the prom committee took the microphone. To my great relief they were Debbie Dinkle and Hank Jeffery. Following the crowning with some rather tacky crowns—they weren't meant to be anything but symbolic— there was the dance for the king and queen. After that Kathy, Eddy's date, took the microphone and asked for silence.

"I have been asked to do a rather unusual thing. Nearly everyone here is dying to know something. And that is . . . what did Jamie say to Emily in the doctor's waiting room that day in the seventh grade."

This was followed by much clapping and cheering. I looked at Emily. "Looks like we're on."

She nodded.

There were broad steps up to the stage and we went up to the microphone. It wasn't such a large gym that one was even needed, but it helped a little.

I took the microphone and said, "First, let me congratulate our prom king and queen."

There were cheers and clapping. Emily was standing beside me and she squeezed my hand. She knew that I had said that because Debbie had been so nice to her. I saw Debbie and she knew, too.

"Now to the story. Please don't fall asleep."

Emily took the microphone and cleared her throat. "I hadn't thought I'd ever tell anyone. It's kind of a treasure to me, but you have all been so gracious to me tonight that I guess I will. The short version is, Jamie said a prayer for me."

There was silence.

"But, I suppose you want a few more details."

Much cheering. It surprised me how that incident was still so much on everyone's mind.

"Here, I'll have to let Jamie start the story."

I took the microphone. "The previous fall we all started seventh grade. I came from the Catholic school and Emily came from a country school. It was all new, big and crowded but we managed. Math class was the only one Emily and I had together. After a few weeks I noticed her, and then discovered I was noticing her more and more. By the end of six weeks I had a giant sized crush on her. She was cute as a button."

Looking at her I said, "And, she still is."

Emily gave me a peck on the cheek.

I spotted Mr. Beecher off to the side. He had come after all. Looking at him I said, "I love my job."

There were some cheers, but I could see Mr. Beecher enjoyed it.

"She seemed popular enough and I knew she didn't know I existed so I looked for a chance to talk to her. To do that I needed two things, the right opportunity and enough courage, and I had neither."

Clapping and cheers.

"This went on and I was going crazy until one day in February I saw her sitting at the end of the table in the lunch room and the place opposite her was vacant—my chance. I approached and asked, 'Is this place saved?'

"'It's a public school so this must be a public table.'

"I sat down and started to eat. We had chili that day. My tongue was in a big knot. Finally I said, 'They make good chili.'

"'They use too much chili powder for my taste.'

"'What's chili powder?'

"'It's what makes chili taste like chili.'

"'Oh.'

"I was already impressing her with my brilliance."

Laughter.

"We spoke about other things and it was going better than I had any expectation it would. At one point she looked right at me and I saw her eyes. Here's a small aside. From when I was the littlest kid I'd go into the woods in spring and look for mayflowers. They enchanted me the way the sprang up out of the brown leaves with no green leaves any-where yet. After they wilted the wild violets bloomed and I liked them, too. For some reason the special color captivated me. I wanted to say she had pretty eyes but what came out was part of what I knew.

"'Oh,' I said.

"She replied, 'What?'

"'Your eyes are so pretty. They're the color of wild violets.'

"'Do you really think so?'

"What I intended was really more of an observation but it came out as a complement. She seemed genuinely pleased.

"'Don't you have wild violets where you live?'

"She nodded and by this time she had finished eating.

"'I should leave so somebody else will have a place to sit down.'

"She left. I had actually spoken to Emily and now was as happy as I could be."

I decided to say nothing about our second lunch so continued, "That was about all we were to each other until that day in March when Mr. Russo said he had had enough. He grabbed my shirt behind my neck and was marching me out to the principal's office to get me expelled. As soon as we left the room the whole class spilled out behind us and Mr. Russo at first was surprised and then got mad. With kids swirling all around him he released me. I moved away behind him. Remember, I had injured my leg at home a couple of days before and was limping. When I was behind him someone beside me punched him in the back. He looked back and seeing me assumed I had done it. He made a fist with his right hand, the one with the big ring on it. He swung it around to backhand me. I saw it coming and ducked and he hit Emily instead of me. I had no idea she was there but I nearly died when I saw her hit. She slammed into the girl beside her and they both fell down. I knew right then that if I hadn't ducked she wouldn't have been hit and I felt terrible. It was my fault that my pretty Emily had been injured.

"When I ducked, I twisted my leg and fell down. It really hurt now. Struggling up, I saw Emily by the wall sobbing as someone held a handkerchief over her eye. She was covered with blood, or so it seemed. At that time the bell rang and the other rooms emptied into the hallway, too. I could hardly step on my leg so decided I'd go home while I still could.

"As I walked along the road, I could think of nothing but Emily so I prayed for her. Half way home I could go no further so I flagged down a car. Luckily it was a neighbor who knew us and he took me home. In the house I told my mother I couldn't walk on my leg anymore and she said she'd take me to see the doctor before he left for the day.

"When we arrived, my mom helped me into the doctor's office. The waiting room was empty except for a little girl sitting alone near the corner. I sat diagonally opposite her. Mom told the nurse why we were there and sat beside me. It was then I saw it was Emily, my Emily. I don't know why but I said, 'Mom, stay here.'

"I hopped over to her and said, 'Emily.'

"She looked up and I saw the saddest face there could ever be. But as she realized it was me she seemed to brighten. She said 'Jamie,' in the strangest tone of voice like she had been waiting for me, or was glad to see me. I crossed my mind that she had been hit harder than anyone imagined and mistook me for someone else.

"I saw the big bandage and the blood on her dress and could sense how bad she must feel.

"'Oh, your eye must really hurt.'

"'I got seven stitches and the doctor said he thinks my eye will be all right, but isn't sure. My dad is in talking to him now.'

"'I'm so sorry, it's all my fault. How could this have happened to *you*?'

"I felt so helpless wanting to do something, anything, but there seemed to be nothing I could do. I couldn't keep standing on one foot so I sat beside her and took her left hand between both of mine. 'I prayed for you all the way home and I'll pray that God sends His angel to watch over you so you get better.'

"I noticed I was holding her hand. 'I'm sorry I grabbed you hand.'

"In the softest little voice she said, 'That's okay; I don't mind.'

"Then she looked at me. I saw her good eye and the right one that was starting to swell shut. 'And I'll ask that God not send just any angel but the prettiest one He has because you're the prettiest girl He ever made. Who else has eyes the color of wild violets?'

"She gave me the sweetest, brightest smile of all time. She was radiant."

You could hear a pin drop; it was so quiet. People were hardly breathing.

"The doctor's office door started to open and I dropped her hand."

Emily was beside me on the stage and she put her arm around my waist and squeezed me. It felt good. She took the microphone and said, "My mascara is starting to run."

Then she began. "As time went on I realized he had a crush on me. In seventh grade I knew him mainly as the boy being singled out for punishment in math class.

"I have to say something about our chili lunch. I was pretty glum that day and when Jamie asked if he could sit down opposite me I was a little surprised because nobody asked, they saw an empty chair and sat down. He seemed interested in me which was another thing that was new. When he said I had pretty eyes and likened them to wild violets it was a thrill that I couldn't explain. People had often mentioned my eyes were an unusual color but not that they were pretty. I excused myself though there was no real need to. It was like I wanted to get away before he changed his mind. I recall feeling warm and, well, good as I walked away and the feeling stayed with me. I tried to tell myself that he was just another boy, but . . . he wasn't just another boy. After that I started to notice him more and began to see he was strong and appealing in ways the other boys weren't.

"Now to the doctor's waiting room. I remember all of it exactly as he said—every word. I was about as blue as it was possible for a person to be. My head hurt, I thought I might be blind in one eye, and I was so alone I thought I'd die. I was off-and-on thinking of Jamie. Maybe it was because he had made me feel good once before and could help me now but he wasn't there so that was an absurd thought.

"Then Jamie said my name. My heart skipped a beat. It was too much to believe. He was the answer to the prayer I didn't say because I saw no hope of it being answered. That taught me never to lose hope. I could tell he wanted to do something for me but was unable . . . and then he touched me." Here she paused a few moments. "He hadn't grabbed my hand. His touch was so light, yet so firm. I desperately didn't want him to let me go. His hands were my connection to survival, to life. His voice sounded so nice, so genuinely concerned about me. Not about my eye or that I might have a scar, but about me, me as a person, me as Emily. He was so distressed for me that my heart went out to him. I began to ache for him; I wanted to do something for him. He wanted to spare me suffering but was helpless to do anything.

"When he said he'd pray to God to send His prettiest angel, he was actually saying the prayer. And, as he said the prayer it was being answered with each word. All prayers are answered but not usually in that way. God chose that moment to touch me directly and He never does things by half. He gives full measure, shaken down, spilling over. I thought my heart would burst with joy. Something like that had never happened to me before nor after. I was smiling so much I though my face would break. It was the only physical way I had to express what happened to me. I remember saying, 'Thank you, Jamie.' God answered the prayer, but *Jamie* had said the prayer for *me*, just for me.

"Oh, yes," Emily continued, "I have to mention this. When the door to the doctor's office started to open, Jamie let go of my had. I instantly knew why. He didn't want my father to think he was making out with his daughter. I always thought that was so dear.

"That's what happened in the doctor's waiting room. Two kids God brought together for a few moments in time. Think of the odds. Chance alone couldn't do that. But, to say a few moments isn't right. The whole thing from when he said my name until the door opened couldn't have lasted more than a minute or two. Yet, every thought, every affective feeling had a chance to start, to glow and to mature. Nothing was rushed.

"It had the immediate effect of picking me up and making me want to get well. I was giddy as I left the office. They said the wound healed faster than normal and it left no scar something that surprised the doctor. Since then I have often thought that what happened in the waiting room was bigger than what I've described but for what reason, to this day, I can't imagine other than, maybe, to tell it to you tonight." She made a small curtsey and bow indicating that was all.

It was silent and then a slow applause started that built to a thunder.

When it was quiet again I looked at Emily and said, "You have your king and queen but I have this beautiful princess."

"Someone yelled, "Are the diamonds real?"

"Where's Nettie?" I asked.

She stepped out from the side by the entrance to the gym and raised her hand. "Come up and let me introduce you."

"This is Nettie Landon, my cousin. Please tell them about the jewelry and the rest."

Emily and I proceeded to the wide steps leading from the stage to the gym floor. Before she took the first step down she squeezed my fingers to signal that she would be counting on me for support since there were no hand rails.

Nettie began. "I'm in a way crashing your party and I thank you for letting me in. I'm from what you would call a well to do neighborhood. A lot more money was spent on my prom than you spent, yet, yours is much nicer. I can feel the spirit and pride you take in what you do. I don't know if you realize how lucky you are. I especially want to congratulate the junior class on the fine job they did in decorating the gym. I really mean that. It's like a magic land."

There was clapping and cheering.

"The diamonds are real. They've been in my family for years. Let me start this way. Jamie had seen pictures of me in my prom dress from two years ago. He told me about Emily and asked if she might be able to borrow it. One thing lead to another. Emily was so enthusiastic and easy to work with that it became a corporate enterprise. I drove up yesterday to start putting her together. The girls will know what I mean."

Clapping.

"My mother drove up this afternoon to bring the jewelry. She wanted to see the prom, too. That was her car, by the way, that Jamie and Emily arrived in. My mom wouldn't be deterred—might as well go the whole way. The car's a 1952 Cadillac Coupe DeVille and don't scratch it or my mom will kill you. She loves that car.

"Mother and I went out to buy me something to wear for my senior prom. We had set a limit on how much we could spend but got carried away. My father almost had a stroke when he saw the bill. 'All that money for one party,' he said about a hundred times. Thank you Emily. Now I can say," she held up two fingers, "two parties."

Laughter.

"That gal can really wear that dress, though, can't she?"

Emily spun around so the skirt flared and as she came around I offered my right hand and she took it with her right hand. Normally I would have offered my left hand to her right but fate was smiling on us. When she stopped she made a deep curtsey almost to the floor and all at once she squeezed my fingers as though she would crush them. It was a signal of an emergency. Not knowing the nature of the crisis I partially bent and partially stooped beside her. As I did I swung her arm over my head so her arm and hand were across my shoulders. Grasping her firmly around the waist I lifted her up. As I did I started to spin her around backwards saying softly, "Apple orchard."

She knew what I was doing so she let her left arm extend gracefully out with the palm up as her skirt swung out. We went around completely twice. As we came around the second time I said, "Time to land."

I stopped and she settled on her feet. There was clapping. She said in a light voice, "Enough of this. Can we have some music, please?"

CHAPTER 50

The orchestra started playing *The Yellow Rose Of Texas* and the dance floor quickly filled with swirling skirts and smiling young people. Still firmly holding her waist we made our way to our table. When we were both seated I looked at her. There must have been horror in my eyes because she said, "Don't worry, Jamie. I got a cramp in the calf of my leg. I practiced that curtsey many times but I suppose after all the dancing my legs are tired. It's okay now."

I let out a long slow breath.

"What did you think was wrong?"

"I didn't know except I immediately thought the worst."

"Which was?"

"Something had come undone with your . . . ah . . . your apparel."

She giggled as she slipped her chair next to mine. Her arms wound around my arm.

"That's why you were holding my so tightly around the waist. You were holding up my apparel." She giggled again.

Then she kissed me on the cheek. I said, "Before this night's over I'll be expecting a better kiss than that, assuming I don't have a nervous breakdown first."

It was obvious that she wanted to say more but she was laughing so hard she couldn't speak. Finally she leaned over to say something to me. I could feel her hot breath on my ear as she whispered, "I promise."

I looked at her and she winked. Up until the wink it had been okay, but the wink was clearly flirting and hence against the rules. Though

nothing was said I knew she expected that I'd forgive her for the infrac-
tion, which I did. Girls were nice and yet so manipulative. Why had God
done that to us?

The next number was *Canadian Sunset* and a guy came and asked
Emily to dance. I saw that Debbie wasn't dancing so asked her and she
seemed happy to accept. As we danced I said, "That was gracious of you
to help Emily down the stairs as we arrived. I'm a bit clumsy and was
concerned about that."

"You're being nice. From that spin as she came up from the curtsey it
is obvious you are anything but clumsy. Her feet were off the floor and it
looked like a ballet."

"Yeah, you're right. It was more than the assistance, it was the acceptance. You might think it was a small thing but it meant a lot. Thank
you for that; I really mean it. She was concerned about what might happen when she showed up in that gown. She only wanted something to
wear to the dance and it turned out to be so extravagant. She never had
much of anything in her life and you should have seen how excited she
was when it looked like she might be able to wear that dress."

She smiled, "We all knew something was going on with you two but
couldn't figure it out. You did a good job of keeping it a secret. I'm glad
your cousin, Nettie, gave her little speech, though. Now, everybody
knows the truth so they don't have the option of making it up." After a
pause she asked, "What is it about you and me and caterpillars?"

"Don't you remember? The third week of first grade you were sitting
in front of me in the classroom and I put a caterpillar on your dress. It
crawled up to your collar and when it transferred to your neck you let out
a scream. I almost got away with it but the girl across the aisle tattled on
me. You told your mother and she told my mother and I caught heck for
that for the next five years."

"I remember it but didn't realize it was you."

We slowly moved across the floor swaying to the music. She looked
at me, "She's nuts about you, you know. It's the way she looks at you,
laughs so easily when you're around."

The music ended and I escorted Debbie to her table and thanked her.
We both knew it was a good bye dance after going to school together
since kindergarten.

We danced fast and slow numbers and it seemed Emily had been honest about her leg because she was having a ball, literally.

I asked Nettie to dance once while Emily was dancing with someone else. And, after some discussion Emily and I went over to where Mr. Beecher and his wife were sitting. Emily asked him to dance and I asked her. Emily was taller than he was in her heels but he was happy to oblige.

All too soon came the call for "Last dance." It was *Love Is A Many Splendored Thing, the April rose that only grows in the early spring.* As we danced Emily seemed to be holding me closer that I was holding her, however that could work. There was an intensity to the way her arm was around my back. We did not have my left arm and her right extended out but folded in against us as we held each other's hand. We weren't quite cheek to cheek but pretty close. My cheek was a little down from her forehead. Not a word was spoken.

After the dance she wanted to go back and get our name card from the table as a memento. When she had left her home I'm sure she was wearing the shawl to cover her shoulders. But it stayed in the car. We stood on the sidewalk and it was cold. In a minute we saw the big Cadillac drive up. Nettie got out and was about to slip into the back seat when I said, "No, Nettie. Come on and sit in the front with us. There's plenty of room."

She came around. Emily got in and then Nettie. I closed her door and went around to the driver's side.

When I got in Emily had the shawl around her. "It's cold," she said.

I wanted to say something about her having too much bare skin but couldn't think of any way to say it without getting into trouble so I let it go.

She snuggled up against me and I put my arms around her. "Let me help warm you up."

She compliantly flowed against me subtly twisting and wiggling as I held her. I was hugging her and it was great.

Her response was, "Hmmm, nice."

"What's going on here? The motor's running and the heater will be putting out tons of heat in a second so break it up, kids."

Emily turned to Nettie and said, "Chaperones can be so annoying."

"Chaperone is a Greek word for sharp-stick-in-the-eye so I can be a lot more than annoying."

I said, "I thought chaperone sounded French."

"You're just high school seniors so what would you know? Now, hands on the steering wheel, eyes on the road and get moving. You're holding up traffic."

Emily unbuckled a slim strap of each shoe and let them drop to the floor as she drew her legs up under her skirt. But, she stayed snuggled up to me and that was okay.

As soon as we were moving Nettie spoke, "When I said be graceful and gracious I had no idea what I was saying. My goodness! For a nickel you could buy this whole town about now. Where did you guys come up with that thing when Emily came up from the curtsey?"

"I got a cramp in my leg and signaled to Jamie that I needed help."

"She squashed my fingers so hard they still hurt."

Emily was laughing. "He thought my dress was falling down."

Nettie laughed, too.

"That's why he took me around the waist and then had to do something so he whirled me around. One day last fall we were out in the Landon's apple orchard and I tripped backward. He caught me and then whirled me around like that only he did it about ten times, then. So, it wasn't something new on the spot."

"I don't believe this."

We all laughed. Nettie said, "This has really been fun. Some of those guys are good dancers. A couple of teachers even asked me to dance."

It was only a mile to the big house where Eddie Norbert lived. He had invited us as well as two other couples and with Nettie it made nine. When we arrived Emily said, "I think I brought flat shoes."

"They're on the floor of the back seat," Nettie replied.

Emily twisted around and leaned over the seat. "Careful!" Nettie said in an almost harsh voice. "There *is* a limit to what you can do in that dress. Here, I'll get them."

Emily turned and settled back on the seat. The light was dim from a street light a half block away but I could see her dress was down a tad, to a point where there was a little cleavage showing. She must have been able to feel it so she grabbed the dress at the top in the center and gave a quick tug upward.

She saw me watching her—it was impossible for me to pull my eyes away—and she gave me a cute fake smile and then a raspberry. "You've been expecting that all night so are you satisfied?"

"Who me? I'm just a guy passing by."

She leaned against me and giggled. "I'm going to take off my flower and leave it in the car so it doesn't get crushed. Is that okay?"

"It's your flower, and that's fine with me."

Since Eddie and I had bummed around duck hunting, trying to make rockets and a few other things I had been in his house before, but never in the living room. It was lavishly decorated. The house was probably built early in the century. As such it had the main living room and attached to it was a smaller room entered though an archway that was what I think would be called a sun room.

Everyone was moving around drinking punch and eating little cookies. Emily wandered into the sun room leading me behind her with one hand. She gently pulled me to the side where there was a small sofa. After we were seated she said, "I keep my promises."

She put her hands behind my head and I engulfed her in my arms. She was wearing the shawl and that was good because my hands were always cold. We kissed. We had stolen a kiss now and then but it was the first serious kiss since the apple orchard. Then I said, "Now it's my turn to kiss you."

When we broke I said, "You have awfully sweet kisses."

"My turn."

About the time we stopped worrying about whose turn it was I heard movement and it was Eddie. "Hey. What's going on back here?"

"We're kissing," Emily said.

"Come on and join us. You can do that any time."

We sat in the comfortable living room and chatted. Nettie was asked a lot of questions about what a prom was like in the big rich city. Everybody had something to contribute. There were frequent peevish remarks about how Emily and I had managed to keep the secret, but it was all friendly. The girls, as one might expect, wanted to hear every detail. They especially wanted to know how she had learned the dress would even fit. Emily said I had given her Nettie's address and they wrote letters and called back and forth. Yes, I had given her the address but only later. She was fibbing so as to shield me from embarrassment. In similar situations I would have expected that everyone would have a laugh at my expense.

While this was going on, Nettie was looking at me with a quizzical smile. She knew it wasn't true and had that wheels-in-the-head-turning look like my mother sometimes had.

When it came to how we had come up with the spin after the curtsey there was no hiding it so Emily told what to her was the apparel story. As she told it she looked at me with sparkling eyes and was giggling so much she could hardly speak. Everybody had a howling good laugh and I didn't mind. Emily was as happy as a person could be and that made me happy.

The whole idea was to stay up until dawn on prom night. Without daylight savings time the sun rose at four-forty-five so dawn came about four. Even at that everyone was hungry so we started breakfast before dawn. Eddie's mother had arranged it so we could have an early breakfast simply by taking some prepared dishes out of the refrigerator and putting them in the oven.

As we ate in the dining area we kidded and laughed. I can't recall what was on the menu but it was good. There had not been a drop of alcohol throughout the whole affair, yet the spirits were naturally high.

The birds were singing as we thanked Eddie and drove away. As a logistical matter we'd drive Emily home and she's shed the dress and other things so Nettie wouldn't have to make another trip.

Emily lived seven miles east of town, but by a different road from ours. Leaving town Emily said, "Are you angry with me for telling the apparel story? Everybody had a big laugh at your expense."

"Of course not. You were having such a good time I couldn't possibly object."

It could cause a little problem, though. The story would be told and retold and by the time we got to school there'd be snide comments about her dress falling down especially after the dance. It'll come mainly from the guys—the dreams of young men.

"Don't worry. If it's mentioned we'll say the spin was all an act that we had practiced which, in a way, we had. And, the dress thing was part of the act. Then question how they could be so gullible as to think I was actually worried about your dress."

Nettie said, "You sound like a politician."

"Were you really worried about my dress falling down?"

"Not so much actually falling down as something going wrong so as to be noticeable and cause you embarrassment. I know women wear strapless dresses all the time, but trains aren't supposed to derail but they do; airplanes aren't supposed to crash but they do. And the way you were moving in it, well, it was beautiful but so is watching a volcano erupt. You never know what might happen."

"Nettie, is he flirting with me?"

"I'd say it was more of a compliment combined with concern."

"I don't know, I think you're flirting with me and that's against the rules."

"Well, when you winked at me that was for sure flirting so you started it. And, if you're so offended, why are you smiling?"

"I didn't say I was offended only that it was against the rules. I'm smiling because I like it. I suppose you didn't like it when I winked at you."

"Oh, shut up."

We all laughed and Emily leaned her head on my shoulder and I felt her soft hair on my face. Now, that could easily be called flirting but I wasn't about to object. And, there was no sharp-stick-in-the-eye from our Greek expert.

CHAPTER 51

A crescent moon was hanging above the not yet risen sun. "Look," I said, "it's the last of the moon of the deep water. That moon has special significance to me."

As we drove Nettie said, "So, you have our interest, what's the significance?"

"Kind of a long story. When I was six, in the spring of 1944, a man walked into our place and asked for a job. He was an Indian, actually an Ojibwe warrior, who had been in the war in Europe. Having been wounded multiple times he was released due to loss of most of his hearing. With the war, all able bodied men were either in the Army or in defense related jobs so a hired man was hard to find. As a result dad took him on. It turned out that he still had a piece of shrapnel in his leg that festered and became infected. Finally, dad took him to the hospital where they operated on him. When he came home that night he had a high fever.

"All the time he was with us he refused to sleep in the house preferring to sleep on the hay in the barn. During the night I woke up and thought about Justin which was the name he used when among white men. His real name was Running Wolf. On an odd impulse I ran out to the barn seeing the brightest moon of my life. It was the moon of the deep water. He was delirious and gasping for water. I ran back to the house and woke mom and dad. After dad had a look at him he called the doctor who drove out to our place in the middle of the night. They wet down all Justin's clothes to reduce the fever. The doctor said he would have died by morning if I hadn't gone out to check on him.

"Anyway, he stayed in the hay mow as he recuperated. At one point during this time he made me his blood brother. It happened like this. He had a strange knife that I was taken with and he let me hold it, but I accidentally cut my thumb. Seeing this he cut his, too, and he pressed his to mine and he said our blood mixed making us blood brothers.

"Some time after that he had a dream visitor, what they would call a *pawágan*, what we might call a grandfather, a spirit or what they know as a person of the other-than-human class. The grandfather gave him an Ojibwe name for me. That name was Little Manknife. There is a basis for that name but it'd take a lot of telling. Where he got the name was important because the name carried a special blessing and power with it having come from a *pawágan*. Their concept of *pawágan* is a little complex because it includes living, as well as dead, and related and non-related old men of the tribe. The true meaning can usually be determined from the context of what is said.

"After that I was counted among the *änícinábek* which loosely translated means human beings. To them only Indians are human beings and everybody else is a white man. So they'd call a Negro a black white man and see nothing odd about it. But, that's a simplistic way of saying it. We talked about stuff like that and little as I was I absorbed a lot. As an example of their thinking, the idea of impersonal 'natural' forces is totally foreign to Ojibwe thought. All natural forces such as wind, thunder and sunlight are alive and frequently viewed as persons of the other-than-human class, collectively called *ätíso 'kanak*.

"I'm kind of babbling, aren't I? Anyway, that's all connected to the story of two kids in a doctor's waiting room."

There was silence. Finally Nettie asked, "How long would it take to tell the connection between you, the Indian and the waiting room?"

"Way longer than we have."

The sun was inching above the trees when three sleepy young people drove into the yard of the farm where Emily lived. Emily took her flower from the top of the dashboard, and the girls made for the house as I waited by the car. Only a minute after the girls had disappeared Emily's mother came out with a jacket over her shoulders. It seemed she had been waiting for us to get back.

We greeted each other. I had met her, of course, so we were acquainted. Smiling she said, "If you aren't a handsome brute all gussied up." She hadn't seen me in the tux. "And, that's some fine car."

"It belongs to Nettie's mother. She insisted we use it for the prom."

"Did you have a good time?"

I smiled, "Any time I'm with Emily we have a good time. But, yes, we had an especially good time. It all went well. She was the belle-of-the-ball." After a pause I continued, "Did you see her as she came into the house? Isn't she lovely? She has that natural beauty and with the dress, shoes, and jewelry she's simply gorgeous. And, on top of that she has that simple graciousness that comes from a kind and gentle heart with just enough mischievousness to drive me crazy."

She looked at me oddly.

"I'm running on aren't I?"

She nodded. "It's okay. Emily's never been so happy. You should have heard those two girls upstairs fitting that dress. I never heard such laughing and carrying on. Later I asked her what they were talking about that could possibly have been so funny. She said, 'Boys.'"

I was leaning against the car and she leaned against it, too. Even though she had worked hard in her life, I could see where Emily got her good looks. "I'll bet she told you she'd wear that shawl to cover her shoulders, didn't she?"

"Yes, she did."

"She promised me the same thing. I'm sorry to say your daughter lied to both of us."

She smiled. "That's a pretty harsh word. When someone tells something that isn't exactly true, and the person being told knows it isn't true, and the person saying it knows the other person knows it isn't true, it isn't really a lie."

"That sounds like something Emily would say. You two wouldn't happen to be related, would you?"

She laughed. "Did you kiss her?"

I nodded.

"How many times?"

"Lost count."

"I thought she said there'd be a chaperone at all times."

"Oh, I think the lump on Nettie's head should heal without leaving a scar."

She give me a questioning look not sure if I were serious.

"Don't worry. There was no violence. As soon as we got to Eddie's place Emily immediately spied a nook where we could sit on a small sofa unseen. But, hey, why am I telling you this? It's personal."

"You're telling because you feel good and have to tell someone. Don't worry, I won't tell anyone—except the whole world!"

She flashed me a mischievous smile. Emily was definitely related to this woman.

"But, I didn't tell the secret of the dress and it almost killed me."

In the next breath she asked, "Do you love her?"

It took me off guard. "You have a way of coming to the point."

She smiled at me, a simple warm smile.

"For certain we loved each other in the seventh grade. Did she tell you anything about the night on the merry-go-round?"

She nodded.

"I doubt she told you this. We were hugging each other and had kissed our first kiss and she said the most beautiful thing. 'I love you and you love me the way young hearts love. It's a simple love not like adult love where they talk about babies and payments to the bank.'"

I looked at her. She shook her head. With a note of sadness she said, "No. She never mentioned that."

"I would guess she didn't because it's one of those treasures she holds in her heart. Maybe I shouldn't have mentioned it. I did mention it because we have come to the age of adult love. My parents as well as you and your husband have done a good job of keeping us apart. We've never had time alone where we could talk and develop something more than a passing friendship. We've never even had an argument and had to say, 'I'm sorry, please forgive me.'"

When she didn't respond I asked, "Didn't Emily ever ask if we could get together now and then, maybe just to walk around the yard and visit on a Sunday afternoon?"

"Many times."

"Then why was it never allowed? Were you so afraid that if we got to know each other I'd sneak up some night and spirit her off to a hay stack?"

"No. I never thought of you as that kind of boy."

"It's nice of you to say that. My parents wouldn't be so kind. But, then, why put a wall between us?"

Again she didn't answer and something occurred to me. "Was it because you thought I was not too smart and a no-good goof-off?"

"There was all that talk that you were always in trouble at school . . . ," she trailed off.

"I guess you never knew that most of the teachers, and most of the town for that matter, blamed me for that teacher going to prison because he hit Emily. If there was something rotten those teachers could do to me they did it. They'd humiliate me, ignore me, do anything they could to make me look foolish. They couldn't give me bad grades if I got the answers right, though. That was tried with my older brother Tommy and a teacher nearly got fired for it. I always had a problem of getting bored easily and when I did I'd do something to distract the class so they found lots of excuses to be hard on me. I did get good grades, by the way."

"Why *did* that teacher hit Emily?"

"He tried to hit me but I ducked and he hit Emily by mistake. He intended to kill me. I was standing behind his right shoulder and Emily was to my left. When he brought his fist around and missed me his arm was soon nearing its limit of travel and was slowing down. Still, look at the damage it did to Emily."

"Then, why would a teacher want to kill you?"

"Quite by accident I landed in the middle of organized illegal activity. That teacher had involved himself willingly and got in over his head. He was going to prison no matter what. That's all I can say about it."

"But, we didn't know."

"It was a sensitive federal case. But, if anyone had asked I would have said this much. I'm surprised you never tired to find out what was going on? After all, your daughter was pretty interested in this screw-up."

She didn't respond. "Through all these years, of the whole town, including my family, there was only one person who was unfailingly nice to me and that was Emily. She was more than nice, she was my angel. There were days when I wouldn't have been able to get out of bed without the thought that I'd see Emily."

We stood there for a full minute saying nothing. Then I said, "That's all beside the point because now it really gets hard. I've worked at a gas station and on road construction and would be miserable doing something like that all my life. If I were unhappy my wife and family would be, too, if I ever got that far. I have to go to college so I can get a job that doesn't bore me to death and that provides enough income so I can afford to get married. Somewhere in there I'll have to spend time in the service. That's forever."

"No it's not. No time in your life will be perfect. If you try, you can enjoy these coming years. Don't wish this time gone too soon—you'll never pass this way again. There'll be sorrow on parting but greater joy on meeting. You're not the first couple in the history of the world to face this. You can do it. The time when you're changing diapers or walking the floor all night with sick kids will come sooner than you think."

I had to smile at Mrs. LaNell's sincerity at trying to make amends. "Don't you see, though, she's ready to get married now or will be in a year or two. She'll go to the city and find a job. She's certainly attractive so there'll be lots of single young men getting an eye on her. The difference will be they'll already have an education. They'll have good paying jobs, be ready to get married and will have something to offer. Just by working with someone on a regular basis she'll get better acquainted with one of those guys in a couple of months than we are after five years. The time for us to have built a relationship was while we were here living in the same community going to the same school. Now, we'll be going our separate ways.

"We'll probably both be home at times, for example at Christmas, and run into each other at church. We'll say a few words like we always have. The next time she'll be with a boy friend, and the next with a husband. I wouldn't blame her."

She seemed shaken perhaps thinking I'd always be around and who knew, maybe I'd even turn into something. "Well, Emily isn't married yet! And, I hope you haven't given up on her. Stay in contact. Write her letters and send little things. Don't forget her birthday or Valentines Day. You'll always be welcome here. Stop by over the holidays."

Mrs. LaNell continued in a softer voice, "However, in the time ahead, I hope you don't forget how important it is understand that a lifetime of happiness starts with a chaste courtship. There's no other way. If you don't respect each other before marriage it's not likely you will after."

"Except that there won't be much of a courtship for the next six or so years. But, that aside, have you told Emily any of this?"

"No. And, I don't know how much good it would do. I don't say that because she's high spirited at times, but because women are fickle. It's important for the man to keep a steady hand. That's not to say you wouldn't both have to work at it."

"Mrs. LaNell, tell Emily what you just said—about our conversation. If there's to be any hope we'll need help and I don't think my parents will be much good in that department."

Before she could say anything the screen door opened. Nettie and Emily came out carrying boxes. Emily was wearing blue jeans, a white short sleeved blouse buttoned to the top, and lace shoes. I keep repeating myself, she was beautiful.

"Safe at last with no train wrecks," I said.

She giggled and said, "You worry too much."

"Jamie, open the trunk," Nettie said.

I reached in and pulled the key from the ignition. Assuming the non-ignition key was for the trunk I opened it and beheld something like the back forty. There was nothing small about that car.

When we were packed and ready to leave, Emily turned to Nettie, "If I had a big sister, I'd want her to be you."

They hugged. It was like two mountain ranges colliding but that wasn't my problem. Emily came to me and I leaned over and kissed her on the cheek.

Nettie took the keys and went to the driver's side while Emily's mother went to the house. I took one of Emily's hands in each of mine and looked at her. "Thank you for a wonderful time."

She slowly slid her hands from mine and gave me a hug and walked to the house. At the door she turned, smiled and blew me a kiss. It was the best kiss ever. Even at that, I had to wonder what the future held for us.

As Nettie steered the car from the driveway onto the gravel road she said, "You've got a tiger by the tail. What ya gonna do about it?"

Staring out the windshield I said, "Not much I can do but let go."

"What? It's impossible to argue with affairs of the heart, I know that. But, from the way she looks at you and you look at her you've both got it really bad. And the way she protected you from embarrassment at the house by lying about how I got her measurements was a clear tip off."

"Nettie, I have college and military service ahead of me. I'll be terribly busy and she'll have a normal life. Friendship can last under those circumstances but when a good looking girl like Emily is of marrying age that's a different story. I don't want to lose her. . . ."

"But, you expect you will."

"Yes, I'm afraid I will."

"Boy, that's tough. All I can say is don't lose hope."

"Oh, I haven't given up hope. It just seems that no matter what we do there'll be difficult times ahead for us."

We drove on. "Nettie, I have a favor to ask you."

"Not another dress," she said with levity in her voice.

"No, but it's for Emily again. I don't know what will become of us, but if it continues to work, or even if it doesn't, she's never had a real girl friend and you two seem to hit it off. Would you be willing to keep in touch with her a little?"

"That's very thoughtful of you. I was thinking I'd do that even if you hadn't asked."

"That's good. I don't know how much she told you about how we first got together, but we were both very lonely. After the waiting room we, well, fell in love. There's no other way about it, as young as we were, we fell in love. I can't describe it to you. It was a thrill just to talk to her and see her smile at me.

"Neither of us were sullen and lonely anymore, we both did better at school, and we more willingly helped out at home. It didn't matter. Both sets of parents were still wringing their hands. They were wishing I had found a boy friend and Emily a girl friend."

She laughed. "Parents are never happy, are they?"

"What I'm saying is she'll be lonely again and having you as a friend will help."

After awhile she said, "Someday I want to hear the connection between a six year old kid, an Indian warrior and a waiting room. That's the price of the dress. Got it?"

I laughed and said, "Got it." I turned my head and saw she was smiling.

We arrived home tired but satisfied. We had pulled it off. Through Emily's determination and natural abilities, the dress and the prom had been a success. It had been a good time for everyone.

NOTES

This tale starts out as fiction but ends as fantasy. In fiction we have a story where if the reader suspends reality in believing what is called the big lie, the rest of the story follows as something that did not happen but could happen. In fiction the big lie is possible. For example in *Treasure Island* Robert Louis Stevenson uses the big lie where there is a treasure buried on a distant island and there exists a map showing where it is. Once that is accepted the rest of the story follows with the characters being introduced in their turn. Each has strengths and weaknesses. The scenes depict the conditions of the real world with good and bad people, hard journeys and various other trials.

In a fantasy the big lie is not possible. In *Alice In Wonderland* by Louis Carol the idea that a small girl could fall down a rabbit hole and find herself in an alien world is the big lie, but it is not possible. We enjoy fantasies and they can seem every bit as enjoyable as life. It is in this light that I say the part about the six year old boy could pass as fiction. The boy-girl part in the seventh grade and especially the senior prom are over the edge for fiction and slip into fantasy.

That being said, the story is roughly based on real events. The descriptions of how we lived are included as a record of ordinary lives at the time. The Landon farm did exist, though the buildings are now gone as are most of the trees. And, some of the anecdotes did happen. The guardian angel stories are true except, of course, the one with the Indian. We had a hired man called Justin and we had one that was and Indian, but they were not the same man. My father did fall and break his hip on threshing day, and I did stab myself in the shin with a pitchfork. I had a crush on a girl and she was most certainly "cute as a button." In my case, though, she never knew I existed. The scene where Emily gets hit in the face is a fictionalized account of something that happened. One difference being that there was no photograph on the front page of the local paper to prove it.

Communism was a real threat and when the USSR broke up the world had access to its records. We learned that Senator Joe McCarthy was not only right in his accusations but understated the case by a wide margin. Yet, even today, McCarthyism is in any desk dictionary and has the meaning of a radical who uses unfounded allegations to malign someone.

During World War II there was a persistent problem with counterfeit rationing stamps. The underground communists or their fellow travelers would have known what the next issue of ration stamps looked like. The communists would sell counterfeit stamps cheaply so they would sell a lot of them. They wouldn't be primarily after money so much as to destabilize society and the government. They wanted to take over in this country like they had in Russia. The sleeper agents as described also existed.

A word about the book's title. Wild violets are often seen mostly as troublesome weeds in the yard or garden. But the flower is delicate and beautiful. Deep inside any woman of any age is the desire to be beautiful and if she's honest she'll admit to wanting to be, at least at times, a little wild, hence *Wild Violets*—wild and beautiful. And, there is about one woman in 1.5 million who has truly violet eyes.

There was an effort to portray young love. This is not puppy love where two sexually mature teenagers are infatuated. It was meant to show where a boy and a girl who are just at the point of noticing the opposite sex become acquainted and then are thrown together by adversity. It's certainly sexual but mostly physiological. It's a friendship that has the boy-girl complication. Maybe it's so rare as to be total fantasy like most of the story.

* * *

A few more words about the prom. In some towns there was a banquet before the dance, but not in Deep Woods during those years. In the story Emily never expected to wear such a fine gown, but it was what was available. And, I hope I showed that she thoroughly enjoyed wearing it. I have always thought that if good things come your way now and then that it isn't wrong, within reason, to enjoy them.

Other than that the whole senior prom sequence was pure fantasy even more so than falling down a rabbit hole. A strapless gown might have been acceptable in an upper class suburb of Minneapolis, but not yet at a small town prom. And, Debbie's ready acceptance of being up-staged by a poor farm girl was beyond even the whimsical. In general, all concerned were well behaved, and showed not the slightest tinge of ego. That's not the school I attended. But, we like to think such a thing could happen, just maybe.

It's important to remember that imagination is a wonderful thing. It can take you places that you could never hope to go. That includes not only exotic places in the past, present and future, but on endearing journeys of the heart which are timeless.

But only if it's . . . *Once upon a time.*

www.ingramcontent.com/pod-product-compliance
Lightning Source LLC
Chambersburg PA
CBHW032140010726
47494CB00002B/301